Caroline Graham was born in Warwickshire and educated at Nuneaton High School for Girls and, later, the Open University. She was recently awarded an MA degree in Writing for the Theatre by Birmingham University. She has also written several plays, both for radio and the theatre, television soaps and two books for children. Her first Chief Inspector Barnaby novel, THE KILLINGS AT BADGER'S DRIFT, was selected by the Crime Writers' Association as one of the top hundred crime novels of all time and has now been televised, with the other hugely popular Barnaby novels, DEATH IN DISGUISE, DEATH OF A HOLLOW MAN, WRITTEN IN BLOOD and FAITHFUL UNTO DEATH, as the major ITV drama series, *Midsomer Murders*.

Caroline Graham lives in Suffolk, where she is currently at work on the next Chief Inspector Barnaby novel.

Death in Disguise

Caroline Graham

HEADLINE

First published in 1992
by HEADLINE BOOK PUBLISHING

First published in paperback in 1993
by HEADLINE BOOK PUBLISHING

10 9 8

ISBN 0 7472 3974 6

Phototypeset by Intype, London
Printed and bound in Great Britain by
Clays Ltd, St Ives plc

HEADLINE BOOK PUBLISHING
A division of Hodder Headline PLC
338 Euston Road
London NW1 3BH

To DAVID,
my son.

That monks can save the world, or ever could,
That anchorites and fakirs do you good,
Is to bring Buddha back before your gaze.
Men do not eat the lotus in our days.

Juvenal. Satire 3.
(trans. Thorold-Roper)

PROLOGUE

No one in the village of Compton Dando was surprised to hear of the murder up at the Manor House. They were a funny lot up there. A most peculiar lot. Weird.

Mr and Mrs Bulstrode were almost the only locals to have a thread of contact with the spiritual community (so called) in the big house. She pushed the parish magazine determinedly through the letter box once a month. He delivered a single daily pint of milk. The tenuousness of this connection in no way undermined the couple's standing as a source of much juicily informative gossip. Now, of course, they were in even more demand and Mrs Bulstrode found herself facing a full house every time she put foot to pavement outside her front door.

Demurring at first: 'I know no more than I did yesterday Mrs Oxtoby . . .', the temptation to embroider and expand proved irresistible. And by the evening of the third day if the inhabitants of 'The Lodge of the Golden Windhorse' had come sailing over their crinkle-crankle wall on broomsticks, the village would have been unastonished if not exactly sanguine.

In the butcher's, buying her lamb's liver and a bone for Ponting, Mrs Bulstrode shook her head in reluctant and judicious revelation. She had seen it coming she told Major Palfrey (two kidneys and a packet of dripping) in a voice that carried. The goings-on at that place you would simply not believe. The queue, more than willing to take up the challenge, followed her to the Post Office.

There Miss Tombs, cushiony cheeks practically taking an

3

impression from the wire grill, passed over Mrs Bulstrode's stamps with a stage whisper: 'You won't be getting over this in a hurry, dear. Your Derek finding a body. Not something you come across every day of the week.'

'Ohhh. . . .' Overcome, Mrs Bulstrode (whose husband had not even seen the body), clutched at the counter's edge. 'It's all rushing back, Myrtle—'

'Devil take my tongue!' called Miss Tombs and watched her customers disappear, clustering like nebulae around their guiding star.

In Bob's Emporium Mrs Bulstrode said that just the way they dressed was enough. Her audience seemed to think this a mite parsimonious. They hung on for a sec then started to drift towards pyramids of Happy Shopper cat food and bags of carrots.

'Can't tell if they're male or female half the time.' Then, gussying things up a bit, 'What my Derek's seen through the windows some mornings. . . . Well – I wouldn't divulge in mixed company.'

'You mean. . . .' A woman in a headscarf with a snout like a porbeagle breathed heavily '. . . *sacrifices*?'

'Let's just say "ceremonies" shall we, Miss Oughtred? Best leave it there.'

Ceremonies! People regathered, quick and solemn. Their minds swarmed with melodramatic images, horrific and banal. Graves yawned, allowing the undead easy access to careless passers-by. Horned Lucifer, yellow-eyed and sulphurous, clattered his hooves at the pentagon's rim. Burning sand and a girl, once beautiful as a Mameluke, staked-out to be eaten alive by marching ants. (Major Palfrey had served with the Desert Rats.)

Next stop was the Crinoline Tea Rooms for half a dozen home-made Viennese fingers. While the assistant silver tong'd these into a bag, Mrs Bulstrode looked around in the hope of further increasing her audience ratings.

But she was out of luck. Only two people were present tucking into coffee and cakes. Ann Cosins and her friend from Causton, Mrs Barnaby. There was no point at all in trying to talk to them.

Ann had a most dry and unimpressed way with her – almost as if she were laughing up her sleeve – that made her quite unpopular. Also she had let the whole village down on one occasion by actually going to the Manor House on a course. The two of them had been seen walking up the drive bold as brass one Friday afternoon, not emerging til the Sunday. To add insult to injury, Ann had then refused to be drawn as to what the place and people were really like.

So Mrs Bulstrode contented herself with a cool inclination of the head and a sniff of acknowledgement, grandly ignoring the gurgling snorts upon which she closed the door. Finally, on the way home, she paused to exchange a few words with the vicar who was leaning over the gate of 'Benisons' smoking his pipe. He greeted her with a look of deep satisfaction, for The Lodge had long been a thorn in the ecclesiastical side. Uncertainty as to its precise ethos had proved no hindrance when it came to firing off a series of mildly hysterical salvos at the letters page of the *Causton Echo* – warning readers against the new idolatrous theology now nestling in the wholesome English countryside, like a maggot in the heart of a rose.

Any religion (wrote the vicar) invented by man as opposed to that plainly emanating directly from the Almighty could surely come to no good end. And so it had proved to be. God, after all, was seen to be not mocked and the Reverend Phipps plus his minuscule congregation had gathered to celebrate the fact with a renewed sense of righteousness and not a little surprise. Now he raised a greying compassionate brow and asked if there were any fresh developments.

Mrs Bulstrode, flattered at the implication that Derek and the CID were as two peas in the same pod, could not bring herself to tell even the whitest of lies to a man of the cloth. She had to admit there were none, adding: 'But the inquest's Tuesday, Vicar. Eleven o'clock.'

He knew that of course. Everyone knew and they were all going, some even taking time off work to do so. Hopes were high that the hearing might last all day and every table in

Causton's Soft Shoe Café had long since been booked for lunch. Compton Dando had not seen such excitement since three boys from the Council Estate burned down the bus shelter and it was confidently supposed that the incendiary quotient in this later drama would be immeasurably higher.

The scene of these dramatic goings-on was a modestly beautiful example of early Elizabethan architecture. Two storeys high, it was built of grey stone horizontally banded with flint and smooth pebbles and was charmingly unsymmetrical. There were Ionic columns at the slightly off-centre doorway, a little porch and forty-six light mullioned windows. The chimneys were huddled together in three separate clumps, some twisted like barley sugar, others appliquéd with vine leaves and convolvulus. Many had star-shaped openings emitting, during the cold winter months, star-shaped puffs of smoke. A huge lump of metal thought to be a meteorite or, less romantically, part of a cannon ball lay near the edge of the roof which had rose-red, moss-encrusted tiles.

The building was the gift of Elizabeth the First to an exiled favourite, Gervaise Huyton-Corbett. The queen and her entourage were frequent visitors during the first five years of his occupancy and this crippling honour brought him, and several near neighbours obliged to absorb the overspill, near to bankruptcy. The descendants of Sir Gervaise (as he was graciously dubbed once brought to his knees by penury) had lived at Compton Manor for the next four centuries but the family coffers never really recovered. Each year the house cost far more to maintain than it had originally cost to build but, so great was their love of the place, the Huyton-Corbetts struggled on – borrowing beyond their means and unable to bear the thought of parting with the family home. Then, in 1939, Ashley joined the Fleet Air Arm. The scion of the house, he was killed at the Battle of the River Plate. In old age and having no immediate heir, his father sold the property and the village suffered the first of what was to be a long line of cultural shocks and setbacks.

No longer was it possible on the day of the village fête to

6

swarm all over the Manor gardens and be entertained by the sight of Lady Huyton-Corbett, gently drunk in georgette and a shady picture hat, bowling for (and frequently hitting) the pig. No longer did the squire present a silver cup for the finest sweet peas, with rosettes for the runners-up.

In 1980 the property was sold again and the house was transformed into a conference centre. The villagers' deep distrust of change and resentment of newcomers was much consoled by the creation of over thirty jobs, albeit of a rather menial nature. Five years later, muddled and inefficient management having forced the property once more on the market, one of Mrs Thatcher's designer gladiators took it on. He also purchased a thousand acres of adjacent farmland with the (concealed) intention of creating a Tudor theme park. Horrified Dandonians of every rank and political persuasion joined forces against this vile despoliation of England's green and pleasant. Neighbouring villages, imagining the hooting traffic jams outside their own front doors if not actually in their own back yards, rallied in support and, after petitions had been handed in and a banner dramatically unfurled in the public gallery of the House of Commons, planning permission was refused and the entrepreneur went off in a huff to attempt malfeasance elsewhere.

Relieved though the locals were to see the back of him, they had at least understood, if not appreciated, his simple profit-making rationale. The present situation was quite beyond their comprehension. For a start the newcomers kept themselves strictly to themselves. The village, sturdily resentful at the slightest hint of seigneurial familiarity from a succession of visiting parvenus, was doubly resentful when no such hint was seen to be forthcoming. It was not used to being ignored. Even the half dozen or so weekenders who drove down from London at the first sign of a clement Friday, Golf GTI boots crammed with bottles of wine and stone-ground pasta, made hopeful attempts at integration in the saloon bar of The Swan – receiving by way of return many a falsely jocular put-down.

But the second black mark against the Windhorse contingent

was much more serious. *They did not spend.* Not once had a resident entered Bob's Emporium or even the Post Office ('Use It Or Lose It'), let alone their friendly neighbourhood local. This had been grudgingly accepted when the community, tilling and hoeing its three acres, was thought to be self-sufficient but when one of them was spotted getting off the bus with two Sainsbury's carrier bags, umbrage was well and truly taken. And so it was with a quite justified sense of grievance as well as happy anticipation that a large crowd trooped into the Coroner's Court to see the drama unfold and justice done.

The dead man, fifty-three at the time of his demise, was named as James Carter. The proceedings opened with written evidence from an ambulance attendant who had arrived at the Manor House following an emergency telephone call to find the body of Mr Carter lying at the foot of a flight of stairs.

'I carried out a brief examination of the deceased,' read out the clerk, 'and contacted my control who sent out a doctor and informed the police.'

Doctor Lessiter gave evidence next. He was a pompous little man who refused to use one word where five could be conjured and his audience soon got bored and turned their attention to members of the commune.

These were eight in number and something of a disappointment. Primed by Mrs Bulstrode, the courtroom was expecting a rare exotic species piquantly marked to distinguish it from the common herd. True, one girl had floaty muslin trousers and a reddish dot on her forehead, but you could see that sort of thing any day of the week in Slough or Uxbridge. Rather peeved, they all tuned back into the doctor's gist just in time to hear the satisfying words 'strong smell of brandy'.

The constable who followed confirmed that he had questioned the ambulance man as to his opinion on the possibility of foul play of which he himself had seen no outward sign. Then the first witness from the Windhorse took the stand. A tall, wide woman clothed in a brilliantly coloured Liberty silk two-piece and presenting a splendid figure. Agreeing that she was indeed

Miss May Cuttle, she recounted her movements on the day in question in greater detail than was strictly necessary. All this in ringing confident vowels that would not have disgraced the chair of the local WI.

She'd had a dental appointment in Causton – 'a recalcitrant molar' – and left the house just after eleven with three companions who required a lift to Spinnakers Wood where they were to dowse for animal ley lines.

'Had to wait at the surgery. Child being awkward. Ducks, teddies, promise of ice cream – wouldn't budge. Persuaded him to think orange – all over in a trice. Hence the saying "good as gold" of course . . . where was I?'

'Molar,' said the coroner.

'Ah, yes! That tackled I went to Hi Notes to collect some music. Boccherini's – the G5 – Sonata and a piece by Offenbach. I always think of him as the Liszt of the cello don't you?' She beamed at the coroner whose half moons jigged on his nose in disbelief. 'Bought a cucumber and a cream bun. Ate them down by the river and drove home arriving a quarter to two and finding poor Jim. Rest you've already heard.'

Asked if she had touched the body, Miss Cuttle replied in the negative. 'Could see he'd already transmuted to the astral.'

'Quite so,' replied the coroner taking a sip of water and wishing it were something stronger.

Miss Cuttle explained that as far as she'd been aware no one else was in the house. People hadn't started trickling back until nearly tea time. Asked if she could think of anything else that might be helpful, she said: 'One odd thing. Someone rang up asking for Jim just after I got home. Very strange. He was hardly ever in contact with the outside world. Quite a reclusive sort of chap really.'

Given permission, she then retired to her seat blissfully unaware that the cucumber and ley lines had come within a whisker of undermining the excellent groundwork laid by the pure silk and the chime of authoritative vowels.

After the first person to see James Carter dead, came the last two to see him alive. Giving his name as Arno Gibbs, a small man with a beard like a little red spade dipped to a respectfully sombre angle explained that he had left the house at eleven-thirty to drive the Master—

'Could you use the correct name, please,' interrupted the clerk.

'I'm sorry,' said the bearded man, 'Mr Craigie and Mr Riley – to Causton in the van. When we left Jim was watering the pots on the terrace. He seemed in good spirits. Said he was going to get some tomatoes from the greenhouse and make soup for lunch. It was his turn to milk Calypso and he'd missed breakfast you see.'

A buzz of speculation *in re* Calypso was briskly put down. Asked about the drinking habits of the dead man, Mr Gibbs said that the community was teetotal although a bottle of brandy was kept in the medicine chest for emergencies. Mr Carter had certainly not been drinking when they'd parted from him.

Next the coroner asked for Timothy Riley but the clerk crossed quickly to his table, murmuring something in a low voice. The coroner frowned, nodded, shuffled his papers and called for Mr Craig.

By now the air in the room was stifling. Faces were runnelled with sweat, shirts and dresses darkly patched. The ancient ceiling-fan's whangee propellors creaked, sluggishly pushing at the heat. Several large bluebottles buzz-bombed the windows. But the man who now came forward to speak looked very cool. He wore a pale silky suit and his hair was pure white (no trace of yellow or grey), and gathered into a rubber band. The resultant ponytail fell to below his shoulders. Mrs Bulstrode was heard to mutter that white hair could be very deceiving and it was true that the man's eyes were not at all rheumy but a vivid cerulean blue and his clear pale skin was hardly wrinkled. When he began to speak the quality of the court's attention changed. His voice, though gentle, had a strange almost revelatory quality as if the most tremendous news were about to be imparted for those who had ears to hear. Everyone leaned forward as if to miss even a syllable might deprive them of something precious.

Yet, after all, he had little that was new to add, agreeing merely with the previous witness that the deceased had behaved much as usual – being cheerful and positive on the morning of his death. He added that Mr Carter was a founder member of the community, had been greatly liked and would be greatly missed. The rest of the gathering then came forward but merely to confirm their own and each other's absence from the scene in question. Then the coroner began summing up.

The jury, now one melting mass on its long hard bench, strove to look impartial, intelligent and reasonably awake. There seemed to be no reason, they were told, to suspect foul play in this instance. All occupants of the Manor House were proveably elsewhere at the time of Mr Carter's unfortunate death. The rucked runner at the top of the landing, and the small amount of alcohol consumed by a person apparently not at all used to it and on an empty stomach, had probably between them combined to bring about the fatal fall. The coroner pointed out the advisability of using some sort of rubber grip or backing between loose rugs and highly polished floorboards, and he offered his sympathy to the friends of the dead man. Then a verdict of Accidental Death was pronounced.

The coroner rose, the fan gave a final apathetic groan and a dead bluebottle fell on the usher's head. The Windhorse group remained seated whilst everyone else drifted towards the door. You could have cut the disappointment with a knife. A murder, people unreasonably felt, had been as good as promised. They looked around for someone to blame but the Bulstrodes – prophets without honour – had already slipped away. The crowd moved, rumbling and grumbling, down the steps and into the car park or off to The Soft Shoe.

Two girls, young and pretty, long golden legs disappearing into stone-washed shorts, hung about waiting to see the witnesses emerge. One of them, staring round, nudged the other and pointed to a shabby Morris Traveller.

'Will you look at that.'

'Where?' A sun-bleached Afro turned and turned about.

11

'You blind? There, dimmo! That's their van.'

'So?'

'Look. . . .'

An indrawn gasp. 'Ange. . . .'

'D'you fancy him?'

'Are you kidding?'

'Chat him up then. I dare you.'

'Kev'd kill me.'

'If you don't, I will.'

'You wouldn't.'

'I'll say the car won't start.'

'We haven't got a car.'

Giggling, pushing each other, retreating, lurching forward, they eventually fetched up against the side window of the van. The one who wasn't Ange nudged her friend and said, 'Go on. . . .'

'Stop laughing then.'

A rap on the glass. The man turned. For a moment all three stared at each other then the girls, suddenly cold, their faces slack with shock, stepped back.

'I'm ever so sorry. . . .'

'Sorry.'

'I was only. . . .'

'We didn't mean anything.' They gripped each other's hands and ran swiftly away.

Back in the courthouse the wearer of the muslin trousers was weeping and being comforted. Her companions crowded round, hugging and patting her slim shoulders. The man with the beard left them, returning a few moments later with the news that everyone seemed to have departed so perhaps they could now make their own way home.

In this he was not quite correct. As the small gathering proceeded soberly through the waiting doors, a young man got to his feet in the gallery. He had been sitting, successfully concealed, behind a roof-supporting pillar. He stood very still, staring down at the coroner's empty chair. Then he took a piece of paper from the pocket of his jeans and read it – seemingly, from the length of time it took – over and over again. Finally he replaced the paper and leaned hard on the gallery rail, apparently in the grip of some powerful emotion. He stood there for several minutes before ramming a peaked cap on his fair hair and turning to leave. But even then it could not be said that he had quite recovered. For as he ran down the stairs his fingers balled themselves into angry fists. And his face was white with rage.

Five days later the ashes of Jim Carter were scattered around the bole of a giant cedar beneath which he had once loved to sit. A prayer for his reincarnation as a Chohan of the First Ray was offered and a wooden frame from which depended tiny bells and fragile twists of glass was held, glittering, up to the sun. There was a bit of gentle chanting then everyone had some lemon balm tea and a slice of Miss Cuttle's iced carrot cake and went about their business.

TWO DEATHS

Chapter 1

Breakfast was nearly over. The Master, who rose to commence his meditation and orisons at sunrise, was never present at this meal – settling instead for a tisane and a caraway biscuit in the Solar once his chakras had been cleansed and recharged. And, beloved though he might be – even worshipped on occasion, (although he would have been the first to rebuke such exuberant nonsense) – there was no doubt that his absence engendered a certain easing of restraint. The little group at the long refectory table was on the point of becoming quite frolicsome.

'And what are you two getting up to this afternoon, Heather?' asked Arno, removing a speck of yogurt from his beard with a hand-woven napkin. He referred to the single free period that their chores and devotions allowed.

'We're going up to Morrigan's Ridge.' Heather Beavers spoke with the eager breathlessness of a little girl, although her hair was long and grey. 'There's a monolith there with the most amazing vibrations. We hope to unlock the cosmic energy.'

'Be careful,' said Arno quickly. 'Make sure you take an amulet.'

'Of course.' Ken and Heather both touched the pyrite crystals suspended from a leather headband and resting, like a third eye, in the centre of their foreheads.

'Last time we had an energy release Hilarion came through with the most incredible power-packed information. He just . . . effloresced. Didn't he, Ken?'

'Mmm.' Ken spoke indistinctly through a mouthful of bran

17

and Bounty of the Hedgerow compote. 'Described our next thousand lives plus an outline of Mars' inter-galactic war plans. Going to be really hot come the millennium.'

'And you, Janet. Do you have any plans?'

'It's such a lovely day I thought I'd take the bus to Causton. May needs some more tapestry needles. Perhaps you'd like to come, Trixie.' She looked across at the girl sitting next to Arno who did not reply. Janet stumbled on. 'We could go into the park afterwards and have an ice.'

The long bony face was lean and hungry. Always either quite blank or flaring with emotion, it seemed incapable of expressing ambiguity. Janet had pale, light eyes, the pupils almost colourless, and coarse wiry hair like an Irish wolfhound. Arno averted his gaze from all that longing. Enslaved himself by Miss Cuttle's grand bosom and liquefacient gaze, he appreciated acutely enslavement in others and poor Janet was a perfect example of subjugation brought to a pretty heel.

Receiving no response, she now got up and began to stack the bulgy, smearily patterned cereal bowls. They were the unfortunate results of her Usefulness Training in the pottery when she had first arrived. She loathed the blasted things and always handled them roughly, hoping for a reduction in numbers, but they remained obstinately indestructible. Even Christopher, slap-dashing his way through May's Daisy Chain Spode, washed them up without mishap.

'As it's Suhami's birthday no doubt you have some treat in store.' Arno smiled shyly at the young man opposite, for everyone knew how sweetly the land lay in that direction.

'Well. . . .' Usually amiable and open-faced, Christopher appeared ill at ease. 'There seems to be an awful lot going on already.'

'But you'll be wanting to take her out? Maybe on the river?'

Christopher did not reply and Janet laughed, a forced rough sound with a scrape of malice, pinching some coarse brown breadcrumbs into a little pellet with her bony fingers. Frequently told as a child that she had pianist's hands, she had never cared to put the supposition to the test.

'Don't you believe in romance then, Jan?' Trixie laughed, too, but merrily, shaking out a mop of blonde curls. Shiny pink lips and thick sooty lashes gave her the look of an expensive china doll.

Janet got up and started to brush some spilled muesli towards the edge of the table. This was so old that the two halves had begun to warp, shrinking away from each other. A few nuts disappeared through the gap and rolled around on the wooden floor. She decided to be unskilful (the word used by the community to denote behaviour liable to cause a breach of the peace), and leave them there. Trixie tilted her chair back, glanced slyly down and made a tutting sound, her rosebud mouth in a kissy pout.

Janet took the bowls away, came back with a dustpan and brush and crawled under the table, the bare boards hurting her knees. Ten feet. Male: two Argyle socks – felted with much washing and smelling faintly of camphorated oil – two white cotton, two beige terry towelling and six sturdy sandals. Female: purple lace-up felt bootees embroidered with cabbalistic signs. Mickey Mouse sneakers over socks so brief they barely reached pert, delicate ankles. Jeans were rolled up to just below the knee and, on lately shaven calves, stubble glinted like gold wire.

Janet's heart pounded as she glanced at, then quickly looked away from the blue-white milky limbs and fine breakable ankle bones. You could crush them as easily as the rib cage of a bird. The brush slipped and swirled in a suddenly sweaty hand. She reached out, briefly touching near-transparent skin, before pushing the Mickey Mice aside.

'Mind your feet everyone.' Aiming for casual busyness she sounded only gruff.

'And you, Arno?' asked Christopher.

'I shall carry on with Tim,' replied Arno. He got up, collecting the square, stone salt cellars and horn spoons. 'We're working on a new straw hood for the hive.' Every member of the community was artisanally virtuous.

'You take such trouble,' said Heather. The words were shrill little pipes. A gymslip of a voice.

'Oh well . . . you know. . . .' Arno appeared embarrassed.

'We had a little astro-ceremony for him last night, didn't we Heather?' said Ken.

'Mmm. We held him in the light for ever so long.'

'Then we offered the auric centre of his being to Lady Portia – the pale gold master of serenity.'

They were so unshakeably positive. Arno said 'thank you' not knowing what else to say. Neither the Beavers for all their ring of bright confidence, nor the Lady Portia could help Tim. No one should. He could be loved and that was all. It was a great deal of course, but it was not enough to lead him from the shadows.

But it would be useless, Arno knew, to point this out. It would be unkind too, for Ken and Heather had brought the practice of positive thinking to a state-of-the-art meridian. No naughty darkling hesitancies for them. If one peeped out it was swept back under the carpet p.d.q. This refusal to acknowledge the grey, let alone black, side of life made them supremely complacent. A problem was barely described before the answer was on the table. Postulation. Simplification. Solution. Each stage liberally laced with Compassion. Soft-centred, honey-coated and as simple as that.

Trixie dragged her chair back, saying: 'I'm glad I'm not on kitchen rota for the grand occasion tonight. I can have a nice long drink in The Black Horse instead. I'm sure we're all going to need one.'

Ken and Heather Beavers smiled indulgently at this roguish whimsy. No one at the commune had ever been into the village pub. Janet emerged and got up rubbing her knees.

'What do you mean?' asked Arno. 'About needing a drink.'

'Mr Gamelin. Don't tell me you'd forgotten his visit.'

'Of course not.' Arno now collected the plastic washing-up bowl from which everyone had helped themselves to muesli. One of the community rules was: Never leave The Table Empty-

Handed, and, although this occasionally meant something vanishing before anyone had had a chance to make use of it, on the whole the system worked very well. 'Will you be making your Quark soufflé Heather?'

'I thought I wouldn't in case he's late. You know what tycoons are.' She spoke with rueful authority as if hot-foot from the Stock Exchange.

'We thought the three-bean lasagne,' said Ken stroking his comanchero moustache.

'That is certainly very filling.'

'Then use up the Quark with some stewed pears. Beat in some of Calypso's yogurt if it won't stretch.'

'Excellent.' Arno beamed as if it really was and thought, there's always the birthday cake.

'I bet he'll buy her an amazing present,' said Trixie.

'What they really like, ruthless tycoons,' said Janet, 'is tearing into a big red steak.'

'Quite a father-in-law you've chosen Christopher.' Ken and his crystal twinkled across the table.

Christopher said: 'Let's not get carried away,' and started to collect the cutlery.

'Well he won't get a steak here.' Heather shuddered. 'How do you know he's ruthless anyway, Jan?' Janet hated being called 'Jan'. Except by Trixie.

'I saw him on the box ages ago. One of those studio discussions. The Money Programme I think it was. He ate the lot of them up in the first five minutes then started on the table.'

'Now, now,' chided Arno. He had not seen the programme. There was no television at the Manor House because of the negative vibes.

But Janet remembered it well. That square powerful figure thrusting forward as if about to smash its way through the screen, crackling with aggression. Head held low and to one side, motionless like a bull about to charge. 'I wish he wasn't coming.'

'Stay mellow.' Ken waved his hands up and down, *diminuendo*. 'Don't forget. Not only is there one of him and ten of us, but we are standing in the light of the divine ocean of consciousness. We understand there is no such thing as anger.'

'He wouldn't have been invited you know,' said Arno when Janet still looked worried, 'if the Master had not thought it wise.'

'The Master is very unworldly.'

'Gamelin doesn't realise the challenging situation he's coming into,' chuckled Ken. 'It'll be a golden opportunity for him to change his karma. And if he's half the man you reckon, Janet, he'll jump at it.'

'What I don't understand,' said Trixie, 'is why Suhami didn't tell us until the other day who she really is.'

'Can't you?' Janet gave another unamused laugh. 'I can.'

'Just as well,' continued Trixie, 'that Chris had already started declaring his intentions. Otherwise she might think he was only after her money.'

A sudden silence greeted this intemperate remark, then Christopher, tight-mouthed, picked up the knives and forks, said 'excuse me' and left the room.

'Honestly Trixie. . . .'

'It was only a joke. I don't know. . . .' She stomped off without carrying as much as an egg spoon. 'No sense of humour in this place.'

Now Ken struggled to his feet. He had 'a leg' which stopped him doing quite as much as he would have liked around the house and garden. Some days (especially if rain was forecast) it was worse than others. This morning he hardly limped at all. He picked up the breadboard, saying 'No peace for the wicked.'

'They wouldn't know what to do with it if there was,' said Janet, and Heather put on her patient Griselda face.

Janet was Heather's cross and a great challenge. She was so left-brained; so intellectual. It had been difficult at first for Heather to cope. Until one day, appealed to, Ken's spirit guide Hilarion had explained that Janet was the physical manifestation of Heather's own animus. How grateful Heather had been to learn this! It not only made absolute sense but brought about an even deeper feeling of caring commitment. Now, using a tone of exaggerated calm she said: 'I think we'd better get on.'

Left alone with Janet, Arno looked at her with some concern. He was afraid he intuited some sort of appeal in the whiteness of her face and the strained rigidity of her hands and arms as she hung on to the dustpan. He wished to do the right thing. Everyone at The Lodge was supposed to be available for counselling at any time of the day or night and Arno, although he was by nature rather fastidious about the spilling of his own emotions, always tried to be open and receptive if needed by others. However there were resonances here which disturbed him deeply and that he did not understand. Nevertheless. . . .

'Is there something worrying you, Janet? That you would like to share?'

'What do you mean?' She was immediately on the defensive, as if goaded. 'There's nothing. Nothing at all.' She was irritated by the word 'share', implying as it did an automatic willingness to receive.

'I'm sorry.' Arno backtracked, unoffended. His freckled countenance glazed over with relief.

'Unless you go around with a permanent grin on your face, people keep asking you what your problem is.'

'It's well meant—'

But Janet was leaving, her angular shoulder blades stiff with irritation. Arno followed more slowly, making his way to the great hall. It appeared empty. He looked around. 'Tim . . . ?' He waited then called again but no one came. The boy had lately found himself a quite impregnable retreat and Arno, appreciating Tim's need to be safe and lie securely hidden, made no attempt to seek him out. When the Master emerged from his devotions, Tim also would show himself – following in his beloved benefactor's footsteps as naturally as any shadow. And crouching at his feet when he halted like a faithful hound.

So Arno put the beehive hood aside for another day. Then he made his way down the long passage to where the Wellingtons, galoshes and umbrellas were kept, found his old jacket and panama hat, and disappeared to work in the garden.

* * *

After everyone had gone and the main house was quiet Tim appeared, edging his way into the hall.

Here, in the centre of the ceiling, was a magnificent, octagonal stained-glass lantern thrusting skywards forming part of the roof. On bright days brilliant beams of multicoloured light streamed through the glass, spreading over the wooden floor a wash of deep rose and amber, rich mulberry, indigo and soft willow green. As the clouds now obscured and now revealed the sun, so the colours would glow more or less intensely, giving the illusion of shifting, flowing life. This area of quite magical luminosity had a compelling fascination for Tim. He would stand in it, slowly turning and smiling with pleasure at the play of kaleidoscopic patterns on his skin and clothes as he bathed in the glow. Now he was poised beneath a powdery haze of dust motes suspended in the radiance. He saw them as a cloud of tiny insects: glittery-winged harmless little things.

Sometimes he dreamed about the lantern. In these dreams he was always in motion, occasionally swimming upwards, parting the spreading shiny light with webbed fingers, pressing it behind him, kicking out. But more often, he would be flying. Then, weightless in a weightless world, his body would soar and spin and dive, looping the rainbow loop. Once he had been accompanied by a flock of bright birds with kind eyes and soft unthreatening beaks. Waking after a lantern dream he would sometimes be filled with a terrible sense of fear and loss. He would spring out of bed then and race on to the landing to check that it was still there.

When Tim had first been brought to the Manor House and it had been impossible to persuade him to take any food, the Master, seeing the transforming effect of the dancing colours, had had two cushions brought and placed on the hall floor. Then, sitting with the boy, he had coaxed him to eat as one does a child – a spoonful at a time on the 'one for me and one for you' principle. He had kept this up for nearly two weeks. Tim was better now of course. He sat at the table with everyone else and played his part in the community as well as he was able, struggling with his allotted simple tasks.

But he never stopped being frightened. And now, when a door on the landing opened, even though it was only Trixie going to the bathroom, Tim ran like the wind to the nearest fox-hole and once more hid himself away.

In the Solar the Master sat, a tisane of fresh mint-and-lemon balm in his hand. Suhami, who had asked to see him urgently, seemed in no hurry to speak now that she was here. Being in the Master's presence frequently affected people so. Whatever disturbance of mind or body drove them to seek his counsel, they would find hardly had they come before him than the matter did not seem so urgent after all.

And in any case thought Suhami as she rested upon her cushion, spine supple and elegantly straight, it was now too late for words. The damage had been done. She looked at her teacher. At his delicate hands, enrapt features and thin shoulders. It was impossible to be angry with him; foolish to expect him to understand. He was so guileless, his concerns purely of a spiritual nature. He was in love (Janet had once said) with the ideal of purity and so saw goodness everywhere. Suhami pictured her father, soon to be on his dreadful juggernauting way, and her distress returned, keen as before.

Guy Gamelin was about as spiritual as a charging rhino and had been known to leave an equivalent amount of chaos in his wake. The Master could not possibly imagine a person so volatile; so alarming when thwarted; so consumed by massive gobbling greed. For he thought there was that of God in everyone and all you had to do to reach it was to be patient and love them.

'I would not have suggested this visit,' (she was quite used to the Master reading her mind), 'if I didn't think the time was right.' When Suhami remained silent, he continued: 'It is time to heal, child. Let all this bitterness go. It will only do you harm.'

'I do try.' She said, as she had a dozen times over the past week, 'I just don't see why he has to come *here*. I shan't change

25

my mind about the money if that's what's behind it.'

'Oh, let's not start on that again.' He smiled. 'I know an impasse when I see one.'

'If you won't take it, it will go to charity.' She added quickly, 'You don't know what it does to people, Master. They look at you, think of you differently. Already—' Her face changed, becoming apprehensive. Soft and blurred. Her mouth trembled.

'Already?'

'You . . . haven't told anyone? About the trust fund?'

'Of course not, since that was your wish. But don't you think your parents—'

'My mother isn't coming. He wrote saying she was ill.'

'That may well be true.'

'No.' She shook her head savagely. 'She didn't want to come. She wouldn't even pretend.'

'A visit on that basis would be worthless. Be brave Suhami – don't seek false satisfactions. Or demand that others comfort and sustain you. That's neither fair on you or them. You have everything you need right here. . . .' And he laid his fingers to his heart. 'How many times do I have to say this?'

'It's easy for you.'

'It is never easy.'

He was right about that. Only once at meditation had she come anywhere near understanding what 'everything you need' really meant. She had been sitting for just over an hour and had experienced first a deep intensification of the silence then an extraordinary gathering of attention which she felt as a strong energetic pulse. Then there was a moment of luminous stillness so sublime that it seemed all her human-ness, all the mess and pain and hope and loss that made up Suhami, vanished – subsumed into some inner core of certain light. A blink of an eye and it was gone. She had mentioned it to no one but the Master who had simply warned her against any zealous seeking of further such experiences. Naturally she had been unable to resist such attempts but it had never happened again.

A year ago she had not even known he was alive and still

occasionally experienced deep tremors of alarm when recalling the haphazard manner of their meeting. If a left turn had been taken instead of a right. . . .

She had been with half a dozen acquaintances in a wine bar off Red Lion Square. It was during the Happy Hour – that early-evening hiatus when the lonely, disaffected and dispossessed can swill themselves into oblivion for half the going rate. They were all smashed, flicking aubergine dip around with bread sticks. Asked to leave, refusing, being threatened with the police was nothing new. They racketed off, arms linked, shouting, forcing people off the pavement in Theobald Road.

It was Perry who'd seen the poster attached to a board by a shabby doorway. The words 'LOVE, LIGHT & PEACE' were prominent as was a large photograph of a middle-aged man with long white hair. For no reason this struck them as hysterically funny. Jeering and snorting with contemptuous laughter, they charged up the worn, mica-freckled steps and through some swing doors.

They found themselves in a small room, sparsely occupied, with a platform at one end. The audience was mostly women, mostly elderly. A few earnest-looking men with rucksacks or carrier bags. One wore a cap with a transparent plastic cover. He kept pursing his lips judiciously and shaking his head, making it plain he was not to be easily impressed. Everyone turned at the disruption and several people 'tutted' and sucked their teeth.

The newcomers clattered along the row of tip-back seats and sat hoisting their feet up. They were reasonably quiet for about five minutes then Perry crossed his eyes in warning preparation and let out a long succulent raspberry. The others shrieked and giggled, stuffing fists into their mouths like naughty children. They put on po faces as people stared and Perry shouted: 'It was him with his hat in a bag.'

Ten minutes later, bored with the game, they got up and left, mocking the man on the platform, kicking the seats on their way out. Reaching the swing doors, one of them – Sylvie – turned and looked back. Half a step away from chaos (as she was later to recognise), something had compelled this movement. She returned to sit quietly on the wooden seat, heedless of raucous beckoning shouts from the stairwell.

The address had soaked into her, warm and soothing as honey balm. Afterwards she had been amazed that an evening which had so utterly transformed her life was so hard to recall in detail. The only complete sentence she remembered was: 'We are all standing in our own light.' Although she'd had no perception as to what the words actually meant they'd struck her then (and did still) as immeasurably profound and consoling. Even in those first moments she had been aware of a longing to take that sideways step away from her old tawdry self. To crack open and shed the carapace of a loveless and ugly past. Those hate-filled drunken days and love-starved nights.

When the talk was over the speaker put on a coat over his long blue robe. In this he was assisted by a small bearded man. Then he drank a little water and stood, looking over the rows of empty seats to where the girl sat. He smiled and she got up and moved towards him, feeling (although she could not then have described it so) the pull of sheer disinterested goodness. She seemed to sense in the slight figure an overwhelming concern for her wellbeing. The sheer novelty of such a situation struck her as unbearably poignant and she began to weep.

The Master watched her approach. He saw a thin tall girl in a lewd outfit. A gleaming silver cake-frill of a skirt and halter top no wider than two ribbons. She had a wild fuzz of pale hair, eyes smearily ringed with kohl and a scarlet jammy mouth. She smelt of gin and strong perfume and sour embittered dreams. As she lurched closer her sobs became more raucous and by the time she reached the dais she was shouting; terrible wails of grief and woe. 'Ahhh . . . ahhhh.' Rocking on high sparkly heels, arms folded tight across her barely covered breasts, she stood and howled.

So long ago now it was hard for her to recall the intensity of that despair. She reached out and took her companion's glass.

'Do you want some more tea, Master?'

'No. Thank you.'

There was a deep crevice between his brows. He looked tired. Worse – Suhami noticed the drooping skin beneath his eye – he looked old. She could not bear the thought that he was vulnerable to the passing of time. For was he not the fount of all wisdom, the never-ending source of blessings? He was there to love and protect them all. If anything happened to him. . . .

As she moved towards the door, Suhami realised that knowing someone was mortal and truly comprehending it were two different things. She had convinced herself he would be there for them for ever. She thought of Tim. What would he do without his beloved protector and companion? What would any of them do? A spasm of fear seized her and she ran back and pressed his hand to her cheek.

'What on earth is it?'

'I don't want you to die.'

She thought he would smile and tease her out of her distress but he simply said: 'But we must. All of us.'

'Aren't you afraid?'

'No. Not now.' And he withdrew his hand. 'I would have been . . . before. But not now.'

I am afraid, thought Suhami. And her face was deeply troubled as she left him.

Flowing from an open casement on the ground floor of the house came a torrent of glorious sound. May seated at her cello, legs sturdily apart, size eights planted firmly on sea-grass matting, was playing the Boccherini Sonata. The bow swept back and forth with fierce élan. Two deep furrows tugged at her thick brows and her eyes were tightly closed. She tossed her head in such an excess of passionate dedication that transparent pearls of sweat flew sparkling through the warm air and one of her plaits, coiled like an auburn saucer over her ear, became loose, swinging vigorously back and forth in three-four time.

She was wearing a loose gown, tie-dyed gamboge and maroon showing the pyramids and a burial cortège sideways on. Not one of the print room's more successful efforts. A mistake had been made with the blocks so that at one point the funeral party – corpse, camels, mourners *et al* – had done a volte-face, colliding with the forward-looking lot head-on.

Above the bateau neckline of this voluminous shift rose May's splendid profile. Cleanly etched, serene, noble, unambiguous in its dedication to the spreading of happiness and health, it was also most attention-catching for May adorned her face as she did her room, her person and every single artefact she owned, which is to say prodigiously. And her palette was as comprehensive as her brush was generous. Cheeks bloomed wanton coral, full lips shiny pomegranate red. Eyelids bright green shading into a blend of sky blue and plum, occasionally patterned with silver dust. Her tea-rose complexion sometimes had quite a solid bloom for, occasionally distracted by other-worldly musings, she would forget she had already put on her foundation and would impasto on a further layer before finishing off with a generous dusting of Coty American Tan.

Now, after a final buoyant flourish of the bow, she laid her hand upon the strings to still their vibration. Was there any other instrument, she wondered, any other creature that could grunt with elegance? She rested her cheek briefly against the glowing wood, leaving a dusty peach-brown imprint, then leaned the cello against her chair and in all her calicoed splendour billowed across to the window.

She stood gazing out at the cedar tree, struggling to maintain the sensation of joyful calm that had possessed her whilst playing. But she had no sooner noted such feelings than joy became mere happiness, and pleasure transmuted quickly into a dullish lack of ease. May sighed and, for comfort, wrenched her thoughts to her recent colour workshop 'There's A Rainbow Round Your Shoulder', which had been over-subscribed and very well received. But even this stratagem was only partially successful. Visions of uplifted participants all thinking aquamarine faded despite all her best efforts to the contrary, and the shadow of anxiety returned. She realised she was not even looking forward to her coming regression and these were often most exciting occasions.

May was extremely cross that this should be so. She didn't have a lot of patience with folk who 'mooned about' as she put it. Fretting over this and that, refusing to get to grips with the problem, never mind putting it right. Rather self-indulgent she thought that sort of thing. Now she was doing it herself. And really without excuse, for there was certainly no shortage of people to go and talk to. Unfortunately one of them (she didn't know which) was the cause of her concern. She would have liked to turn to the Master even though it was not usual to bother him with temporal matters. The fact that in this instance she could not caused her genuine distress. It was as if a constantly reliable source of warmth and light had been unkindly doused. She felt not only bereft but also rejected – which she knew to be unreasonable. The difficulty was that her beloved guru – innocently and unwittingly she was sure – was partially to blame for this sense of unease.

It had happened like this. Two days after Jim died May had been passing the Master's chamber on her way to the laundry room. Although the door was ajar his beautiful passe-partout zodiac screen was positioned in such a way as to conceal any occupants. Low voices were chuntering on, stopping, starting again and May assumed a spiritual-growth stroke chakra-cleansing session was in progress. Then, suddenly a voice cried out: 'Oh God – why couldn't you have left well alone! If they do a postmor—' A vigorous shushing cut this short.

The resulting silence seemed to May, standing as if bolted to the floor, quite stifling. Of a smothered, tightly wrapped quality. Then she understood from the rustle of a robe, rather than any footfall, that someone was coming around the screen. She jumped aside just in time, flattening herself against the corridor wall, and the door was firmly closed.

Trembling with surprised distress, May continued to stand there. She had hardly recognised the Master's voice, so choked had it been with emotion. Whether anger or fear it was hard to say. Could have been either. Or both. She struggled to persuade herself that she had misunderstood or that the words, taken out of context (and she had heard none of the context), could have quite a different meaning from the one apparent. But to what could the words 'post mortem' apply except Jim's death? The inference was surely inescapable.

In the laundry room, pouring ecologically sound enzyme-free pale green washing granules, May silently railed against the malevolent sprite who had directed her steps that morning. For, like the majority of the community, she firmly believed that the shape and disposition of her day was ordered not by herself but by her stars and she couldn't say she'd not been warned. Zurba, moon of Mars, had been skidding about from here to breakfast all week.

When the time came to take out the dripping piles of brilliantly coloured washing, May couldn't help reflecting on the contrast between their freshly rinsed unstained perfection and her own darkly blemished thoughts.

And then, about a month after this, another almost equally disturbing thing occurred. She had been awoken in the middle of the night by a soft bump in Jim's room, which was next to her own. This was quickly followed by two more as if a chest of drawers was gently being opened and closed. May had heard someone moving around there on a couple of occasions during the day but had thought nothing of it, assuming that whoever it was would be about the sad task of sorting out Jim's things preparatory to their disposal. But this nocturnal prowling was something else. Guessing at burglars, she had bravely taken up her heaviest tome (*New Maps of Atlantis and Her Intergalactic Logoi*), crept along the corridor and, holding her breath, with fingers pinched tight around the handle, gently tried Jim's door. It was locked.

Silent though her pressure had been, May heard a sudden flurry of movement. Although alarmed she stood firm, holding *New Maps* high above her head. But the door remained closed. Uncertain what to do next, still listening, she heard a metallic grating sound and realised it was the window latch. She rushed back to her room but by the time she had put down the book and reached her own window it was too late. Next door's casement gaped wide and she was convinced she saw a shadow, a dark disturbance, at the end of the terrace.

This made her rethink her assumption that the next step would be to raise the alarm. For whoever it was had not made for the street and the outside world. It would have been easy enough for them to do so for, like many other large Elizabethan houses, the Manor was only a modest distance from the main village street. There had been a bit of half-hearted vandalism a few months before, (some bulbs uprooted, rubbish thrown in the pond) and the Lodge had purchased a halogen lamp which switched itself on after dusk if a person or vehicle appeared on or near the drive. It was not on now.

Doubly disturbed, May rested on her window seat and gazed out into the perfumed night uncomforted by the rich complexity of garden scents or shining perfection of low hanging stars. It was a moment of extreme isolation for her. Not the bleak, four-in-the morning intensification of solitude when the possible time and manner of one's death presses like a blindfold on the mind. Hers was a humbler but no less terrible sensation. She had discovered that in her Eden – for so happy was she at the Golden Windhorse no other name would do – was a serpent. Double-faced and -hearted, double-tongued.

Who it was she as yet had no idea, but she believed – no, she *knew* – that the person fleeing from Jim's room had re-entered the house. Her mind backtracked to that earlier disturbing snatch of conversation. She was convinced, even whilst chiding herself for such dramatic silliness, that the two incidents were connected. The temptation was to put them both aside. Carry on as usual in the hope that nothing else peculiar would happen, then in time the whole thing must surely fade from mind. The phrase 'mind your own business' was perhaps not entirely inappropriate here. But that sort of attitude was completely against the ethos of the community. The whole point of living in such a way was that everyone constantly minded everyone else's business. That's what caring was all about.

And so May's thoughts treadmilled back to the well-worn theme of the mystery prowler and the mystery voice. Fretful and distracted, she had been tightly pleating her skirt. Now, released, the camels sprang forth giving a more than fair impression of a living caravan.

If only she had been able to learn the sex of the person the Master was addressing. She would then simply have confided in someone of the opposite gender.

She jumped to her feet almost growling with crossness, for May could not bear to think there was something wrong that couldn't be fixed. She started to pace up and down, calling silently but with great force on Kwan-Yin, the pale peach lady master, under whose guidance and sublime patronage she had been placed during a charming ceremony involving a basket of fruit, some folds of clean white linen and an extremely substantial cheque. But although from then on Kwan-Yin had never stinted when it came to giving advice and firing off mother-of-pearl rays to refresh and comfort, today she remained absolutely unforthcoming.

Arno was hoeing the broad beans and struggling with his koän. It was a very difficult koän, having been set originally by the Zen master Bac An. 'What is the sound,' the great sage had inquired, 'of one hand clapping?'

Step by rational-thinking step would, Arno knew, avail him naught. Illumination according to the *Teach Yourself Satori* shelves of the library (Theo/Psych/Myth: Oriental Sub-Section 4:17), though sudden and blinding, would be vouchsafed only after months – perhaps years – of gruelling meditation and reflection. And that wasn't the half of it. The disciple must closely attend to every moment of every day, living always with full awareness and one hundred per cent physical, mental and spiritual involvement in any undertaking no matter how humble. Arno had many little ploys to trick him back into the present when attention strayed which it did all the time. Now he pinched his arm to banish daydreaming and concentrated once more on the weeds. He grasped the handle, wholly experiencing the satiny warm wood, stared intently at the rusty blade and scrutinised the minute white flowers of the chickweed. Even the dark-tipped stamens were assiduously noted.

Arno did all this with no feelings of pleasure. Descartes' notion of man as master and proprietor of nature struck no answering chord in his breast. He did not enjoy or understand the garden at all. It seemed to plot ensnarement, being full of grasping brambles and secret squishy places cunningly concealed beneath firm-looking grass. It was full of insects too: leather-jackets and chafer grubs; pea thrips and eelworm. All strongly motivated and growing fat on Arno's vegetables which, truth to tell, were not much cop to start with. Having no idea of soil husbandry he planted carrots in clay, beans in soggy ground and potatoes over and over in the same plot.

He was aware of course that such agricultural ignorance could be remedied and had at one point bought a book for the purpose. It was very thick and crammed with black and white drawings, many of them illustrating to perfection Arno's scabbed, forked and furry emblements. Boredom smothered his mind the moment he first glanced upon the closely packed hectoring paragraphs and the volume quickly got lost behind balls of twine and old seed packets at the back of the potting shed.

Naturally he had remonstrated when given the position of gardener, assuring the nominations committee that he had no talent at all in such a direction. But that, it was patiently explained, was the whole reason behind the allocation. His own wishes must not be secondary, not even last, but of no account whatsoever. No pandering to the ego (that slavering, ravenous beast). No picking and choosing. To grow in grace was to shrink in self-interest and there were no short cuts. Arno sighed and winkled out a bit more groundsel.

But then all irritation vanished for, humming across the lawns and pond and the rhododendron walk, came a mellifluent flow

35

of sound. Arno put aside his hoe so as to give the music played by the darling of his heart his full and rapt attention. One of Arno's deepest fears was that if by some miracle his ego, constantly starved of accedence to its desires, withered away entirely, his love for May would disappear as well – taking with it all cause for future joy.

It had been borne upon him gradually that he would never speak of his magnificent obsession. This wasn't always the case. When he had first arrived, not having grasped the full splendour of May's bountiful personality and remarkable musical gifts, and possessed by a wistful lust for attention, he had presumed to press his artless suit. This had consisted of a series of overtures so quiet, subtle and introspective that no one noticed them, least of all May. And this despite her penchant for divination.

But realising quite quickly that his ambition had wildly overleapt itself and that his beloved was one of those extraordinary beings put upon this earth not for the comfort of one solitary soul but of all mankind, Arno withdrew to settle, almost content, for a lifetime of devoted service.

He had so nearly missed knowing her at all having arrived at the Golden Windhorse by a very chancey and roundabout route. He was quite alone in the world, his mother with whom he had lived since his father ran away thirty years before, having recently died. The protracted and undeservedly cruel manner of her death, for she was the gentlest soul alive, had left him bitter, lonely and in despair. After the funeral he had shut himself away in the little terraced house in Eltham like a wounded animal. He practised only the minimum grooming and feeding necessary to stay alive and look reasonably presentable when going out for food. Apart from shop assistants he saw no one for weeks at a time for he had given up his job at the Water Board Authority to nurse his mother in the last stages of her illness.

Most days he would lie curled up in bed, a ball of dark steely pain, his cheeks slobbered with tears. Salt water ran into his ears, his nose clogged and his throat was sore. His mother's friends, and she'd had many, would tap on the window and occasionally, meeting him abroad, ask him around for meals. Sometimes he found little cardboard boxes containing tins of soup and instant whip on his doorstep. Weeks went by when he hardly got up. The blinds were permanently drawn and day ran into night ran into day with merely a rim of brightness round the window frame to indicate which was which. Once he had found himself frying bacon at what he thought was breakfast time only to discover it was three in the morning.

Then, one afternoon, he started to read again. He had made some coffee but instead of slumping back on to the bed as usual to drink it, he had sat up at the kitchen table, opened some Bourbon biscuits from one of the gift boxes and picked up *Little Dorrit*. He and his mother had both loved the Victorian novelists although she had preferred Trollope.

Later that day, having finished shopping he'd called in at the second-hand bookshop and spent some time browsing in the philosophical section. He supposed now, looking back, that he had been hoping to obtain some insight into the reason for his mother's prolonged agony. He didn't of course. He took half a dozen volumes home but they were either so abstruse he could not make head nor tail of them or so glib and silly that they would have made him laugh had he been capable.

Shortly after this he attended several spiritual meetings where although his mother did not 'come through', he had obtained a degree of comfort, paradoxically by observing the suffering of others. Several people present had lost young children and the sight of their anguish and the small toys they sometimes brought along to encourage the shades of their dear infants to draw nigh helped Arno put his own bereavement in perspective. His mother had, after all, been nearly eighty and by her own admission tired of life.

And so, gradually, the sharper edge of Arno's misery was transformed into a dull bearable ache. But his loneliness remained, unassuaged by the shallow day-to-day exchanges that were his lot. He yearned timidly for a wider, more intimate acquaintance whilst being unsure quite how to bring this state of affairs about. His only hobby was reading so he could hardly follow the ubiquitous advice to join a club whose members shared his interests. Even so he felt the vague cautious friendliness he was starting to feel vis-à-vis the wider world should be encouraged, so he signed up for a Literary Appreciation course at the nearest technical college.

But then, walking home from the enrolment evening, he had called into Nutty Notions for some honey and seen a card on the noticeboard advertising a psychic weekend 'Hearing From Your Loved One'. Whether it was the nursery comfort of the words 'loved one' or simply the idea of a weekend away from the cheerless shell that his home had now become, Arno decided to go. It was rather expensive (he noted from the travel agent's window that he could have had a week in Spain for the same amount), but he felt it might well be worth it for the chance of getting to know new people.

As things turned out the 'high-grade channeller' (a Hopi Indian) promised on the card came down with a low-grade bout of flu but 'Man – the Cosmic Onion!' proved a not uninteresting alternative theme to occupy the serious inquirer's mind.

The opening address was given by Ian Craigie, Founder Emeritus of the community. Arno was impressed and mildly entertained at the idea of himself as multi-layered with the 'god self' at the very heart of things. He enjoyed the company of the other guests and was intrigued by the variety of remedial courses: Colour Therapy, Harmonic Tuning, Tear Up Your Negative Script, The Care and Cleansing of Your Astral Body. An initial consultation was included in the cost of the weekend and he had almost decided on a harmonic tune when the door of what he now knew to be the Solar opened and, with a thrilling rustle of iridescent taffeta, Miss May Cuttle swept in.

He would never forget that first sight of her. So tall, with gleaming auburn hair flowing down her back. Her features were assembled with a rare degree of spatial symmetry. The end of her large gently hooked nose was displayed cleanly against a powdered expanse of olive skin adorned by a very fine silky moustache. Her cheek bones were flat and broad and her eyes, which had translucent glowing pupils like circles of amber, had a Magyaresque tilt.

After supper she played her cello. Entranced by the nimble fluidity of her bow and the floridly emotional music soaring to the high beams, Arno knew not only that he loved her but also that in some mysterious, impossible way he always had. He discovered her subject (Colour Healing), put himself down for a workshop and revelled in the warmth of her enthusiastically humane and generous nature. She sorted out his aura, wardrobe, sleeping habits, diet and attitude to the cosmos in a twinkling. Arno attended three more retreats then sold his house and moved to the Manor for good.

All this had been eighteen months ago and the happiness he had felt on first arriving had proved accumulative. Gradually he had shed his loneliness like an old skin, carrying it half-heartedly for a while – a rough barbed little parcel – and then one day just putting it down for good.

Of the members present when he had entered the commune, only May and the Master remained. The others, as is the way of communicants, had joined other groups or reverted to the nuclear.But replacements had arrived and now The Lodge was thriving. Indeed so satisfactory was the balance sheet that it was able to offer bursary help to the impecunious. Most months there was even a small surplus to send to Eritrea or wherever was the greatest need.

Arno gave an irritated 'uurgh' and pinched his arm hard. He had done it again. He had drifted off. He wondered not for the first time if he had made a mistake in choosing Zen as his discipline. He had been so attracted by its concrete day-to-day practicality – so resolutely non airy-fairy – but it was jolly diffi-cult. Even without the koän. Clenching his teeth, applying himself determinedly to the task in hand, he tried the Master's suggestion of verbalising the moment positively and loudly.

'How wonderful, how miraculous!' he cried, rootling away with

39

the metal blade. 'I am hoeing the radishes and now the broad beans. What joy!'

But it was useless. In no time at all he was picturing May and longing to be in her presence. Serving, adoring. Turning the pages of her music, making lemon tea on her little spirit stove. Or just blissfully basking in the charm of her company under the shining bright protection of her radiant eye.

Every day around mid-morning Ken, in his rôle as Zadkiel, planetary light worker, got down to some serious channelling. Sitting upright in the way of the Lotus, nostrils fluting with extra-sensory verve, eyes humbly crossed, he and his supra-conscious mind would attempt to penetrate the Outer Screen of Life and plug into the Inner Matrix of Reality. To assist him in these endeavours Zadkiel wore his nuclear receptor. This was a small gold-plated medallion covered in tiny pyramids which trapped all toxic energies (from microwaves, acid rain, carcinogenic radiation, Janet's negativity etc.) then manipulated the body's DNA vibrations until all toxicity was defused and harmonised.

Heather (or Tethys as she was astrally known) sat beside her husband breathing noisily and nasally, off about her own cosmic business which might run from a basic recharging of her energies through the great Devas of the Crystal Grid to a full-blown trip to Venus renewing friendships with other ascendant souls who, like herself, had escaped the drowning of Atlantis.

Sometimes Hilarion, Ken's contact on the other side, would come straight through (a single abracadabra), other times he would go in for quite lengthy teasing, wispily hovering about and hinting portentously in capital letters of revelations to come. Today he spoke almost before Ken had taken one pure breath from the Ascended Master Realms.

'I am here Earthling. Do you accept the Concentrated Flame of the Presence of the Sacred Fire?'

'Greetings beloved Hilarion. I accept the Authority of the Flame and promise to perfect, protect and beautify the Cosmic

Cause and work only to establish the Spirit of Love in all Mankind.'

'It is well. Know that they in the High Realm, the Shining and Invincible Ones, desirous of assisting in the precipitation of God's Perfection in the World of Form, Bless thy Sincere Endeavours.'

'Please convey my heartfelt gratitude to these all-powerful supreme authorities, great Hilarion.'

There was quite a bit more of this, plus instructions on how to keep 'the spiralling energy-vortice of our sweet planet earth' consciously tuned and magnetically cleansed. Hilarion's voice was very like Ken's and he was inclined to giggle. When these puckered-up sniggers had first escaped from between Ken's lips, he had been very surprised – not expecting one of the Lords of Karma to have anything as earthy as a sense of humour. The content of these sessions varied and truth to tell this a.m. it was all rather dull. Mainly about How To Throw Off Discordant Accumulations into the Interplanetary Matrix of Violet Light.

What Ken really enjoyed were the rare occasions when the old wizard offered a really unusual suggestion for some imaginative sortie which would somehow lead Zadkiel and Tethys towards a new appreciation of the glorious Cosmic Heartbeat. For instance only last week he had vouchsafed that if they chose, in the right and proper frame of mind, to trace each abandoned railway line in England to its source, they would obtain proof positive that Jesus – the Cosmic Christ – had visited their country in the latter half of the twelfth century.

'I have a prophecy, Zadkiel.' Ken sat up and Heather, who was by now on her way back, sat up too. 'By happenstance this night at the rise of the crescent moon the goddess Astarte will take upon herself a fleshly vestment to move amongst all denizens of the lower planes and disseminate lunar wisdom.'

'Gosh,' said Heather cogently.

'I suggest you bethink a circle of light around your whole being in readiness. Also call upon the countless legion of Violet Elohim for support. Visualise yourself within the electronic pattern.

Keep the rhythm of invocation going at all times. And don't offer her any refreshments.'

'Of course not, great Hilarion.' As if they would be so crass. 'Have you any idea of the exact—'

But he was off. Back over the aeons to the galaxy of his choice. At one once more with the burning stars and solar fire of divine alchemy. Briefly the words 'I AM' burned in the heavens then they too were gone and Ken gave a great sigh as he sloughed off his ethereal persona and returned to the thorny old work-a-day world. He looked across at Heather.

'How was it for you?'

'Ohh . . . Unity of Life as Light in the Sisterhood of Angels. A new core Avataric message – God Ego equals Vestal Virgin. A bit samey to tell you the truth. But Hilarion . . .' Heather tried not to sound miffed. 'Giving you a prediction. . . .' Ken blushed, shrugged and regarded the sole of his upturned left foot. 'Do you think we should tell the others?'

'Certainly,' replied Ken. 'It would be unfair not to. Imagine their surprise otherwise. And we have to consider the Master. He is old and frail. An unadvised shock of this magnitude might well be too much for him.'

Suhami was milking Calypso, resting her cheek against the goat's cream and chocolate flanks, gently squeezing dark wrinkled teats. The milk spurted into a plastic bucket.

When not tethered about the place Calypso lived in an out-house. This was clean and whitewashed with a two-part stable door. There were rows of apples on slatted shelves. Though scabby, the fruit smelt very wholesome as did Calypso's straw which was changed every day.

Suhami loved this place. The quietness. The golden warmth of the morning sun as it bounced off snowy walls. It reminded her of the Solar where they gathered for meditation – having the same charged, beneficent brightness. Even while noting the comparison she smiled. Nothing very spiritual about an old byre full of goat. But the Master had said that God could be present anywhere if the heart was open and humble, so why not here?

'Why not Cally – hmn?' Suhami shook off the last drips of milk and stroked the goat's warm mottled udder. Calypso turned her head, lifted a rubbery lip and gazed at her milkmaid intently. The pupils of the goat's eyes were yellow horizontal slits and she had a slight beard, girlish and feathery. Her expression never changed. She always looked ruminative and self-satisfied, as if guarding an important secret. A back hoof shifted slightly and Suhami moved the bucket out of harm's way. Calypso's bell gave a petulant honk. There was nothing she liked more than kicking the milk over.

In a moment Christopher would be here to take her out to graze. The habit was to move her round and about the vast lawn where she would nibble away producing a nap like velvet. This idea of establishing goat browsage rights had been voted for almost unanimously after a petrol mower was judged to be environmentally unsound. Only Ken, who was allergic to the milk, abstained.

Suhami slipped Calypso's leather collar on, gave her an apple and put a second in the lovely tapestry bag resting against the milking stool. The bag was a birthday present from May. The embroidery of glowing sunflowers and deep purple irises against a background of earth and red-brown leaves was almost identical to the design on May's own bag which Suhami had long admired. Only the sunflowers were different. A shade paler, for the shop in Causton had run out of marigold wool and could only offer the slightly less rich amber. Suhami had been very touched, picturing May secretly sewing in her room, motivated solely by the wish for someone else's happiness, hiding the work if Suhami came by. Suhami had received so much kindness since moving to the Manor House, in addition to the supreme kindness of the Master's teaching. So many offerings of quiet concern, conversations where someone really listened, gestures of comfort, tasks shared. Now they knew who she really was all this would change. Oh – they would try to carry on as usual. To treat her just the same but it would be impossible. Eventually money would drive a wedge. It always did.

Suhami's lips twisted ironically as she remembered how excited and hopeful she had been at the idea of choosing a new name and leaving her old self behind in London. A naïve and childish way of going on, for how could one shed twenty miserable years or become another person by such an ingenuous device? Yet it had helped. As 'Sheila Gray' she had presented a new face for new friends to write their affections on. Then her growing interest in and determined practice of Vedanta, coupled with a deepening commitment to further change, had suggested her present title. Now her days were filled with quiet gratitude which she took for happiness, for it was as near as she had ever been.

And then Christopher joined the commune. They had slipped almost immediately into an easy jokey friendship. He would tease her – not unkindly (he was never unkind) – crossing his hands over his heart in a mock languish of love, swearing he would waste away if she would not have him. This was in front of the others. When they were alone he was quite different. He would talk then about his past, his hopes for the future, of how he wanted to get out from behind the camera and write and direct. Occasionally he kissed her, grave sweet kisses quite unlike the heartless mouth-mashings she had previously endured.

When she thought of Christopher's inevitable departure Suhami had to remember very hard the Master's maxim that all she needed to sustain her was not out there in the ether, or residing in another person's psyche, but right in her own heart. This struck her as a tough and lonely dictum and she'd been alone enough already. As she pondered, footsteps disturbed the gravel outside and Suhami's fingers trembled against the wooden stool.

Christopher leaned over the stable door and said, 'How's my girl?'

'She's been eating apples again.'

As always Suhami was both exhilarated and perturbed by the sight of him. By the soft black hair and pale skin and glowing, slightly tilted grey-green eyes. She waited to hear him say, 'And how's my other girl?' for this was a well worn bit of cross-talk. But he simply pushed open the stable door and crossed over to Calypso, taking hold of her collar saying, 'C'mon old fat and hairy.' He had hardly smiled and in a moment they would both be gone.

Suhami said: 'Aren't you going to wish me happy birthday?'

'I'm sorry. Of course I am, love.' He wound the chain about his wrist. 'Happy birthday.'

'And you haven't declared your undying passion for nearly a week. It's not good enough.'

Struggling to keep her voice light, to make a joke of it, Suhami heard the echo of a hundred similar questions in a hundred other scenes. Won't you come in for a minute? Shall I see you again? Would you like to stay the night? Will you give me a call? Must you go already? Do you love me . . . do you love me . . . *do you love me*? And she thought: Oh God – I haven't changed at all. And I must. I must. I can't go on like this.

'I know you only do it in fun. . . .' She heard the pleading note and loathed the sound.

'It was never in fun.' His voice was harsh as he tugged at Calypso's chain. 'I said come *on*. . . .'

'Not . . .' Suhami stood up, dizzy and weightless. She stared at him in disbelief. 'Not in fun? What then?'

'Does it matter.'

'Christopher.' She ran towards him shaking with emotion, putting herself directly in his path. 'What do you mean? You must tell me what you mean.'

'There's no point.'

'The things you said. . . .' Almost exalted, she took hold of his chin and wrenched his face around, forcing him to meet her gaze. 'They were *true*?'

'You should have told me who you were.'

'But this is who I am.' She held out begging arms. 'The same person I was yesterday. . . .'

'You don't understand. I fell in love with someone and now I

45

find she's someone else. I'm not blaming you Suze – Sylvie—'

'Don't call me that!'

'But I feel completely thrown. You know my situation. I've nothing. Well, nothing compared to the Gamelins—'

'Oh God. . . .' Suhami cried out, jerking back her head as if from a blow. 'Am I going to have this all my life? *Gamelin Gamelin Gamelin*. . . . I hate the word. I'd carve it out of myself with a knife if I could – I'd *burn* it out. Do you know what it means to me? Coldness, rejection, lack of love. You've never met my parents but I tell you they are hateful. All they care about is money. Making it, spending it. They eat and breathe and dream and live money. Their house is disgusting. My father is a monstrous man, my mother an overdressed dummy kept going by pills and drink. Yes! my name is Sylvia Gamelin and it'll be the bloody death of me. . . .' And she burst into a torrent of abandoned weeping.

Christopher seemed for a moment unable to speak. Then he stepped forward and folded her into his arms. After a long while he dried her tears, saying: 'You must never, ever cry like that again.'

Chapter 2

Guy and Felicity Gamelin were in the doorway of their much-photographed town house near Eaton Square. The door, blinding pillar-box red, stood open beneath the Georgian fanlight. Smart bay lollipops grew in tubs on the black and white tiled step.

Guy and Felicity were saying goodbye. That is to say, Felicity was murmuring vexedly at the sight of her reflection in the writhing tangle of Mexican glass that was the hall mirror, whilst Guy fluently cursed Furneaux – at that moment stuck in a traffic jam in Chester Row. Neither addressed the other. Anything of import had long since been said. Or shouted, or shrieked and screamed. Now Felicity was careful, Guy indifferent. He had wondered once, on one of the rare occasions when he paid her any mind, why she bothered to go through this air-kissing, hand-waving ritual every morning, never thinking that his departure might be the one certain moment of satisfaction in a treacherous and hazard-ridden day.

Felicity shook out her silvery-tipped apricot mane and briefly imagined it netted in a Botticelli chignon of gold thread and pearls. Guy's invective rose to fever pitch. He had a mind like a well-stocked cess pit and never minced his words, which were full of spite and filthily inventive. The car finally arrived and Furneaux, grey-capped and suited, stone deaf from choice, parked and got out to open the nearside door. Immediately a queue of hooting vehicles formed. Guy gave a 'yah boo' smirk and leaned on the Roller's thickly padded door. It did not occur to him, thriving as he did in the narrow blank-eyed fastnesses of

47

the city where respect was index-linked, that the queue might be under-impressed by the magnificence of his equipage. This tiny victory, the first of the day (for he had long since ceased to regard his wife as a foe of any merit), cheered Guy up considerably as he settled back into the ivory leather and lit the first of his forbidden Dom Perignons.

Left alone Felicity drifted into the drawing room. This time, these first few moments after her husband left, would decide the shape and flavour of the hours to come. And – she recalled his overnight case – the evening, too. She prayed for a good day. Not happiness, never that. Just a bland unfolding of ordered assignations hedged about with the usual conventions. Where 'How are we Mrs Gamelin?' and 'Lovely to see you again' were never spoken from the heart and so, thankfully, demanded no sincere response. She had all sorts of little dodges, fail-safe mechanisms to set her on the right path. Or at least keep her off the wrong one.

Charity lunches, private views, dress shows, tastings of exotic foods and fine wines. The invitations were always there. Come as you are and don't forget your cheque book. Today was an auction of Russian icons and a yearling sale at Newmarket. Otherwise she might ring a gossipy acquaintance and ask questions about people in whom she had not the slightest interest. She would force brightness into her voice, and darkness out, like some effervescent actress/housewife in a washing commercial.

Her movements were becoming vague; a dangerous sign. Keeping busy, they had said at the clinic, was most important. By this she assumed they meant physically busy for her mind was never still. When she had first come home many people offered advice that frequently concluded with the words 'Whatever happens you don't want to go in there again.' Felicity felt it impolite to disagree and could imagine the amazement had she told them the truth, which was that she had been as near to contentment in the hermetically sealed warmth and comfort of Sedgewick Place as she had been in her entire adult life.

Drugged at first, then gradually weaned into a more subtle

dependence, each day had been one long highlight. Flowers would arrive followed by exquisitely arranged trays of delicious food. Smiling people bathed her, then combed her hair with slow languorous strokes. Doctors heard out her sorrows, and the cruelties of the outer world beat on the clinic walls in vain. Nothing was real. She felt like an imprisoned princess in a high and mysterious tower. The phenomenal cost had not even grazed the surface of her fortune.

They called it a nervous breakdown. A neat phrase explaining many antisocial actions – from bursting into tears at Harrods to clawing one's face in a convulsion of self-loathing. She had done both and in the same day, too. A terrifying escalation of abandonment and despair. But that was all in the past. All in the past, Felicity.

She said her name aloud a lot. It helped to counteract the frequent sensation that she was constituted so vaguely as hardly to make a complete person at all. Artificially brisk, she strode down to the basement, her heavy cream satin robe slapping at her calves.

In the huge Italian-designed hi-tech kitchen, the smell of chocolate brioche hung melting on the air. *Verboten* if she was to stay size ten. Guy had eaten four. Weight looked good on a man.

He'd been lean and hungry when they'd first met; slinking round, low-bellied like a starving cur. All she'd had to do was crouch down, extend the palm of her soft white idle hand, show him the words 'McFadden and Latymer' and smile. In those days there'd been a quick lightness in the turn of his head and a neck-or-nothing set to his wide, slightly turned down lips. He'd reminded her of a handsome frog. A young Edward G. Robinson.

Felicity grabbed at still warm pastry and rammed it into her mouth, knuckling in the overhanging fragments, hurting her lips. She chewed and chewed and sucked and chewed, voraciously extracting all the buttery, chocolatey vanillary essence, then spat the pulp into the disposal unit and ground it away. Then she lit a cigarette and stared up through the basement bars at the sad pollarded plane trees. She pictured them growing straight and tall, tender leaves uncurling high above London's muck and murk. All these poor things had were a few twigs sprouting from scaled over wounds. Someone walked by glancing down. Felicity dodged away and hurried upstairs.

Her bedroom was on the third level. She locked her door and sank, panting, on Guy's bed as if she had been pursued. They still shared a room, whether out of cussedness or malevolence on his part she could never quite fathom. It was not a comfortable experience. Guy was restless, his face on the pillow usually expressing some extreme emotion. Sometimes he laughed in his sleep and Felicity was sure he was laughing at her. On his bedside table was a photograph of their daughter in a mother-of-pearl frame. Felicity never looked at it. She knew it by heart. Or would have done if she had a heart to know it by. This melodramatic reflection made her eyes sting with self-pity and she screwed them up tight.

Foolishly she picked up the frame and slid further into ruinous introspection. As she stared into the wide hazel eyes the face seemed to dissolve, regressing in a flowing series of images into babyhood. Sylvie's first clumsy efforts at ballet class, her bewildered tears at being sent away to school and terrible anguish when Kezzie, her adored pony, died. Felicity slammed the photograph down, splintering the glass and thought, Christ I need a drink.

A drink and a couple of Feelgoods. The brown bombers. They should do the trick. Strictly for emergencies the clinic had said, but if being alone and in despair at nine on a terrible bright sun-ridden morning in deepest Belgravia wasn't an emergency what the fuck was? And a bath. That should help jolly things along. Felicity wrenched at the delicate golden taps and scented water gushed out.

She drew on her cigarette and saw her mirrored cheeks cave into corpse-like hollows. A web of fine lines spun out from the corner of her eyes. So much for the embryonic serum for which so many unborn lambs had given up any chance of skipping about

50

the greensward. She stubbed out her cigarette in the honey-coloured gel. A hundred and fifty, and for what? A web of fine lines. She traced the network with the tips of her index fingers then suddenly thrust the nails hard into the delicate skin, leaving cruel half moons. Then she picked up the tranquillisers and returned to the bedroom.

Taking out a half bottle of champagne from the tortoiseshell and ebony armoire which Guy had had converted to an ice-cool receptacle for his bed-time tipple, she put the tranquillisers on her tongue and tipped back the sparkle, letting it run all over her face and throat. In the bathroom the perfumed water overflowed, soaking the carpet, oozing outwards to the door.

Felicity, having drunk two more bottles, curled up, shrinking and dry-mouthed on a low brocaded chair. She was trying to avoid touching the fabric which had taken on the aspect of a mysterious landscape: spiked trellises; dissolving lovers' knots running into crimson lakes; clouds like blue-bunched fists. It was all sinisterly vivacious and filled her with foreboding.

The encroaching tide, the slap-slap at the edge of the bath, finally attracted her attention. She tried to stand up. Her limbs were heavy and her head ached. She blinked at the water which seemed to be vigorously on the move. Feeling bereft and frightened she started to cry.

Outside in the street a pneumatic drill started up. *Drrrrrrrrr r. r. r.* . . . Felicity rammed her fingers in her ears but the sound continued, splitting open her skull. *Drrrrrrrr.* . . .

She lurched over to the window, flung it up and screamed, her voice cracking like a wet sheet in the wind, 'Shut up you bastards . . . *Shut up!*'

The drill stopped independently of her intervention. She was about to withdraw when a voice directly beneath her said: 'Mrs Gamelin?'

Felicity craned out further. Standing on the black and white steps, looking up at the house with an expression of covetous respect, was a perfectly strange young man. She ran down and opened the poppy-red door. The young man jumped back no doubt recalling the manic shrieks from the upstairs window. Behind him, parked at the curb, was a van inscribed 'Au Printemps: Luxury Dry Cleaning & Invisible Repairs.' He produced a piece of paper.

'From the desk of Mr Gamelin, Mrs Gamelin.'

Felicity gave a hawk of laughter at such pomposity but she took the paper, which listed various items of clothing and read them out. 'One navy pinstripe suit, one grey chalk-stripe, one cream linen dinner-jacket. To be collected.' And a signature: 'Gina Lombardi'.

'Wait.' She left him on the step knowing he'd be in the hall the moment she was out of sight, and climbed back upstairs. In Guy's dressing room she pulled out the clothes noticing, as no doubt she was meant to do, the lipstick on the tuxedo lapel. An unnecessary directive. As far as Felicity was concerned Gina could have him not only mounted but stuffed.

She walked to the landing and looked down. The front man for Au Printemps was examining his zitzy complexion in the Mexican sunburst. Felicity shouted 'Catch' and threw down the clothes, watching their ballooning descent.

The young man flushed. He moved quietly into the hall where he knelt and folded each item with ostentatious neatness. Felicity was sorry for her rudeness. She had been brought up always to be polite to inferiors which, her parents had led her to understand, included everyone but the Queen, the heir apparent and, on Sundays, Almighty God.

He did not reply. He was checking the pockets, pulling the linings out, tucking them back. He was not really put out by her behaviour. Everyone knew that the rich, like the very old, did and said just what they damn well liked. And for the same reason. Nothing to lose. This one was well away. He could always smell champagne. It would be something to tell Hazel when he got back. They always said in the office he was a proper little Nigel Dempster. Whilst half hoping for a further tasty burst of obscenity to round the story off, his hand came into contact with a pale green envelope. He took it out and placed it carefully on the hall table. She made a sound of inquiry.

'We're trained to check all the pockets, madame.'

'I say,' said Felicity, hanging over the banisters. 'Is it a long course?'

When he had gone, slamming the door behind him, she went back down and picked up the envelope. It was not like Guy to be careless. He had a shredder in his study at home as well as in the office. True he had been very distracted the last couple of days, but even so. . . .

The envelope was recycled. She turned it over. It was addressed to them both. Strangely this perfidious concealment evoked a response far stronger than any sexual or social infidelity might have done. Her fingers trembled as she drew out the paper. What a bloody cheek! Her letter, *her letter*. She read the note several times, at first shaking with anger, not really taking it in. When she had fully absorbed the information she sat for a long time as if in a trance. Then she went into the sitting room, picked up the telephone and started punching.

'Danton? You must come over – right away. . . . No – Now! This minute. Something incredible has happened.'

The loudest sound in the Corniche convertible now inching its way round Ludgate Circus was the bump lurch stagger bump of Guy Gamelin's heart.

The calming technique of deep breathing suggested by his man in Harley Street had been impatiently and sketchily resorted to as had the muscle-relaxant drill. Neither had much effect. Guy performed both routines with a deep grudging resentment and then only because he could not bear the thought of paying for advice and not taking it. The fact was he refused to admit that such protective exercises were at all necessary. He was as vigorous now as he had ever been. At forty-five, still shaking hands with youth.

There was a flutter in his chest. An extremely delicate oscillation like a vibrating feather. Guy rested his fingers against his inside breast pocket feeling the outline of a brown glass bottle without which he had been told never to travel; not even from the bedroom to the loo. He swung out the walnut drinks cabinet, poured a dangerously generous ice-cold Tom Collins and placed a tablet on his tongue. Soon the fluttering ceased and although Guy didn't relax – he never relaxed – he sat a little more easily on the puffy upholstery. Then he disconnected the phone and let his mind go. Immediately it started to write anticipatory scenarios for the evening's confrontation, now only hours away.

Normally when riding out to face an adversary, Guy's blood would be fizzing with exhilaration. For, more than anything else, he loved a fight. Embattlement was his normal state of mind. He woke each morning from dreams of bloody conquest ready to charge through city boardrooms leaving a trail of wounded enterprises in his wake. Caparisoned by Savile Row, laved and barbered by Trumpers, he saw himself as a twentieth-century merchant prince. In truth he was a robber baron although his lawyers would have crucified the first man bold enough to say so.

Guy could not bear to lose. He had to be the best at buying and selling; the best at laying waste. His horses must run faster, his yacht be the most splendid. The racing cars he sponsored only came second under his patronage once. 'Show me a good loser,' he would bawl into the driver's sweating, oil-streaked face, 'and I'll show you a loser.'

But although he bought and sold men like so many peanuts and bent whole companies and countless women to his will, there was one area in which, up until now, he had not yet succeeded. Even in this instance, though, the word 'failed' was never uttered. The love of Guy's life, and his greatest torment, was his daughter Sylvie.

Naturally when Felicity first became pregnant Guy had wanted a boy. He was so used, even in those early days, to getting his own way, that the birth of a girl had devastated him. The measure of his disappointment at this insult to his manhood alarmed his wife, her parents, the hospital staff and anyone else who came within singeing distance. For all he knew, (too late, too late), it had even alarmed the baby.

Guy simmered down over the first few weeks but resignation was not in his nature. He despatched someone to glean the latest information on genetic research from scientific and medical journals and bought the best advice available. It seemed from what he had read that the point had been as good as reached when it was possible to choose the sex of one's child in advance, and he did not intend to be cheated by nature a second time. But, as it turned out, all the gleaning and expenditure, and bullying confrontations with specialists, were a waste of time and money – for Felicity never conceived again.

Guy had taken his first mistress during his wife's pregnancy and suspected that Felicity's consequent wilful refusal to give increase was a deliberate act of revenge. Later, when this point of view became medically indefensible, he was faced with what was, for a man of his sensibilities, an appalling dilemma. Either he went through life the father of one female child or he began again with another partner, thus announcing to the world that his marriage was a failure.

To understand the absolute impossibility of such an admission would be to understand what an astonishing, breast-beating triumph his capture of Felicity had been in the first place.

Her family, of course, had seen him for what he was. They had investigated his background and been appalled. She, fresh from a Geneva finishing school, presented with a collection of suitable young and not so young men had found them all pallid in comparison to Guy – who had thrilled and alarmed her in equal measure. Aware of this, he skilfully kept the fear quotient at just the right level. High enough to keep her intrigued, low enough for her to believe that he was tameable if the right girl took him in hand. She was wrong and he destroyed her.

But their life together, if one could so call such an empty baroque extravaganza, must be seen to continue. He would not be bought off and they had all tried. No one would ever say of him he could not hold what he had won.

His daughter's childhood held no interest. He hardly noticed her. There had been nannies (one or two deliciously satisfactory), and occasionally other children in the house. Once Guy came home and found hordes of them with balloons and carnival hats and a man in a harlequin suit riding a one-wheeled bicycle. Sylvie had thanked him gravely on that occasion for a magnificently attired four-foot-high doll that he had never seen before. But mainly she did not impinge and how could Guy, who had no imagination, perceive the passionate longing for love and praise or just simply attention that possessed his daughter's lonely heart?

And then, just after her twelfth birthday, everything changed. He remembered the day and time almost to the minute. She had been asked to play something on the piano. Music was on the curriculum at her very expensive boarding school so music she had to learn. Sylvie had no talent for the subject but, compelled to have lessons and practise during term time, had inevitably acquired a rudimentary technique. She had chosen 'The Robin's Return', an old-fashioned, tinkling rather sentimental tune. Guy had been leaning on the mantelpiece wondering if he had been right in sensing a wind of change in Blue Chip Trusts when he glanced across at the white Steinway and saw, as if for the first time, his daughter's face.

Pale, intense, rigid with anxiety. She was frowning and her lips were bitten together in a narrow line of concentration. Thin arms arched high over the keyboard, her shining brown silky little girl's hair was caught back from her face in a velvet-covered slide. She had been wearing a blue and white striped dress with a large white collar and bow that had fluttery, dark blue streamers. All these things appeared to Guy with such vivid and dazzling clarity that he might only that second have been awarded the gift of sight. And then, before he could become even slightly familiar with this almost hallucinogenic prospect, a second and even stranger thing occurred.

He became overwhelmed by a torrent of extraordinary emotion. Drowning in it, swept away, he gripped the mantelpiece, deeply alarmed. He thought he was ill so violently did his body react. His heart felt as if it were being squeezed, his guts looped and tangled. And more, and worse. For when this wave of feeling ebbed away it left behind a terrible residue. It left him with the gift of understanding.

He received and appreciated, compressed into the briefest space of time, all of his daughter's despair, her aloneness, her desperate hunger for love. And then knew an immediate agony of protective tenderness towards her. The newness and strength of this pain, that any father could have told him was par for the course, pierced him like a knife. He drank in her downbent serious face and realised how rarely he had seen her smile. (How could he not have noticed that?) He felt unbearably moved at this revelation of her sadness and then consumed by a desperate need to make amends. To offer all his love.

Yes – he recognised the emotion, even though he had never received any himself, for what it was. He vowed to give her everything. Find time to do all sorts of things, to make up for the lost years. When the music faltered and, after a few more hesitant notes, stopped entirely, he applauded, striking his hands together too loudly. Felicity stared, amused and disbelieving.

'That was very good, Sylvie. Marvellous, darling! You're coming on really well.' He was surprised how naturally the words sprang from his mouth. He, who never praised a living soul. He waited for her response, indulging in a little fatherly contemplation, imagining her pleasure at this enthusiasm. She closed the piano lid gently, got up from her stool and left the room. Felicity laughed.

Guy had pursued his daughter from that moment on. He took her away from boarding school so he could see her every day. Each weekend he devised outings that he thought might please and entertain. He poured presents into her lap or hid them in her room or rolled them up in the napkin by her plate, sick with apprehension lest they should not find favour. She rejected all these attempts at gaining her affection not harshly or vigorously – he could have handled that, there would have been an opening to build on – but simply turning from them with an air of quiet, well-mannered resignation. Occasionally she would look at him and her eyes were like pale blue stones.

Only once did she respond with any show of emotion and that was when, in a renewal of remorse at the years of neglect, Guy had struggled one day during an outing at the zoo to put his shame and regret into words. To unload perhaps, however unfairly, a fraction of the guilt. He had hardly started to speak when she turned on him shouting: 'Stop it, stop it! I don't *care*.'

He had desisted of course and they had spent the rest of the afternoon silent and apart although, he reflected painfully, no more apart than usual. Everywhere he looked that day there seemed to be fathers holding their children by the hand or carrying toddlers shoulder-high. One boy who looked no more than sixteen wore a canvas sling cradling a tiny baby. It was asleep, its scarlet crumpled profile resting on the boy's hollow chest. I could have done that, thought Guy, looking down in anguish at the narrow parting of his daughter's hair. Christ – I don't even remember picking her up.

He never again attempted to burden Sylvie with a declaration of his feelings although he had once struggled to put them in writing. He had not given her the letter of course, just locked it away in his desk drawer with a lock of her hair, some photographs and school reports. As the months and then the years went by his bitter regret inevitably, given her continued indifference, became less sharp. He could not ease up though. Doggedly he conversed till his throat ached; asking questions, making suggestions, commenting on day-to-day affairs. Once he had got the idea that it was Felicity's presence that was causing the child's restraint. That if he and Sylvie lived just with each other, they would by some happy miracle of familial osmosis breathe warmth into each other's lives and hearts. He had suggested it to Sylvie, not caring by that stage that such a move would broadcast to the world the failure of his marriage. She had appeared puzzled, frowned and pondered for a moment then said: 'But why would I want to do that?'

Then five years ago everything changed again. On the morning of her sixteenth birthday Sylvie disappeared. Walked out of the house as if going to school, never arrived, never came home. Guy, mad with terror, was convinced she had been kidnapped. Then, when no ransom call was made, he concluded that she had been the victim of an accident or murderous attack. He had contacted the police who, once they had been given Sylvie's age, were irritatingly unalarmed and said she was probably staying with friends or just wanted to be on her own for a bit.

Knowing this could not possibly be the case, Guy had visited the school and asked if he could talk to anyone with whom his daughter was particularly close. He could not give a name for Sylvie had never discussed her friends nor, for many years, brought any of them home.

A tall girl with narrow, supercilious eyes had been brought to the principal's office. She informed Guy that Sylvie had always said she couldn't wait to be sixteen so that she could leave home. 'She told me,' said the girl with feigned reluctance, 'she'd always loathed her parents.'

That night Felicity, home after her third cure and already over the yardarm, heard out her husband's pain-filled revelation and said: 'God, you're so dense about everything except making money. She's hated us for years.'

Guy had tracked Sylvie down fairly quickly. She was living in a squat at Islington. Quite decent as squats go. Water, electricity, off-cuts of carpet on the floor. He had gone round with the bloodstock papers relating to the three-year-old racehorse that was his birthday gift. She had appeared in the doorway and immediately started to shout and yell abuse at him, almost spitting in his face. After the years of bloodless unresponsive introversion it had been like receiving an electric shock. He had stepped back alarmed, amazed and – yes he had to admit it – exhilarated. Then she had flung the papers over the basement railings and slammed the door. They must have been picked up later, though, for the horse was sold the following month for two-thirds of the original price.

Oddly enough, after becoming almost resigned to what was

virtually a non-relationship, this brawling encounter reawakened in Guy all his previous yearnings. He could not believe any of the half dozen sponging troglodytes smirking behind her in the open doorway gave a damn for her wellbeing.

Over the next few years she moved around a lot. Guy employed a firm of private detectives, 'Jaspers' in Coalheaver Street, and always knew where she was. She never lived alone, sharing sometimes a mixed flat and occasionally with just one man. These liaisons, if such they were, never lasted long. Guy wrote to Sylvie regularly, asking her to come home, always enclosing a cheque. A very large cheque at Christmas and birthdays. She never replied to the letters but the cheques were always cashed so at least he was still good for something. Once she was twenty-one and could draw on her trust fund, even that small usefulness would be denied him.

Of course she was getting her own back, he thought. She has bided her time. She has waited and waited until she could humiliate and reject me as I, for years, did her. He recognised with an almost elated surge of recognition: *She is just like me.* And then, with a terrible falling back, *And I would never forgive.*

He wondered sometimes, to comfort himself, if perhaps her mind had not devised some cold and cruel symmetry. Could she mean this punishment, this banishment to last for precisely twelve years as his had done? She'd be twenty-eight then. Married, perhaps, with children of her own. She might be living anywhere. Abroad even. Thinking this, Guy had the shameful and traitorous notion that he could have borne it better if she had died.

He took to hanging around near her current apartment, discreet and self-conscious, like a thwarted suitor. Once, getting into a cab, she had spotted him in a doorway and gestured with crude and vigorous panache like a lustful navvy. Another time – and this was much worse – he had seen her come out of the building hanging on to the arm of a bored-looking man in a tweed jacket. She had been chattering brightly, laughing up into his face, her whole posture that of someone desperate to please. Half way across the road the man shrugged her off and Guy, even whilst appreciating the irony of the reaction, could have killed him.

Then she disappeared for the last time and much more thoroughly. In receipt of this disturbing intelligence Jasper himself took on the task of trying to trace her. Posing as a debt collector he had called at her last place of residence only to be thrown down the stairs by an Amazonian domestic. A female operative was then employed, at first with equal lack of success.

During this time Guy was in a pit of despair. Until he found himself totally ignorant of his daughter's whereabouts, he had not appreciated how crucial this knowledge was to his peace of mind. Bitterly estranged from him she might be but at least he had known she was 'all right' in the most basic sense of the words. After she vanished he became aware in his days and nights – and especially in his dreams – of a great yawning darkness that, in unguarded moments, threatened to engulf him.

Once when these fears seemed to be almost eating him alive he had briefly thought of talking to the Press. They would find her. 'GAMELIN HEIRESS VANISHES!' They had photographs a-plenty on their files, she would be hunted down and flushed out. Someone, somewhere knew where she was. But although such action could hardly damage the father-daughter relationship further, it would surely tip the balance against the chance of any future reconciliation. An eventuality in which Guy, hope triumphing wildly over experience, still unreasonably believed.

Sylvie had been gone about three weeks when the distaff side at Jasper's picked up a crumb of information. The investigator had the bright idea of booking an appointment with Sylvie's regular hairdresser. Seated there, her wide-eyed and gushing assumption that Felix and his rollers must be privy to half the top-society secrets in London flattered the stylist's tongue into looseness. Once he had determined that no one sporting such a ghastly home-made jumper and suburban haircut could possibly be writing a gossip column, he gladly dropped the odd name and juicy titbit for her to take away and thrill her boring little chums with in Ruislip or wherever.

Two of the items related to Sylvia Gamelin. Apparently she was sick of Hammersmith ('and who wouldn't be, darling?'), and was moving somewhere quiet, clean and peaceful. Pressed as to the possible place of relocation, Felix replied, 'She just said the country. And we all know how big that is don't we? She may not even have meant the Home Counties.' Snipping scissors faltered at the enormity of such a prospect.

'She did say she'd met a marvellous man, tho' whether the two things are connected. . . .'

Although these fragments of information yielded naught for his comfort Guy, starving, fell on them and instructed Jasper's to fan out and redouble their efforts. But no further lead could be discovered and six more sterile months dragged past, affecting Guy adversely. The fierce relish he had once obtained from the grab and grind, and cut and thrust of the market place became transmuted into a numb unfocused longing to inflict pain. This in turn affected the clarity of his judgement. He bought and sold clumsily and, for the first time in twenty years, started to lose money. Then, a few days ago, the letter had arrived.

After the first violent jolt of disbelief, inevitable when something yearned for over a long period of time seemingly drops into the hand, Guy had been overwhelmed with excitement. Although the communication was not in Sylvie's handwriting (was not, in fact, from her at all), it was *about* her and, even better, contained an invitation. Guy made to touch the letter which had come to hold almost talismanic powers for him. It was not where he expected it to be. He tried other pockets, slapping and pulling at his clothes in an excess of panic before remembering that since putting it away he had changed his suit. No matter. He knew the address and every line of the contents by heart.

Dear Mr & Mrs Gamelin, Your daughter has been staying with us for some time now. We will be celebrating her birthday on August the seventeenth and would be happy if you could both be present. Perhaps arriving around seven-thirty? We eat at eight. With kindest regards, Ian Craigie.

Guy had lain awake all the previous night, excited and intrigued, turning over each phrase and intimation in the brief note, extracting solace where he could. The 'us' consoled him greatly. For a start it didn't sound as if Craigie was the marvellous man for whom Sylvie had left London. The word implied plurality to the extent of at least a wife, perhaps even a family. And there was something a bit formal and middle-aged about 'your daughter'.

Naturally Guy had not mentioned the invitation to Felicity. Her dislike of Sylvie, the relief she had not troubled to conceal when the child left home, her indifference to her daughter's welfare – she never even mentioned Sylvie's name – made it unthinkable that she should accompany him. Guy decided to say that she was ill. That seemed simplest. And who would be any the wiser?

Danton Morel was one of the best-kept secrets in London. No one who employed him ever told a living soul, so jealously did they guard the advantages his ministrations gave. In spite of this whenever the rich and glamorous, famous and infamous were gathered together in celebration's name, there would most likely be present, taking the collective breath away, at least one example of Danton's sorcery.

His card described him with becoming modesty as *Coiffeur et Visagiste* but the dazzling transformations that his art contrived far exceeded the simple 'making over' techniques shown in magazines or on television. Danton magicked up not only dramatically transfigured flesh, but also an apparently dramatically transfigured personality too.

As well as these fairy-godfather abilities, Danton was blessed with the most mellifluous cream-and-brandy voice. And when not speaking, the quality of his silence was warmly, encouragingly, receptive. Consequently people felt compelled to tell him things. All sorts of things. Danton would listen, smile, nod and continue on his designing way.

He had started out twenty years ago as a mask-maker and puppeteer and would often ironically reflect that he was still in the same line of business, although his devotees would have been mortified had they known he thought so. His private life was one of extreme simplicity. He lived vicariously, nourished by information received from muddled emotional outpourings, confessions and confidences, and by the descriptions of sybaritic events so much larger than life that his heart would glow with envious excitement. Because he never gossiped everyone assumed he was discreet and in that one respect he was. But he wrote everything down and was now in the tenth year of keeping the diaries that he hoped would make him disreputably wealthy. He was helping himself to some fresh bay leaves when Felicity opened the door. She looked wild. Her hair was standing on end as if she had been tugging at it, and he could have been a stranger so blank was her stare.

Once upstairs she began pacing about, lamenting; long expensively tanned legs flicked in and out of her housecoat like deep-brown scissors. She had thrust the letter into his hand the moment he entered the house. Danton, having read it, sat down and waited.

'The deceit of it Danton . . . *the deceit*. . . . My own daughter! As if I wouldn't want to see her. . . .'

Felicity gasped out the words. Her shoulders twitched and she kept brushing at her arms as if being attacked by a swarm of insects. She said again: 'My own daughter!' in a loud accusatory voice as if Danton were somehow at fault. She had awaited his arrival in a positive torment of emotions. Amazement at the very fact of the invitation, fury that she had not been informed and a growing queasy awareness that, having discovered the envelope, she would now be compelled to make some sort of decision regarding its contents. Coming and going in this boiling mess was a needle-sharp surprise at the letter's compulsive power. She had been quite sure that her love for her daughter was long since dead. She had ground it into oblivion herself, devalued it over the years until now it was a tawdry thing of no account.

Sylvie had never wanted her mother. As a baby she would struggle and strain away when Felicity tried to cuddle or even hold her. Toddling, she would direct her steps towards her nanny, the au pair, or even casual visitors to the house. She would go to anyone – or so it seemed to Felicity – but the person who loved her best. Later, when it became plain that Sylvie not only didn't love her mother, but also refused even to like her, Felicity began the slow pulverisation of her own affection. This had caused her great pain for she had already guessed at the arid landscape that her marriage would prove to be and had seen the child as an antidotal source of comfort and joy. Now, so many years later, how could she let hope in? She would not dare.

'It's some sort of practical joke I suppose.'

'Why do you say that Mrs G?'

Danton was always being asked by his clients to use their Christian names and he always declined. In Felicity's case the diminution of her surname was as far as he was prepared to go. She disliked it intensely, thinking it made her sound like a Cockney char in some rubbishy play but would not have risked offending him by saying so.

'We haven't seen or heard of her for five years.'

'Didn't you say once she comes into some money when she's twenty-one? Perhaps he's a solicitor and you both have to sign something.'

'We don't. It's perfectly straightforward. All tied up by my parents when she was small. Anyway – we're asked for dinner.'

'Is it a lot? The inheritance.'

'Five hundred.'

Danton mentally added the missing noughts and shivered with envy. Felicity stopped pacing and sank on to an over-stuffed footstool, wrapping icy satin tight around her knees. She said: 'I shall go,' and felt the enormity of it. As if she had leapt into an abyss.

'Naturally,' said Danton. 'The point is, what will you go as?'

Felicity looked mystified, then startled. The truth was she had summoned Danton automatically, simply out of need for his assiduously attentive ear, thinking no further than that.

'You can't just stroll along Mrs G.'

'Can't I?' The fact of having made the decision seemed to Felicity more than enough to be going on with. What she would wear, how she would look had simply not entered her mind. And yet now that the matter had been raised she could see how important it was. Already her mind, nervous and vulnerable, had cast whoever else might be present at the dinner in antagonistic rôles. And if her expectations were correct she would need to be not just simply covered, but armoured against a formidable collection of adversaries. On the other hand. . . .

'Nothing extreme, Danton.'

'Surely you can trust me on that score.'

She had offended him. Hastily Felicity apologised. Danton got up.

'Well – better get on. Clothed and in your right mind don't they say?'

A cruel slip, if deliberate, which of course it couldn't have been. You didn't charge your clients a hundred pounds an hour for your services and then insult them. Felicity followed him on to the landing and into her evening room. She would have liked another drink but was fearful of appearing sluttish. Danton never drank alcohol and nothing containing caffeine. Sometimes a little spring water might pass the lips. His teeth and the whites of his soft brown eyes dazzled by their purity.

Felicity's wardrobe was contained within three rooms. One for night, one for day and one for other things which were not so easily categorised: cruise wear; bikinis and cover-ups; barely used sports equipment. Tennis racquets, skis, golf clubs. (She had taken up golf and got bored with it in a single morning.) The wall facing the door in each case was mirrored and metal rods had been suspended about four feet from the ceiling to hold the clothes.

Danton and Felicity wandered along these rails pushing and pulling at the padded hangers, instigating rustles of taffeta and silk, and soft, soundless collisions of velvet. Under a dozen recessed 'daylight' bulbs they took out and scrutinised Muir and Miyake, Lagerfeld and Bellville Sassoon. Chanel and St Laurent.

Creations were unhooked, discussed, dismissed. A tangerine flamenco dress: full frilled dancing skirt, no back, hardly any front. 'I shouldn't. It can get nippy after eight o'clock.' Narrow black velvet with a little train and white band around the neck. 'You're her mother not her father confessor.' Beige wild-silk chemise stiff with seed pearls and golden thread. 'Costively dull.' Raspberry georgette and feathers. 'Too Fred and Ginger.'

And so it went on until having covered the territory and started to double back, Felicity remembered the Karelia. She went away, returning with a bulky swathe of white cotton inside a see-through cover. 'It was for a first night at the Garden.' She tugged at the poppers and Danton held the bottom of the bag preparing to pull. 'The people I go with,' continued Felicity, 'always have a box, but this time for some reason we were in the dress circle. There's no way I could have got along a row of seats so it's never been worn.' Felicity kicked the wrapper aside. 'It was Pavarotti.'

'You *must* wear this.'

'Oh. You don't think it's a bit—'

'We're talking celebration-dinner in a country manor. Everyone's bound to dress up. What else is there for them to do poor beasts, down there in the sticks?'

Actually Danton thought the dress *was* 'a bit' if not quite a lot, but it was also sensationally inspirational. Just looking at it made his fingers twitch. A dream number made to float down a Busby Berkeley staircase between ranks of adoring, top-hatted males.

Layers and layers of transparent chiffon in every possible shade of grey, from the merest wisp of smoke to deepest anthracite foaming over petticoats the colour of tarnished silver. The satin bodice and tight pointed sleeves were smothered with loops of ribbon, each anchored into place by a single dark pearl.

'Put it on.'

Without embarrassment Felicity took off her robe.

'Do me up. . . . Well – what do you think?'

'Oh my. . . .' He stepped back, bursting with anticipation. 'What time will you have to leave?'

I suppose. . . . end-of-day traffic, half six.'
'Will you be having lunch?'
'I couldn't swallow a thing.'
'Right. Then we'd better get started.'

Chapter 3

Shortly after lunch, Suhami and Christopher went out to move Calypso. This had to be done at fairly frequent intervals for she nibbled at speed and with ferocious heartiness.

How Calypso loved the grass! Weed killers were forbidden so it was rich in cinquefoil and burnet and succulent dandelion. She did not feel she had quite exhausted her present territory when Christopher prised up her steel peg, and he had to wind extra links of chain around his forearm to tug her elsewhere.

Calypso's assessment of her handler's muscularity was spot on and she was inclined to bolt if she thought it a bit on the skimpy side. Only the other day she had shot off at a fair old lick down the drive, out of the gates and into the High Street where she'd been found ten minutes later standing patiently in a queue at the fish shop.

'You're a very foolish girl,' May had scolded, walking her back. 'You don't even like fish.'

'Do you want to hang on or drive in?'

'Hang on,' said Suhami, seizing the studded collar.

'Watch out for yew berries, then.'

Christopher hammered while Calypso butted the air and kicked up her back legs in a fit of rage. But, once tethered, she quickly simmered down and began to munch, just occasionally lifting her head to give the world one of her enigmatic stares.

Christopher said: 'We have to do some talking Suze. Isn't that right?'

She turned from him. 'I don't know.'

'I love you.' He stepped in front of her again, caught the shadow on her face. 'Well . . . nice to be wanted.'

'I do want you – I do. It's just. . . .'

When she didn't continue, Christopher put his arm through hers and moved towards the giant cedar. 'Let's sit down and I'll—'

'Not there.' Suhami held back.

'OK.' Looking puzzled, he turned and they began to walk towards the pond.

'I know it's silly . . . and they'll long ago have disappeared but Jim's ashes were scattered there. I can't help seeing it as some sort of grave.'

'Arno told me about that. Must have been very upsetting.'

'It was at the time. And yet – it's a bit sad really – how quickly one forgets.'

'I suppose that's usually the case. Unless the person was very close.'

'He was such a nice man. Quiet and devout. When he'd finished his chores he'd just go to his room and read or meditate. He didn't really fit into our sort of commune at all. Sometimes I used to think he'd be happier in a monastery.'

'Wasn't he a secret drinker though? I thought someone said—'

'Oh no. He didn't drink at all. That's what made it so peculiar. As a matter of fact—'

'Hullo..o.o.' A call from the terrace. May was waving, already walking towards them.

She came with a comforted heart. Almost as comforted in fact as if her troubles were already over. For Kwan Yin had come up trumps after all. And the solution, once proffered, was so strikingly obvious that May could have kicked herself for being so blind. The person to talk to was, of course, Christopher. He had not joined the Windhorse till some time after Jim's death and so could not possibly have been involved. But although May was relieved, this did not mean she was not concerned as to what his response might be. For instance he might suggest going to the police and May knew, if such were to be the case, that she would feel as guilty as if the decision had been her own.

She hoped to find him by himself but it was Suhami who waved back, calling: 'Did you want something, May?' May gestured vaguely in an attempt to suggest that, even had that been the case, by now she'd quite forgotten what it was. The gesture was an awkward one for May was hopeless at pretending, being by nature as guileless as a kitten.

'It's you I really wanted, Christopher.'

'So now you've got me.'

'Yes . . . um . . . well. . . . We're doing the honey at the weekend and the steriliser's on the fritz.' May closed her eyes as she spoke and gabbled the words. The lie still sat awkwardly in her mouth like an ill-fitting tooth.

'Working fine last time we used it.' All three were now strolling back towards the house. 'Mind you – that was a bit ago.'

As they entered, May was still wondering how to prise the young couple apart. Various unimaginative ploys occurred to her, but she knew she would present them with such transparent lack of conviction that they were more likely to make Suhami suspicious than get her out of the way.

'I'll do it after tea.'

'Do what?' May stared blankly at Christopher.

'What you asked me to do all of ten seconds ago, May. Have a look at the steriliser – after tea – OK?'

'Of course!' cried May. 'Tea! Suhami – I shall need to take my ginseng and I've left them on my bedside table. Would you be a dear girl – save my legs. . . .'

As Suhami sped off, May seized her companion's arm and pulled him further into the hall until they were standing directly beneath the lantern. Then she whispered: 'Christopher – I have to talk to you.'

Christopher looked huntedly around and whispered: 'I zink zey know our plans.'

'Be serious.'

Christopher laughed. 'Sorry. If you like I'll look at the steriliser now and we can talk in the kitchen.'

'There's nothing wrong with the steriliser. I couldn't think of anything else on the spur of the moment. I had to see you alone. I've been so worried. There's something going on here . . . something wrong. And I'm sure it's to do with Jim's—' She broke off and looked up at the gallery. It appeared to be empty. 'What was that?'

'I didn't hear anything.' He followed her gaze.

'A click. As if a door was closing.'

'Perhaps it was. What is all this May?'

'Better talk outside.'

Christopher allowed himself to be dragged down a corridor towards the kitchen. 'This is all a bit MI5. You're not recruiting by any chance?' They had arrived at the back entrance to the house, a glassed-in door leading to the terrace. 'I'm not swallowing any microfilm, May,' Christopher continued. 'Not even for you.'

They stepped outside and Christopher turned to pull the door. May was standing a couple of paces ahead of him on old uneven flagstones seamed with yellow stonecrop. Moving to join her, he became aware of a heavy rumbling noise. Thunder? A skywards glance showed no sign of darkness. Then there was a bump and a big, black rounded object appeared teetering on the guttering.

Christopher yelled and pushed. May shot forward, tripped over the hem of her robe and went hurtling into a flower border. Christopher jumped back into the opening. The object fell between them, smashing a flagstone. A web quickly ran out from the breaking point; chippings of stone flew.

So rapid had been the descent, so violent the connection that for a few seconds the two of them remained motionless with shock. Christopher gradually became aware that someone was standing behind him calling his name. It was Suhami.

'Was that you shouting? What is it? What's the – *May* . . . !'

May, her scratched face further impressed by the woody stems of a lavender bush, was struggling to her feet. As Suhami hurried to help her, Christopher slipped back into the house. The stairs and gallery were still deserted. Everything was quiet.

Swiftly he ran up to the gallery and around the three sides, knocking on doors, opening them and looking in when there was no response. All the rooms were empty.

At the far end of the right-hand section, concealed behind a velvet curtain, was an archway, the stone soaring to an exaggerated point. Directly behind this arch were a dozen steps turning back on themselves in a savagely tight corkscrew and leading to the roof. There were signs of recent disturbance. The dust on the steps was scuffed and marked by flakes of old green paint from the skylight's metal frame. Christopher remembered that Arno had been up there a couple of days before cleaning bird mess off the lantern. He crouched down on the top step which was very close to the glass, pushed the nearest half of the skylight open and fixed it into position with a rusting strut. Then he raised his head cautiously above the opening and looked around.

The place appeared deserted. Climbing out, he at once felt disoriented – the twisty steps having left him unsure which way faced where. To get his bearings he turned a slow circle. There was the vegetable garden, so the section of the roof directly over the back door must be on the far side.

As he hesitated, a cloud slid across the sun, leeching colour from the surrounding brick and slate. A breeze sprang up and Christopher shivered although he was not cold. *Someone walking on my grave.* He wondered how the phrase had first arisen, for the dead, snug in their wooden cocoons, were the last people to give a damn who walked, skipped or even danced a jig above their mouldering heads.

The roof seemed crowded with chimneys though in fact there were only three sooty stacks holding four pots each. Christopher found himself disturbed by their proximity. Inanimate, they yet gave an impression of convergence. Some were cowled and, as the breeze intensified, several metal hoods swung creaking in his direction. His feelings of unease deepened and he was seized by the nonsensical conviction that the hoods concealed active organisms that were observing him.

Telling himself not to be stupid, he started making his way towards the opposite edge. His passage was not quite straight-forward. The roof was in three steeply sloping sections separated by narrow paths between two of which reared the great iron ribbed lantern.

The only way to progress, so narrow were the walkways, was to place one foot directly before the other on the blue-black sheets of buckled lead in a heel-toe fashion, and this is what Christopher did. Once across, he peered over, aligning himself precisely with the smashed flagstone. He could see from the dent in the guttering where the metal object had gone over. And a lightish circular unstained patch to indicate where it had for so long been standing. This was about two feet from the edge on a completely flat surface. There seemed to him no way that any-thing of that size and weight could have rolled off of its own volition. Indeed it would have been far from easy for a single person to drag it to the appropriate point let alone heave it over. Yet that must have been what happened.

But in that case – Christopher sprang up quickly and turned around – how had whoever it was vanished with such speed? Could anyone be so fleet of foot as to scramble across the roof, replace the skylight, negotiate the twisty steps, and run down-stairs in the brief moments between the lump of iron falling and himself re-entering the hall? Frankly it seemed impossible.

The cowls creaked again and Christopher recalled his previous sensation of being overlooked. Perhaps he had hit on the expla-nation. If the would-be murderer (for what else could you call someone who aims a great lump of iron ore at a human skull?) had not left the roof at all but had stayed concealed, hiding. . . . *Was maybe still hiding*.

He became keenly aware of the yawning space behind his back. Nothing but air. Oxygen, nitrogen and carbonic acid gas, excessively unsupportive. Fit only, when you came to think of it, for falling through. Just when he needed them most, Chris-topher felt the bones in his legs leak into his bloodstream.

He moved quickly from the edge to the nearest chimney stack.

It concealed no one. Nor did the second. Silently, heart bumping, he approached the last. Four lemon barley-sugar twists thick with soot. Soft-footed he began to circle the base. Half way round he had a wild desire to laugh, recognising the action from a score of spooky movies where the comic lead tiptoes round a tree followed by a man in a gorilla suit. But there was no one there. They must have climbed through the skylight, thought Christopher, while I was checking the gutter.

He was turning to go when he noticed something sticking out from the gap between the chimney pots. It looked like the end of a metal rod. He tugged at it, slowly pulling out the whole thing. It was a crowbar.

By the time Christopher had descended from the roof and made his way to May's room, it was crowded with people. Standing in the doorway he did a quick count. A full house.

He faced a most dramatic scene. Quite painterly in a Victorian narrative sort of way. Like one of those allegorised intimations of mortality showing an aged patriarch breathing his last, surrounded by tearful family and retainers, plus a mopey-looking dog.

May reclined on a chaise longue looking, for her, quite pale. Someone had placed a fringed shawl of peacock-blue silk across her knees. Behind her the Master, white hair fairly sparkling in the sunlight, rested his hand lightly on her forehead. Suhami knelt at her side. Tim squatted on a footstool. Arno hovered, wringing his hands (really wringing them, like pieces of washing). Janet and Trixie, looking with but not quite of the group, stood a little apart.

The Beavers were at the foot of the couch. Heather had brought her guitar and was quietly activating a few rather lachrymose chords. Ken said: 'We've got a lot of healing to do here,' and touched first his magnetic crystal then the sole of May's foot with great solemnity.

'I'm all right,' said May. 'Accidents happen. Don't fuss.'

Heather started thrumming with a little more attack and now

broke into a shrill quatrain, making them all jump.

> 'O!, zenith ray of cosmic power
> Pour forth from thy celestial bower
> Bright radiance in a golden shower
> Sustaining here our star-born flower.'

Ken stroked his crystal again and looked sternly at everyone, then at the curtain pelmet as if accusing it of concealing vital information. At length he turned back to the recumbent figure and spoke. 'You are now enfolded deep in Jupiter's psi-probe and bathed in his miraculous healing influence.'

'Well I know *that*.' May twitched at the silk shawl. 'We are enfolded in miraculous healing rays at all times whatever the source. Now – I need my rescue remedy and some arnica for bruising. They're in the little shell box. Would someone please. . . . ?'

Arno moved first, saying as he handed it over, 'Perhaps you'd like some oxymol too, May?'

'Why not? Honey never hurts. Thank you, Arno.'

Delighted at being under instruction from the queen of his heart, Arno hurried off. He would use the most fragrant honey – wasn't there some Mount Hymettus left? – and the freshest, lightest vinegar all in a beautiful cup. There must be a beautiful cup somewhere. Should he pick a few flowers? Surely under such circumstances the house rules could be relaxed.

About to turn into the kitchen he halted. The back door was still ajar. Arno stepped over the threshold and stood by the shattered slab and great lump of iron. He looked at the lavender, flattened and snapped off where May had fallen. Seeing how close it must have been, he experienced a terrible quiet thrill of fear. He suddenly envisaged the world without her. Sans colour and warmth, without light, meaning, music . . . harmony. . . .

'But it didn't happen,' he said firmly. May would be extremely cross if she caught him thinking along such soggily pessimistic lines, for she always saw the best in everything. The silver lining, not the cloud. The rainbow, not the rain.

When Arno returned, having found no more elegant container, he bore a hefty mug of oxymol. May was sitting up and looking once more serenely infallible. She had shaken her rescue remedy to indigo and rubbed some on her wrists – scenting the room with a woody fragrance. He stepped forward with his offering and, as the mug was transferred, May's fingers touched his own. Arno's freckled cheeks blushed and he hoped no one was looking.

'I was never in any real danger,' she was now assuring them all. 'My guardian angel was present as he always is. Who d'you think placed Christopher so close behind?'

Christopher received several grateful smiles in silence. He was still feeling uneasy about the decision he had taken when on the roof. Once the shock of finding the crowbar had receded he was left with the problem of what to do with the thing. Should he replace it? If he did this the attacker would remain unaware that he was rumbled and, confidence unimpaired, might well soon try again. On the other hand if Christopher removed the crowbar the man would be on his guard and perhaps doubly dangerous. On balance Christopher had decided on the latter course of action. The bar was now wrapped in a blanket and hidden beneath his bed. Later, he planned to remove it to Calypso's byre.

Conversation had moved from May's wellbeing to the lump of iron itself and the curious fact of how it came to be up there in the first place. Heather, the only person to have familiarised herself with the chronicles of the Manor House via a booklet in the kitchen drawer, said that it was first mentioned at the time of the Civil War when it was believed to be a large fragment of a Roundhead cannon ball. Later, due no doubt to increased scientific and astronomical knowledge, a meteor fragment was diagnosed. But, whatever its origin, it had been up there with-standing all that nature could throw at it, plus man-made bombardment in World War Two, without shifting an inch. How strange then, concluded Heather, that it should fall today.

A long silence followed this remark. May, angelically protected though she might be, still looked a bit perturbed. Trixie rolled her eyes behind everyone's back. Ken seemed rather excited by the mystery and Heather guessed he was looking forward to channelling Hilarion's views on the matter. Tim, sensing the inexplicable, curled up a little more tightly.

The silence lengthened and then, one by one, people turned to the Master. The whole room seemed full of a grave and supplicatory expectancy. *He* would explain these discordant harmonics, their faces confidently declared. *He* would know. The Master smiled his oblique smile. He bent for a moment to stroke Tim's golden head, for the boy had started to tremble, and then he spoke.

'Many things agitate the vacuum energy-field. The nether stratum of dynamic force is far from stable. Subatomic particles are in constant motion. Never forget – there is no such thing as a still electron.'

So that was it. The falling object was nothing more than an emblematisation of the general liveliness of matter. People started to nod and smile, or shake their heads in acknowledgement of their own slow-wittedness. Ken struck his forehead with the heel of his hand and said what an idiot he was. No one demurred.

Shortly after this the Master said they should leave May to rest. 'And to give thanks to her guardian angel in the proper manner.' He moved away then and Tim followed, almost stepping on the blue robe in his anxiety not to be left behind. At the door the Master turned. 'I'm rather concerned about your regression this evening May. These journeys can be quite demanding. Would you care to put it off till another time?'

'Certainly not, Master,' said May sturdily. 'It is the time of the new moon and, we have heard from Hilarion, most propitious. How would I feel if a manifestation from Astarte arrived and I hadn't taken advantage of all that extra-dynamic energy? And in any case,' she sat up, drank a little oxymol and beamed at them all, 'I am already quite myself again.'

Chapter 4

It was half past five. At dinner the Craigies would be present. Afterwards there might not be an opportunity to catch Sylvie on her own. So Guy had arrived early at Compton Dando. His slight anxiety that this might cause annoyance had been easily subsumed beneath a general surge of excited anticipation.

In fact, being driven down, he had managed to convince himself that, reading between the lines, what Sylvie's letter was really about was a decision to forgive him. She couldn't write herself, Guy appreciated that. She had been badly hurt and would not for a moment assume a petitioner's vulnerability. Neither would he wish her to do so. But that the invitation had been issued, not just with her permission but at her instigation, he now had no doubt. His years of lonely sorrow were nearly at an end. Standing by the main door of the Manor House, a bouquet of sweetly scented flowers with a card reading simply 'With love' in his hand, happiness broke over Guy. He was bathed in it, like perspiration.

He looked around for signs of life. There was a big Gothic key in the lock and a vertical iron rod fixed to the wall, attached to a rusting bell. He put his finger through and tugged. The bell was quite loud but no one came. He waited a while, gripping the flowers awkwardly. There were two wooden seats in the porch flush to the wall, worn and smooth like those often found outside old country churches. Guy put his bouquet down on one of them and stepped back for a better view of the beautiful and imposing house.

It hadn't occurred to Guy that she might simply not be there. Should he check into his hotel and come back? Gina had booked a room at Chartwell Grange, the only halfway decent place within miles. Guy had decided that, whatever direction the evening took, he did not wish to return home afterwards. He wanted to be by himself to absorb, digest, relive and, surely, to celebrate. And although Felicity knew nothing of the invitation, and in any case would be zonked out of what was left of her mind by the time he got back, Guy still felt a trace of disquiet at the idea of being in her presence so soon after parting from their daughter.

Reluctant to give up, he strolled down the side of the house. What a mess the border was. Flowers that should have been upright trailing in the dust. One immensely tall many-spired blue thing had collapsed entirely and was spread all over the gravel. He came to a shaggy yew hedge running parallel to the right-angle wall. At one point the branches had been chopped away to make an opening. Guy stepped through.

He was standing on a lawn, very large and multi-starred with daisies and white clover – some of which were being eaten by a stoutish goat. In the centre was a vast cedar of Lebanon which looked as old as the house itself. At his feet was a rectangular pond full of lively darting fish. Some striped like tigers, others smaller with spiny backs and transparent snail-like horns. At the far end of the lawn were a lot of bamboo wigwams and a general air of leafiness indicating some sort of vegetable garden. And at last, a sign of human life. Someone raking or hoeing. Perhaps Ian Craigie?

Guy started off again but had not gone far when the man stopped work, threw back his head and started to declaim. It sounded like blank verse and it was very loud. He gestured, too, throwing his arms about and gazing at the sun. Guy retreated, much perturbed.

Back at the porch he decided to give the bell a final try but then, reaching upwards, changed his mind and on impulse turned the iron ring handle. The door opened and he stepped inside.

He was in a huge hall with an arched soaring roof punctuated by brilliantly painted bosses. A grand staircase with elaborately carved newel posts and banisters led to a three-sided minstrel's gallery. The place was sparsely decorated with very plain bits of furniture. Two large wooden chests, one of which had a splintered lid, some rush-bottomed chairs, a round nondescript table which could have been from any period and a tall, free-standing cupboard. The only attractive item visible was a large stone Buddha, about five feet tall, on a plinth. Its head was covered with curls so tight and small they looked like pimples. There was a glass jar of lupins on the plinth and a little pile of fruit.

The air smelt disagreeable. Floor polish, unsavoury cooking and dampish clothes. An institution smell. He should know. He'd been in enough. All overlain by a pungent rather sickly odour which Guy feared might be incense.

The table held two wooden bowls, each supporting an exquisitely written card. These read 'Feeling Guilty?' and 'Love Offering'. Inside the guilty bowl was five pence. There were also lots of pamphlets which proved to be hand-cranked, hugely exclamatory, full of unnecessary italics and oddly situated quotation marks. Guy picked up *The Romance of the Enema* by Kenneth Beavers: Clairaudient: Intuitive Diagnostician FORW. Behind the door through which he had just entered was a green baize noticeboard. Guy walked over to have a look, making his footsteps louder than was strictly necessary.

The material displayed was uninspiring. Rotas mainly. Cooking. Cleaning. Feeding and milking Calypso. He read quickly through the list but Sylvie's name was not there. He didn't know whether to feel encouraged or frustrated. There was also a large poster: '*Mars & Venus: Longing To Help But Are We Ready?* Talk: 27th Aug Causton Library. Book early and avd. disappointment.'

Was it some daft quasi-religious set-up then? The rota listed both males and females so that ruled out a nunnery. Or a monastery either, come to that. Perhaps it was some sort of retreat. The thought of Sylvie in such a place was frankly risible. And where did Craigie come into it? 'Have dinner with us.' Was all this lot 'us'? Guy didn't like that idea at all. He had no intention of sharing his reconciliation with a load of freaks. He looked around for further clues.

There were two corridors leading off the hall and a door marked 'Office'. Guy opened it and peered inside. The room was windowless, full of stationery and files, some stacked on the floor, some on shelves. A Gestetner stood on a card table and, in a tall-backed leather chair, a further sign of life.

Long blue-jeaned legs, glorious tumbling amber hair with a fine golden fuzz clustered around the pale brow. A board creaked under Guy's foot and the figure turned. He caught a brief glimpse of her face before she scrambled up and ran towards a dusty tapestry wall-hanging which she seized, wrapping it around herself as if she were naked.

She was the most beautiful thing he had ever seen. Perfection. Guy gaped like a fool. It was half a minute before he recollected himself and when he did it was to realise she was terribly afraid of him. As she stood pressed against the wall, her breath was snatched and rasping like a cornered animal's. Guy mumbled into apologetic speech.

'I'm sorry . . . I didn't mean . . . It's all right. I'm a visitor. Here to see my daughter. . . .'

It made no difference. She was panting now, scented with fear. Guy backed off, attempting with smiles and shrugs to show how safe he was. Then, in her agitation the curtain slipped. He saw her face again and got a further shock. His stomach gave a queasy flip and his forehead became cold and clammy. He looked away sick with disenchantment and disgust, for the girl was crazed.

Deep-blue eyes rolling wildly round in her head, lovely lips dribbling with slime, grimaced and pushed forward into a grisly tight circle. Then, for the first time, Guy noticed the size of the jawline and the large brown hand ferociously splayed against the wall and realised that the figure was not female at all but that of a young man. His disgust deepened and he almost ran from the room, slamming the door behind him.

What the hell sort of place was this? Guy had been willing to give the first chap talking to the empty air in the cabbage patch the benefit of the doubt, but there was no mistake about the demented second. He felt a deep sense of alarm at the thought of his daughter living here.

He returned to the central area of the hall where it seemed that, at last, his appearance had been noticed. Following the rattle of wooden curtain rings a girl had appeared in the gallery and was hurrying towards the staircase.

She had long dark hair in a plait and wore floaty muslin trousers which billowed as she moved like wide white mothy wings. The muslin was caught into anklets from which hung tiny bells tinkling in a delicate manner. She sped along on bare feet which seemed hardly to touch the ground, and descended the stairs like a piece of thistledown. As she came closer he could see that her plait was threaded through with small white flowers and that a red spot marked the precise centre of her forehead. Standing before him, she placed her hands together in a prayerful salute to greet him: 'Welcome to the Golden Windhorse,' and bowed.

Guy, absorbed his third shock in almost as many minutes yet recognised the moment for what it was. Fraught with danger, rich with opportunity. He looked down at her hair parting – which was also powdered with reddish dust – reached out and touched her shoulder very gently. Then he said, 'Hullo Sylvie.'

'My name is Suhami now.' Even her voice was different. Gentle, colourless and curiously muffled as if strained through layers of cotton wool. 'It means little dancing wind.'

Guy considered several rejoinders all of which seemed primed with the potential for misunderstanding so he kept silent. Just nodded and hitched the flesh in the lower half of his face up into a smile. Was this too bold a response? The bland downcast-browness gave nothing away. She said, 'You are early.'

'Yes. I hoped we might be able to talk before dinner.'

'I'm afraid that won't be possible.' She appeared disturbed at the very thought. A frown pleated the red spot.

Guy stood, ill at ease and uncertain, staring helplessly. Only

Sylvie could reduce him to such a state and, for the first time ever, he felt a flash of resentment that this should be so.

She was going away without another word. Fluttering off across the hall, disappearing down a corridor. Surely she must mean him to follow. Guy lumbered off in pursuit feeling, in contrast to all that floss and cobweb, quite exceptionally gross. The corridor ended in a glass-topped door opening on to a terrace. Just before this on the left was a row of wooden hooks supporting an old mac and a peg bag. Beneath were assorted wellies and a paraffin stove. Facing this wall three shallow stone steps descended, ending in a further door from behind which came the sounds of crockery and the chink of teaspoons.

Turning the handle, Guy entered a kitchen, square with a low ceiling. The tiles and sink were cracked and old-looking, and there was a long iron range as well as a more modern gas cooker. Sylvie was making tea. She took some sprigs of mint from a flat raffia dish, put them in a small teapot and poured on boiling water. Guy hoped this was not for him and then hoped that it was.

She crossed to a rack of assorted knives, took one down and started chopping at a large piece of shiny, tacky-looking hard stuff. Her father, who had recently seen a drugs documentary, thought it looked like cannabis resin.

'What's that?'

'Rambutan crunch.'

'Ah.'

Now she was laying a tray. Obviously the tea was not for either of them. Any minute now she was going to pick up the lot and vanish, perhaps for good. Guy studied the composed profile, searching for some reaction to their meeting. How was it possible for her to remain so calm? Did she really not understand the significance of the moment? Whatever he had expected it was not this. She was like a stranger. His daughter yet not his daughter.

Maybe she'd been brainwashed. Perhaps this was the head-quarters of some weird cult – that would explain the wafty costume, the silly bells and that ridiculous red daub. Guy, having no historical point of reference for the transformation, resented it on principle as he did any change in the quotidian made without consulting him.

He noticed she was handling all the implements on the tray in an exceptionally mannered fashion. Over-precise and unnaturally concentrated, inclining her head in a solemn deferential manner between each movement. Like all rituals its effect was to exclude the mere looker-on. All this serenity was getting on Guy's nerves. He longed to jolt her into a natural response even whilst appreciating that any such move might be extremely unwise. He didn't think that she might simply dread his company.

'A beautiful house Syl . . . er . . . Suzz . . . um. . . .'

'Yes. I'm very happy here.'

'I'm glad – oh! I'm glad you're happy, Sylvie.' He saw her shrink from this intrusive exuberance. Moderating his voice he added: 'Why is that? What is it about the place?'

'I've found peace here.' A graceful hand movement encompassed the old grate, cupboards and shelves. 'And people who really care for me.'

Guy took the blow, barely winded.

He could see she was sincere, he could tell that. Or thought so which was really the same thing. That, no doubt, was what the face denuded of all emotion, swoony drifting movements and humble bow were all in aid of. Guy loathed humility. In Guy's opinion you could stick humility right up your fart-hole. She was speaking again in that sexless, ripple-of-silk voice. '. . . so when the Master suggested that you should be invited down we all discussed it and thought my birthday might be the right occasion.'

The second blow so lightly delivered marked Guy much more deeply than the first. To be frank, it had him on the ropes. It was not her idea then that he should visit. The suggestion had come from some bunch of sharing, caring peace-dispensing Venus-watching nutters. He was here under their sufferance. Guy felt sick with wounded pride at the thought. And jealousy. Unthinkably, he wanted to be unkind. To hurt her for bringing him to such a pass.

'I expect it will wear off.'

'What?'

'All this peace and stuff.'

'No it won't.'

'You're very young, Sylvie.'

'I'm older than I look.'

The words were full of bitterness. He looked across at her and the gap closed. Honesty flowered and the room was suddenly full of wretched agitation. Opportunities lost, gestures never made, songs never sung. Guy moved towards her and she sprang away.

'I'm so sorry, Sylvie. Please . . . believe me. . . . *I'm so sorry.*'

'Oh, why did you come here!' Her dignified composure vanished. Eyes glittered with sudden tears.

'I got a letter—'

'I mean why did you come *now*? Why couldn't you just turn up at half past seven as you were asked?'

'I told you. I wanted—'

'You wanted, *you wanted*. Can't you just once in your life simply do what someone else wants. Is that so impossible?' She broke off and turned away, her hands covering her face.

There was a long silence. Guy, deeply distressed by this rapid and alarming descent into animosity, bowed his head. He recognised that it was all his fault. What matter that this opportunity to meet with his daughter had been set up by strangers? He had been given the chance – that was what counted. And, finding himself in a strange milieu, had assumed hostility and snatched the operational reins into his own hands. He thought, *I've ruined everything*, and immediately quenched the idea. One false step didn't mean disaster.

He looked at Sylvie, still with her back to him. The thick blossomy plait had fallen forward, leaving the defenceless hollow at the nape of her neck clearly visible. This at least had not changed. It seemed as tender and snappable as it had when she was very young. The executioner's deadline he had once heard it called and was as chilled as if the trade had been his own. He stumbled into speech again.

'I'm afraid I've done the wrong thing but it was only because I wanted so much to see you. And now I have I don't seem able. . . .' His throat closed on an excess of helpless, remorseful longing.

The rigid line of his daughter's back slackened. Suhami was already experiencing a sense of shame at her uncontrolled outburst. This was not what she should be about. What was the point of all her meditations, of struggling to walk in the light and send out loving rays to all sentient beings if she could not even welcome a single one of them with courtesy. Her father was a hateful man but she must not hate him. He had done her immeasurable harm but she must not seek revenge. The Master had counselled her to this effect and she knew that he was right. To harbour malice damaged only oneself. Her father was to be pitied. Who in the whole world loved him? But I – Suhami took a long and consoling breath – I have known love. From the Master, friends here, Christopher. I have been nourished and comforted. Should I not be kind in my turn? She turned and faced him. He still looked bullish but post-picador, his chin sunk on his chest.

'I'm sorry too. You mustn't think. . . .' She struggled to find something honest to say. 'Everyone is intrigued at the thought of meeting you.'

Guy responded quickly. 'And I'm looking forward to meeting the Craigies.'

'The . . . ?' Suhami looked puzzled then laughed as if he had said something really witty. 'Oh – it's not like that.' She lifted the plait, letting it fall once more down her back. 'It's not like that at all.' Then she picked up the tray. 'I must take this to the Master.'

'Won't it be cold?'

'I shouldn't think so.'

Guy realised then that they had only been in the kitchen a few minutes. In fact it was barely ten since they had met in the hall. Ten minutes to roller-coaster through a meeting that had obsessed his every waking moment for days.

On the steps, she turned – indicating the glassed-in door by the Wellingtons. 'You can go out that way. I don't know if you'd like to look round the gardens? Or there's a library.'

'I think I'll go and dump my bag and have a shower. I've booked into a hotel.'

'A hotel?'

'I decided to stay over. I thought it might not be convenient here. I don't want to be any trouble.'

Suhami stared at him for a moment then smiled. The smile was prompted solely by amused surprise at the idea of her father not wishing to be any trouble, but Guy saw it as uniquely and transparently affectionate. All his previous confidence, vanquished by anger and distress, surged back. Everything would work out. All he had to do was play it her way. He could manage that. He would agree with everything and like everybody, and if he didn't he would dissemble. As he watched his daughter leave, Guy felt quite proud as if he had pulled this impossible achievement off already.

Sylvie would see that he could change and perhaps eventually would be able to acknowledge that his love for her was true. Excited and hopeful, he made his way past the old stove and wellies and out into the sunshine.

Chapter 5

'There's someone on the terrace.' Trixie moved her cheek on the windowpane. It made a soft squeaky sound but the man did not look up. 'I suppose it's Suhami's father.'

Janet crossed over and, hand pressing lightly on Trixie's shoulder, also looked down. Trixie moved away saying, 'He looks like a gangster.'

He did a bit. Chunky enough head-on, foreshortened, Guy was practically cuboid. The bloom on his jowls, mauvey-grey directly after shaving, was now the colour of hot-house grapes.

'And what a foul suit.' So, eagerly allying herself, did Janet dismiss the Gieves & Hawkes double-breasted silk and mohair. She observed the powerful, surprisingly shapely head covered with dark curls squatting on wide, meaty shoulders. He seemed to have no neck at all. 'I bet he wears a toupee.'

'Course he doesn't.' Trixie dropped into a green flock armchair swinging her legs over the side. She was wearing a thin nylon housecoat and little else. 'I think he looks rather virile actually. A bit like that strange man in your book. The minnator.'

'Minotaur.' Too late Janet could have bitten her tongue.

'Should have been a teacher.' Stitchings of malice pointed up the subtext. Dusty blackboard, scornful or indifferent pupils, lonely nights marking careless homework. Lengthy unappreciated preparations for the following day. 'Always picking people up.'

'Sorry.'

'What do you want anyway?'

'I came to borrow some cotton.'

The truth was that Janet just loved being in this room, even when Trixie was not present. Sometimes she thought she preferred those occasions. She could be more herself then. Relax. Drink in the heady atmosphere: face powder, perfume, cheap hairspray, a bowl of roses. Once she had smelt cigarette smoke. This commingling of scents produced a slumbrous ante-bellum atmosphere with a base note of sweet decay. The roses were illicit. Garden flowers were meant to be cut only on special occasions and then displayed in public rooms where everyone could share them. But Trixie always did as she liked, banking accurately on the communal reluctance to criticise.

Janet pulled open a drawer and pretended to look for the cotton. She disturbed a peachy satin slip, gossamer tights and some garments made of oyster satin that she had once referred to as cami-knickers. An archaism she was not likely to repeat. The second drawer held two boxes of Tampax and several half-cup wired lace bras.

'You won't find what you're looking for in there.'

'No – how silly.' Janet's long bony face crimsoned and she dropped the filmy skimp like a burning coal. 'I meant to put it on Arno's list.'

One day, she thought, when I come in for a plaster or an aspirin, a tissue or a safety pin, she's going to challenge me and say that she knows I really want none of those things. That I am here simply to breathe in the air that she exhales. Or touch the things that touch her skin.

'I can't get over those muscle-packed shoulders.' There was always a curl of anticipation in Trixie's voice when she planned some unkindness. Janet recognised it now and braced herself. 'I wonder what he's like in bed.'

What does she expect me to say? What can I say? Laugh it off? Make some all-girls-together joke? 'There's only one way to find out?' But of course, if I could do that, she'd never have asked the question.

Pictures flared in Janet's mind. Pale delicate limbs twined

around swarthy, hirsute rutting masculinity. Hands gloved by black hair, roaming, probing. Thick blunt fingers squeezing tender breasts, knotting honeyed curls. Nauseous, near to tears, she glanced across at the armchair and caught a stone in the sling smile.

'I really fancy screwing a millionaire. Everyone says power's an aphrodisiac don't they?'

'Who's everyone?' Trixie was like Cleopatra, dowsing for gold.

'I bet it's true. This one really looks as if he's built to do damage.'

It was the perfect opening for a sharp reply. For when Trixie had first joined them it was plain that a fair bit of damage had only recently been inflicted. Her arms and neck were badly bruised, her lip cut, her hair tufted patchily. But, in spite of Heather's frequent early attempts to corner her for some compassionate one-to-one counselling, Trixie had never even referred to, much less explained, these injuries. Dare Janet refer to them now? She came timidly close.

'Don't tell me you're one of those people who enjoy being knocked about by men.'

Trixie laughed: A spontaneous shout of amusement, as if Janet had said something completely ridiculous. Then she swung her milky legs forward again and stood up. 'If you only knew. . . .'

'Knew what?' Janet stepped hungrily forward at this hint of a possible revelation into the other girl's past. Perhaps Trixie would explain the letters that sometimes came in cheap blue envelopes. Or the phone calls where she hung up if anyone came into the room.

But Trixie just shrugged and sauntered over to the window. Guy was still there, chunkily looking about him. He had moved to the terrace steps which dropped to the herb border and was gazing over the lawn. Trixie lifted the latch.

'What are you doing?'

'What's it look like?'

'But you're not . . . at least put something. . . .' Janet watched helplessly as Trixie perched on the window ledge, holding her

91

robe bunched lightly at the waist, the fabric slipping from her left shoulder. She glimpsed Trixie's daring excited profile and saw how fascinated she was.

'Hullo..o.o.' Then, after a pause, 'Up here.'

'Hullo.' He had smiled but you would never have known from his voice which was harsh, graceless and impersonal.

The gown slithered and slipped again as Trixie leaned out a little further. 'Isn't anyone looking after you?'

Janet opened the sweater drawer, saw the colours blur. She started to rummage furiously.

Trixie said: 'How d'you like this weather?' nodding at the drooping flowers and limp-leaved shrubs. As she spoke she agitated the loose drawstring neck of her blouse revealing, then concealing, a creamy freckled upsurge of swelling delights.

'Hot for me.' There was a suggestion of an upturn on the final word. It could have been a question.

Trixie laughed, husky, sassy. 'I should think it is in that suit.' She was standing on the terrace, a shade closer than normal civility required, her feet firmly on the ground and set slightly apart. The challenging stance of a principal boy.

'A drink might help,' continued Guy.

'There's some lemon-balm tea in the fridge.'

'I meant a real drink. I'm just going to check in at my hotel. We could get something there.'

'Ohhh. . . .' This is so sudden said the quickened breath and downswept baby-doll lashes. 'I don't know about that.'

Trixie's confusion, which Guy immediately labelled an attack of the cutes, was not entirely faked. Flinging on some clothes, running down to the terrace she had been driven by nothing more complicated than a childlike wish to gaze at someone rich and famous. But not long after introducing herself – and they had been talking for about ten minutes now, mainly about Suhami – she became aware of a not unfamiliar physical agitation. Her remark about money being a turn-on, made half in jest and half from a wish to irritate Janet, had proved to be compellingly accurate.

Trixie had never heard the saying the rich are different from us only in that they have more money, and if she had would have profoundly disagreed. Guy seemed to her a most mysterious being. The personification of a character previously only encountered in power-packed soap operas. Wheeling and dealing, making and breaking lives, glittering at the top of a shining dynastic tree in sultanic splendour.

They walked towards the car. Trixie stared at the diamond-hard mirror-bright perfection of the sweeping fuchsia chassis. At the huge headlamps, dazzling whitewall tyres and the hood that was like the furled sail of a yacht. It did not occur to her to pretend to be unawed. She said: 'How absolutely beautiful. You must be very rich.'

To which Guy replied simply, 'I'm as rich as God.'

Furneaux, seeing their approach, put down his *Evening Standard*, donned his peaked suede cap and jumped out to open the rear door. Trixie climbed in and perched on the edge of the seat with great delicacy as if it were made of spun glass. But once they had moved off she gradually edged back until, by the time they entered Causton, she was nestling in the corner, one arm lying casually over the side ready to wave should she, in fact or pretence, spot an acquaintance.

Guy, working on his usual principle of never doing one thing when you could be doing half a dozen, was edging his hand ever closer to Trixie's knee, looking into her eyes and questioning her further about the commune.

'What's he like then – this guiding light?'

'The Master? All right. That is kind and . . . you know . . . well, *good*.' It surprised Trixie, now that she was asked, to realise how little she could think of to say. Guy still looked expectant. She scraped around for another morsel. 'He's wonderful to talk to.' Everyone said this so it must be true, though Trixie's own occasional tête-à-tête with the magus had left her feeling exposed and nervous rather than comforted. 'He spends a lot of time in meditation.'

Guy snorted. He was deeply contemptuous of anyone not fully engaged in the chaotic cut and thrust of the working world. He himself, as he constantly pointed out, worked a forty-eight-hour day. Felicity said he made it sound as if he were breaking stones.

Trixie was much more interested in hearing about Guy's life than talking about her own, but before she could turn the conversation round he said: 'You must know more about him than that.'

'No, honestly.'

'Come on – you're an intelligent girl.' Guy smiled into the slightly blank unfinished face. 'For instance – does he own the place?'

'I don't know. There's a committee runs things.' His hand caressed her knee. 'May, Arno. People who've been here a long time. Don't.'

'Don't what?' The vulgar energetic pounce in his voice was almost unnerving. His powerful bulk gave off a multiplicity of scents: tobacco and liquor, hair oil, sharp lemony cologne inadequately masking male sweat. He closed the gap between them and whispered in her ear. Trixie gasped.

'That's an awful thing to say.'

'I'm an awful man.'

Guy's hand ascended a little higher, exploratory, determined. He did not agree with the superstition often held by soldiers and athletes that linked sexual intercourse with a depletion of physical reserves. Sex left Guy clear-headed, drained of troublous humours and smartly on his toes. He would need to be all those things if the evening were to go as successfully as he had planned, and he regarded Trixie's appearance as fortuitous in the extreme. He took her hand, turned it over and scratched the palm with his nail.

When, with some difficulty, Trixie unglued her gaze from that of her libidinous companion, it came to rest on Furneaux's back. Although the line of his body was slide-rule straight and his eyes, reflected in the driving mirror, fixed squarely on the road ahead, she got the strong impression he was laughing.

Guy pressed his full, red, hot lips to Trixie's ear, slipped the third finger of his right hand between the third and fourth fingers of her own and pushed it, more and more quickly, back and forth. Trixie tried, not too determinedly, to move away. She did not appreciate that it was only the fact and duration of the journey that caused her to be exposed to all these rousing preliminaries. Guy's usual idea of foreplay was to check if the girl was awake.

The car swung into the winding drive of Chartwell Grange and Trixie smoothed down her hair. Furneaux parked and unloaded the bags. The reception area was huge with many glazed-chintz sofas, deep armchairs and little tables holding magazines of a sporty or countrified nature. There were also two magnificent flower arrangements perched on Corinthian-style columns.

If Guy had been the sort to apprehend other people's sensitivities, he might have spotted a certain coolness behind the 'Welcome' sign at reception. Little Jill Meredith, who had taken the Gamelin reservation, had been most distressed at his secretary's manner. When Jill politely inquired if both guests required a double en suite the girl had drawled: 'Don't be bloody stupid. Haven't you got an annexe or something? Put the chauffeur in there.'

There was no call, Jill's boss had agreed whilst comforting his employee with an iced Malibu, to take that tone. Politeness cost nothing. Jill nodded and wished she'd thought of such a witty comeback at the time. Now she handed over the keys without a smile. A pageboy in a musical comedy get-up with white gloves under one epaulette went off with Guy's case.

'Now the drinks – hmm?' Guy turned to his companion. Keeping his arm tightly round her waist.

Trixie nodded, looking up at him with a thrilled, slightly nervous possessiveness. She was sure that everyone in the hotel must know who he was and consequently believed her own status to be elevated accordingly. But middle-aged businessmen bringing secretaries, personal assistants, girl Fridays or just companions of the night were regular features at the Grange. These youthful appendages were described by the staff as excess baggage and universally despised, not on any moral grounds but because they never tipped.

'Some Scotch. . . . Gin. Ice. Soda.'

'When would you—'

'Now.'

'Would that be in the Tally Ho lounge, sir?' asked reception.

'If you want it emptied in five seconds flat.' Jill Meredith blushed. 'Otherwise outside my door.'

'All the ice'll melt,' giggled Trixie as they entered the lift, blissfully unaware that the lightning and brutal rapacity of Guy's technique would hardly give a single cube as much as a chance to sweat.

Hands up her skirt before the lift door closed, grandstanding crotch rubbed her thigh. Once inside the room he was on her like a wolf. Tearing, pinching, nibbling, biting. Non-stop obscenities poured from his mouth. Unzipped but fully dressed, he drove into her with effortful satisfaction. At the last, forcing her head towards his groin.

'*No*,' squealed Trixie. . . . 'I'm not doing that –'

'Go down. . . .' Guy grasped her hair and she shrieked with pain. '*Go down you obstinate bitch. . . .*'

When he had finished Trixie ran into the bathroom, opened the complimentary brush and toothpaste kit and scrubbed her teeth and gums, her tongue, even her lips. Then she gargled, rinsed several times with mouthwash and drank a tumbler of water. But the taste of him remained.

She stared at herself in the glass. At her bruised and bitten breasts and at the red weals on the stinging flesh of her arms. She walked stiffly back to the bedroom, picked up her torn pants and rag of a blouse and looked around for her skirt.

She sat down on the edge of the bed, becoming conscious of an agonising cramp in the muscles of her back. Not wishing to look at Guy, she focused on a bowl of fruit. The card read:

Having a wonderful time? Great. Tell your friends. If not tell us.
Best wishes, Ian and Fiona.

Guy had brought in the drinks and was mixing a large Scotch.
He took a deep draught then removed a wallet from his inside
pocket, extracted a note and dropped it on the bed saying, 'There
you go.'

He always paid for casual sex. There was no come-back then.
No one owed anyone a thing. No rubbish about meeting again
and keeping in touch or giving each other a bell. And no dreary
monologues about unhappy childhoods. In and out. That was it.

Trixie stared at the money. Guy took off his jacket, hung it
on the back of a chair and started tugging at his tie. He took
another swig of Scotch and jerked a thumb at the tray: 'Help
yourself.' Receiving no reply he said: 'What's the matter?'

'The matter? *The matter*?'

'Fifty's all you're getting if that's what you're yelping about.'

'I don't want it.' Trixie crouched, hunched and shuddering. 'I
don't want any of it.'

'What's this then?' He grinned, stretching froggy lips. 'Free
bonking for millionaires' week? Go on – take it. Buy yourself a
new top. Not much of that one left.'

'You're . . . you are. . . .' She wrapped her bruised arms tight
across her chest as if for protection. 'Hateful . . . you're hateful.'

Guy stared at her, genuinely puzzled. 'I don't get any of this.'
He pulled off his tie and started unbuttoning his shirt. 'But I'm
already bored to death. Now you can help yourself to a drink
and start behaving normally or fuck off. I'm indifferent either
way.'

He disappeared into the bathroom, turned on the shower and
came back to remove his trousers and underpants. Trixie
watched, sick with rage and self-loathing. How could she ever
have let him as much as touch her? He was repulsive! Shiny with
sweat, covered all over with flattened, long black hairs. Even his
dong, she'd noted sourly, looked hairy; dark and sleek like a
rat's pelt. He was peeling off his socks.

Trixie outsmarted, outgunned closed her eyes and sought

refuge in fantasy. She took the Scotch and smashed it down upon those closely sheared curls then rammed splinters of glass into his eyes and mouth. Possessed of superhuman strength she leapt upon him in the bath, seizing soapy, slimy shoulders, forcing his head under the water till the bubbles ceased. Then she had an inspiration and called across the room: 'I forgot to tell you – I've got Aids.'

Guy looked at her briefly, sharply then laughed. 'Dear, oh dear. I was telling better ones than that before I was born.'

'It's true.' But they could both hear the weak, almost pleading undertow. Guy gave a slow contemptuous shake of the head.

But then, her mind filled with yet more bloody scenes of annihilating splendour, Trixie came across a weapon of devastating accuracy. At the time this seemed accidental. Later she remembered their conversation on the terrace and the shadow on Guy's face as he had talked about his daughter. She sat up.

'Funny Suhami being at the Windhorse, isn't it? With her background. And all that money. . . . You'd think she'd have everything she'd want at home.' The change in Guy's expression frightened Trixie, but the longing to get even forced her on. 'Of course she thinks the world of the Master. I suppose he's a sort of father figure. A bit peculiar really. Not as if she hasn't got one of her own.'

Trixie faltered on the last words for Guy was walking towards her. She willed herself not to shrink back into the pillows. He shoved his face close to her own. She could see the open pores, the thready veins and spiny hairs in his nose.

'I'm going to have a shower now. Wash the stink of the gutter off. When I come out I want you gone. Five minutes – OK?' He spoke in a whisper but the whisper was so gorged with hatred that his breath scorched her skin.

As the door to the bathroom closed, what there was of Trixie's courage vanished. Legs trembling, she got up and stumbled over to the dressing table. In the mirror she saw that her cheeks were wet. She hadn't realised she was crying. How was that possible? To weep and not to know. She released a moan of self-pity, immediately silenced although there was no way it could be overheard.

She listened to him soaping and splashing. There were some tissues in a velvet-covered box. She took some and scrubbed at her face. She had far too much make-up on. The result of a frantic re-embellishment before running downstairs. Flinching at the recollection, Trixie attempted to moderate the damage that tears and perspiration had wrought. It wasn't easy especially as she was without her handbag and consequently – it struck her for the first time – without money.

How was she to get home? The thought of approaching the chauffeur, first having to ask at the desk for his whereabouts, brought the shakes on again. In any case he wouldn't take her anywhere without Gamelin's say-so. Trixie recalled her previous intuition – that the man had been laughing at her. He probably thought she was some sort of prostitute. Perhaps they all did! Trixie turned from her reflection, overcome by shame.

She could still hear water but two minutes had already gone by. What would he do if he came back and found her there? Physically chuck her out that's what. He couldn't give a monkey's about causing a scene. Money meant never having to say you're sorry.

She stared at the fifty-pound note lying on sheets still pungent with the reek of loveless copulation and was disgusted to find herself briefly, treacherously, inclined to take it. Not for the sex but as compensation for bruised breasts, painful back and tender aching limbs. Compulsively, perhaps needing to protect herself from this dishonourable rationale, she seized the note and tore it in half. Then into four and finally into as many tiny pieces as she could manage. About to toss these scornfully into the air she noticed a wallet protruding from his jacket pocket. She pulled it out and began stuffing the bits inside. This childish occupation ignited a brief flicker of satisfaction. She pictured him, perhaps in some smart restaurant, searching for his credit card and releasing a cloud of fiscal confetti.

Replacing the wallet, Trixie felt something small and

lump-like. She drew it out. A bottle, very thick brown glass. She unscrewed the foil-lined cap. Even without the label she would have recognised the contents. *Glyceryl Trinitrate.* Her father had carried just such tablets to keep the shadow of death at bay. He would never have left them in another room while taking a shower. Trixie tipped the tablets into her hand, replaced the top and returned the bottle to its original place. The water stopped running.

She stood staring at the white painted door. Behind it a clatter, then a sharp rap. A coathanger bouncing against the wood. He was putting on a robe. He was going to come out and find her. Not gone in five minutes but standing there with his life-support system, a little ball of sweaty white gravel, in her hand. Then a loud buzz. A shaver. Reprieved, Trixie felt a quick rush of energy and simultaneously a terrible apprehension of the seriousness of what she had done. It could even be criminal. She must put them back. Indeed their very removal now seemed to her an act of absolute madness.

But she had only taken a single step when the room was filled with the loud shrilling of the telephone. Guy switched off his razor. And Trixie fled away.

In the beechwoods which bordered the fields at the rear of the house, Janet paced furiously back and forth, kicking at leaf mould, stamping on fallen twigs. The dark interior with its sombre canopy of light-excluding branches suited her mood entirely. Tears splashed on to her lace-up walking shoes and her breathing was harsh and jerky. Occasionally she gave vent to a peculiar hacking sound. Something between a cough and a groan.

How Trixie had hurried, agonised Janet. God – how she'd raced about! Rubbing on lipstick, squirting clouds of scent every-where – even down her panties. Winking at Janet. Singing: 'Mon*ee* makes the world go round . . . the world go round . . . the world. . . .' Swaying off with her seraglio walk.

It had been horrible. Pitiable and degrading; like watching the poor scrabble for bread. Janet recognised the exaggeration but the principle was the same. I could have given her money. She's welcome to all I have. Janet scrubbed at her cheeks with a wisp of stolen lace.

He'd looked such a thug. She stopped in her tracks at the recollection and sat down on a fallen log. Built to do damage, Trixie had said. What sort of damage might he do? She was so vulnerable. Always trying to appear so . . . what was the word . . . streetwise? But really not much more than a child. Which was why Janet felt so protective.

That, of course, was all she felt. She was absolutely not in any way at all in love with Trixie. Never in a million years. Because that would make her some sort of . . . well . . . lesbian. And Janet would have been distressed and horrified had she been so described. Because she would never actually *do* anything. Could not imagine doing anything under any circumstances whatsoever. In fact was utterly revolted at the thought. Defensively, she regarded her more emotional friendships (and weren't all true friendships emotional?) as being similar to the idolatrous pashes so germane to the plots of old-fashioned school stories for girls. *Maisie Saves The Day. Sukie Pulls It Off.* That sort of thing.

She had been picking absently at the rotting bark – it was soft like flakes of chocolate – struggling to regain some sort of equilibrium. Silly to get into a state. They'd probably just gone off somewhere for a drink. And he was only around for an hour or two. After dinner he'd be gone and that would be that. Surely?

Her scratching had disturbed some woodlice. Dozens fell to the ground and started scurrying about. One fell on its back and scurried with its legs in the air. Janet turned it over with her thumbnail then looked at her watch. Trixie had been gone for nearly an hour. She could be back at any minute. Might be already.

Springing up, Janet walked quickly to the edge of the wood and climbed the stile. She let herself into the grounds through the old door that opened into the orchard. As she did so, she was struck by a fierce urgent compulsion that something was wrong. That Trixie needed her. Was crying out for help or comfort. Janet began to run, stumbling across the lawn, tripping on tussocks of grass, using her arms like pistons – elbows tucked in – as if she were in a race.

As she burst through the gap in the yew hedge, a taxi drew up at the front door and Trixie got out. Calling her name, Janet ran across the gravel to lean, panting, on the bonnet of the car. Trixie appeared quite calm but was pale and clutching at her blouse in a rather odd way.

'Sort out the cab for me would you, Jan?' She hurried into the house calling over her shoulder: 'Pay you back.'

Janet asked the man to wait while she found some money then, after he had driven away, she went upstairs and tapped several times very gently on Trixie's door. But there was no reply. Eventually Janet gave up and went downstairs to help prepare the birthday dinner.

Chapter 6

Utterly transformed, Felicity sat quite still staring into her dressing-room mirror. She and Danton were enclosed inside a black *faux marbre* horseshoe supported by a cluster of grave-faced caryatids. The surface of this creation was invisible beneath a crust of glittering glass – jars, flasks, bottles – and metal – lipstick cases, aerosols, tins. The images in this small space, so grossly given over to a worship of the vanities, were multiplied a hundred times by the judicious arrangement of mirrored screens set at angles in the walls.

As his client rose, Danton moved away, hands lifted in a curious Kabukiesque manner. This gesture encompassed both pride and disbelief as if he could barely comprehend the perfection of his art. Felicity's complexion was drained of all colour but for a pearly pink glow on her cheekbones. Huge eyes were shrouded in violet and silver shadows, her shoulders gleamed and shimmered beneath a wrap of iridescent mussel-shell silk. Lips the colour of rich dark wine were parted in dismay.

'I look like the angel of death.'

'Mrs G . . . Mrs G. . . .' What a compliment though, thought Danton. From the first the dress had said to him 'think ceremental', and what an inspiration it had proved to be. 'You need some more champers.'

'No.' Felicity shook her head but the heavy mane of ashen curls barely moved. 'Too much already.'

'A line then.' Danton always carried an emergency repair kit for his clients.

Felicity hesitated, 'I've been off it for a bit.' She watched Danton unscrew a thin tortoiseshell case. 'Anyway – even if I do by the time I get there—'

'Take it with you.' Deftly he slipped the box and the glass fistula into her bag. 'Chances are if you know it's there, you'll be OK.'

'Yes.'

Already Felicity knew she was not going to be anything remotely like 'OK'. She stared at herself in apprehensive disbelief. How on earth had matters come to such a pass? All she'd done was make a phone call. But from the simple action, plus her decision to take up the invitation, had arisen this capricious and bizarre metamorphosis. She felt she had been ambushed and yet surely there must have been a point at which she could have called a halt? A rejection of the dress perhaps – how wildly unsuitable she now saw it to be. Or the moment when Danton, after studying her newly washed hair from every angle, had finally cried, 'Cold cinders.'

But that point had long been passed. In fifteen minutes the car would arrive. A terrible inertia now entrapped her. A pall of fatalism. She seemed to have no will of her own. Having been launched on a journey, she must continue. She saw herself at the dinner table. A spectre at the feast, like Banquo's ghost. Guy would laugh at her as he did in his sleep. Sylvie would be distressed and ashamed. After it was over Felicity would haste away, cloaked and hooded, cast quite out.

'Fragrance.' It wasn't a question. Danton's fingers hovered in a familiar way about the jewelled stoppers. '*L'Egypte.*'

Very apt, thought Felicity. Heady and oppressive. Sealed tombs, dried-up corpses, dank lifeless air. He sprayed lavishly then re-swathed her hair in the misty scarf: 'I'll take your case down.'

She had gone along with the suggestion of an overnight bag and change of clothes, for protesting seemed onerous. But she knew she would not stay and planned to keep the hired car at the door to facilitate her flight.

Danton returned and stood behind his client. A final touch to the earrings, a rearrangement of a curl. Felicity bowed her head as if for a *coup de grâce*

'Don't look like that Mrs G,' said Danton. 'You'll have a wicked time. Wish I was coming.' In the street a horn blared. 'That'll be us.' He tucked away his cheque and flourished her velvet cloak like a matador. 'Ring me the second you get back and tell me all about your marvellous evening. I'll be in knots till you do.'

At 6.55 precisely the Corniche drew up once more at the Manor House and Guy pulled once more on the iron rod. He was making no mistakes this time. Sylvie – no Suhami, he must remember this changeling name – had rung Chartwell Grange to say that the Master would see her father at seven o'clock for a brief talk before dinner.

Guy had been elated at the sound of her voice. He was already longing to see her again, greedy for an opportunity to repair the damage done this afternoon. But softly, softly. . . . He must feel his way along. Be careful not to offend. Keep his opinions to himself. It would be bloody difficult but he would do it because he had found her and she must never be lost again.

At that moment a pillar of fire came round the corner. Scarlet and orange draperies floated, flared, flickered and flamed. They were encircled by a belt studded with stones like embers. It shimmered to a halt and spoke.

'You're not wearing indigo.'

'I never wear indigo,' said Guy. 'What's indigo?'

'You should. You're over-aggressive. Too much red.'

'I never wear red either.' Guy thought, look who's talking, and felt some perturbation as if the conversation was already out of control.

'In your aura, man. Positively seething. Plus a hole in it big as a cantaloupe.'

'Is . . . is there?'

'Etheric leakage is no joke.' May looked stern as she opened

105

the door. 'There's also a lot of murky spots. You're not a miser by any chance?'

'Certainly not,' replied Guy peevishly, following her into the hall. How could anyone who had treated himself to a Rolls-Royce Corniche possibly be called miserly?

'Well, I see a grave imbalance, Mr Gamelin. Too much of one activity I suspect. I have no wish to pry. But if you crave worldly success—'

'I have worldly success. I crave nothing.' Except a daughter. *Ah Sylvie – my grave imbalance. My life.*

'I'm here to see—'

'I know all about *that*. I'll take you. This way please.' She surged off, with Guy in hot pursuit. They were passing the door behind which he had discovered the mad boy when she spoke again.

'Are you staying over?'

Guy mumbled something about a hotel.

'Excellent. Tomorrow you must come and choose some bottles and I'll get you on to a corrective regime.'

Guy wasn't at all sure about that. The words 'colonic irrigation' sprang to mind. He asked what the consultation might involve.

'I start with the chakras. Give them a good rinse, clear the nadis. Then I try and get in touch with one of the grand Masters. Mine is inestimable. She's a first chohan of the seventh ray you see.'

'But you have a master here already,' said Guy, struggling to keep a straight face. 'Couldn't we just ask him?'

He was intrigued by May's response. She appeared flustered and the rhythm of that splendid stride was momentarily broken.

'Oh – I couldn't do that. He's . . . tired at the moment. Hasn't been too well.'

'My daughter didn't mention it.'

'Really?' May had stopped in front of a carved door. She knocked and waited. Then, apparently answering a response which to Guy was inaudible, she opened the door and said: 'Mr Gamelin is here, Master,' and ushered him in.

The impression first received was of a quite large room but Guy quickly realised that this was because the place was nearly empty. It reminded him of a Japanese interior, pale and uncluttered. A negation of a room. There were two cushions on the floor, a screen near the window and a wooden frame over which stretched a piece of silk dyed in fabulous bird-of-paradise colours.

A man arose from one of the cushions in an enviously supple way and came forward to greet him. Guy looked into eyes so compelling that it was a moment before he noticed any other details of the man's appearance. When he did so, he was immediately comforted. Long white hair, blue robe, sandalled feet – a pathetically transparent straining for spiritual effect. A drawing by a hack artist. Astroth: Master of the Universe. Guy shook hands forcefully and grinned.

Invited to sit, he lowered himself with some difficulty on to a cushion, remaining bolt upright, hands flat on the floor behind him, legs sticking straight out. He regretted the discomfort whilst appreciating the strategy. Craigie obviously had more orthodox seating (no one lived in a shell this bare), but had deliberately removed it to place his audience at a disadvantage. A fakir's version of the 'look who's in the highest chair' manoeuvre. It'll take more than that, Craigie. Guy looked with a fierce and challenging encouragement, *mano-a-mano*, at his companion, who smiled faintly in return but did not speak.

The silence lengthened. When it began, Guy was restless – his mind, as always, furiously thrusting and parrying, plotting the destruction of opposing hordes but then, as the seconds and then the minutes slid by, all his whirling aggravation became first muted and then displaced. He could still hear his bombastic inner voice but faintly, like the sounds of battle beyond distant hills.

Guy was not usually at ease with silence. He liked what he called 'a bit of life', by which he meant a bit of noise. But now the quiet was affecting him strangely. He seemed to be settling into it as into a huge, consoling embrace. He was tempted to let go. To rest safely. A burden seemed to have been lifted from his back and all motion stalled. He felt that he should comment on this extraordinary state of affairs, but the language needed to express such sentiments seemed to be unavailable, so he continued to sit. There seemed to be no hurry for anything and he no longer felt uncomfortable.

The room was filled with light from the setting sun and the strip of silk caught fire. As Guy stared at it, the zinging colours developed in intensity – glowing to such an extent that they seemed almost to be alive and pulsing with energy. He found it impossible to take his eyes off this luminous transformation and began to wonder if he was being hypnotised. And then the other man spoke.

'I'm so glad that you could come and visit us.'

Guy collected himself, attempted to ball up the soft spread of his attention. It wasn't easy. 'The gratitude is mine. For your kindness to my daughter.'

'She's a delightful girl. We are all extremely fond of Suhami.'

'I was very worried when she disappeared.' Rule One. Never acknowledge a weakness. 'Not that we were close.' Rule Two. Or admit failure.

What was wrong with him? This was the adversary. The father figure that Sylvie thought the world of. Guy struggled to reactivate his previous sensations of jealousy and revenge. Without them he felt naked. He stared into the brilliant blue eyes and calm expressionless face. The flesh had fallen in at the side of the nose. It was sharp and pointed, an old man's nose. Hold fast to that. He's decrepit. One foot in the grave. But what about that jaw? A soldier's jaw. A soldier's jaw in a monk's face. What was being signalled here? Guy felt completely at a loss.

'Even in the closest of families young people must break away. It is always painful.'

There was something about Craigie's presence, perhaps the deep concentration of his attention, that demanded a response. Guy said, 'Pain is putting it mildly.'

'These rifts can be healed.'

'D'you think so? Do you really think that's possible?'

Guy leaned forwards, hands clasped. And started to talk.

Streams of resentful reminiscence poured from his lips. Torrents of remorse. Floods of self-justification. On and on it went, seemingly without end. Guy heard it all with feelings of incredulous disgust. Such loathsome black fecundity. And yet – the ease with which it flowed! As if it had been waiting all these years in a pounce posture on the back of his tongue.

When finally it was over he was exhausted. He looked across at Craigie who was looking down at his hands. Guy tried to read the other man's expression which struck him as one of concerned detachment, but this could surely not be the case. You could be one or the other but not both. And certainly not both at once. Guy sat for several moments more until the longing to evoke some sort of response became too much for him. He struggled to gather his wits then added a vindicative coda.

'I gave her everything.'

Ian Craigie nodded sympathetically. 'That's understandable. But of course it doesn't work.'

'Can't buy love you mean? That's for sure. Otherwise there'd be no lonely millionaires.'

'My point is that ultimately *things* cannot satisfy, Mr Gamelin. They have no life you see.'

'Ah.' Guy did not see. Surely things, acquisitions to display and use, were what it was all about. How else did people know what sort of man you were? And surely on the most basic level one needed a house, food, warmth and clothing. He said as much.

'Of course this is true. But there is a fourth great need which we ignore at our peril. And that's the need for intoxication.' He smiled, correctly interpreting Guy's translation of the word. 'I refer to emotional and spiritual intoxication. We see it at the games sometimes. Hear it in music. . . .'

'I understand that.' Guy recalled the crowding glass canyons of the city. The dramatic rites of passage. Smoke-filled boardrooms; daggers noiselessly drawn. That was bloody intoxicating if you like. 'But I don't see how, here. . . .' He gave an all-inclusive wave.

'Here we are in love with prayer. And the pursuit of goodness.'

A disturbing hint of irony. Guy disliked irony, seeing it as a weapon needed only by the smart-arsed weakling. 'You sound as if you don't take it seriously.'

'I take the quest very seriously. But people, no. At least only rarely.'

Guy felt suddenly cold as if a source of comfort had been capriciously withdrawn. Had the warmth, then, the understanding that he was pouring out his sorrow to an empathetic and receptive intelligence been no more than an illusion? Guy felt aggrieved. Cheated even. 'The pursuit of goodness? I don't quite understand.'

'No. Abstract nouns are always difficult. And dangerous. I suppose the plainest way to put it is that once the idea that such a thing truly exists . . . that it is perhaps available and we can experience it – once that idea has pricked you, it never afterwards leaves you quite alone.'

Guy thought of his all-consuming love and understood completely.

'We spend most of our time here falling by the wayside of course, like everyone else.'

'And is this . . . pursuit what Sylvie wants, do you think?'

'She believes so at the moment. Her meditations have brought her a measure of content. But she is very young. We try on many masks throughout our lives. Eventually we find one that fits so well we never take it off.'

'I've never worn a mask.'

'You think not?' There was a rap on the door. He called out: 'A few minutes May,' and turned back to Guy. 'We haven't even touched on the problem of your daughter's inheritance, which was one of the principal reasons that I asked you down.'

'The McFadden bequest? Not with you, Craigie.'

'She wants to give it all to the community.'

Guy gave a strangled groan and the Master leaned forward anxiously. 'Are you all right Mr Gamelin?'

Guy lifted his face. It was stamped with an expression of

stupefied dismay. His jaws gaped. The Master surveyed this pitiable spectacle then smiled, but without parting his lips. These
were firmly clamped together. After a few moments he spoke
again.

'Please don't distress yourself. The money will not be accepted.
At least not at the moment. Your daughter is overly grateful for
our affection, as children are who have not known love. Also
the bequest reminds her of past unhappiness which is why she is
determined to offload it, if not on us, elsewhere.' Guy became
pale, even his port-wine nose blanched.

'This vulnerability is what I hoped to talk about with you. I
wondered if some procedure could not be opened whereby I can
appear to accept it but actually make some arrangements for it
to be securely held, perhaps for at least another year. She may
of course still wish to dispose of it but my experience,' the irony
was plainer now, 'leads me to the belief that she will not.'

The rap came again. May put her lips to the door frame.
'Master – we're awaiting dinner.'

'We'll come back to this, Mr Gamelin. Please don't be alarmed. Something can be worked out.'

Behind this impeccably courteous response Guy sensed that
his reaction had caused amusement, and he resented it. What
man in his right mind would not be alarmed at the thought of
half of a million smackers disappearing from the family vaults!
Loathsome though the McFaddens might be, their money was
still as good as anybody else's. He struggled to his feet and all
his previous displeasure at being forced into such an undignified
posture returned. Craigie did not move. 'Aren't you coming?'

'I eat at twelve.'

'Only then?' You must get very hungry.'

'Not at all.' There was a withdrawing of attention that was
almost palpable. A folding-in. Guy could have been in an empty
room. 'And now you must excuse me. I need to rest.'

In a massive tailback on the M4, Felicity's hired car rested
motionless between a much-welded Cortina and a BMW. The

111

man in the executive job had stapled his finger to the horn. Felicity slipped off her shoe and gave the dividing panel a sharp crack with its rhinestoned heel. The driver jumped and showed a nervous profile.

He'd been keeping an eye on her since just after they'd left Belgravia. In fact, if he'd any choice in the matter, he wouldn't have picked her up at all. Not only did she look like Vincent Price's bit on the side, but she'd also been acting most peculiarly. Constantly pulling her scarf off then winding it back on, humming, waving through the window. He eased the sheet of toughened glass aside.

'I told your firm I had to be there at half past seven.'

'Can't help the traffic, Mrs Gamelin.'

'You should have come earlier.'

'I came the time I was booked to come.'

'But they should have known what it would be like.' They'd had this conversation many times. He kept a weary silence. 'The letter said half past seven to eat at eight, you see. The Manor House, Compton Dandon. It's terribly important.'

No need to tell him the address. It was tattooed on his brain. She'd hardly stopped repeating it since getting into the cab. He'd also got it written down.

'Can't you pull out or something and overtake?'

The driver smiled, nodded and closed the panel, noticing with some trepidation that she kept the shoe in her hand.

'Further to our earlier discussion, Mr Gamelin. . . .'

Guy, once more tacking after May along the corridor, did not hear. He was struggling to regain his sense of self which had mysteriously, subtly, been first fractured then destroyed in that quiet room. My God he thought – if *I* could learn to do that. What a weapon it would be!

'I have a colour workshop in September. Still a few places left.'

Craigie – that frail and near-silent man – was a magician. A trickster. That must be it. What other explanation could there be? All this talk of goodness and spiritual intoxication was absolute balls. A cloak of benign mysticism concealing a secret imperator. As for this pretence of not accepting Sylvie's money. A brilliant bluff. Guy was not unfamiliar with brinkmanship but had never seen a move so close to the edge. Quite breathtaking! As was this arranged 'consultation' with her parents. Set up purely to reinforce Craigie's pose of selfless affection. The clever sod. *Father figure.* I'll give him fucking father figure! He doesn't know who he's taken on. He doesn't know he's born. By the time they reached the dining room, Guy was completely himself again.

There seemed to be an awful lot of people. They were all seated at a long table. One or two wore expressions of suffering restraint. Guy supposed he should apologise for keeping them waiting, reasoned that it wasn't really his fault, but thought it might annoy Sylvie if he didn't – so he mumbled a few conciliatory words in their general direction.

'I expect you'd like a drink.'

May was leading him to an armoire on which were two glass jugs. One full to the brim with dark pink liquid the other, half-empty, held something pondy green. Working on the principle that the natives always know best, Guy inclined towards the latter.

'Now,' said May with a conjurer's wave at the jugs. 'Which is it to be?'

'Whichever's strongest.'

'The bullace is bursting with silenium. On the other hand, with turnip top you have a smidgen of iodine, quite a lot of vitamin C and a good thrust of manganese.'

'I meant strongest in alcohol.'

'Oh dear.' She gave his arm an understanding pat. 'Are you desperate for a fix? That explains the auric slippage. Don't worry,' filling a stone beaker, 'it's never too late. I had an alcoholic here a few months ago. Couldn't stand up when he arrived. I gave him a dowsing with the pendulum, working him over with the violet ray of Arturus, gee'd up his chakras and

113

taught him the salute to the sun. Do you know where that man is today?'

Guy realised he'd left his hip flask in the car. He followed his hostess, sipping at the green liquid. The stuff tasted better than it looked but it was close. He was delighted to see an empty chair next to Sylvie but, veering towards that section of the table, he was skilfully deflected by May who popped him into quite a different chair, taking the other place herself.

He started to call after her, 'Can't I sit . . .' when he was interrupted by a woman on his right.

'We always keep the same seat. It's a little way we have here. A little discipline. You are in the visitor's place.'

Guy stared at her with some dislike. A receding chin, long greying hair held back by an Alice band, eyes bulging with sincerity. She was wearing a T-shirt declaring: 'Universal Mind: The Only Choice' and no bra. Her breasts, huge with big nipples, sagged nearly to her waist. The man sitting opposite her on Guy's right hand (for he was at the end of the table) had on a shepherd's smock. He passed Guy a plate of cow pats.

'Barley cake?'

'Why not.'

Guy took two, forced a smile and looked over the rest of the food. A dismal sight. More jugs of Château Ponderosa, torpedoes of bread spattered with blackish-brown gravel and a dish of gluey-looking stuff in which a metal spoon stood upright as if in a state of shock.

Guy thought gloomily of the dinner menu in his room at Chartwell Grange. Pan-fried Thwaite Shad nestling on a bed of Almond Rice bedecked with Dawn-gathered English Mushrooms and Tiny New Potatoes. This divine assemblage to be followed by either a Chariot of Crisp Cox's Orange Pippins, Hearty Fenland Celery or *Tarte Judy* according to the consumer's inclination and stamina. No doubt Furneaux was at this very moment cutting a swathe. The things I do for love, thought Guy – glancing towards his daughter, hoping for a smile.

Sylvie was wrapped in a beautiful apple-green and rose-madder sari. With her grave young face newly imprinted by a shiny dot and her dusky anchorite's hair, she seemed to him like a child strangely cast in a school play. He could not credit that she genuinely believed all this quasi-religious tommyrot. She was sitting next to a youth with long dark hair who was addressing her with quiet intimacy, sometimes whispering into her ear. Perhaps this was the 'marvellous man' for whom she had left London. If so, he seemed to have got a head start.

Guy noted his falsely tender smile. Plainly a fortune-hunter. The poor girl was surrounded by them, bloody vultures. He did not recognise the paradox in the assumption that his child, beloved by him for herself alone, must be beloved of others only by reason of her presumed inheritance.

May was making inroads into a shallow tin dish, swooping and slicing with great panache. As she lifted the servings, long, pale yellow strings stretched back to base. She was talking as she served to the table at large.

'. . . whole point about cataracts of course that the medical profession just will not see is that they are purely psychosomatic. The elderly cannot cope with modern life. Computers, street violence, large supermarkets, nuclear waste. . . . They can't bear to look at it. Ergo – the eye films over. I mean – it's so simple. Guy?'

'Thank you.' His plate arrived heaped with mysterious matter. A mosaic of red and brown and khaki, plus some black loops of rubbery-looking ribbon. Guy picked up his irons, noted a measure of surprise in the gathering and put them down again. Waiting for the others to be served, he began to sort people out.

Gnomish man with bright red shovel-shaped beard; woman with coarse bushy hair and a morose expression. That poor fool of a boy who sat on the far side of Sylvie. Guy noticed with deep revulsion how gently she spoke to the wretched creature, once going as far as to lay her hand on his arm. People like that, flawed with disease, should be put away, not let loose to make their grotesque demands on the innocent and tender-hearted. Of his afternoon playmate there was no sign. Guy didn't know

115

whether to be glad or sorry. Strangely, for him, a flicker of unease had appeared soon after Trixie's departure. He still didn't understand her problem: she'd made herself available, he'd taken up the offer and paid on the nail. And for all the wails of wounded pride, the fifty quid had disappeared when she did. No – Guy's worry was that she might tell Sylvie and, in doing so, misrepresent the truth. Perhaps even make out she wasn't willing. So he decided, when he saw the girl again, to go out of his way to be friendly. Maybe even go as far as to apologise, although for what he still had no idea.

Once the serving was over a brief silence ensued during which everyone looked down at their plates. Guy looked down at his cow pats which looked faecetiously back. His neighbour sprang into speech. He had removed his smock and was now also sporting a T-shirt which instructed the reader: 'Respect My Space'.

'Hey . . . how about a getting-to-know-you people hunt? I'm Ken "Zedekial" Beavers. And that's my divine complement, Heather' said the grey-haired man. 'Or Tethys, in astral terms.'

'Guy Gamelin.' They all shook hands, then Guy agitated his dinner somewhat with a fork. 'What actually is all this?'

'Well, that's lasagne obviously. Goes without saying. This little heap is chick-pea purée and that,' indicating the black coils, 'is arame.' Ken pronounced the word in a very odd way, raising his soft palate and honking like a goose. 'Where would we all be without the ocean?'

'What?'

'Arame's a seaweed. From Japan.' He pronounced, 'Harpahn'. 'Eat enough – you'll never have shingles again.'

Guy, who had never had shingles in the first place, nodded vaguely and put down his fork. Beneath the hum of conversation he noticed music. Or rather a saccharine reconstruction of nature going about her business. Birds tweeting, trees whispering and a persistent ripple of water. Listening to it was like having your ears syringed.

No doubt it was regarded as conducive to tranquillity. It seemed to work. The whole atmosphere was abnormally serene. All the

116

voices were gentle. No one grabbed for what they wanted. Just gestured tenderly and murmured low. Guy wondered what they did with all their anger. Everyone had some after all. Part of the kit, along with liver and lights, teeth and nails. Did they meditate it away? Sublimate it under a blanket of kind deeds? Or – with a single babbling incantation – send it winging off for ever into the cosmos. What a load of jelly-bellied wimps. Huddling together, running away from the dark and from themselves. He became aware that he was scowling and, hurriedly adjusting his expression to one of polite interest, turned to his neighbour.

'And what do you all do here at the Windhorse?'

Heather gave her long hair an abandoned fling. 'We laugh . . . we cry. . . .' She cupped her hands then opened them with a bestowing fling as if releasing a racing pigeon. 'We live.'

'Everyone does that.'

'Not in the deepest chalice of their being.' She passed a dish of green stuff. 'Some carracol?' Guy hesitated. 'A fine mincing of comfrey, marjoram and just a little hempnettle.'

Guy shook his head, concealing his disappointment well. 'The one thing I'm not allowed. Hempnettle.'

'Condensed sunshine,' assured Ken, nodding at the fine mincing.

'In what way?'

'Impregnated with solar light.' His crystal winked and twinkled, backing him up. 'Don't tell me you've never heard of the five Platonic solids.'

'Heard of them?' said Guy. 'I'm eating them.' He smiled to show it was a joke then, sotto voce and with malice definitely aforethought, asked if there would be any meat.

This led to a long lecture full of warm sentimental invective from Heather, concluding with the information that 'at any given moment the colon of any given carnivore would have at least five pounds of animal protein fermenting in it.'

'*Five pounds*.'

'Minimum.'

Guy whistled and Ken, perhaps to underline the sweet

117

workability of his own gut reactions, let forth a whiffy crepitation. Guy wrinkled his nose. Heather changed the subject, offering Guy some more of the ersatz poteen that he had privately labelled 'Château Scumbag'.

Having failed to persuade him, she asked: 'And what do *you* do all day?'

'I'm a financier.' *As if you didn't know.*

'Heav..e.e.'

'Not if you've got the balls,' said Guy pleasantly. There was a sticky hiatus. 'Oh dear – have I offended? I thought you were all terribly close to nature down here.'

'Certainly we favour the visceral over the cerebral.'

'The dark night of the intellect,' interrupted Heather, 'is drawing to a close.'

It certainly seems to be in your case, thought Guy. 'I enjoy a spot of cerebral cut-and-thrust myself,' he said.

'We are all millionaires of the spirit here,' said Ken. 'And think the rat race is for rats.' This repartee was delivered through a mouthful of multi-coloured gubbins.

'I'm surprised to hear myself referred to in such terms. Especially as a guest in your community.' Ken turned scarlet. Guy was suddenly sick of them both. He leaned forward, contriving to speak with quiet confidentiality, secure in the knowledge that he couldn't be overheard by the rest of the table.

'Listen thunderbum, people do not abandon the rat race. It abandons them. The ones without fire in their bellies. And they crawl away leaving someone else to man the ship.'

Ken smiled and reached out forgivingly. 'It makes me sad to hear—'

'It doesn't make you sad to hear. It makes you bloody livid but you haven't the courage to say so. And take your hand off my arm.' The hand leapt away like a startled salmon.

'Where would we be,' Guy pushed his luck, 'if everyone decided to slink off and contemplate their navels. No doctors – no nurses – no teachers . . .'

'But that would never happen,' protested Heather. 'The

number of people wishing to lead reclusive lives of a moral and philosophical nature – a spiritual élite if you will – must by the very nature of things be small. It is an intensely disciplined regime.'

'I notice you take advantage of modern technology.' No one, thought Guy, who had an arse like an elephant had any call to bandy the word 'discipline' about. He knew the time had come to shut up. 'Has it never occurred to you that while you're up there on your pillar of virtue, some poor sod's on his knees down a mine so you'll have coal to burn?'

'But that's his karma.' Guy picked up a ripple of irritation. 'He would be at a very low level of incarnation. Probably working his way up from a mole.'

At the other end of the table people spoke amongst themselves. Janet wondered if she should go up yet again to see if Trixie could be persuaded to come out. May asked if anyone else thought the chick peas tasted rather odd, and Arno said on no account was she to have another morsel. Tim continued to eat globbily, stopping from time to time to stroke the amber sunflowers on Suhami's birthday bag.

Suhami herself ate little. She sat watching her father in a condition of growing unease. To someone who did not know him he was giving the impression of the perfect dinner guest. Nodding, talking, listening, smiling – although not eating much. Pretending? Of course. Brutal duplicity was his coinage. He played his games with little else. And there was something now about his glance and the set of his head that she did not like. She felt a sudden rush of panic and wished that she could perform a violent exorcism and vanish him entirely. Heather was speaking. Suhami strained her ears.

'. . . and we believe that the only true happiness is to be found in forgetting the self. So we try to lose our individuality in a concern for others. The sick or dispossessed . . . the poor . . .'

'*The poor* . . .' Guy's voice exploded. Tormenting memories, long suppressed, struck fire. A young boy, kneeling before an electricity meter. Penknife jammed in the slot, unable to get knife or the money out and so feeling a length of chain across his shoulders. The same boy scavenging for fruit and vegetables from splintered boxes behind market stalls receiving great clouts around the head if he was spotted. A hollow belly occasionally crammed with cheap greasy piles of starch so that when the boy grew up he ate nothing that was not an invitation to a cardiac arrest. Richly sauced red meat, towers of chocolate and whipped cream. Lobster Thermidor.

'. . . have to be strong . . . get out . . . get away . . . or you go under . . . .' Guy trembled and stared blindly around him, carried away by the intensity of his recall, hardly able to form his words. '. . . lice . . . the poor . . . they're lice . . . .'

'No . . . you mustn't say that.' Arno leaned forward, pale but determined. 'They are human beings and so to be valued. And helped, too, for they are powerless. Doesn't it say in the Bible that the meek shall inherit the earth?'

'They've done that all right.' Guy gave vent to a goaded yelp. 'There are mass graves everywhere full of them.'

A stunned silence. Everyone looked at each other unable to believe that they had actually heard such a shockingly cruel remark.

Guy sat motionless, his mouth still open, experiencing a thrill of horror. What had he done? How could he let himself be taunted into such intemperance by a couple of aging hippies when there was so much at stake? He lifted his head, cold and heavy as a stone, and stumbled once more into speech. 'I'm sorry . . . forgive me.' He got up. 'Sylvie – I didn't think . . . .'

'You can't leave anything alone can you?' Suhami, her face frozen, had also got to her feet. 'Anything kind or beautiful or good you have to drag down to your own poisonous level. I was happy here. Now you've ruined everything. I hate you . . . *I hate you* . . . !'

Tim cried out in alarm and cowered in May's lap. Christopher, grasping Suhami's arm, said, 'Don't darling . . . please . . . don't . . . .'

The others crowded round them all talking at once. Suhami

started to cry: 'My birthday . . . on my birthday. . . .'

Christopher stroked her hair, May stroked Tim's hair and Ken and Heather swung shiny beams of bright-eyed sanctimony at Guy who stood at the far end of the table – spurned and despised like the plaguey inmate of some lazaretto.

Then, as the soothing babble abated, he became aware of an extraordinary quality in the ensuing silence. The group had pressed more closely together and gave the impression of being both excited and alarmed. Guy felt a cool draught on the back of his neck. He turned and saw a woman standing in the shadow of the open doorway.

Phantom-like she rested against the jamb. She was wrapped in draperies the colour of fog. A huge bunch of cellophaned, beribboned flowers depended from one hand. She moved forwards, slowly dragging in her wake huge swathes of silk and tafetta which shushed and hissed on the bare boards. Half way towards the others she came to a halt, pushing back the misty scarf. At the sight of her huge-eyed, deeply hollowed face and tumbling mass of clay-grey hair the group drew even closer.

Ken murmured in wonder and disbelief: 'Hilarion's prediction. It's come true. . . .'

The visitor looked round uncertainly and cleared her throat, making a sound like the rustle of dry leaves. 'I rang the bell.' A voice so timorous it was almost inaudible. She held out a square of green paper as if in support of such importunity. 'I was invited.'

Guy, recognising the letter, gave a gasp of outrage and disbelief as he watched his wife, swaying like a narcolept, make for the nearest support, a low backed canvas chair. Reaching it she sank down, storm-cloud skirts billowing, and appeared overwhelmed with satisfaction at this simple feat.

Ken and Heather approached, praying hands to the fore. A few feet away they knelt down, foreheads touching the floor.

'Greetings Astarte – Goddess of the Moon.'

'Crescent Queen – lunar radiance.'

'A thousand humble welcomes.'

121

Felicity stared at them and blinked. Then Suhami, pale with embarrassed recognition, said: 'Mother?' She crossed to the seated figure. 'He said you couldn't come.'

Guy winced at the dismissive impersonal pronoun. He watched Felicity's blackberry lips shake with the effort of forming a reply. Instead she offered up the bouquet. Suhami took it, read the card and said: 'How lovely – thank you.'

Guy recalled his own flowers forgotten in the porch, then realised that these *were* his flowers. Of all the barefaced gall! Nothing he could do now. To rush forward and claim them would appear petty in the extreme. Sylvie would think he had brought no gift at all. She was saying something else.

'He told us you were ill.'

'My dear,' said May, 'you *are* ill.'

Not her, thought Guy. Snowed-under or drunk as a skunk. Come down to gloat if things go wrong. Or throw a spanner in the works if they seem to be going right. Just look at them all clustering round. Like some bug-eyed natives in a Tarzan film creeping out of the jungle. Hail white god in iron bird from sky! Christ – what an evening.

'You poor thing,' continued May. 'You look dreadful. Suhami – get your mother a drink.'

'Oh, yes please,' cried Felicity and heard her husband laugh.

She caught his eye, her glance unfathomable. He saw it as triumphant and said, 'You joined the living dead then, Felicity?'

'There's no need for all that.' May produced a tiny plastic bottle from the pocket of her robe. 'Your wife is quite distrait. Now – hold your hands so. . . .' She poured a few drops into Felicity's cupped palms. 'Inhale please.'

Felicity did and started to sneeze. May said, 'Excellent,' and 'Could I have a napkin?'

Ken and Heather, still on the moony trail, crowded close to Felicity and asked her if she knew what day it was. Felicity, who hardly knew what year it was, attempted to shake her head. Suhami came along with the drink. Felicity put her hand out two or three times but made no connection. Heather said, 'Astral space is different.'

May took the glass and folded Felicity's fingers gently round it. Felicity drank a little then, mind and tongue finally synchronised, started to explain her late arrival. She sounded anxious and defensive as if such tardiness might cost a stack of Brownie points.

Everyone said: 'never mind – it really doesn't matter,' and 'super that you're here at all.'

They were getting used to her. Arno, closing the front door, found a pigskin case and brought it in.

Guy was right, of course, in thinking Felicity was not ill. The fact was that she had taken a line just before leaving home and a second in the car. Normally things went better with coke. You got a spiralling zing of light and airy confidence wafting you up on a stairway to Paradise. High-kicking the glitter dust en route to the stars.

But this time the reverse had happened. Felicity was experiencing a monstrously exaggerated sense of her own vulnerability. She felt like one of those poor soft-shelled creatures washed up by an ebbing tide and left dying on the sands. She shrank from the figures looming over her. They had hot stretchy eyes and rubbery mouths and kept changing their shapes. One reached out and touched her, and Felicity howled in terror.

Guy said: 'Bloody hell,' and they all turned on him again.

Just over an hour had passed since the dramatic advent of Felicity's arrival. The first course had been cleared away to make way for an egg custard and Suhami's birthday cake. The latter was a square 'cider' cake made by Janet with apple juice and soya marzipan. It had an 'S'-shaped candle and a frill of recycled sludge-green toilet paper.

Nine people sat down for dessert. May had withdrawn in preparation for her regression but Trixie had been persuaded to join the company. This had been achieved partly through Janet's persistent keyhole-cajoling and also by her cunning stimulation of Trixie's curiosity. Janet, knowing Trixie's passion for clothes, had dwelt long and inventively on the dazzling spectral beauty of Felicity's evening dress. She had also, instinctively feeling it would please, described the row with Suhami and Guy's subsequent discomfiture.

Trixie had not meant to come out till he had gone for good. Crouched in her room in a sweating funk, she had pictured a thousand times Guy's fury on discovering the loss of his Trinitron. In each subsequent recreation he became a little angrier and more violent so that, by now, she was braced for him to come tramping up the stairs bellowing 'Fee Fi Fo Fum', smash her door down and eat her alive.

Then, when Janet said he hadn't changed for dinner, Trixie began to entertain the hope that he might not yet have noticed the pills' disappearance. And even if he had would he wish to upset Suhami further by causing another scene? Also (and this is when she decided to go down), what was to stop her saying she knew nothing about the matter? No one could prove otherwise. Certainly the things couldn't be produced for she had thrown them out of the taxi window in guilty panic. So now here she was, sipping a little bullace supreme, gazing emerald-with-envy at the dress and occasionally sliding an apprehensive glance down the table at Guy. Eventually she caught his eye and received such a grotesquely false smile and vigorous wave that she wished she had not.

Christopher was talking. Telling them all about his last assignment (a documentary on Afghanistan), and the endless troubled trekking in the Chagai Hills, when a soft booming sound like a foghorn out to sea was heard.

Heather said, 'The conch,' and turned to Felicity adding kindly, 'we have to go.'

Ken and Heather had by now reluctantly accepted Felicity's corporeity whilst still regarding her as 'sent' in some mysterious and omened way. Since May had left the table, Heather had taken charge: filling Felicity's mug (half warm goat's milk, half Acorna) and also, from the overflowing goodness of her heart, doing some discreet counselling. A homely blend of psychological uplift, astrological prediction and tips on recycling negative vibrations. Felicity had listened with an expression of intent seriousness on her sleepwalker's face, interrupting only to clap her hands when the cake was cut.

'Come along then.' Heather helped her up.

'Where?'

'We're going to the Solar. You'll see the Master. Won't that be nice?'

'Yes,' said Felicity, screwing up her eyes in an attempt to discover precisely where the edge of the table was. 'Will there be dancing?'

'Spaced out,' said Ken, taking the other arm. He added in an aside, 'Picture the Bangladeshis that dress would feed.'

The others were already moving off. Trixie laughing, talking loudly, linking arms with a surprised but delighted Janet. Suhami with Christopher who was carrying her bag and Tim who stopped in the hall to gaze entranced at the lantern and refused to move until Suhami promised he could come back afterwards. Guy wandered alone, somewhere beyond the pale.

Arno, noticing this, overcame his natural aversion and joined the man, introducing himself. He even held out his hand but with such an air of brave and self-conscious resolution that Guy looked for a lion tamer's chair in its fellow.

Arno. What sort of name was that? Neither one thing nor the other. Like one of those far-flung islands that turned up in the shipping forecasts. Force 9 gales in Ross, Arno and Cromarty. Guy ignored the hand, saying coldly, 'You've got custard on your beard.' Then he defiantly produced a Zino Anniversaire, the baguette of the cigar world, and lit up.

The Solar was at the far end of the gallery. A long room with high beams and a floor of black bitumen. Placed upon it in two impeccably straight rows and precisely equidistant were twenty-four large, thinnish cushions in loose covers of coarse bleached cotton. These parallel lines directed the eye to a small dais raised on three steps and covered in oatmeal tweed carpet. There was

125

a chair on the dais with a carved back and at the foot of this a small collection of objects: the conch shell, a little brass gong and a much larger wooden fish so highly polished that the scales gleamed like a caramel toffee. As it was getting dark, the light – concealed inside a low hanging paper lantern – was switched on.

The Master, wearing white, was already in situ, resting on the carved chair. Tim ran across the room and curled up at his feet. The rest disposed themselves either sitting on the steps or standing behind the enthroned sage.

Guy was relieved to find he was not once more expected to squat on a cushion. He turned to look at Craigie who was welcoming Felicity with a smile of concerned sweetness. Noting the man's fragile looks and snowy hair veiling his stooped shoulders, Guy marvelled at his own previous gullibility. How could he have been taken in, even briefly, by such an obvious poseur? Now, seeing that everyone was settled, Craigie was picking up the fish. He parted its widely hinged jaws and brought them together with a loud clack.

May appeared in the doorway. She was wearing a plain mauve linen shift and had removed all her jewellery save for a silver unicorn pendant. Her broad feet were bare and her hair, unbound and brushed smooth, hung almost to her waist. She walked towards them in a slow, very measured way – carrying herself tall and straight as if balancing an invisible amphora.

On the floor, in between the furthest six cushions and about ten feet from the dais, an appliquéd quilt had been spread out. May lay down on this, assuming a sacred expression, and folded her arms across her breasts. Then after a moment she sat up again.

'Actually, I got a bit cold last time in that Viking longboat. Do you think I could have my little pelerine? It's in my bag.'

On the platform Christopher reached down.

Suhami said sharply, 'That's mine.'

'Of course it is. Sorry.'

'Over by the door,' called May.

Christopher collected May's bag and took it to her, opening it as he went, pulling out a cream ribbed cape. 'Is this the thing?' He placed it round her shoulders where it lay in little folds like uncooked tripe.

May said, 'Splendid,' and tied the fastening. Then she lay back again, her dark eyes closed, and started to breathe deeply, pushing the magnificent cupolas beneath her shift up into the stratosphere. Arno gave a stifled moan of enchantment and was glad when the Master said 'Lights' and, hurrying to the switch, he was temporarily distracted.

'Shall I stay here, May?' asked Christopher, squatting by her left shoulder. 'Then I can hold your hand if things get sticky.'

'If you wish but I'll be quite all right. One always returns safely you know.'

Once the light was out everything looked different. In the greyness the unmoving figures became drained of their humanity. They looked mysterious, their edges ill-defined, like statues in the garden at dusk. May's breathing became more audible; deep regular sighs with a longer and longer pause between each exhalation.

When the Master wanted to know if she was ready, May replied on a sonorous note: 'I Am Ready.' Next she was asked to locate the very centre of her being and, after several more slow and even deeper breaths, laid the flat of her hand on her tummy.

'How do you see that centre?'

'A ball . . . a golden ball.'

'Can you propel that ball down? Down . . . and out through the soles of your feet . . . that's right – push it away. . . .' May gave a small grunt. 'Now bring it back and push upwards. . . .'

May propelled the very centre of her being up and down, further and further away each time until it had expanded from a little ball to a great shimmering golden skin pressing against the walls like a giant helium balloon. Then, released, it suddenly floated free. Briefly May glanced down, seeing the twisty chimney pots and mossy slates of the Manor House roof and then she was

127

off. Over the hills, over the clouds and far far away.

'Where are you now, May?'

Where indeed? Below her things were changing fast. The terrain was now rough and wild. Forests and large areas of scrubland. Then some circles of tents within a high stone wall.

'Tell us what you see?'

Descending, the tents became larger. One was rather grand. Bigger than all the others and flying a pennant, purple and gold. An eagle rising.

'What is inside the tent?'

A pair of wooden pattens materialised, tied with strips of rag on to filthy masculine feet and raising them from the earth. In the right hand of the owner of the feet was a lump of dripping meat.

The place stank of sizzling fat, spilt wine and burning pitch from the torches. There was the most tremendous row going on. Men were yelling at each other, laughing, shouting. Dogs snarled, fighting over bones. Somewhere in the middle of it all a singer, accompanying himself on a small drum, struggled to make his lyrics heard.

The reeking air made the General's taster sick. He put the bear flesh into his mouth, chewed on the sinews, forced it down then placed the remains on a metal dish. A new skin of wine had just been uncorked and he swallowed some of that. The General's slave, a very young blackamoor, took the plate and goblet and placed them at the end of a line of similar dishes all rapidly congealing on a stone slab. The General never had hot food (not all poisons being quick to take effect, time must be allowed). On the other hand he was still alive.

The General was finishing sheep's kidneys now. Belching, farting, wiping his greasy fingers on the negro boy's woolly hair, tossing back some wine. Aping his betters he rested on his right elbow. His rough tunic was in disarray and everyone could see his knickers made from the hide of his favourite stallion and gleaming like wood chestnuts.

Mushrooms came next. The taster hated all forms of fungus.

It was well known that some varieties were deadly and although these had mostly been isolated (thanks to various self-sacrificing predecessors), the odd one could still slip through. In which case the lives of both the cook and the taster would be forfeit. But the General loved them, believing that they made him potent in love and invincible in battle.

The mushrooms were stewing in a small four-legged bronze skillet, their juice a vivid unpleasant colour. The taster put a single stalk and a spoonful of the violet liquid in his mouth. Immediately he choked. The muscles of his throat became numb, his stiff coal-black tongue stuck out. Eyes bolting, he fell and upset the skillet, scalding his arms on a steaming mass of food.

He briefly comprehended startled faces and the slave running, then paralysis spread downwards to his chest and life closed up inside him like a fan.

'*May . . . May. . . .*' The words were knotted with terror as Arno heard the strangled choking. He was first from the dais, flinging himself on his knees at her side. Other people followed, crowding round. Even Felicity, looking dreamily puzzled rather than alarmed, drifted over to glance down at the figure wrenching itself into such terrible loops and arches on the appliquéd quilt.

'Do something!' cried Arno. 'Someone . . . do something. . . .' He snatched May's hand from Christopher's grasp and started to chafe and rub it between his own.

'Give her the kiss of life.'

'She's not drowning.'

'How do you know she's not drowning?'

'Shouldn't we loosen her belt?'

'Look at her face!'

'Take the pillow away. Lay her flat.'

'She can't breathe as it is.'

'Ken's right. That'll just make things worse.'

'We need some agrimony.'

'I'd have thought there was more than enough agrimony here already.'

'Remarks like that are not particularly helpful, Mr Gamelin.'

'Sorry.'

'This is actually an emergency in case you haven't noticed.'

'I'm sorry – all right?'

May drew back her lips and gargled horribly.

'What would she say if she could speak?'

'Think colour according to the cosmic law.'

'That's right she would. What day is it?'

'Friday.'

'That's violet.' Heather leaned closer and shouted, 'May – can you hear me? Think violet. . . .'

May shook her head with great force and, struggling to form the words, finally cried out: 'Mush . . . mush. . . .'

'What does she mean – *mush, mush*?'

A puzzled silence then Arno cried, 'Dogs. She's calling a dog team. May is in Antarctica.' He pulled off his jumper. 'That's why she's shaking. She's freezing to death. Quick everyone. . . .'

They all removed an item of clothing. Felicity offered her shiny mussel-effect scarf. Everything was piled up on May and finally, it seemed, to good effect. The gargle became a ripple then a mere bubbling sigh. The rasp of her breathing softened almost into inaudibility, her chest rose and fell in a calm, even motion. The hem of her shift stopped vibrating.

'It's worked.' Arno turned a radiant face to them all. 'She's better.'

As he spoke, May opened her eyes, gave a great yawn and sat up. 'My goodness! The most exciting adventure yet, I do believe. What on earth are all these things?'

'We thought you were cold.'

'You were shivering.'

'Nonsense. Sweltering in that tent. Someone put the lights on and I'll tell you all about it.'

Christopher went to do so. As light flooded the room, people started to pick up their bits and pieces and don them again. May called across to her mentor: 'Well, Master that was quite—' She broke off and gave a loud exclamation. Attracted by this the others, too, turned and stared.

The Master was standing just in front of his chair. Slowly and seemingly with great effort he lifted his right arm. A finger pointed. Then he fell, very gracefully with a slow turning movement so that he came to rest face upwards with his milk-white hair spreading over the oatmeal carpet. He lay cruciform, arms flung wide and in his breast a knife was buried. Right up to the hilt.

SOME INTERVIEWS

Chapter 7

Detective Chief Inspector Barnaby was cooking *Moules à l'Indienne*, pounding away at some cardamom seeds in a stone pestle. He wore a long cotton tablier of the sort favoured by waiters in speakeasy type dives and had a glass of Frog's Leap Chardonnay to hand.

It had dawned on Tom the hard way, and over many years, that Joyce, his beloved prop and mainstay, was not going to (indeed saw no reason to) improve her cooking. Take it or leave it was her attitude and the fact that on the whole he left it was not apparently reason enough to instigate reform. And as she had once said, poking him none too playfully below the belt, you didn't get up to thirteen stone by going without. She was neither defiant nor aggressive; just simply did not understand his point of view. Joyce ate her own cooking quite happily and now ate her husband's, when he had time to do any, just as happily – but without any indication that its quality was at all superior to her own. Barnaby had long ago decided that she suffered from the gastronomic equivalent to being tone deaf.

'What's for starters?'

'Tarragon eggs.'

'Are they the ones in brown puddles?' Joyce took a deep swallow of wine and beamed encouragement. 'I like those.'

'I'll put more gelatine in this time.'

The making of aspic had come into part seven, 'Raised Pies and Galantines', of Barnaby's 'Twelve Cookery Lessons for Absolute

Beginners' at Causton Tech and was one he had missed, due to being on call. He had taken to the art straight away, really looking forward to Tuesday evenings when he could once more get to grips with scales, knives, pots and pans. The only male in a class of seventeen, he was left relatively in peace once his fellow students had got used to his lumbering masculine presence and tired of pulling his leg. Only one lady, a Mrs Queenie Bunshaft, still persisted in asking archly where he was hiding his truncheon and which of them was going to be his dish of the day. Barnaby threatened to run off with Mrs Bunshaft when Joyce got particularly obstreperous.

The meal was to celebrate his daughter's engagement. Both parents had been pleased but surprised at Cully's emotional declaration some weeks ago. Barnaby had been quite caustic when shown the ring, a pretty white-gold love knot studded with Victorian garnets.

'I thought he just moved in these days with a toothbrush and a packet of peppermint-flavoured Mates.'

Cully had smiled dreamily and looked demure. *Demure*! The first time, as Joyce said later, since she'd abandoned nappies. Nicholas looked simply stunned as if he could not believe his luck, which was quite true.

'Students,' moaned Joyce once they had danced away. A Hollywood pavane complete with dry ice and string accompaniment.

'Not for much longer.'

'They've no money.'

'They've as much as we had.'

'At least you were in a proper job. The theatre, Tom . . . of all things. . . .'

'They're only engaged, not married with five kids. Anyway – she's enough confidence for fifty that one.'

'You don't know what it's like.' Joyce emptied her glass and reached for a bowl of coconut.

'Leave that alone. I've weighed it out.'

'Don't start throwing your weight about with me. You're not at the station now, you know.' Joyce put some of the white shreds in her mouth. 'It's going to be all right for Sunday, isn't it Tom?'

'Fingers crossed.'

At the moment matters were quite sluggish. No shortage of crime (when was there ever?) but for the past few days it had been seedy, run-of-the-mill stuff. There were occasions – not many, never long – like this. Other periods seemed to hold such an escalation of smashing and grabbing; of screaming, squealing tyres and breaking bones that Barnaby sometimes felt he had been sucked into an ever-spinning maelstrom of brutality. He marginally preferred these times. This acknowledgement gave him neither pleasure nor comfort but neither did he attempt to duck the fact.

In the hall the phone rang. Joyce got up saying, 'Oh no.'

'Probably Cully. . . .'

'Bet it isn't.'

Barnaby started to chop some chillies, half an ear to the door. Joyce reappeared, expressionless. Barnaby pulled at the strings of his apron and turned off the gas. Five minutes later Joyce was helping him into his jacket.

'Sorry, love.'

'I don't know why you keep up this fiction of saying sorry, Tom. You've been doing it for nearly thirty years and it wouldn't deceive a child. You already look twice as sparky as you did in the kitchen.' Barnaby buttoned up and kissed her. 'Where is it, anyway?'

'Out Iver way.'

'Will you be late?'

'Looks a bit like it.' He added, pointlessly, for she invariably did, 'Don't wait up.'

She called after him down the path, 'Shall I ring Cully and cancel?'

'Not yet. See how it goes.'

Troy had taken to wearing glasses for driving. Glinting, squared-off steel rims which made him look like Himmler. Weaving and

137

snaking, foot down, they were already half way to the Manor House.

'Break up anything special did it, Chief – this caper?'

'Not really.'

Just rustling up a few *Moules à l'Indienne* for my daughter's engagement dinner. Barnaby smiled to himself, imagining his sergeant's response. The concealed disdain behind a courteous, 'Oh yes, sir?' And the limp-wristed mock-up of a chef portrayed later in the staff canteen when he was safely elsewhere.

To Troy, cooking, like hairdressing and making clothes, was a pursuit fit only for women. Or poofters. It was his proud boast that he had never as much as toasted a slice of bread or washed a sock in his entire life. Start doing that sort of thing, he'd say, and you'd got women left with time on their hands. And women with time on their hands got into trouble. Known fact.

'Course a baby went quite a way to solving that problem. His own was now nearly one. Incredibly bright. Troy wondered if this was the moment to pass on what she had said at breakfast. It was so clever, so advanced. He had told everybody at the station; one or two people twice. But with the Boss you never knew. Sometimes you'd think he was paying attention then discover he hadn't heard a word. Sometimes he jumped down your throat. Ah well – worth a try.

'You'll never guess what she said this morning, Chief.'

'Who?'

Who . . . ? *Who*? For a minute Troy was so flabbergasted he could not reply. Then he said, 'Talisa Leanne.'

'Hmn.'

Could have been a grunt. Or a cough. Could even have been a sigh. Only the most besotted parent would have taken it as encouragement to continue.

'She was eating her Weetabix . . . well, I say eating . . . flinging it about's more like it. . . .' Troy laughed, shaking his head at the wonder of it all. 'Some in her bib . . . some on the wall . . . there was even – '

'Let's get it over with, Sergeant.'

'Pardon?'

'What did she say.'

'Oh. Yes. Well – it was "ball".'

'What?'

'Ball.'

'*Ball*?'

'True as I'm sitting here.'

'Good grief.'

The sky was almost dark. A rim of crimson seeped into the horizon's edge as the car swung with great panache into the village. Barnaby half expected to see an ambulance on the Manor drive but there were just two police cars and George Bullard's Volvo.

As soon as Barnaby climbed out he heard the howling. Terrible agonised cries like an animal in a trap. He felt his skin ice over.

'Jesus!' Troy joined him in the porch. 'What the hell is that?'

A constable positioned inside the hall became alert in recognition. 'Everyone's upstairs, sir. Along the gallery to your left. Far end.'

Troy stared around as they climbed, too disturbed by the dreadful sounds to experience his usual knee-jerk resentment when entering what he presumed to be the environment of the upper crust. He sniffed and said, 'What a stink.'

'Joss sticks.'

'Smells like cat mess.'

They found Scene of Crime in a long room almost bereft of furniture. Controlled businesslike people moving with quiet efficiency. A photographer sat on some steps, a Pentax with an attached flash dangling from his neck. A second constable was at the door. Barnaby asked who was making all the row.

'One of the people who lives here, sir. Apparently he's a bit mental.'

'That should cheer things up.' Barnaby crossed over to the dais and crouched by the white robed corpse. Some blood had oozed from the wound in his chest and lay in a long narrow crinkle, glistening like newly set plum jam. 'What've we got then, George?'

'As you see,' said Doctor Bullard. 'A blade artist.'

'Neat.' Barnaby took a close look then nodded in the direction of the howling which was dying into a series of tormented moans. 'Can't you give him something? It's enough to drive a man to drink.'

The doctor shook his head. 'As far as I can gather he's already on quite complicated medication. Not wise to mix it. I've suggested calling their own doctor but they say they haven't got one. Do it all themselves with herbs and moonshine.'

'They must have. How does he get his stuff?'

'Hillingdon at Uxbridge by all accounts.' He got up, dusting his knees unnecessarily.

'On the way to bed was he Doctor Bullard?' asked Troy, winking at the body. 'In his nightie.'

'How long, George?'

'An hour at the most. But this time you don't need me to tell you. Apparently they were all here when it happened.'

'What. . . . You mean they were playing about? This is some sort of accident?'

Troy recognised a trace of disappointment in his chief's voice. Briefly Barnaby looked betrayed. Smiling to himself, the sergeant looked down at the dead man, noting the refined passionless features and tissuey skin. And get a load of that hair. He looked like something out of the ten commandments. You could just see him as Moses in the wilderness shouting: 'Let my people go.' Or was it 'come'? Troy and the Bible were not close. Barnaby was now talking to Graham Arkwright, Scene of Crime. The sergeant tuned in.

'. . . a lot to go on, I'm afraid. We found this behind that curtain over there.' He indicated a small embrasure and held up a plastic bag containing a bright yellow glove. 'Might get something on the knife for you, there's a bit of thread attached. Know anything about this set-up, Tom?' Barnaby shook his head.

'My wife came here on a weaving course. Took me for ever

140

to get rid of the scarf. I gave it to a jumble sale in the end. Turned up later in the window of Oxfam. She wouldn't speak to me for a week.'

'I'd call that a result myself,' said Troy.

Barnaby took the glove and a second bag containing the knife and said, 'I'll drop these off later at Forensic – OK?'

A flash bulb flared and the two officers made their way towards the man standing in the doorway.

'You first here, Sergeant?'

'Yes, sir. Arrived same time as the ambulance. On patrol with Policewoman Lynley. Notified the CID and stayed here with the body. She's got the others downstairs. The big room far side of the hall.'

'How did it strike you – the set-up?'

'Well . . . much as you'd expect really. They were all standing round looking gobsmacked. Apart from the idiot boy who was yowling his head off. I did ask if the dead man had been touched and they said no. I couldn't get anything out of them after that.'

'Right.' Barnaby lumbered back downstairs. Troy, slim as a whip in his worn leather blouson and tight grey pants, running ahead opening two doors before finding the right one.

It was quite large with a 'feathered' ceiling made of wood, as were the panelled walls, so that one had the impression of being in a large carved box. There were a lot of shell-like polystyrene chairs on thin metal legs and an imperfectly cleaned blackboard. A place for lectures and seminars.

The communalists were all bunched together with the exception of one man who stood some distance away by the French windows. Bunched fists rammed into his pockets, he looked baffled and full of rage. There was a long scratch beaded with fresh blood down his left cheek. Barnaby thought he looked vaguely familiar.

Troy clocked the WPC (never see thirty again and dumpy with it), and then the rest. A weeping girl in a sari being comforted by a man in jeans. The wailing boy, his head in the lap of a bold-featured woman wearing blue. A dolly, dolly blonde and a

141

harsh-faced pepper-and-salter in corduroy pants. Two fat pathetic-looking hippies with lumps of rock in the middle of their foreheads and a woman in a mad frock who looked only marginally more life-like than Stiffy upstairs. Plus a round little geezer with a beard the colour of tomato sauce.

Barnaby introduced himself and asked if any of them could tell him precisely what had happened. There was a long, long pause. Troy got the impression that the girl in the sari was struggling to control her sobs preparatory to speech, but then everyone (bar the man by the window) turned to the woman in blue. Still stroking the head of the crying youth, she gave a reluctant inclination of her head and made to stand but the boy clung so tightly to her knees that movement was impossible. When she spoke her voice was very tight. Low and calm but unnaturally so as if large reservoirs of emotion were being strenuously damned.

'The Master has left us. He has entered his body of lights and is now at one with the over soul.'

Oh dear, oh dear, thought the chief inspector. It's going to be one of those. Troy wondered what the chances were of slipping out for a quick drag before things got going seriously. He'd cut down to five a day, had smoked the first four before breakfast, and the need for a long cool inhalation was driving him up the wall. A greatly extended two minutes went by without anyone saying a dicky bird. Then the tart with saggy boobs started yammering whilst opening her arms wide, before flinging them across her chest as if to keep warm.

The sergeant regarded these flamboyant obsequies with irritation and dislike. You'd have thought they were a load of foreigners the way they were cracking on. Italians. Or jabbering Caribbeans. His hand reached into his pocket and closed wistfully over a lighter and packet of Chesterfields.

Barnaby quickly realised that questioning en masse would get him nowhere. All he had ascertained so far was the dead man's name. It was like talking to captured prisoners of war. So he asked for a separate room and they were offered what appeared to be The Lodge's office.

A workmanlike place – boxes of stationery and manila envelopes, filing cabinets, an old fashioned duplicator. On the wall a reincarnation advisory poster: *Ever signed a cheque 'William Shakespeare' then wondered why?* It was an internal room with no windows which made it especially satisfactory from a policeman's point of view. The combination of an unknown interrogator and the complete disappearance of the outside world could mean you were already half way there.

Barnaby sat at a little round table with a stack of rough paper and some pencils, his plastic bags by his feet. Troy strolled about. A further patrol car had arrived, releasing the constable on the front door who was now seated with a Biro and notebook, his chair positioned so as to be invisible to the person being interviewed. As the gathering had remained schtum, the chief inspector was not able to follow his usual procedure of taking the most useful witness first so he had started with their spokesperson and was already ruing the day.

Barnaby had been of the belief that, after thirty years in the force, he had come across just about every type, colour, sexual proclivity and variety of political and religious zealot that his country had to offer. Within minutes he realised he was mistaken. The woman facing him gave her full name, her astral name ('Pacifica') and her opinion that Barnaby should be writing on yellow paper rather than white – to allay confusion and harmonise his spleen. Barnaby, who had been doodling, put down his pen.

Asked about the death in the Solar she explained that the term was inappropriate. The Master had been magnetically transmuted and was now an ariel tapping into the interplanetary pool; a lord of all the Elohim and a droplet in the great field of cosmic consciousness.

'Be that as it may, Miss Cuttle. . . .' (Oh, very witty thought Troy.) 'What I'm trying to get at is who was responsible for sending him there.'

'Oh no, no, no – it wasn't like that at all.' She bestowed on him a sweet but slightly patronising smile. Barnaby felt he might be advised any minute not to worry his pretty little head.

'How was it then?' asked Sergeant Troy.

'Well. . . .' May settled herself more comfortably, resting her bag like a kangaroo's pouch in her lap. 'It all started with my regression.' She broke off noticing the increased strain on Barnaby's rugged features. 'Oh dear . . . it's so difficult explaining to outsiders. Suffice it to say that we have all been on this earth many times before and, under the guidance of the Masters, I relive incidents from one or the other of these lives the third Friday of every month except for Feb. when there was a Psychic Self Defence Workshop.

'There is always a great deal of energy humming about at regression times but today was really outstanding. I had an accident, for instance, this afternoon which I see now was not an accident at all but a metaphor. A chunk of iron fell off the roof—'

'Could we stick to this evening, Miss Cuttle?'

'Oh. Very well. Continuation of same, really. A symbolisation of Astarte, goddess of the moon. Then later during the actual regression, nebulæ crashing about, stars colliding, darts of silver light showers and showers of golden rain, spinning moons. . . . The passing of an arahat is of gigantic astral significance and cannot be accomplished by mere common or garden dynamism. It is no casual or accidental matter.'

'Certainly not accidental.'

'I see you're hankering after some sort of human intervention.'

'That's the line this investigation will be taking – yes.'

'When you came out of this trance or whatever it was you were in,' said Troy, 'what exactly did you see?'

'I've just explained all that. Moons whizzing—'

'I mean in actual fact.'

'Those are the facts.'

Barnaby continued, determined to tighten his questions in such a way as to leave no loophole for further astrological whimsy. 'Now Miss Cuttle—'

'Taster to the General.'

'Pardon?'

'That's what I was tonight. In Roman Britain.'

'Really?' Never strong on ancestor-worship, Barnaby pressed on. 'Could you tell me – or better still show me – where he and the others were sitting before you began.' He pushed over a pencil and sheet of paper, adding hurriedly as she opened her mouth, 'White is all there is.'

May said, 'Music's my forte you know. Not art.'

'A rough sketch will do. Use crosses if you wish. But don't guess. If you're not sure leave a blank.'

She drew like a child, concentrating fiercely, her tongue peeping out. Barnaby looked at the results.

'And had these positions changed when you . . . um . . . were yourself again?'

'Oh yes. Everyone was crowding round me. Arno was crying – silly man.'

'Why?'

'I'd been poisoned. When I was tasting some mushrooms. They will worry so. He should have known I'd be all right. Once I was bound to a chariot wheel—'

'You say everyone,' said Troy. 'Did that include Craigie?'

'No. But I didn't realise that till Christopher put the lights on.'

'Where is he on this?' Barnaby took the drawing.

'Nowhere. He stayed with me.'

'You mean it was dark?' inquired Barnaby.

'Duskish.'

'That's handy,' said Troy.

May frowned. 'I don't understand.'

'Who suggested putting them off?'

'No one. It's always done for meditative practices.'

'So what did you see once they were on again?'

'The Master was standing in front of his chair –'

'Still on the dais?' Barnaby glanced down at the sketch.

'Yes. Then he just sort of toppled down the steps.' The voice faltered and her lips trembled with remembrance. 'His bosom had already received the celestial lance.'

The chief inspector's patience was wearing thin. Brutally he picked up the first polythene bag and pushed it across the table. 'Your lance, Miss Cuttle. Do you recognise it?'

'My. . . .' She picked up the bag. The stains had already oxidised to a rusty orange. 'But that's one of our knives from the kitchen.' She put it down again. 'How could . . . ?' For a long moment she stared at him, her forehead tuckered deep with puzzlement, her eyes bewildered. Then they cleared.

'Of course.' The cast-iron confidence was back. 'We are unawakened ones here, Inspector. We strive, we pray, we struggle for perfection, but it is a long and troubling discipleship. None of us, apparently, are ready for the revelation of divine wisdom. Knowing this, the Gods in their ineffable kindness have transmuted their sublimely mysterious weapon of dispatch into a humble household implement. Something all we acolytes can easily assimilate and comprehend. I've no doubt at all you'll find a karmic fingerprint.'

Troy snorted. Barnaby, feeling perhaps that this analysis lacked a certain rigour, produced his second bag. 'And is this from the kitchen too?'

'Yes. Janet wears them. She has a mild skin disorder, gradually giving ground to my Mallow and Horehound salve. What are you doing with it?'

'It was found behind one of the curtains in the Solar.'

'How odd. You can't wash up in there.'

Given her conviction of a mystical assassin, there seemed little sense in pointing out the evident connection. 'Did you see anyone cross to the window at any time?' May shook her head. 'And these regressions – do they usually take such a dramatic form?'

'Varies. I succumbed to the Black Death once and screamed the place down. Next week – a whizzo time with Henry the Eighth. You just can't tell.'

Good question, thought Troy. Very shrewd. Because if people knew there might be a possible distraction on the way. . . . He put a question of his own. 'Was anyone present who was unfamiliar with this routine?'

'Yes indeed. Mr and Mrs Gamelin were strangers to us.' (*Gamelin*, thought Barnaby. That's who it was.) 'They'd come down for their daughter's birthday. Poor child.'

Her accent really stuck in Troy's craw. Toney. British racing green. Born to order others to jump to it. Or thought they were which came down to the same thing. You could get away with being bonkers if you sounded right. But you couldn't get away with murder. The chief was asking about the structure of the commune and who would take charge now.

'We're equal here, Inspector Barnaby, although, as in all groups, I suppose you will find a natural hierarchy.' Barnaby nodded, thinking how rarely people who used the phrase saw themselves at the bottom of the heap. 'I have been here longest and I suppose you could call me the bursar. I do all the ordering from the soya beans to Calypso's hay. And the banking. I'm allowed to sign cheques.' She went on to list the other members of the organisation, the order of their arrival and length of stay.

'And the boy?' Barnaby nodded in the direction of the door. The moaning had now quite died away.

'Tim? Oh – he was . . . found.' She appeared uneasy. 'I don't know the details. Arno would never tell me. He got quite upset when I asked a second time. One day he and the Master simply brought Tim home. How he will bear this . . . poor boy. The Master was his life, his whole existence. I fear for him, I really do.' She got up. 'If that's all, could I go? I'd like to see—'

'One more question,' said Barnaby. 'Has anyone changed their clothes since the regression?'

After she had replied in the negative and been allowed to go, the three men exchanged bemused glances. Barnaby said, 'Calypso's hay?'

'They'll all be vegetarians, sir,' said the young constable.

'Get every word of that did you, sunshine?' said Troy.

147

'Course not, Sergeant,' said the PC, going very pink. He had an absurdly fluffy moustache like a strip of duckling feathers. 'Just the relevant details.'

'They had plenty of time to get together on this before the patrol car turned up, Chief. Maybe this supernatural garbage is going to be the official party line.'

'I doubt it. They can't all be as batty as that one.'

There was a knock and the woman with the long grey hair came in, followed by the man with the *Hey Viva!* moustache. They had taken off their headbands and wore expressions of exalted mourning. Their eyes were sharp and interested. She carried a tray with three cups and he a plate which could easily have fitted on the tray.

'We thought you might appreciate some refreshment—'

'A cup of Acorna—'

'A really excellent coffee substitute—'

'And some cake.'

Barnaby, taking a cup, asked their names. Then he said, 'Well perhaps as you're here you wouldn't mind answering some questions regarding Mr Craigie's murder.' He named the deed deliberately just so everyone knew where they stood.

Plainly this was the whole point of the exercise and they were both sitting down in a flash. Ken opened by saying, 'You can't call it murder.' Adding kindly, 'Not as a layman would understand the term.'

'There's only one way to understand the term, Mr Beavers. The wanton destruction of human life. You can trick it out in whatever airy-fairy jargon you choose. Murder's what it is.' He responded to a brace of pitying headshakes by pushing over the paper and pencils and explaining about the sketch. He added, 'No conferring' and watched them start to draw.

Their diagrams, like their clothes and hairstyles, were almost identical. He could just see them in the winter in matching sweaters and matching bobble hats on their matching pointy heads. Troy was struggling with his refreshment, which as a piece of cake would have made a great foundation stone.

Ken returned the paper saying, 'Perhaps I could meta-comment on your last verbalisation.'

'By all means. But speak plain if you would. I haven't got all night,' replied Barnaby, fearing very much that he had.

'The knife was inserted by a mortal hand.' Very grudging. 'But that hand was divinely guided. To tell the truth both of us were more than a little upset at not being chosen—'

'We would have been honoured—'

'No followers could have been more devoted.'

'However,' Ken sighed sniffily, 'it was not to be.'

'You should be grateful it was not to be, Mr Beavers. Unless you fancy spending the next ten years in a prison cell.'

'Where are you *coming* from on this?' cried Heather, tossing her head back and revealing briefly an embryonic suggestion of what might have been, in the fullness of time, given intensive exercise and a great deal of hugely expensive plastic surgery, the whimsical beginnings of a chin.

Ken said, 'There is no such thing as a cell in the life of the spirit.'

This was when Barnaby passed over the two bags. The one with the knife was handled with intense reverence by Ken, murmuring . . . 'Vibrations still present . . . subtle but potentwise . . . wow. . . .'

'He can be of real assistance, Inspector,' said Heather. 'Try and think of him as your cosmic tuning-fork.'

What a pair of piss-artists, thought Troy. Right off the wall. He asked what form this assistance might take.

'My husband is a sensitive.'

'A sensitive what?'

'It is a term used to denote a soul in tune not only with the fathomless depths of their own being but with all the vibrant currents of the hidden universe.'

'That a fact?'

'A side effect of this,' said Ken with a grave and modest lifting of the shoulders, 'is that I was chosen to be a channel for Hilarion. One of the greatest minds the world has ever known.

Transmuted many times, you might know him better as Samuel the Prophet of the Lord. Or Merlin. Better still as Francis Bacon, Son of Elizabeth the First and Robert Dudley –'

'What I'd really like . . .' Barnaby determinedly tried to stem the wave of rôle-playing.

'—the true author of the so-called Shakespearean plays—'

'*What I'd really like*. . . .' He could glare to great effect when the occasion demanded and did so now. They sat up smartly. 'Is to ask if either of you have any idea why this murder was committed.'

'It wasn't like that.'

'Assuming,' Troy leaned over speaking loudly into their faces, 'it was like that.'

'Impossible. Everyone loved him.'

'At least one person obviously didn't, Mrs Beavers,' said Barnaby. 'Now, I know there wasn't much light but did either of you notice any sudden movement during the regression?' He glanced down at the drawings. 'Anyone sitting on the steps for instance?'

'Well of course we all got up because of May. And rushed down to her.'

'Simultaneously?'

'Pretty much wouldn't you say, Heth?'

Heather nodded. Barnaby suspected this might be the first of many similar opinions. A darkened room. People concentrating on the horizontal figure. Everyone looks one way, the sleight of hand takes place in quite another. A common conjuring ploy. Even so it was a daring thrust. So why choose such a dangerous time? At this stage the question was plainly unanswerable so he changed course, attempting to fill in more of the background.

'How many people live here?'

'There are ten of us in permanent residence but of course we can accommodate many more. Sometimes at retreats or workshops there can be forty . . . fifty people.'

'Can't be easy,' said Troy, 'living that close. Must be arguments and upsets.' Two cloying smiles and headshakes. 'A clash of personalities? Rows about money?'

'Materialism is not our bag.'

'What is money but the concretisation of etheric force?'

There was a bit more of this then Barnaby let them go. He and Troy were being discussed adversely before the door had even closed.

'Those guys . . . from another planet . . . you know?'

'Not listening at all. Just hearing the words.'

'I must remember to tell Maureen that next time she tries to up the housekeeping,' said Troy. 'How'd it go – money's the concrete what . . . ? And speaking of concrete – have you tried this cake?'

'I've taken enough risks for one night,' said Barnaby. 'I drank the drink.'

'Not what you'd call leaping ahead are we, Chief?' Troy perched on the table, fielding Barnaby's sour glance with a winning smile. 'What about the conspiracy theory? The old dingbat deliberately lays on the drama to draw attention from the dais . . . they all rush down thus allowing the other half of the combo—'

'Exactly. They *all* rushed down.'

'Yeh . . . well . . . look. . . .' Troy turned May's sketch round. 'There's what . . . nine of them? It's dark . . . ish. Nine people do not move as one. Obviously somebody lags behind, does old Obi Half a One Kenobi, then brings up the rear. How long would it take? A second? Two? And with her yelling and carrying on, no one'd hear even if he did cry out.'

'Mm. It's a sensible theory.' Troy smirked with pleasure. 'Not sure I buy the conspiracy bit, though. Well – let's talk to—' he turned the sketch back, 'Christopher Wainwright. He stayed with the Cuttle woman throughout the regression so, like her, had a head-on view. He may have seen—' A brief tap and the thirty-something policewoman put her head round. 'What is it?'

'There's a Miss McEndrick outside, sir. She says she has some urgent information about the incident upstairs.'

The officer had hardly finished speaking before Janet pushed her way into the room. She stood screwing up her eyes with nervousness and blinking, bony shoulders hunched before bursting into a flurry of speech. The words tripped each other up, fell over themselves.

'I'm sorry – I couldn't wait till you sent for me – sorry – it's just that I saw something – I'm sure it's important – that you'd want to know before wasting your time on other people – sorry. . . .'

Everything about her was remorseful. She seemed to be asking forgiveness for her height, her unappealing clothes, her angle-poised body, her very existence. Yet she had forced her way in. Imposed herself upon a stranger in a position of authority. That must have taken some doing.

Barnaby asked her to sit down. She did so saying, 'I know who did it. He wore a glove didn't he? A washing-up glove?'

'What makes you think so?'

'Behind the curtain, wasn't it?' She paused and Barnaby said, 'Go on . . .' noting the lack of grief in the intelligent, wide-apart eyes and the jumping-jack nerve in her cheek.

'He pulled it out of his pocket. I was watching. He'd been glancing round the room as if waiting till he was unobserved, so I looked the other way – pretending to be talking to someone – but I caught him!'

'Caught who, Miss McEndrick?'

'Why – Guy Gamelin, of course.' She was struggling to speak evenly but there was a current of triumph in her voice that could not be disguised.

Of course? This is personal thought Barnaby and wondered why. Perhaps, like his sergeant, she was simply one of those people consumed by envy in the presence of the very rich. Somehow the chief inspector didn't think so. He asked what her opinion was of Mr Gamelin.

'Me?' She flushed an ugly crimson. 'I have no opinion. I only met him today.'

'You had dinner together.'

'Hardly together. There were nine of us.' Barnaby nodded,

looking expectant and encouraging. The silence lengthened but the expression of concerned interest upon his features did not change. One would have to be a churl not to respond.

'If you really want to know, I thought Gamelin quite obnoxious. Full of himself – like most men. Putting us right when he wasn't putting us down. Laughing at our ideals and the way we try to live. Of course some people are easily impressed by power. And money.'

'The majority perhaps?'

'More fool them.'

Barnaby explained about the sketch, and offered her some paper, but Janet said, 'Why? I had nothing to do with this.'

'You are all being asked.'

'But isn't it over now? I mean – why don't you just go and arrest him?'

'You any special reason for wanting that, Miss McEndrick?' Troy stalked behind her chair.

'No. . . .' The word whipped out. Janet screwed her neck round, seeking the questioner. She took in the bristling red hair and thin mouth, and sensed a cold unkindness that alarmed her. She turned back, almost with gratitude, to the older of the two men. 'It's just that I thought whoever used the knife must have worn a glove because of fingerprints. When I saw him hiding it—'

'You put two and two together?' suggested Troy.

Janet started on her map. Barnaby observed her downcast head as she drew. Noted the pin-thin scrupulous parting – not a single hair straying to the wrong side of the tracks. Battleship-grey metal grips cruelly scraped the scalp. He could just see her brushing the wiry mass night and morning without fail. Fifty hard, punishing strokes. Nothing to do with beauty, more with self-flagellation. A wish to drive the demon out. Or was he being fanciful? Which demon, he wondered, might it be? Jealousy, despair, sloth . . . lust? The sketch was returned, looking (a brief glance down) pretty much like all the others. He jumped into the dark.

'Do you like living here, Miss McEndrick? Get on all right with people?' She looked wary. He sensed a retrenchment. 'Yes. I suppose so.'

'Do you have a particular friend perhaps?'

'*No!*' In one swooping motion she had left her chair and veered towards the door. Opening it, she turned a tormented face to Barnaby. 'I'll tell you something else about Guy Gamelin. The Master pointed him out when he was dying. Pointed him out to us all. That's how guilty he is. Ask him . . . . Ask anyone. . . .'

Chapter 8

'I had a sports teacher like that,' said Troy when Janet had departed. 'Knobbly knees, plimsolls, no tits, whistle round her neck. They really turn me up, dykes. All members of the buggerocracy, come to that. Don't they you?' He directed his question at the note-taking constable.

The young man glanced across at Barnaby who, head down, was still writing busily and decided to play safe. 'Never really thought about it, Sergeant.'

'Going to have Gamelin in now, sir?' asked Troy.

'I prefer to hear what everyone else has to say. See what we can build up.' He sent the constable after Christopher Wainwright.

'I don't suppose he's used to being kept waiting.'

'Bring a little novelty into his life then, won't it?'

Troy admired that. He knew plenty of officers (some far senior to Barnaby), who wouldn't have kept Gamelin waiting longer than it took to polish the seat of the visitor's chair. I shall be like the chief, vowed Troy, when I'm DCI. No one'll push me around. I shan't care who they are. That he would be operating from a position of psychological weakness, rather than strength, did not occur to him.

Christopher Wainwright looked to be in his late twenties. The pallor of his face was somewhat exaggerated by the solid blackness of his hair. He wore tight jeans and a short-sleeved sports shirt with a little green alligator patch. If he was devastated, he concealed it well. Although he looked at both policemen frankly enough, there was about him a controlled caution that puzzled

Barnaby. What could the boy have to be worried about? He was one of the two people in the room who could not have delivered the fatal blow. Was he concerned on someone else's behalf? The weeping girl he had been holding in his arms? Barnaby asked if he had seen anything at all from his uniquely helpful viewpoint. Christopher shook his head.

'Most of the time I was watching May. The last few minutes holding her hand. In any case we were a good ten feet from the others. And there wasn't a lot of light.' Asked to do a sketch he said, 'It'll be rather vague. I hardly remember where anyone was. A murder puts that sort of detail right out of your mind.'

'Do you have any idea why Craigie was killed?'

'Haven't a clue. He was a most inoffensive man. Genuinely kind unlike one or two people here who talk about love a lot but fall down somewhat on the practice.'

'Aren't you in sympathy with the general attitudes of the commune?'

'With some, not others. I suppose you'd call me an inquirer with an open mind. I was on holiday in Thailand last year and was tremendously impressed by the spirit of the people. By the temples and the monks. When I came back I started reading Buddhist literature then I found a three-day course here – a meditation on the Diamond Sutra – listed in the *Vision*. I signed up for it and six weeks later I'm still here.'

'And why is that, Mr Wainwright?'

'I . . . met someone.'

Barnaby saw the shoulders loosen and the watchful tightness around the eyes smooth out and thought, so he's not concerned on behalf of the girl. It was something else. He seemed to want to talk about her and the chief inspector let him.

'I couldn't credit it at first.' He appeared rather shamefaced as if admitting to a hidden vice or weakness. 'Falling in love.' He attempted to sound ironical and failed. 'One has had affairs of course . . .' he shrugged. 'But the real thing . . . never. To be honest my first inclination was to scarper. I liked my life the way it was. Nice little flat, no shortage of female company. But

I hung on just a fraction of a second too long and there I was . . . trapped.' His pale skin flushed. He didn't look trapped. He looked happy and hopeful. 'I didn't know who she was then.

'I took a month's leave – I'm a BBC cameraman – which was due. When that ran out, I asked for a three-month sabbatical which will also soon run out. By the time it does I hope I'll have persuaded Suze to marry me. She's frightened of the step, I think. The Gamelins have been at each other's throats for years. Her childhood must have been diabolical.'

'So, Craigie's death,' said Barnaby, 'could be said to work to your advantage. Her environment being now far less secure.'

'Yes. It's sad and naturally I regret what's happened but I do feel it might tip the scales in my direction.'

Jammy devil, thought Troy. Talk about falling on your feet. Didn't know who she was. He must think they were born yesterday. Obvious to anyone with an ounce of brain what happened. He picks up on the telly grapevine where poor little rich girl's hiding. Comes down, makes a play and pulls it off. Once they're hitched with a joint bank account she won't see his Ferrari for gold dust.

This imaginative projection, linked with Barnaby's thoughts on the motive, gave Troy an idea. 'Where actually is the light switch Mr Wainwright?' he indicated the just-completed sketch and Christopher obligingly put a cross. Troy looked over his shoulder. 'I see. So to reach it, you'd have to pass quite close to the platform.'

'Not really. To get from here to here,' he drew a diagonal line, 'that's the quickest way.'

'And is that the way you went?'

'Of course it is.' Christopher stared at the sergeant. 'What are you getting at?' Then, realising, he laughed. 'Oh come *on*. . . .'

The sergeant snatched up the sketch and studied it closely, eyes hooded to conceal his anger. Troy could stand anything he told himself, (untruthfully), except being laughed at.

'I believe,' said Barnaby, 'that the dying man pointed at someone before he fell.'

157

'He was standing with his arm stretched out, yes. Whether he meant to indicate anyone special, I don't know.'

'Doesn't seem much sense in it otherwise.'

'It's been suggested,' Troy replaced the paper, 'that he was fingering Gamelin.'

'Who by?' Receiving no reply, Christopher continued, 'Well you can understand that. He's the outsider. No one can bear to think it's one of us.' He was shown the knife and glove and agreed that they both came from the kitchen, then said, 'Suze has some ideas about what really happened. Quite honestly I think they're a bit on the wild side. What I wanted to ask was, can I stay when you talk to her? She's still pretty upset.'

'Provided you don't interrupt.' Barnaby gestured towards the door.

'Is that a good idea, Chief?' said Troy, once Christopher had left.

'I think so. The more relaxed and coherent she is, the sooner we'll be through and on to the next one.'

'Tell you something about that bloke – he dyes his hair.' Troy presented this perception rather touchingly, as a dog might bring along an absurdly shaped bone. Barnaby, who had already noted the fact, said nothing. 'Now he's not the sort to try for street cred. He's too young to be going grey. So why do it?'

The Gamelin girl must have been waiting outside for they were back already. Fresh tears lay on her cheeks and she was still in great distress. Barnaby never enjoyed questioning the grief-stricken but there was no doubt that it could be very fruitful, circumspection usually being the last thing on their minds. And so it proved now. No sooner had the girl sat down than she launched into a flood of anguished guilt-infested speech.

'. . . it's all my fault . . . he was only here because of me . . . and now he's dead . . . the most wonderful man. He was a saint . . . he loved us all . . . he had so much to offer the world . . . so much to give . . . you've no idea what has been destroyed here today . . . wicked . . . so wicked. . . . Ohhh I should never have come here. . . .'

She continued for a while longer. Wainwright held her hand and Barnaby tried to sort out the various 'he's'. Eventually she calmed down a little and wiped her eyes with her sari which already had many damp patches.

'So you think this is all down to you, Miss Gamelin?'

'My father would not have been here otherwise.'

'You believe he was responsible for Mr Craigie's death?'

'I know he is . . . *I know he is*. . . .' She had leapt to her feet. 'No one else would have done it. They had no reason. We all worshipped the Master. He was the centre of our world.'

'So this "knowledge" is based on nothing more than emotional supposition?'

'It's based on proof. The Master when he was dying pointed directly at my father. It was unmistakeable.'

'Were there not a whole group of people crowding round Miss Cuttle at the time? He might have been indicating any one of them.'

'No.'

'And the weapon?' Barnaby pushed over the knife.

She looked at it and shuddered. 'It was on a rack in the kitchen. He was in there this afternoon. That was my fault too. I actually left him alone while I carried some tea upstairs. He took it then. He must have been planning it all along.'

'And the motive?'

'Ha! The motive behind everything he does. *Money*. I came into a trust fund today . . . my twenty-first. Half a million.'

Christopher gasped. 'You didn't tell—'

'Mr Wainwright. . . .' Barnaby held up his hand and nodded for her to continue.'

'I didn't want it. It was just a burden.'

My God, the rich, Troy thought, the bloody rich. The idle fucking rich. *A burden.*

'So I decided to give it away.'

Well look no further, lady. Here I am.

'I wanted the commune to have it. The Master thought that was unwise. That I'd be sorry. He suggested I talk to my parents.

Apart from the question of the money he thought we could heal our differences.' She laughed again, another grating humourless syllable. 'He was so naïve. He didn't understand how terrible people can be.'

'Tell me, Miss Gamelin—'

'Don't call me that! It's not my name.'

'Did your parents actually meet with Mr Craigie?'

'My father did. They talked together for half an hour at seven o'clock. My mother was late arriving'

'Do you know anything of the outcome?'

'Only that they were going to carry on the discussion later. I don't think much of the Master's influence rubbed off. My father was absolutely bloody at dinner.'

'How did he react when you told him your decision about the trust fund?'

'I didn't. I left that to the Master.'

Barnaby glanced down at the sketch. 'You recall him then, your father, as standing directly behind Mr Craigie's chair?'

'Yes. You can see why now. All he had to do was lean over and . . . and. . . .'

'It's not quite as straightforward as that, is it? For instance you've just said that your father knew nothing of your decision to hand over the money until he talked to Craigie.'

'That's right.'

'At seven o'clock.'

'Yes.'

'So why would he take the knife at five o'clock?'

'Oh. . . .'

Troy wondered how she'd cope with that one. Always pleased to see anyone disconcerted, he strolled over and placed himself behind Barnaby to watch.

'Well . . . the money need not have been the only reason. I'd been talking about this place. Telling him how content I was.'

'Surely no one could take offence at that?'

'You don't know him. He's terribly jealous. He can't bear me to be happy with anyone. After I left home he used to hang round in doorways and spy on me.' She reached out and picked up the bag with the glove. 'Did he wear this as well?'

'We're presuming whoever handled the knife wore it, yes.'

'It's a left-handed glove. He's left-handed. They were in the kitchen as well. What more do you want? And May getting upset was the perfect distraction.'

'Trouble about that, Miss Gamelin,' perching on the table-edge, Troy repeated her name with some satisfaction, 'is that it rather works against the premeditation theory. As he hadn't been here before, how was he to know things would take such a dramatic turn?'

'You're going to let him wriggle out of it aren't you?' She glared at Troy with contemptuous disgust as if he were infinitely bribeable. 'I should have known. Money gets you off any hook.'

Troy was furious. He was a lot of awful things but he was not corrupt, nor would he ever be. 'You keep your bloody insults to—'

'All right. Enough.' The words were quietly spoken but Troy connected with the chief inspector's gaze, slid off the table, turned away.

Barnaby realised that the determinedly exclusive cast of his present witness' thought made further questioning pointless. Running out of factual evidence, there was a real danger she'd start dreaming something up. He let them both go and turned on his bag carrier.

'What do you think you're about, Troy? Letting yourself be provoked by a bit of a girl?'

'Yeh . . . well. . . .'

'Well what?'

'Nothing. Sir.'

Barnaby checked his list and sent the young constable for Mr Gibbs. Troy stood, stiff-backed, staring down at the old Gestetner. It had a yellow sticker refusing Nuclear Power with a polite 'No Thanks'. The mildness of Barnaby's reprimand in no way mitigated, to Troy's mind, its hurtful timing. To be pulled up like that in front of a policeman still damp behind the ears, plus two members of the public, was unforgivable. Crashingly insensitive to the feelings of others, Troy's own sensibilities were fragile to a fault. He was on his high horse at the merest hint of criticism.

'See if you can get some water. I'm parched.'

'Right.' Troy moved with Jeevesian formality towards the door.

'And refuse all alternatives. Especially that unspeakable substitute for Ronseal. I wouldn't clean my drains with it.'

When Troy opened the door, Guy Gamelin was there. He moved forwards and the sergeant immediately took several steps back.

'I'm returning to my hotel now. I should be there until tomorrow morning. Chartwell Grange, outside Denham.'

Barnaby rose to his feet. 'Mr Gamelin,' and indicated the empty chair. 'A few things I'd like to ask before you leave.'

The two men sized each other up. Guy remained standing. He also remained uncooperative, saying, 'Can't say' or 'No idea' to Barnaby's first few questions. And he declined the invitation to draw a sketch.

'I don't remember where I was, let alone anyone else. With the exception of that stupid cow mooing and rolling about on the floor.'

'You don't have a lot of time for this organisation then?'

'A load of self-deceiving weak-minded histrionic wankers.'

'In that case you can't have been pleased to find your daughter living here.' At this remark, Guy's formidable jaw thrust forward slightly and his breathing quickened. But he did not reply. 'I understand,' continued Barnaby, 'that you and she have been estranged for some years.'

'If you choose to believe the gutter press.'

'Isn't it true then?'

'Moderately. Not that it's any of your bloody business.'

The adverb seemed inappropriate. Gamelin struck the chief inspector as a most immoderate man, the sort to fly from one extreme of heightened emotion to another.

'Tell me – had you met Craigie before this evening?'

'No.'

'What was your opinion of him?'

'He was a con man.'

Takes one to know one. Troy was staring enviously at the watch on Gamelin's wrist. A glittering oval of pale gold and crystal with an immaculate display of Roman numerals all on a platinum trellised band. Cost me a few years' salary that, thought the sergeant.

'He was trying to take Sylvie for half a million. But I've no doubt you've discovered that by now.' Barnaby went in for a bit of ambiguous throat-clearing. And waited. 'I've come across some shysters in my time – the City's full of them – but he was something else. He not only tried to dissuade Sylvie from giving the money. He asked me to talk her out of it as well.'

'Wasn't that a bit risky?'

'Not at all. You don't understand how these fakers work. That's the final move. Like the end of a haggle in the market place. The customer walks away knowing he'll be called back because he's got the whip hand. All this pretence made Craigie look good, y'see. Reinforced the saintly image.'

There was something in the voice and in the bloodshot piggy eyes that did not quite ring true. Or marry with the words. What was it? Envy? Disappointment? A failure of belief? It could even have been, thought Barnaby, desolation. Gamelin was speaking again, vindictively shoring up the character assassination.

'What Craigie was into, was what all these guru types are into – money and power. That's how they get their spiritual rocks off.' Black misery coloured every word.

'You've not seen the light then, Mr Gamelin?' asked Troy.

'I've seen the dark,' replied Guy. 'It's preferable believe me. You know where you are in the dark.'

'That why you killed him, Mr Gamelin? Because of the money?'

'*You what*. . . .' So quiet. Words with no sibilants yet making a sort of hiss. Gamelin leaned forward, clenching the table's

163

edge. He pushed his face – a meatball of congested flesh – to within an inch of the chief inspector's. 'Listen to me. You watch your fucking step. I've eaten people twice your size. I sharpen my teeth on men like you.'

Spittle coated his bristling chin as his expression of frustrated rage intensified. Fury flowed untrammelled across the narrow space between the two men. Barnaby sat quite still, a clot of saliva on his tie, unimpressed by the third-rate dialogue but very impressed indeed by the measure and quality of Gamelin's ferocity. He had never had a boiler explode in his face but felt the time might well be nigh. Beneath his hand the table shivered.

Troy, who had been on the point of moving forward, stayed where he was and watched. They could have been a pair of great bull moose at the start of the season. Shoulders solid, foreheads low. Troy observed his chief's impassive unflinching profile with a stirring of collaborative pride. He thought as he turned his attention to Gamelin, you've picked the wrong one there boyo.

Barnaby produced the glove. 'We believe whoever used the knife wore this. You were seen hiding it.'

'Who told you that?'

'Do you deny it, Mr Gamelin?'

'No.' He was drawing his rage back. Hoarding it now. Barnaby noticed a blue rim on the inside of the slack lower lip. Gamelin sat down breathing carefully, evenly. His hand rested briefly on his breast pocket. Came away.

'Do you want something to drink, Mr Gamelin? A glass of water?'

'No. Nothing.' He sat quietly for a while then said, 'The glove. After the bearded dwarf with the stupid name had gone to the phone for an ambulance and the others were staring at each other not knowing what to do, I reached for a handkerchief and the glove came out with it,'

'Someone must have noticed that surely, sir?' asked Troy.

'I didn't think so at the time. I was on my own you see – at the far end of the room. Persona non grata. Been like that all night. They wouldn't even let me sit by her at dinner. Said they always kept to the same seat.' He made to touch his cheek. 'I put it straight back. It was plain what had happened. Whoever killed the man was planning to incriminate me. I went over to the window, waited until I thought I was unobserved, then stuck the glove behind the curtain.'

'Are you left-handed?'

'As it happens.'

'I can see that may well have been as you describe, Mr Gamelin. But there's also the matter of the dying man pointing you out. . . .'

To Barnaby's surprise Gamelin made no attempt to deny or explain the fact. Nor did he attempt to bluster it away.

'Yes. I can't understand that. Plays perfectly into the murderer's hands of course. Backs up the glove to perfection.'

'Perhaps . . .' Barnaby tested the water, offered a way out. 'If you were part of the group . . . ?'

'No. It was me all right. I was standing a little away from the others. It's funny but I thought at the time he was trying to tell me something.' He shrugged, appearing slightly confused. 'A bit thin but that's it.'

Bloody thin, thought the chief inspector. Trouble was, Gamelin didn't seem like a man to dissimulate. He just didn't give a cuss what anyone thought or felt or said about him. A position of extreme strength or extreme arrogance according to your point of view. The chief inspector, a modest way along that path himself, naturally favoured the former. He asked if Guy had any ideas of his own on who might be guilty.

'None at all. I don't know enough about the set-up here. Quite honestly I wouldn't have thought any of them had the guts to swat a fly.' He was silent for a moment then said, 'I'm ideal, aren't I? The outsider bringing in all the nasty ways of the wicked world. All the hands here, whiter than white. Mine, redder than red. You've got to hand it to the cunning buggers.' His throat released a short explosive clatter. 'Praahh.' Belatedly Barnaby recognised a laugh.

'Do you believe then that you were invited specifically for that purpose?'

'Of course not. I was asked down by Craigie himself. He's hardly likely to collude in his own death. Unless . . .' he looked across at Barnaby, alert and interested, the boiling fury of a minute ago apparently quite forgotten, 'unless my visit was suggested to him by someone else, which means this was all planned some time ago. Perhaps . . . at the last minute . . . he understood. That could be why he was pointing me out . . . as a warning. . . .'

Troy had come across some smart examples of thinking on your feet but for sheer nattiness that took some beating. Guilty as hell and giving them a twinkle-toes runaround. He couldn't understand why the chief was even pretending to go along with it. Both men were getting up.

Barnaby said, 'I shall want to talk to you again, Mr Gamelin. Tomorrow.'

Gamelin did not reply. He walked to the door, his exit vastly more restrained than his arrival. His massive shoulders slumped and there was tiredness in his step. When the door had closed, Troy said, 'Why didn't you arrest him?'

Barnaby waited for the tag line. Open-and-shut case. Handed on a plate. Bang to rights. Short and curlies. In the matter of the well-worn apothegm, Troy stood alone.

'We can pick him up in the morning. We'll know more clearly where we are when we've finished the interviews. So far it's pretty circumstantial.'

Behind the Boss's back, Troy shook his head in disbelief. How much plainer could anything be? *Obviously* Gamelin was going to say the glove was planted. Who wouldn't? Talk about snoringly obvious! But he'd got the motive, opportunity, both to take the knife and use it and, most damning of all, the murder victim had fingered him. The man was over a barrel. For a traitorous moment Troy wondered if he had been wrong about his chief's imperviousness to the seductive power of wealth.

Barnaby was muttering now, apparently to himself. Troy listened, thinking he might not have heard aright. Something about always being sorry for Caliban. He remembered the earlier request for water and moved off.

By the time the sergeant returned, Arno was being questioned. He was sitting nervously hunched up, looking intently at the chief inspector. Encouraged to do a sketch, he had produced a host of stick figures – one flat on its back, toes turned up, hands crossed on breast and a 'Smiley' face. Barnaby having ascertained Arno's position in the commune and noticed his extreme agitation, left the dark heart of the matter temporarily aside.

'Tell me Mr Gibbs, what do you think will happen here now? To the Manor House for instance.'

'I don't know. I just don't know.' Arno sounded deeply melancholic. He was ashamed to admit, even to himself, that once having absorbed the distressing fact that the Master was no more he had thought of little else but his own possible future. How would things fall out if the commune broke up? Who would look after Tim? And, most important of all, how on earth could *he* survive without the robust and serene presence of his dear love? Denied that radiant gaze that lit and sustained each awakening, and benevolently solaced the going down of the sun, his own life would hardly be worth the living.

'You have no idea how the property is entailed?'

'No. Actually I don't think anyone has. Somehow it was never discussed.'

'Did members have to buy into the organisation? Shares – that sort of thing?'

'Not at all. We just pay our way. The Lodge made money from courses and workshops. We were planning to apply for charitable status actually. Become a trust but. . . .' He gave a defeated shrug.

'Did you know about Miss Gamelin's bequest to the commune?'

'No. I do now – they were just talking about it.'

'And this evening. . . .' Arno braced himself. 'What do you think actually happened?'

167

'God – I don't know. It was so terrible . . . so confusing. . . . One minute he – the Master – was guiding May through her regression – '

'You mean verbally?' Barnaby interrupted.

'Yes.'

'First we've heard about that,' said Troy severely and Arno looked abashed as if he were personally at fault. 'How does it work?'

'He asks questions – what do you see now? Where are you? That sort of thing. And May replies. This time she touched down in Roman Britain. He asked if she could describe anything and she began to tell us about the tent. I think that was the last time he spoke. Shortly after that she began to make the most dreadful noises. Of course we all ran to see if she was all right.'

'Why "of course", Mr Gibbs?' said Troy. 'We've been led to understand such reactions were not uncommon.'

'Oh, it's never been as bad as that before. But she *will* persist. She has the bravest heart and an unquenchable thirst for knowledge.'

Troy noted a tremolo in the vocals and the sudden emotional ducking of the little red beard, and thought, hullo – we've got a gruesome twosome in the making here or I'm a monkey's uncle. If middle-aged people in love knew how grotesque they looked they might take up something more seemly. Like exposing themselves in the park.

'We were warned that today would be special. Ken – speaking as Zadekiel that is – said the cosmic energy released was tremendous. And of course there was the omen. They have to send one you know – the Karmic Board – if a grand master is to be withdrawn from the physical octave. Unfortunately we didn't see the link until it was too late. The others thought they'd sent Astarte, goddess of the moon, in the shape of Mrs Gamelin. My own feeling is that the omen was May's accident – '

'Yes, Mr Gibbs. She told us about the accident,' said Barnaby.

'Oh. I beg your pardon.' Arno looked at them both then added: 'I must say you seem to be taking it very lightly.'

'We've got a murder to concentrate on,' said Troy. 'Now, are

you of the opinion that Craigie pointed out Guy Gamelin before
he died?'

Arno was gravely hesitant. 'Well . . . you know . . . one is
reluctant to say anything that might . . . but yes. That was my
impression. But that's not to say the gesture was an accusation.'

'What else do you think a murdered man is going to use the
last seconds of his life for?' asked Troy.

Arno looked deeply upset at this and became even more so
when Barnaby said, 'We shall have to talk to this retarded boy
I'm afraid. I understand you know something of his background.'

'Oh you can't do that! He's withdrawn, hardly coherent. It'd
just be a waste of time.'

'He's a witness, Mr Gibbs.' Barnaby glanced down at his
sketches. 'Actually sitting at Craigie's feet. Closer to him than
anyone. He may have seen something.'

'He's asleep. Please let him rest.' Arno's freckled skin was
beaded with luminous sweat. 'His world has come to an end.'

'In the morning, then.' Arno's alarm was palpable. Barnaby
added gently, 'We're not monsters you know.'

'Of course not. I wasn't meaning to imply . . . oh dear. Could
I be present?'

'In the case of the mentally ill someone has to be, Mr Gibbs.
And if you think you're the best person – by all means.'

They talked to Mrs Gamelin next and the conversation, though
not short on entertainment value, was in all other respects an
absolute frost. May, leading the police towards the communal
sitting-room, described Felicity as 'rather poorly and resting'.

Troy had already volunteered the information that the lady
was a smackhead. As they walked along he added, 'Crashed the
car. They found some stuff. Lost her licence. It was in the *Sun*.'

'Surely not,' replied Barnaby.

'Bet she's tranqued out of her skull.'

Face to face with Felicity, Barnaby felt his sergeant might
well be right. Her huge eyes beneath smudged purple lids swivelled and slipped all ways. The hands made delicate broken

movements. Up as if to touch her face, changing direction, plucking at her dress, scrabbling in her tangled hair. Her face was shrunken and seemed to fold in on itself, pinched and tiny, like a worried marmoset's.

Felicity became aware that people were present. One was talking rather persistently and his voice rattled inside her head, making no recognisable sounds. He pushed a piece of paper of a pleasant pale shade her way. Felicity admired it politely and handed it back. He offered it again with a pencil and seemed to be urging her to try it out. She smiled, quite agreeable to this suggestion for she had loved drawing as a child. She spent a long time bending over the paper and the result, Barnaby had to admit, was not unattractive. Several quite charming horses, one with only three legs and a garland of flowers big as cabbages round its neck.

Felicity then asked for a drink and Troy got her some water. She hadn't meant water and poured it over his trousers. Shortly afterwards the interview came to an end.

While it was going on, and directly overhead, Trixie was walking up and down. She had been chain-smoking and the air was acrid and stale. 'Why are they taking so long?'

'I expect they want to talk with everyone. It's only been . . .' Janet turned the Snoopy alarm round, 'an hour and a half since they first arrived. That's not bad.'

'You're not waiting are you?'

'I don't know why you're getting into such a state. You didn't have anything to do with it.' She crossed to the window and pulled aside a curtain to reveal a low hanging sliver of moon. Cold and sharp, like a scythe.

'Don't do that. You know I hate the night.' Janet let the curtain fall. 'What are they like?'

Janet recalled narrow lips, a fiery brush cut. 'All right.'

'Are you sure you told them about the glove?'

'I've already said a dozen—'

'And that you were the one who saw him hide it?'

'*Yes.* How many more times?'

'Then they should have arrested him, shouldn't they? I don't understand it.'

You and me both, thought Janet sadly. But I know it all goes back to this afternoon. After the first fierce rebuff she hadn't questioned Trixie again, but it had not been difficult to guess at the reasons for the girl's smeared make-up, milk-white face and held-together clothes. So Janet, guessing at revenge, understood when Trixie had explained what she wanted her to do.

'The thing is Jan – I saw him hide the thing. I really did. I wouldn't ask you to tell otherwise. The trouble is, once Gamelin knew who shopped him he'd tell them I was making it up out of spite and they'd believe him.'

'Why?'

'Because he's rich and powerful, stupid.'

'Then why can't we both say we saw it? I'd back you up.'

'I don't want to be in it *at all*.'

So Janet had told her lie, still not sure if Trixie spoke the truth but sympathising with, indeed almost sharing, her friend's need to exchange a hurt for a hurt.

There was a knock at the door and a policewoman asked if Miss Channing could spare a few moments.

'They're very civil, aren't they?' said Trixie. 'I wonder what they'd be like if I told them to take a running jump.'

'Don't antagonise people unnecessarily. And don't take those cigarettes. You've already had—'

'Oh for heaven's sake, stop clucking. You're like a bloody old hen.'

Troy had no complaints about the cigarettes. As wreaths of smoke surrounded Trixie's blonde curls, his nostrils flared – sucking in such wisps as came his way. It helped to take his mind off his soggy trousers. She sat, knees very close together, gripping a golden box of Benson's and a lighter.

Barnaby could see she was frightened. Smell it too. A scent both sour and intemperate. He'd met it before, had attempted to describe it once and the nearest comparison he could find was to the smell released when digging out old nettles. He asked if she'd been at the Manor House long.

'A few weeks. Why? What's that got to do with all this?'

'Could you be more precise?'

'No. I've forgotten the exact date.'

'Do you like it here?' His tone was courteous yet she took immediate offence.

'I suppose you think I don't belong. Just because I'm not wearing a wafty frock and chanting hallelujah.'

Troy chuckled. Trixie looked at him in surprise, then mistakenly believing his response to be sympathetic, with sly interest. She then assured Barnaby that she could not help at all regarding the death of 'our poor Master', though her sketch showed her to be sitting very close.

'But it was kind of dark, you see. We rushed to help May then the light came on and it was all over. He pointed Guy Gamelin out. But I expect everyone has told you that.' She looked at him expectantly.

'There seems to be some difference of opinion there,' lied Barnaby.

'Oh no – it was absolutely clear. Directly at him.' She flushed, recognising her insistence on the matter. 'Also I heard upstairs he was seen hiding a glove. It must have been the one he wore to hold the knife.'

'Had you met Gamelin before today, Miss Channing?'

'Blimey – I don't move in those circles.' Then, as if remembering her persona, 'They're so materialistic, aren't they?'

'You seem to be quite sure that he's the guilty party.'

'I don't see who else it could have been.'

'May Cuttle is of the opinion,' said Barnaby, 'that the despatch was brought about by supernatural means.'

Trixie laughed. A spontaneous robust shout of amusement, fear momentarily flown. Troy said, 'You're not a believer then?'

'Oh—' A devout expression appeared with such speed as to make her look positively silly. 'Yes – I'm a disciple of course. Just not that far along the road.'

If you're a disciple, my girl, thought Barnaby, taking in the perky breasts, glossy lips and flashy triple wedges, I'm Joan Collins. She was back on Gamelin again.

'Is . . . um . . . is he still here?' When Barnaby became engaged with some papers and did not reply, she added, 'We need to know you see . . . if someone's staying overnight.' Another pause. 'To make up the bed . . . and food. . . .'

Finally the chief inspector took pity on her. 'I believe Mr Gamelin has returned to his hotel.'

'You let him go!'

'I shouldn't worry about it,' said Troy. 'We keep a close eye. On everyone.'

Grumbling that it wouldn't be of any use, Trixie did a sketch and then Barnaby released her. As the door closed, Troy said, 'A worried girl, Chief.'

'She's hiding something that's for sure. So're Wainwright and Gibbs. Yet when I pressed the murder button none of them jumped. Now why is that?'

'Wheels within wheels, I'd say.'

'It was Gamelin set her off. Claims she's never met him before today, yet can't wait to stuff an apple in both ends, truss him up and bung him in the oven. If there's one thing I can't stand,' he got up, moving stiffly, 'it's being railroaded.'

'Talk to him again in the morning?'

'Oh yes. We'll bring him in I think. Meanwhile – drop these off at Forensic on your way home.'

Troy took the plastic bags. The lab was not on his way home. In fact it was not on anyone's, but if it *was* on anyone's way home then it was more on the chief inspector's way home than it was on his sergeant's way home. . . .

Saying 'Right you are sir' he foisted them on to Constable Fluffy and reached thankfully for the fifth cigarette.

Guy was slumped in a wide deep armchair in front of the flickering television set. He had undressed but he had not bathed. He had called his lawyer but he had not cleaned his teeth. He was wearing socks, boxer shorts and a sweat-stained unbuttoned shirt.

Links removed, the cuffs flopped down – covering the backs of his hands.

His body was motionless apart from occasional movements towards a freshly filled ice bucket, but his mind stormed and raged. He felt nauseous, although whether this was because of what he had drunk (the bottle of whisky ordered that afternoon was almost empty), or because of the foul, seething blackness inside his head, he neither knew nor cared.

He was devoured by thoughts of Sylvie. Obsessed by the recollection that it was she who had been closest to him when they had all been bending over May. And on his left; side sinister. The side on which the glove was found. Her flowing robes could have concealed it perfectly as they could the knife. This fact, coupled with the knowledge that it was only because of her he had been there in the first place, pointed to the agonising assumption that he might have been set up. And struggle as he might against the idea, within his fog of alcohol and morbid introspection, Guy was unable to put it quite aside. His skull ached with the effort of trying to do so and the muscles in his neck were like knots of steel. The more he twisted and turned, the more remorselessly logical did the hot depths of his imaginings seem to be.

It explained why she had lured him into the kitchen and left him alone – so that he should have easy access to the knife and glove. And most terrible of all, her instant accusation. For, after the first hellish seconds when the lights went on and they had all stared immobile and disbelieving at the falling white-robed figure, Sylvie had turned on her father, shouting, 'You . . . you . . .' and struck him across the cheek, her nails searing the flesh.

Someone had restrained her and Guy had backed away, assuming the position and rôle of pariah in which the police discovered him. Had it formed then – the first suspicion? The evil little canker. Guy groaned and reached for more ice, rummaging in the bucket with his glass, using it like a shovel. He poured whisky over the cubes. It slopped about, some going into the bucket, some on to the tray. The room reeked of it: a peaty, raw-paper smell. He drained the stuff in two gulps.

Muddied in with the dreadful apprehension of his daughter's treachery was a mixture of irritation and resentment against the dead man. They had been going to talk again. Guy had wanted that. Although there had not been even the faintest trace of the judgemental in either Craigie's attitude or conversation, Guy knew he himself had not come out of their earlier encounter well and the knowledge rankled. He felt that he had come across simply as a man with an out-of-control super-ego. But there was more to him than that. And life, in any case, had made him what he was. No one who hadn't been there knew what it took to climb out of the gutter. The energy and determination, the terrible transforming cost. A moment of weakness and you were face down again in the sewage with a dozen spiked boots ramming the back of your neck. If he could have told Craigie that. . . .

Guy remembered the stillness in that empty, quiet room. The feeling that he had briefly laid down the burden that was Guy Gamelin. A burden he had not even realised he carried. If he went back, if he were allowed to go back, would the silence still be there? And could it really heal?

Even as he posed the question he became angry at the gullibility that provoked it. Craigie was a trickster, right? *Right*. An impresario putting on a show with a bit of silk and sunlight. Remember that.

'Remember that.' Nodding vigorously in self-convincement, Guy returned his glass to the bucket and unscrewed the whisky bottle.

Seeking distraction he applied himself to the television set, screwing up his eyes in an effort to distinguish and separate the blobby shapes on the screen. A woman washing up, a little girl with shining hair standing next to her on a box. They were having a serious conversation about cutting grease. The woman gave a false 'maternal' laugh and placed a sparkly bit of foam on the tip of the child's nose. Guy zapped channels but the damage had been done.

Renascent deprivation gripped his heart and with it the final cruel apprehension that it really was too late. That what he wanted, what he yearned for, was not his daughter – that tall duplicitous stranger – but the child that she once was. Flesh of his flesh. The utter hopelessness of this desire quite overcame him and his face became disfigured by grief.

He caught sight of himself in the cheval glass across the room. Swags of flab hanging over the elasticated band of his shorts, wet matted chest hair, face the colour of uncooked pastry and running with perspiration, whisky stains down his shirt. As he stared at this gross and repulsive figure, a powerful visceral queasiness made itself felt. Then an overwhelming sensation of physical heat. Guy put his head between his knees.

The room tilted and slid first one way then the other. He sat up again, hanging on to the braided edge of the armchair. He was going to be sick. Struggling, heaving and pushing, he somehow got to his feet and started towards the bathroom. Half way there he felt an astonishing fierce tearing sensation in his chest as if someone was ripping it open with a bill hook. He cried out and stood swaying, looking round.

The pills were in his jacket. Guy moved slowly, dragging legs weighty as marble columns. A step away, a second tear knocked him off his feet. He lay on his back till the worst was past then forced himself up on one elbow and, raising his other arm, grabbed the table. He got the edge of the fruit bowl, dislodged a small card. Apples and oranges, pears and bananas rained down, hit him in the face and bounced off.

Impossible to try again. The pain was back, this time in iron hoops. Guy fell back against the carpet and let it devour him.

A LIE WITH
TRUE INTENT

Chapter 9

By eight-thirty next morning Barnaby was at his desk sifting, thinking, looking over his multiplicity of statements and sketches. Most of the latter showed some blanks but everyone seemed to know where they and their immediate neighbours had been, and from these incomplete drawings Barnaby had composed a large complete one of his own, now blown up on the wall.

He was studying this when the door opened and a pale-faced wraithish creature with eyes ringed like a panda's appeared hanging on to a tray.

'Is that my tea? About time.'

Barnaby had had five hours' sleep. He never needed more than six and was in fine form. Troy got to bed at three a.m. The baby woke at four and cried, on and off, till seven-thirty when her dad got up and dressed, whereupon she had fallen into a deep sleep. She had been doing this sort of thing every night for a week. Such a degree of vindictiveness in one so young was giving Troy serious pause for thought. He gave Barnaby his tea, put three sugars in his own, stirred and drank. Barnaby drank too and pulled a face. 'No sugar.'

'You said you were cutting down.'

'Down not out.' Troy took over the bowl and the chief inspector helped himself liberally, grinning up at his sergeant. 'Ah – the joys of fatherhood.'

'She's lovely. Beautiful. But. . . .'

'But not in the middle of the night. I remember it well.' He and Joyce had taken turn and turn about when Cully had six-week colic. He wondered what sort of helping hand Maureen got.

'I expect eventually I'll learn to sleep through it.'

'I'm sure you will, Gavin.'

Encouraged by the voice of experience and enlivened by his sweet tea, Troy went over and studied the chief's sketch.

'That it then?'

'Yes. Although just how important all those positions are I'm not sure. We'll look again when we get the PR report. See the angle of the knife and so on.'

'I've been thinking about that, Chief.' Troy scraped out the last of the melting sugar with his spoon. 'Quite long it was and bloody sharp. Even if you could conceal it about your person I shouldn't think you'd feel all that safe or comfy. I wondered if it was stashed in the Solar ahead of time?'

'Not much in the way of a hiding place. Plus you'd have to retrieve it.'

'I was thinking of those cushions.'

'Bit of a risk. Might have a bum on at the crucial moment.'

'Then you sit on it yourself.'

'But no one did.'

'True, true.' Troy was loath to let go his theory. He wandered over to the window, fingers twitching, longing for a ciggie to set off his cup of tea, and stared out hoping for distraction. ''Course that would mean Gamelin knew in advance where the regression would take place. We could find that out when we talk to him this morning.'

Barnaby, lost in the pile of statements, did not reply. About to return his cup to the tray, a movement in visitors' parking caught Troy's eye. 'Hullo, some smart money's spreading itself out there.'

Barnaby, glad to stretch his legs, joined his sergeant. A magnificent Bentley the colour of bitter chocolate had driven to an immaculate standstill. A man climbed out with some difficulty and walked towards the main building. Watching his slow and stately progress, Barnaby thought it took a tailor of genius to make a paunch like that look distinguished and not disgusting.

'Who the hell do you think that is?'

'I've got a very good idea.'

Shortly after this a constable from the main building came in with an excessively plain engraved card which Barnaby read aloud. 'Sir Willoughby St John Greatorex. OK, Troy – better wheel him in.'

The CID was quite separate from the station proper, connected by a high glassed-in walkway. It was quite a distance although not nearly such a distance as Troy made it seem. He took Sir Willoughby through Traffic Control and up two unnecessary flights of stairs, proceeding always at a brisk pace until, by the time they arrived at Barnaby's office, the great man was gasping for breath. Troy announced him po-faced but casting a derisive eye at the ceiling. Barnaby introduced himself and offered coffee. Sir Willoughby pressed a paisley silk square to his perspiring forehead and declined.

'It's very good.'

'I'm sure it is, Chief Inspector. Unfortunately I'm limited to one cup a day which I've already had three times.'

Barnaby, a martyr to indigestion, nodded not entirely sympathetically. His own unruly gut was simply reacting against years of ropey home-cooking and greasy fry-ups in the works canteen. He suspected the Greatorex intestines were finally giving out after an equivalent period of superb business lunches and evenings toying with a morsel of pâte de foie gras and a glass of Margaux.

Sir Willoughby really was the most extraordinary shape. Like a huge tweedy pear. Everything about him was pendulous. His nose, his jowls, the thready pouches under his eyes. Even his ear lobes looked as if the slightest breeze might set them dancing. He was speaking again.

'On the other hand it appears I may be involved quite soon in a lengthy and rather unpleasant disquisition, so perhaps a further bending of the rules might apply.'

No discipline these people, thought Troy, going off to get the desired brew. No self-control at all.

Soon, sipping delicately, Sir Willoughby said, 'Perhaps you could explain exactly what the situation is regarding Mr Gamelin. The telephone call I received last night was a little incoherent.'

What exquisite tact! Barnaby imagined the torrent of oaths and vitriolic abuse that must have poured out of the Greatorex receiver. No doubt the size of the Greatorex bill would be commensurate. He explained exactly what the situation was.

Sir Willoughby heard out the man lately described to him as 'a truculent bugger with a face like a side of beef.' Then he rested long, surprisingly slender fingers on the elegant camouflage of his trousers; winced and returned his nearly full cup to the chief inspector's desk. Turning to Troy, Sir Willoughby said, 'Do you think I might have a glass of water?'

Perversely the man's courtesy irritated the sergeant far more than haughty condescension would have done. Even so there was no way the words 'Sir Willoughby' were going to cross his lips. Even a simple 'sir' used without a second thought to any half-way adult and reasonably sober male member of the public remained unuttered. Muttering, '. . . Right . . .' he left the office.

'I understood,' said Sir Willoughby, 'when discussing this matter late last night that Mr Gamelin had been formally charged.' ('The fuckers have stitched me up, Will.')

'That is not the case although we will be questioning him again this morning. As Mr Gamelin's solicitor—'

'Please.' Sir Willoughby's hand made a weary gesture of disassociation. 'I am the McFaddens' solicitor and am here primarily to support and protect Mrs Gamelin.'

Barnaby felt a fleeting sympathy for Guy. The poor sod must have worn his trotters down to the ankles scrambling for a foothold in that tight little clan. The water arrived. Troy put it on the far corner of the desk and removed himself to the window.

Barnaby continued, '—You're welcome to be present.'

The offer was not entirely disinterested. An attendant solicitor helped keep the story straight. Saved trip-ups if things got as far as court. Sir Willoughby smiled, stretched way out for his water, drank a little and gestured again, this time with such stylish ambiguity that it could have meant anything, everything, nothing or all three simultaneously.

They're going to throw him to the wolves, Barnaby thought, and decided to question Sir Willoughby about the previous evening's phone call. Normally asking a suspect's solicitor if he could help the police with their inquiries would be about as daft as trying to milk a mouse and with much the same results. But Sir Willoughby considered the request seriously.

'Well, it was fairly rambling. There was something about a glove and colourful descriptions of the food and company. The murder of course. And a long lament about his daughter.'

'What did he say about the murder?'

'Only that he'd had nothing to do with it.'

'Did he mention the trust fund?'

Sir Willoughby sat up. Or as nearly up as his avoirdupois would allow. 'No.'

'I understand Miss Gamelin intends to give it all away.'

'Ah. . . .' He recovered so quickly the anguished little twist of sound might never have been uttered. 'Well, of course it's her money and she is of age.' He then rose after a certain amount of rocking to and fro. 'I have to be in court this afternoon . . . so. . . .'

'Will you be driving Mr Gamelin over here later, Sir Willoughby? Otherwise we'll send a car.'

'I really can't quite say when we'll be meeting. I shall be going straight from here to the Manor House to see how Sylvie and her mother are. So I shouldn't rely on me.'

Yes, thought Barnaby. Definitely to the wolves.

Troy detailed Policewoman Brierley to show Sir Willoughby out and watched the Bentley depart with a curl of his lip, thinking, *Sinjhan*. If I'd got a name like a Paki newsagent I'd keep it to myself.

Nobody had slept much. Breakfast was proving hardly worthy of the name. Everyone was saying to everyone 'You must eat

183

something' whilst going without themselves. Earlier in the hall (no one could bear to enter the Solar), they had gathered in a circle to recharge. But even ten minutes' controlled breathing into Universal Mind had little effect. Grief had disunited them and they mourned individually, hutched in invisible cages of sorrow. Even Janet, whose respect and admiration for the Master stopped well this side of devotion, was dismayed by how disconsolate she felt.

Christopher poured fruit juice, Arno crumbled a barley cake, Heather had carved herself a slice of marmalade the colour of treacle toffee and laid it to rest on some burnt toast. Ken, on Hilarion's instructions, was just about to retire to the garden with a straightened-out metal coat hanger to dowse for whatever etheric traces of the Master's spirit might remain, a sortie he referred to as Operation Karmalight.

May sat at the head of the table, proud shoulders drooping, wonderful hair loose and unbrushed. She had been crying and her eyes were still bright and swimmy. Without make-up her face looked haggard. She looked ten years older; a faint facsimile of her former self. Arno's heart almost broke at the sight and he had never loved her more.

She had been up most of the night with Tim. Arno had taken over at four o'clock. When he came downstairs he had left the boy still in bed lying in a rigid foetal loop, arms locked round knees, eyes screwed tight shut, refusing to acknowledge wakefulness.

Janet said, 'Shall I make some more tea?' No one replied. Heather asked where Suhami was.

'She won't come down,' said Christopher. 'She blames herself for bringing him here and can't face anyone.'

'Poor child.' May got heavily to her feet. 'Someone should go to her.'

'You won't get in. She talked to me through the locked door.'

'Oh dear.' Subsiding, May looked inquiringly at Janet and said, 'Trixie's not here either.'

'No.' Janet's pulse ticked a little faster at this supposition that she would be the one to know why. 'She's still asleep. I looked in on my way down.'

'It's for ourselves we grieve of course.' May's face twitched as she returned to the subject on all their minds. 'For him it's over. He is in the ranks of the illuminati.'

'And already born again,' said Heather with a watery smile.

True though this might be, no one was much comforted. It was too soon. The total awfulness of not only the matter but also the manner of their Master's demise lowered, a dark pall around their heads. Forced to believe, no one could quite believe. It was simply incredible. Like finding blood on the yellow brick road. Only May, still convinced that an immense supernatural force had spirited her teacher away, escaped this added dimension of despair. 'We must undreary our minds,' said Heather. 'I'm going to make a supreme effort - it's what he would have wanted.'

'You're right!' Ken jumped up as springily as his gammy leg allowed. 'There's a lot of loving needed here today. And I vote we start things off with a heart-centred hug - check, Heather?'

'Check.' His wife got up and the couple stood facing, arms locked round each other's waist.

'Direct eye contact.'

'Heads together.'

'Full body contact.'

'Breathe slowly and gently.'

'. . . s.l.o.w.l.y . . . g.e.n.t.l.y. . . .'

'Flow of compassion. . . .'

'My heart chakra to yours. . . .'

'F.l.o.w. f.l.o.w. . . .'

'Squeeze.'

'Release.'

They broke apart, smiling. Ken's trousers looked better already. No one else had gone in for the heart-centred hug. Arno drank a little juice and broke off a bit more barley cake. 'I think what would help - what would also help I should say,' he glanced apologetically at Heather, 'is to keep busy. I mean after a. . . . After something like this aren't there all sorts of things to organise?' He was remembering his mother's death and friends and relatives endlessly coming and going. The letters to be answered, the funeral tea.

'Be a post mortem I expect,' said Christopher. 'There's not much we can do till that's over and the body's released.'

This blunt remark caused May to gush fresh tears. Arno reached out to take her hand but at the last moment his courage failed and he let his own freckled paw lie in mute but companionable support a finger's width away. The thought occurred to him that she might (absent-mindedly, of course) take hold of it and he came over quite wobbly.

'For now I suppose we should carry on with our usual routine. It's what the Master would have wanted. In the long run. . . .'

'What do you mean?' asked Ken. 'The long run.'

'I suppose what he means,' said Janet, 'looking at it from a practical viewpoint, is what will happen to the house?'

'I don't understand.' May looked bewildered.

'Well, May,' Janet's voice softened. 'Assuming The Manor was his to leave, he might not have left it to the community.'

There was a long disturbed silence while this new idea spread its ripples amongst them. Then May spoke. 'He must have. We were his family – his next of kin. He said that to me once.'

'To me also,' said Arno.

'Don't either of you know how the house is entailed?' asked Christopher. 'You've been here longer than anyone.'

Arno shook his head. He was feeling rather depressed at the rapidity with which this 'nuts-and-bolts' conversation had taken off. 'We discussed everything else. Administrative matters, setting up courses, funding. But that just never seemed to come up.'

'There was no need for it to come up,' said May. 'Until now.'

'Did he have a solicitor?'

'He's never spoken of such things. His bank – The Lodge's bank I should say – is the National Westminster in Causton.'

'Ask them, May,' said Ken, 'next time you go in. You handle the accounts after all. They know you.'

'Certainly my signature is accepted,' admitted May. 'But only on communal matters. I don't see why they should tell me anything about the Master's personal business.'

'At least they could tell us if there was a mortgage.'

'A mortgage!' Ken was dismayed. 'Gosh – I'd never thought of that.'

'He was so other-worldly,' sighed Heather. 'It's just like him never to have made a Will at all.'

'I don't agree,' said Arno. 'He'd have considered us and left his affairs in order.'

'He would certainly,' said May, 'have considered Tim.'

'Our continuation here though,' argued Christopher, 'doesn't just rely on who owns the bricks and mortar, surely? All communities whether secular or religious need a guiding spirit to which they can conform. Ours resided in him. Who else here can lecture as he did, recharge people, give spiritual advice?'

'I'm a qualified counsellor.' Heather looked quite pouty. She had five framed certificates on the walls of her room including one for successfully completing a course in Venusian Temple Disciplines.

'Christopher's right,' said Janet who was fully conversant with Heather's idea of counselling. The procedure usually consisted of Heather sitting rather complacently while her 'client' explained the problem. Then, after pointing out that all dis-ease, whether mental or physical, was the external result of internal spiritual ignorance she would briskly offer an astrally oriented solution. After the recipient had paid their bill and left, Heather complained they'd drained her dry.

'After all,' continued Janet, 'we are the laity here. Our tasks have been mostly practical. Making things and running things. I feel our numinous gifts may be a bit on the skimpy side.'

'Speak for yourself,' said Ken.

Arno interrupted an uncomfortable pause. 'Has anyone looked in on Mrs Gamelin yet?'

'I should let her rest,' said May. 'It's still barely eight. She'll probably sleep for some time. I gave her a betony tisane.'

187

'God, that woman is in such *need*.' Heather braced her shoulders and held the bridge of her nose between thumb and little finger in a manner that suggested some wonder-working power source coiled within the cartilage. 'I really don't know if I can cope.'

'No one's asked you to cope, have they?' said Janet. She got up and poured some more tea.

In the end it was May who attended to Felicity. At nine o'clock she gently opened the door of the Oriel room, peered round and saw, beyond a foamy explosion of grey stuff in the middle of the floor, a narrow figure in a satin slip perched on the edge of the bed staring at the wall.

Felicity was in a turmoil and feeling very strange. She was trying to understand her state of mind. To separate at least one strand of emotion, draw it out, have a good look at it. But no sooner did she pinpoint one singular sensation than it bolted, swept away in the rush of half a dozen more. It seemed a long while since her arrival at the Manor House. She had not closed her eyes until the dawn and then only fitfully which no doubt contributed to the mental chaos.

At first the extraordinary and frightening events of the previous evening had touched her not at all. Things had seemed very bright, and clear and interesting, but also somehow unreal as if they had taken place on a stage some distance away. Or behind a thick glass wall. (She had taken a third line in the downstairs cloaks before going into the Solar.) Then, shortly after the police arrived, the effect wore off and fear, mess and muddle came roaring in, sweeping away this protective viewpoint. Self-knowledge loomed. She became aware that she was somehow involved in terrible things and that she looked ridiculous, having allowed Danton to turn her into a sideshow whilst she paid massively for the privilege. The click of the door made her jump and she stared at May whom she did not remember.

May was carrying a delicious cup of steaming tea. Visitors' rations (Earl Grey bags, coffee beans and other decadent goodies) were always to hand in a special cupboard. She had slipped in a few drops of a gem remedy to aid Felicity's recovery. May placed the cup on the bedside table, sat down and took Felicity's hand.

Felicity looked dreadful. Her face was a splodged mess as if a child had gone to town on it with mixed crayons. Yesterday's excessive mousseing, spraying and gelling had left her hair a lifeless mat. May stroked Felicity's hand, smiling encouragingly and, after a while, persuaded her to drink.

Felicity tried but her mouth was trembling so violently that her teeth chattered against the rim of the cup and the liquid spilled. May went back to the hand-holding. There was not much else she could do at the moment, given Felicity's emotional state and feeling far from robust herself. Gently, gently was the way. That a great deal of help was needed, May could see – for Felicity's aura was quite splintered. One of the worst cases May had ever come across.

After a while May approached the open pigskin case. She was looking for some fresh underthings, intending to run Felicity a bath, and found a large pink and gold jar of cream. Using this, she cleaned Felicity's face with slow rhythmical movements. After the third attempt the wastebasket was full of tissues and Felicity's original ivory pallor was revealed.

May returned briefly to her own room, rummaged in the fluorescent bowels of her wardrobe and found a silk robe in deepest blue. (No colour refreshed the spirit more.) Then she picked up a tub of mallow shampoo and a fluffy towel, and returned to wash Felicity's hair.

This proved much more complicated than cleaning her face even though Felicity bent meekly over the basin and kept quite still, holding a face flannel to her eyes. For a start there was so much of the stuff. The hand basin was full of it. May felt she was wrestling with a lion's mane. This was partly explained when, at the second wringing, a large piece of the back section came away in her hands. Briefly horrified (had she discovered a mallow allergy?) May then realised the hair was false. She wrang it out, draped it over the back of a chair and carried on shampooing. So much awful gunge. How could anyone bear to have all this ticky-tacky on their head? Eventually the water ran clear. May wrapped Felicity's hair in the soft towel and patted it gently. Then she combed it back and tied it with a piece of Kumihumo braid from her pocket.

'Now,' May bent down until her face was level with Felicity's and smiled, 'doesn't that feel better?'

Felicity made a sad little sound, like a hungry kitten.

'There, there,' said May. 'Now I suggest . . .' she took Felicity's arm, 'that you lie down until just before lunch time. Then you can have a bath and something very light to eat.'

Felicity sat down numbly on the bed and gazed at May with dark, pain-filled eyes.

'It's all right. Everything will be all right now. We'll look after you.' May leaned forwards and kissed Felicity on the cheek.

While these tender ablutions were going on, Janet was washing up, banging her hand-made cereal bowls around as usual in the stone sink. As she slopped water about she wondered about lunch. Suhami's name was on the rota but she had still not emerged and it was now ten o'clock. It was going to be a disorganised day, the first, Janet suspected, of many. The utter finality of the Master's death struck her with renewed force and she was sure that no matter how hard they all struggled to carry on as normal, things at the Manor House would never be the same again.

What would happen to them all? Where would they go if the house did prove to be no longer available? Would they try to live together somewhere else? Would she want that?

Janet knew she had no gift for the vigorous meddling in other people's lives that seemed to be the commune's definition of friendship. Philosophically, too, it was a struggle to conform. She was not at home with wild inexactitudes or fantastic suppositions and thought it sentimental to pretend all problems could be solved. Also she liked a bit of a grouse now and then, which was much frowned on. Only the other day, making some mildly derogatory comment on the weather, she had received a lecture from Heather on the lines of how she should be grateful she was not blind, or suffering from multiple sclerosis in a tower block.

Irritated by these recollections, Janet decided to break the house rules and make some real coffee. Stimulating uplift – that's what she was in need of, and to hell with pancreatic cancer. Or was it liver fluke? She would take some up to Trixie as well. And perhaps some biscuits.

In the visitors' cupboard she found a commercial and sinfully inorganic packet of Uncle Bob's Treacle Delights. She ground some beans, inhaling with pleasure, and undid the biscuits. The wrapper, with a fine relish for the cultural cross-reference, showed a Chinese girl in a sombrero with corks dangling from the rim. Janet selected a blue flowered plate for the Delights, put it back, got out a little glazed mustard number with a spray of crimson blossom, put that back and finally settled for a pale pink trellised-edged look. She carefully arranged several syrup-coloured biscuits in overlapping circles then, while the coffee brewed, snipped an Albertine rose (a perfect match for the plate) from outside the kitchen window.

Entering the hall with her laden tray, stomach looping an apprehensive loop as she anticipated rousing Trixie from slumber, Janet came to a full stop. There, at the bottom of the staircase, were May and Arno talking to a huge man in a speckled suit. As Janet hesitated, May and the man turned and went upstairs.

'Who was that, Arno?'

'The Gamelins' solicitor.' His eyes were already slipping after May and he brought them back to Janet with an effort. 'Something awful's happened. At least I suppose normally one would say it was awful. I can't help wondering if it's a blessing in disguise. He was found dead this morning in his hotel room.'

'What . . . Guy?'

Arno nodded. 'Apparently he'd asked to be called at nine. The maid took some tea up and he was just lying there. Hadn't even gone to bed. They seem to think it was a heart attack.'

'How dreadful.' Even as she made the expected response Janet knew that she was glad. He had been a terrible man. Avaricious and unkind. The world was well shot of him. And what a piece of news to offer Trixie. What a sweet token of a gift! Better than the real coffee and Uncle Bob's Delights. Better even than the rose. Arno was saying something else.

'May thought Suhami might be better able to receive the news. Her mother is still not quite . . .' He trailed off tactfully but Janet was already climbing the stairs.

Trixie was not sleeping after all but curled up on the window seat and smoking again. 'Has the post come?'

'Yes.' Janet put the tray down on the chest of drawers. She wondered if Trixie was looking for another letter in a blue envelope. 'Were you expecting something?'

'Not really.' Trixie was wearing an apple-green silk dress. Her face was unmade-up, the skin thick and smooth like cream. Inside her arms, Janet could see yesterday's scarlet pinch-marks transformed to little violets as the bruises came out.

'I've made you some real coffee.' She filled two mugs.

'You'll be for it. We're in a caffeine-free zone here.'

'And opened some biscuits.' Janet put her own mug aside and took the tray over to the window. The rose now looked rather silly not to mention superfluous. She had forgotten Trixie already had a bowlful. 'Drink it while it's hot.'

Trixie told her not to go on and Janet accepted this routine castigation with the patience of one who knows it is within her power to spring a big surprise. She made some headway into her own mug. Heavens – she'd almost forgotten how utterly delicious the real thing tasted! Was a squeaky-clean colon worth the sacrifice? 'Is it OK?' she asked timidly.

'Lovely. It'll warm me up.'

Janet didn't understand. The sun was streaming in and Trixie was bathed in it.

'Is there any news? I mean from the police.'

'They're here now. With the Gamelin solicitor.' Janet paused, her gaunt ardent face cloaked with anticipation. This was the moment. Still she hesitated, for the news could only be given once and then her purse would be empty. She could not tantalise, coyness not being her nature. In the end she just blurted it out.

'Guy Gamelin's dead. He had a heart attack.'

She remembered always what happened next. Trixie jerked violently upright as if she'd received an electric shock. The coffee spilled down her apple-green dress and bare legs and the mug clattered to the floor. She gave a wild shout, which was cut off as she clapped her hands over her mouth. Then she cried, 'Oh God – what am I going to do?' and started to scream.

About half an hour after this dramatic and sensational display, the police arrived to interview Tim. Arno led the way slowly and with the utmost reluctance along the gallery towards the boy's room. As they approached the door, his steps became more and more sluggish until finally he stopped, turned to Barnaby and laid an urgent, detaining hand on the chief inspector's sleeve.

'He won't be able to help, you know.'

'Please, Mr Gibbs. We've been through all this downstairs.'

'If you're determined . . . would you . . . ?' Arno had moved some small distance away, beckoning. When the two men joined him he continued, lowering his voice. 'I feel I should say something about his background. No one else here knows but it might help you to understand and be. . . . You see I met him – well found him might be a better way of putting it – about six months ago.'

He paused, cupping his hands round his eyes like blinkers for a second, then continuing. 'I'd driven the Master into Uxbridge – he was a hospital visitor, Thursday was his regular day – and we'd arranged to meet back at the car. There's a public toilet nearby which I needed to use. As I went down the steps, three men came up. Big men. One of them had tattooed arms, red and blue. They were laughing – great rough shouts. Not humorous laughter but ugly.

'I used the urinal thinking the place was empty, then I heard whimpering coming from one of the cubicles. He was in there –

Tim. His trousers were round his ankles and he was bleeding from the anus. They had . . . used him.' Arno's voice had sunk almost to a whisper. Barnaby leaned forwards, barely able to hear. 'Some money as well . . . a five-pound note . . . there. I mean, wedged. . . . It was vile.'

Arno broke off unable to continue. He produced a handkerchief and rubbed his eyes, turning his back while he did so. Picturing the scene, Barnaby felt the pity of it and even Troy was moved to sympathy – thinking, life's a bugger and no mistake. After a few moments Arno apologised for the break in continuity and carried on.

'He was in such pain and he didn't understand. I'll never forget how he looked . . . his eyes. . . . It was like finding a child violated. Or a baited animal. As soon as he saw me, he started to scream. I tried to help him but he just hung on to the lavatory, his arms locked around it. I didn't know what to do. I ran to the car park where the Master was waiting and told him what had happened. He came back with me. Tim had fastened the cubicle by then. The Master talked to him through the door for over an hour, even though he got some odd looks from the two or three men who came in during that time.

'You never heard him speak, of course, Inspector – but he had the most remarkable voice. Not just mellifluous but with a great promise of kindness . . . of happiness even. And so compelling. You felt whatever he told you must be true. Eventually Tim unbolted the door. The Master comforted him, stroked his hair. Then after a little while we helped him dress, took him to the car and drove him here. May put him to bed and we cared for him. And have been doing so ever since.

'Everything had to be sorted out with the Social Services of course. We all got a thorough going-over which I thought a bit ironical considering how the boy had been neglected before. Turfed out of the hospital, shoved into a bedsitter and visited once a week, if he was lucky, by a care assistant. We got his benefit book and details of his medication and that more or less was it. I think the fact that we're a sort of religious organisation swung it. They said we'd be checked up on from time to time but no one's ever come. I expect they're glad to have one less on their list.'

Arno paused then, with a look that plainly hoped this sorry tale would deflect Barnaby's intention. As it became clear this was not the case he said: 'Better come along then. . . .'

Tim's room was nearly dark. Through a gap in the heavy velvet curtains, sunlight leaked to form buttery puddles on the sill. Arno pulled the velvet further apart. Only a little, but the humped form beneath the quilt twitched and shivered. The air was so smelly and stifling Barnaby longed to open the windows.

Arno approached the bed, uttering the boy's name: a syllabic croon. He drew back the quilt, the floss of golden hair glittered on the pillow and Tim looked up, his eyes flying open like those of a mechanical toy. Barnaby heard a quick intake of breath behind him and was not unmoved himself – for the boy's beauty, even disfigured by tears and grief, was remarkable.

'Tim? Mr Barnaby would like to talk to you for a moment – it's all right. . . .' The boy had already started to cower. Tim shook his head. There was a throbbing vein like a thin turquoise worm in his alabaster forehead.

'I shall stay here,' continued Arno.

Barnaby took a chair so that he would not be looking down on the boy and sat near the opposite side of the bed to Arno. At a nod from his chief, Troy withdrew to a far corner of the room, producing a notebook but without much hope.

'I know you must be very unhappy, Tim, but I'm sure you'll want to help us if you can.' A ring dove's voice, purling. Troy thought the station'd never credit this. Even so, Tim reached out and seized Arno's hands in what appeared to be an absolute frenzy of alarm.

Arno had said the previous evening that this was his usual condition. But it seemed to the chief inspector, cautious though he had been, the boy's fear was intensifying by the second. His staring eyes were shadowed by it and the throbbing vein became more pronounced. Barnaby gave it five then continued.

'You understand what's happened, Tim? That someone has died here?'

Another long pause then, on the palely illumined pillow, the anguished face turned. Tim's cheeks were slobbered with tears. Brilliant dark blue eyes touched Barnaby's, slid away, returned. The procedure was repeated many times. Finally the connection held and he seemed to be getting ready to speak.

'Ask . . . ask. . . .'

'Ask who, Tim?'

'Ask . . . her . . . don. . . .'

The voice was but a tangled filament of sound, but Barnaby did not make the mistake of leaning closer. He just repeated his question, adding, now that he had a gender, 'Do you mean May, perhaps? Ask May? Or Suhami?'

'Neh, neh . . .' Tim shook his head fiercely and the nimbus glittered and shone. 'Askadon . . . askadon. . . .'

Barnaby said, 'Are you saying "accident"?'

'No, Chief Inspector. He just—'

Arno broke off as Tim made an urgent strangled copy of the chief inspector's words.

'. . . mean ackerdent . . . ack . . . si . . . dent. . . .' Having got it right, Tim repeated the words more and more quickly, rising higher and higher on the scale until the three syllables became transformed into a stream of meaningless babble. His body was a single bolt of flesh beneath the quilt and his eyes rolled wildly. Arno gave Barnaby as near to a glare as a man of such equable temperament could muster, then stroked Tim's forehead with an air of resentful protectiveness that said quite clearly, now look what you've done.

Barnaby sat stubbornly on for a further thirty minutes, even though he suspected that Tim would not speak coherently again. Although the boy soon grew quiet, slipping into a self-protective doze, the measure of Arno's indignation did not abate and Barnaby felt the warmth of it across the narrow space.

He refused to feel guilty. He knew he had been right to question Tim and that he had done it in a tactful and humane way.

The fact that the boy was mentally disturbed did not mean he was incapable of noticing what was going on. Of course Barnaby had not realised quite how disturbed he was. Even so. . . .

At this point in his reflections he caught Troy's eye. As was his wont, the sergeant immediately blanked out any expression that might give away his true feelings. His lids fell but not before his superior officer had caught an impatient and derisive gleam. Barnaby accurately translated: What a waste of frigging time.

But he was not at all sure that he agreed. It was hardly unimportant that Tim, closest of all to Craigie on the dais, saw his death as an accident. And surely there was, in Arno's attitude, a much deeper anxiety than that caused by mere protectiveness?

No – Barnaby finally got up and moved towards the door, not a waste of time at all.

Hearing the news of Gamelin's death, Christopher went searching for Suhami. Her room was empty and he finally discovered her on the terrace leading to the herb garden. May had tried to dissuade him from searching, saying, 'She needs to be by herself. To take things in.'

Suhami did not turn as he approached but continued to stand motionless like a pillar of salt. He studied her profile. She looked very calm, wrapped in her own thoughts as tightly as the sari enwrapped her slender figure.

'How are you feeling?'

'I don't know.' She turned then and he saw that she was not as composed as he had thought, but rather dazed. 'I feel I've lost something but I don't know what. Certainly not him . . . not him.' The repetition was charged with a disconcerting mixture of bewilderment and satisfaction.

Christopher felt ill at ease. Her stillness seemed to him unnatural. He took her hand and said, 'Let's walk.'

They moved down the steps, avoiding outcrops of sempervivum and thrift, and into the garden proper. It was already very hot and the air was thick with the thrum of bees foraging among pink lavender and borage.

His future with Suhami was overwhelmingly on Christopher's mind. Had the fact of her father's death not arisen, he would have tried to discover how she now felt about leaving the commune. For it seemed to him that it was above all the presence of Ian Craigie that had held her there. Perhaps, even now, she would choose to stay. If that proved to be the case he would stay too for he was determined not to give her up. They sat down on a tiny circular lawn. A Catherine wheel of silver thyme and camomile.

'How's your mother taking it?'

'She doesn't know. Will told me first. He thought I'd be better able to handle things. I'll break it to her when we go back. Or this afternoon. It's not as if there's any hurry. . . .'

'Is it true they were unhappy?'

'They always seemed so. I can't imagine anyone being anything else living with him.' She turned, her expression strained. 'Perhaps we'll get like that.'

'Never, ever.' Christopher smiled, greatly encouraged by the 'we'. 'Other people's lives. This is you and me. This . . .' he placed his hand on the back of her neck, brought her close and kissed her. 'Is you . . .' his lips still hovered on her own, 'and me.'

He was upset by her lack of response. Just the day before she had danced in his arms, almost ecstatic. He reached in the pocket of his jeans and tugged out a flat box wrapped in magenta tissue.

'I bought these for your birthday. Before I knew who you really were. Then I felt I couldn't offer them.'

'But you were wrong.'

'Yes.'

'Who I really am.' The box lay in her lap, ribbon looped around her finger. 'That's what the Master said we should find out. That's what matters isn't it, Christopher? Everything else is shifting sand.'

'You can do the philosophical bit when you're ancient. There's no answers to the big questions anyway. Open your present.'

Suhami put the earrings on, delicate sprays of filigree, trembling little pearls. She turned her head this way and that.

'You're like a lovely temple dancer. Ahh, you're so pretty Suze.'

She hung her narrow head, surrendering gravely to disbelief. Not protesting as pretty girls usually do.

'What can I say to you?' he despaired. She lifted her slender shoulders and laughed with humorous resignation. 'Yesterday in the byre—' he tried again.

'Yesterday you saw how I used to be. Frightened, desperate, grabbing at happiness, at people. Frantic in case I was left alone. I can't live like that any more Christopher, I just can't. And I won't.'

'But there's no need to be frightened. I'd never leave you—'

'You say that now, perhaps it's true. But people are no different from all other forms of life in that they're changing all the time.'

'That's a bit pessimistic.'

'No, it's realistic. Obvious. Change in the only constant and I don't want to live in fear of it.'

'What about faith and hope?'

'I'm not sure they're relevant.'

'That sort of stoicism's for old men on the battlefield. Or neurotics. Afraid to start any sort of relationship in case it goes wrong. Ending up lonely and half-alive like—'

There was a long silence. The bees thrummed louder than ever. One of the fish jumped in the pond and plopped back. A breeze sighed. Suhami said, 'I shall never end up like my mother.'

'I'm sorry.'

'You're angry aren't you?'

'Of course I'm angry. I can see our future disappearing down the drain.'

'You haven't understood.'

'I don't think you know what you do want.'

'I want . . .' She recalled that single moment of illumination in the Solar. The Master's words when they had talked together only twenty-four hours ago. His powerful conviction that beneath the restless tangled surface of her life lay all she would ever need to comfort and sustain her. 'I want something that doesn't come to an end.'

'Everything comes to an end. Lesson One, Stoic's Handbook.'

'No, there's something. It can be discovered and called on. I know that's true. The Master called it the pearl of great price.'

How very unoriginal of him, thought Christopher. He reached forward and took hold of her plait, teasing out the soft hair that smelt of frangipani into a silky fan. 'Why can't we discover it together then? I'm interested in these matters too, you know. Why do you think I'm here?' He tugged her closer. 'We could go on a retreat for our honeymoon if you like.'

'Honeymoon.' Behind the word a flash of longing. Encouraged, Christopher pressed on.

'You don't have to be in a religious community to live a religious life. There are plenty of lay people who make room for prayer and meditation. Exist quietly and harmlessly. Why can't we be like them?' Suhami frowned. She seemed uncertain, a little confused. 'Don't you think in any case esoteric knowledge is written on the wind? If you're facing the right direction on the right day, fine. If not. . . .'

Suhami gave a half smile. She quite liked that way of putting it. It echoed the Master's proposition: that the pursuit of the dream was not only useless but counter-productive.

Christopher returned the smile double, triple, manifold. His own was quick and bright; full of confidence. He had time on his side. And youth. And passionate determination. Surely in the end she would be his.

Returning to the house they found a confab going on in the kitchen. Everyone sat round the deal table making hay with Uncle Bob's Treacle Delights whilst absorbing pungent distillations from the Arabica bean. After the proper expressions of surprise and pleasure at the sight of these secular delicacies, Suhami and Christopher helped themselves to coffee and shared the last biscuit. The conversation was about Trixie but directed at Janet who sat well back in her chair, looking more than a touch at bay.

'Are you sure,' Arno was asking, 'that you got nothing intelligible out of her at all?'

'She must,' argued Heather, 'have said something that made sense.'

'People having hysterics don't make any sense.'

The scene in question had been chewed on for nearly an hour and Janet was getting sick of it. The others had taken over the distressing and frightening episode in just the bustling and concerned way they seized on every opportunity for service. They didn't seem to know the difference, Janet thought crossly, between benign interventions, bossiness and bullying. Mind you, it could be said she'd bullied Trixie pretty violently herself, though that had not been her intention.

When the shouting had started, Janet had rushed across the room calling out 'Don't, don't!' and stupid things like 'It's all right'. Then she had seized Trixie's shoulders, or tried to. But Trixie had wriggled and wrenched herself free, flailing her arms wildly, striking Janet on the side of the neck and making non-stop fear-filled shrieks. Her mouth was opening and closing like a fish and her blank eyes stared. It was the eyes, Janet thought afterwards, that made it possible for her to do what she had done – for there was no trace of Trixie in them at all.

Janet hadn't meant to hit so hard. The palm of her hand still stung. She must have pulled her arm right back for, when the blow connected with Trixie's cheek, the girl staggered two steps sideways and fell against the wall. It worked though, just like it always does in the movies. Trixie immediately stopped screaming, understanding came back into her eyes and a huge red patch flared on her cheek. Then the others arrived and Janet was pushed into the background.

Outside on the landing, trembling, gripping the gallery rail, she repeatedly relived the moment of violence. Previously sure she had acted on desperate impulse (anything to stop those awful, soulless cries), now other more complicated motives threaded their way into her consciousness. If she was honest she had to admit that the connecting moment had not been entirely without a certain satisfaction. Even a vengeful satisfaction. How terrible! Janet felt sick with shame at this insight. She had been unaware that her dry and profitless love cloaked hostility. Trixie was right to reject her friendship. She became aware that Arno was regarding her anxiously and forced a smile.

Actually Arno's anxiety, and there was a lot of it, was pretty widely distributed. The fact that his gaze happened to alight on Janet was almost by the way. The largest object of his concern was, of course, the murder. Like most of the others, he believed Gamelin responsible and couldn't decide whether the man's death was a good thing or a bad. *Good* if the police also agreed that he was guilty, as that would remove the need for a trial and all the attendant publicity. *Bad* if they were not sure, for that would mean the investigation dragging on, and doing even greater damage to the community than had already been done.

Then there was this extraordinary business with Trixie. Arno had been very disturbed by the wild intensity of her reaction to Guy's death. He was not at ease with the inexplicable or with sudden explosions of emotion, especially those that seemed to have no logical launching pad. After all, she'd hardly known the man. Even the lightning realisation, on hearing the sound of Janet's single hand connecting so forcefully with a curved cheek, that he had at long last solved his koän, did not console. It simply threw the loss of his dear teacher into more painful perspective as he recognised with what joy he would have hurried to break the marvellous news. Arno turned back into the conversation – where it seemed Heather was expressing aloud the first of his concerns.

'If only we knew what happened between them yesterday.'

'Confucius he say to know is to know that to know is not to know,' said Ken. He spoke in his ageless-wisdom voice and lifted the skin at his temples to make almond eyes.

'No wonder he was confused,' replied Janet.

The previous evening's tragedy was not touched upon. Perhaps the feeling was that any sort of speculation would be rather crass with Suhami, who was now swishing spinach round the sink, being present. Heather proffered a consolatory thought-brick.

'I was meditating in the orchard this morning. Sitting oh so still and oh so quiet calling down the yellow flame of Cassiopea as it's Saturday and you'll never guess what happened?' The table waited, all agosh. 'A beautiful bee settled on some clover near my hand. A real Mr Bumble. He stayed and stayed, whirring his little wings just as if – and you can call this pneumatic synthesis if you like – but just as if he was trying to tell me something. Well, eventually I thought nothing ventured nothing gained, so I reached out and he actually let me stroke his furry back with my tiniest finger. Wasn't that incredible?'

May said, 'What do you think he was trying to transmit, Heather?'

'I think – and I mean like this is pretty earth-centred, OK? – but my perception of the situation was that the Master's transmutation having been so recent, etheric wisps of his astral body must still be about. Why couldn't said Mr Bumble have traces on his wings? Because what I was getting from that dear small furry creature was the most overwhelming sensation of comfort.'

'That could very well be,' said May. 'Certainly, if he was able, that is what the Master would wish to impart.'

'Perhaps,' said Suhami, now wringing out green leaves in a tea towel, 'the bee *was* the Master. A reincarnation.'

Ken and Heather exchanged amused glances. Ken spoke. 'I hardly think that a supreme arahat, after a life of devoted service to his fellow man, is going to reincarnate as an insect.'

'So you can buzz off for a start,' whispered Christopher, who was packing the spinach in an iron cauldron, and Suhami laughed.

'Heather's right,' said May, 'about left-over matter. I felt it myself this morning. There was a crowd of Elohim chattering away beneath my window. We must watch out for mischief. There's nothing they like more than hitching a ride on the aura. Ah well . . .' she pushed back her chair, 'it's nearly twelve. I must go and run Felicity's bath. Do you think you could take over the main course for lunch, Janet?'

'Surely.'

'And we'd better finish our chores,' said Arno to Ken. 'I think we're both on the garden this morning.'

'My leg's playing up a bit actually, Arno.'

'Well . . . there's always the hoe.'

'Bending just seems to compound the problem.'

'You haven't got a back as well as a leg have you?' Janet sounded quite pithy.

Ken gave her an all-forgiving smile. Poor old Jan, projecting again. If the group had had a pendulum reading when she first arrived, as he'd suggested, at least they'd have been forewarned. 'Oh, I have plenty to occupy my time.'

'Like what?'

'Hilarion has warned me to expect a mass incarnation of god-beings from Pluto. I plan a lengthy star-seeding session under my Chela pyramid in preparation. And then I thought I'd give the giant bonsai a trim.'

Chapter 10

Ian Craigie's effects had been released and Troy had gone to pick them up. The scene-of-crime report could not be far behind. Barnaby half hoped there would be something solid from Forensic to support the so far purely circumstantial evidence against Gamelin. If there wasn't, or if he was found to be straightforwardly not guilty, then the chief inspector had a case that looked fair to being one of the most interesting and complicated for a long time.

Almost his first reaction when hearing of his major suspect's demise was overwhelming relief. He had been quite near at one point the previous evening to taking the man in. Any custody death resulted, quite rightly, in a complete and careful investigation amidst the by now inevitable cries of 'police brutality'. Imagine the descent from above on Guy Gamelin's behalf: the tony lawyers, the Bill's top brass, every press man who could stand upright, photographers, probably questions in the House. . . . Gratitude had welled up in Barnaby's breast at the gods' collusion in this near miss.

Troy entered, a grey plastic bag in the crook of his right arm. 'Got our mystical dude's stuff here, Chief.' There was a nudge of anticipation in the words and his eyes shone. With slow dramatic movements he pulled out sandals, a bloodied robe and some cotton underpants. Then he paused looking alert and expectant.

'If you're waiting for a drum roll you'll be standing there till the cows come home. Get on with it.'

Troy at once delved into the bag, this time producing a long fall of shining white hair. Barnaby reached out. The wig was beautifully made. Real hair on a base of fine gauze.

'Very nice. Expensive.'

'Makes you think don't it, Chief?'

'It does indeed.'

Barnaby's pulse quickened. For the first time the dead man had revealed something of himself. Until now information had all been second-hand. What others remembered, thought, believed. But here was a direct revelation from beyond the grave. A primary source. Barnaby laid this basic staple of the actor's artillery aside and said, 'I wonder how many people knew he wore it?'

'No one I bet,' said Troy. 'I reckon this bears out Gamelin's theory. Part and parcel of the con man's gear.'

A not unreasonable assumption. In fact quite tempting. What need, pondered Barnaby, would a genuine pietist have of such a tricky accoutrement? No sooner had this thought occurred than he recollected the splendid dressage of priests and prelates to the world's more orthodox religions. A simple hairpiece appeared modest in comparison.

So Craigie used artificial aids to project an image that would reassure his followers. This did not necessarily argue that his teachings or persona were false or that some chicanery was afoot. And yet. . . .

Gamelin had been so definite. Was this simply, understandably, because of the trust fund? Or had it, as Troy supposed, been like genuinely sniffing out like? No harm in running a trace on Craigie, although nailing a con man was always bloody hard work. For a start they were forever on the move and had as many names as they had off-shore bank accounts. Second, the really fly ones, having never been nicked, would not be in the computer at all. Still, no harm in trying.

'I got an idea about the glove as well, Chief,' said Troy. 'Something Maure said at breakfast.' His voice took on a slightly sour tinge as he recalled the first meal of the day. The meal which was supposed to gird the family breadwinner's loins till lunch time. This morning it had been cornflakes and tea and that not freshly made. One small baby and suddenly it was too much trouble to scramble some eggs, put a bit of bacon under the grill, fry a few mushrooms and sling some bread in the toaster. He'd had to shell out for a burger and chips in the canteen. Second time this week and it was still only Thursday. And now the desk was giving him dirty looks.

'Problem, Chief?'

'*Glove*.'

'Oh – yeh. She was washing up, grumbling that the gloves never last five minutes. I wasn't listening – well, you don't do you? But I heard, "It's always the left one goes first." That clicked because ours was a left-hander. She said, "I used to have all these odd things piling up till I found you could buy them to fit either hand." So I thought, what if ours was like that?'

'Might be. Although there's nothing to stop a left-handed murderer wearing a right-handed glove. Or vice versa just to confuse the issue.'

'Makes holding the knife a bit more awkward, though. And that is a very slick mover we're talking about.'

'True.' Barnaby got up. 'Might as well get a check for Craigie started. They usually stick fairly closely to the original name. The initials might be the same for instance.'

'What'd he be . . . fifty-five? Sixty?'

'I'd say. Maybe a bit older. I'm going over to the path lab. See how they're doing.' He took his lightweight jacket from the peg. 'Then we'll try Felicity Gamelin again. See if we can get some sort of sensible statement.' He turned at the door. 'Get your aura read while we're at it.' Troy made a winding movement directed at his forehead with his index finger. Barnaby grinned. 'Your horoscope, then. What is it you're supposed to have been born under? Sirius the dog star?'

'If I was,' said Troy, 'I'll bet the little bugger was cocking its leg.'

Arno, having done a modest bit of gardening and eaten a piece of fruit to clarify his mind, was now wrestling with a haiku. His thoughts were all of May (the poem was of course for her). The haiku – three lines of five, seven and five syllables in which to compress a single illuminating thought – is not an easy form. The floor around Arno's chair was covered with screwed-up little balls of paper.

He sighed deeply, frustrated at the elusiveness of Thalia the poetic muse and at the general intractability of the English language.

> Beloved blossom
> Light-winged music-maker
> Spirit of flame.

He couldn't give her that. To start with it sounded incomplete, like the opening to a much longer work. Then there was that 'beloved'. These endearments would creep in. All the abandoned pensées had at least one. And let's face it, thought Arno moodily, if a person was addressed as 'bosom's ease', 'angel fluff', or 'honey cuddle-bun', sooner or later, however unsophisticated that person might be, she was going to deduce something a tad warmer in the offing than mere friendship or respect.

Cross, and dry in the mind, Arno gave up pro tem and went over to the basin to wash his hands which had become rather stained. He had bought the finest parchment, a bottle of sepia-coloured 'Indian' ink and a calligrapher's pen, feeling that only the very best materials would be worthy of his sacred task. But, being normally a Biro man, he couldn't get the hang of the nib and the ink had spattered everywhere.

Scrubbing at his hands and knuckles, a depressed Arno stared at himself in the small flaky mirror. He would never be reconciled to his appearance, never in a million years. If only he were tall and handsome as the full moon! He would sweep her off her feet then; gallop away with her over his saddle on a wonderful barrel-chested white horse with jewelled harness and reins of gold.

Arno smiled at these imaginings. His mother would have called it 'going all rhapsodical'. He studied his face and tugged his beard, parting it experimentally, curling the ends around his fingers.

He had tried a Blakeian beard, quiverful of life, tumbling all over his chest. But it hadn't suited him. He'd looked like a dwarf with a doormat round his chin. The one he had was . . . well . . . neat. And at least it shone, for he treated it with henna regularly. Sometimes he thought he might look younger if he shaved it off.

Before turning away, Arno bathed his face in greenish water taken from a small bowl half full of saxifrage. Heather had assured him that it was superb for fading freckles but he'd been using the stuff for over a month now and he honestly couldn't see much difference. He dried himself and put the towel back neatly. It was almost time for lunch.

With ten minutes to go, Janet had just got some sort of main course together. She had peered half-heartedly into the store cupboard, taking things out, putting them back before deciding on a packet of Sossomix. There was a drawing of granulated sausage shapes sizzling in a pan and Janet noted, not for the first time, the perverse labelling techniques adapted by firms catering to that ever-growing section of the population who loathed eating meat.

Nut Steaks, Veggie Burgers, Cashew Roast. Down at the Karmic Pulse, they offered Tofu, shaped like chicken legs and covered with soya grits. Quite indistinguishable, the cling wrap proudly assured customers, from the real thing.

Wool-gathering, Janet had poured too much water in the granules. Instead of being a nice firm malleable lump, it was all sloppy. Trying to drain off the excess, she'd allowed some of the mix to slip away. Fed up with the whole business, Janet dumped the bowl on the draining board and went back upstairs to try and talk out Trixie.

After practically pushing everyone who was trying to help from the room, Trixie had locked the door. Nothing odd in that but she would usually answer when someone knocked, if it was only to ask why people just couldn't leave her in peace. But today – not a sound.

There was something so solid about the silence, thought Janet, rapping gently and calling, 'Trixie – lunch. . . .' It was so absolutely total. Not so much as a carpeted footfall. Hard to believe there was even a heart beating in there.

Looking round to check that she was unobserved, and still feeling vulgarly inquisitive, Janet knelt down and peered through the keyhole. All she could see was a section of Trixie's unmade bed. Blushing, she scrambled up again.

When she got back to the kitchen she found that Christopher, who had slipped out to the village, had returned with a sinfully large chocolate cake 'to jolly everyone up'.

'But Heather's done a tapioca roulade for pudding with a fig glaze,' she pointed out.

'Exactly!'

Janet laughed and was further cheered to discover that the Sossomix had absorbed the remaining water and was firm enough to shape and fry. She lit the gas under the spinach and suggested Christopher call the others.

He found Heather on the terrace in a royal-blue track suit. She was intoning, arms stretched high to connect with telluric energy lines.

> 'I take movement into my very essence
> I take runningness and jumpingness
> I *am* run . . . I *am* jump. . . .'

She started to bound about on the spot then, her huge bosom and bum quivering like giant jellies. About to call that lunch was ready, Christopher was halted by an explosion of lyricism.

> 'Every little cell in my body is happee. . . .
> Every little cell in my body is well. . . .'

Christopher was familiar with Heather's paen to holistic positivism. She taught it to all her clients no matter how dreadworthy their disease. He placed himself in front of her and mouthed 'food'.

She panted, 'Kenny . . . office . . . go . . .' and pogoed off round the side of the house.

Ken was organising some posters for their next marriage workshop (On A Clear Day You Can See Each Other), resting his aleatory limb on the desk whilst the Gestetner chugged along.

'Lunch is ready,' panted his spouse, popping her head round the door.

'About time,' said Ken. 'I'm starving.'

'Sorry but things are sure to be a bit chaotic on a day like this.' Heather wheezed in, picking up a poster. It was pale blue and showed two doves, one with long eyelashes wearing a pinny, the other stark-naked but for a fair smattering of white feathers. This one had its wing around the other one's middle. Beneath it were Ken and Heather's names and after Ken's (in brackets) 'Intuitive Diagnostician, Writer, Channeller'. Heather was down as 'Healer, Writer, Priestess'. She said, 'This should really bring them in. I hope it'll still be on – I mean with all this upset.'

'I resonate with that, Heth,' said Ken, easing down his leg, 'but hang loose. I've something to share.'

'Oh – what is it?' Heather sat with some difficulty, cross-legged on the carpet.

'Well, you know my theory – never do one job when you could be doing three.' Heather nodded. 'So, while I was producing this lot, I also used my thought-energy web to tune into Hilarion about our future here.'

'Brilliant. What did he say?'

'Wouldn't tell me, the old reprobate – oops!' Ken put his head in his lap and covered it with his hands as if protecting himself from a rock fall. 'Sorry, Hilarion . . .' he called through his fingers. 'Only joking.' He sat up then and continued. 'But he did zero in with some info of his own. Nothing less than a complete world-overview of the cosmic and global situation. There was a special reference to the holes in the ozone layer and – talk about a paradigm shift – *they are nothing whatsoever to worry about.*'

'What? I can't believe. . . .' Hope and incredulity fought it out in Heather's shining face.

'It's true. Comes directly from the Original Silent Fourfold Column. You know how the waters break when a baby's born? Well, this is precisely the same process. As we all know, there's a great spiritual outpouring from the angelic realms at this particular moment in time. Now, how can this get through if apertures are not made in the heavens?'

His wife clapped her hands in wonder. 'I never thought of that.'

'Talk about profound. The old fox.'

'So all this changing aerosols and fridges and things — '

'Complete waste of time.'

Heather galumphed to her feet. 'We must share this with the others.'

'And then with the world.'

Crossing the hall towards the dining room, Ken checked the 'Feeling Guilty' bowl as he always did when passing. There was no money in it today, but he did find something else. A key with a tag on reading '25'. The key to Trixie's room.

The afternoon was hot. Both the windows in Barnaby's office were open but there was little breeze. It was Policewoman Brierley's twenty-second and someone had had the wit to lob in ice and a huge bag of lemons as well as assorted cakes and pastries. The chief inspector had a frosted glass of tart, freshly made lemonade in one hand and was eating his doughnut in a very circumspect manner, trying to keep the filling off his shirt and off the mass of material om his desk, which included the recently delivered scenes-of-crime report.

A chorus of 'Happy Birthday' wafted through the half-open door and he could see his sergeant perched on Audrey's desk. Troy was holding some computer sheets and singing away, his eyes on her black-stockinged knees.

She'd come on a lot in the last three years had little Audrey, thought Barnaby. Earlier on she'd been really shy, not knowing how to handle flirtatious come-ons or chauvinistic put-downs, which in any case often came joined at the hip, like unkind Siamese twins. The girls that stuck it toughened up. As Barnaby watched, catching scarlet confectioner's jelly just in time, Troy leaned forward with a predatory leer, murmuring something, winking. Audrey winked and murmured back. There was an explosion of laughter and the sergeant walked away.

'She used to be really sweet, that girl,' he said angrily, flourishing the print-out. 'Dead feminine – know what I mean?'

'I think she's quite sweet now, actually.'

'Pay them a compliment – jump down your throat.'

The compliment had gone as follows. Troy: 'I'll take you for a drink to celebrate. Somewhere really smart. How about that snug little place on the river? You'll have a good time. They don't call me up-and-coming for nothing.' Audrey: 'Use it to stir your tea, Gavin.'

'Women who are coarse just show themselves up – don't you think, Chief?'

Barnaby, reading, said: 'No Craigie on these.'

Troy made an effort to become unchagrined. 'I checked on similar names as well. There's a Brian Craig in there. Insurance fraud. Died in Broadmoor.'

'Must have been some territory.' Barnaby rarely made a joke. This one died on its feet.

'There's more to come. I'm waiting on a Cranleigh and Crawshaw.' He sounded very bright and positive. 'I'm convinced Gamelin was right. Feel it in my bones.'

Troy was always feeling things in his bones. They were about as reliable as a Saint Bernard that had been at the brandy.

'Anything in scenes-of-crime, sir?'

'Not a lot.'

Troy read the two closely typed sheets. Nothing on the glove – which was to be expected. And nothing on anything else much either. A magnified picture of the fibrous thread which had been caught up on the knife.

'Bit of a pisser, that,' he said when he'd finished. 'Doesn't look as if it came off anyone's gear.' Mind you – not everyone was wearing the sort of clothes that could conceal it. May Cuttle's dress had long floaty sleeves but she's out. Could have passed it to somebody though. Hey – maybe she slipped it to Wainwright. Because there's no way he could have brought it in himself. Tight jeans, sneakers, short-sleeved shirt.'

'He didn't go near the dais either.'

'So who's left? The dykey woman wore trousers – she could've brought it in. The blonde might have found it difficult. Gibbs could have had it up his jumper. Gamelin and the Beavers could have hidden it and that lad with one oar out of the water. He wore a baggy sweater. Or Gamelin's wife – she could have had a whole canteen of cutlery in that dress. Same goes for her daughter in the sari.'

Troy's mouth pursed with a *moue* of distaste. If there was one thing that turned him up, it was white women dressing like blacks. 'If that girl was mine,' he muttered, 'I'd drag her home, wash that red muck off under the tap and give her a good clout.'

'But people are not "ours", Sergeant. They're not cars or washing machines. You've forgotten someone.'

'No I haven't.' Barnaby pointed to the wall sketch. '*Craigie*?' Troy laughed in disbelief. 'Well, he's not going to give the murderer a hand by smuggling a knife in, is he?'

'He was there. We shouldn't exclude him. What do we keep, Troy?'

'An open mind, sir,' sighed Troy, thinking some people's minds had been kept so open their brains had fallen out.

'Have a look and see if there's any more of those doughnuts.'

Janet was searching Trixie's room. She knew there was no point. She had searched it twice already, first in a whirling hawk-eyed frenzy of disbelief then more slowly, systematically turning out every drawer. She looked beneath the mattress and rugs and through pages of books and, once, in a moment of barmy desperation, pulled out the basket in the fire grate. But she found no clue as to where Trixie might have fled.

What Janet was really looking for, of course, was a letter. But there was no trace of any such thing. Not even thrown-way scraps from which an address might be pieced together. And there was nothing on file in the office either. Trixie's first inquiry was by telephone, and this had been followed by a weekend visit which had extended itself indefinitely once bursary help was found to be available.

Janet was almost as distressed by the intensity of her misery as by the misery itself. How had she let herself get into such a state? The progress had been so insidious. At first she hadn't even liked Trixie. The girl had struck her as shallow and silly, and they'd had nothing whatsoever in common. Then, gradually, she had started to admire and eventually envy the younger girl's soubrettish character. Her assurance and smart backchat. Born into a tradition of polite reticence, Janet frequently found herself either tongue-tied or constrained by good manners from speaking her mind.

She had realised quite early on that Trixie was not a true seeker. Was not in fact very interested at all in the higher realm. She had attended meditation, had interviews with the Master and slipped a few genuflective remarks into various semi-religious discussions but Janet knew her heart wasn't in it. It struck her once that Trixie only went this far to be sure of keeping her foot in the door. Janet had often longed to ask why she was at the Windhorse in the first place but had never dared. Trixie always said that if there was one thing she could not stand it was nosiness.

Now, sitting at the dressing table, the roses still blushing in their bowl and feeling quite ill with loss and longing, Janet opened the top drawer for the umpteenth time and regarded all that was left of Trixie. A half-full packet of Tampax, a pink lacy angora jumper smelling under the arms and some 'airport' novels, ill-written and virtually (Janet had dipped into a couple) porno-graphic, although any virtue seemed to have been vanquished by page seven.

Janet was sure that Trixie had disappeared because she was afraid. And that it was something to do with Guy Gamelin. Even in death that monstrous man exuded the power to harm. Janet pictured Trixie alone and frightened, running, running. Had she any money? Surely she wouldn't try to hitch a lift. Not after all the terrible stories one heard. She must have left sometime between half eleven and twelve. Perhaps creeping through the hall with her blue-wheeled suitcase while Janet was just a few feet away in the kitchen. Oh God!

She sprang up, her arms wrapped straight-jacket-tight across her chest. Now more than any other was the time when Trixie would need her friendship. And Janet had so much to give. She could feel it lying, a great heavy lump, where her heart should be. She seemed to have been carrying it all her life and it grew heavier every day.

She caught sight of herself in the glass. Her hair was wild, skin stretched tight over beaky nose. She faced the thought that Trixie might never return and a terrible sensation of time passing snatched at her throat. A concentrated sense of loss. The bleakness of it almost brought her to her knees. She felt she was facing a long, unendurable twilight without ever having known the glory of the day.

She'd read once that the intensity of a really powerful emotion could kill recollection. Janet felt she could handle such oblivion. Loving Trixie in a poignant cauterised way, like a misplaced memory. There was something clean and austere about this conclusion. The absolute certainty of naught for your comfort was almost a comfort in itself. She would walk alone bearing in mind the harsh and deeply unsatisfactory epigram that the only sure way to get what you want in life is to want what you get.

'Settle' was the term her mother would have used. 'I'll settle for that' Janet remembered her saying about a length of fabric or a piece of meat or a knitting pattern. Janet had always understood the phrase to mean 'It's not what I want but it's better than nothing.'

But no sooner had Janet decided to settle for nothing than an agonised longing for human contact, for a flicker of warmth to light the way, devoured her, and she buried her face in the scented roses and wept.

Christopher and Suhami were in the study. She gazing out of the window, he sitting at the barley-twist one-legged table at which Barnaby had conducted the interviews. There was a small pigskin case by Christopher's feet and on the table a large unsealed brown envelope. Three days' neglect of the room had occasioned a layer of dust over everything.

The couple were talking about death. Suhami in the driven, irritable manner of one who is drawn to reinvestigate an unhealed wound. Christopher, who was also getting irritable, with great reluctance.

'It's impossible, isn't it?' she was saying, 'to imagine what it's like to be dead. You picture yourself looking down at your funeral. People weeping, all the flowers. But you have to be alive to do the imagining.'

'I suppose. Can't we talk about something else?' When she did not reply he hefted the case on to a hard-backed chair. 'We could get your father's things sorted.'

'What is there to sort? It's only clothes. Next time someone goes into Causton they can take them to a charity shop.'

'There's this envelope as well.'

'I know, I know. I signed for them didn't I?'

'Calm down.' He shook out the contents. Guy's wallet, his keys, handkerchief, cigar-cutter and lighter. An empty brown glass bottle. A small card, crumpled as if someone had clutched it tight, holding an engraved message from Ian and Fiona (Props). Christopher turned the card over. An elf in curly toed shoes pointed a little wand at a line of italicised prose: *Our true intent is all for your delight. Wm Shakespeare*. There was something else in the envelope. Right at the bottom.

Christopher slid in his hand and removed the watch. It lay on his palm, dazzlingly splendid; nothing but jewels and facets of light. He gasped (he couldn't help it) and knew she had turned

217

round. When he looked up, Suhami was watching him, the expression on her face unreadable. He lay the watch down and it blazed like a star against the dusty rose-brown wood. When he felt that he could speak without avarice shining through he said, 'What do you think? Should we give these things to your mother?'

'Hardly.' Suhami came over. 'The last thing she needs is that sort of reminder. It's because of him she's in the state she is.'

'This bottle's empty.'

'Heart pills.'

'He had time to take them, then.'

'So it seems.'

'There's something stuffed in this wallet.' Silvery cream and fawn alligator scales, it bulged slightly on one side. Christopher placed his finger into the aperture and a cloud of confetti-like stuff flittered out. He caught some pieces in his hand. 'It's money.'

'How grotesque.' Suhami stared down at the scattered fragments. She felt irrationally frightened. 'He would never do that. Unless. . . .' Briefly she entertained a vision of Guy *in extremis* finally apprehending the useless futility of his massive wealth and symbolically ripping apart a high-denomination bank note. Almost immediately she rejected this sentimental indulgence for the nonsense that it was.

'Unless what?'

'I don't know. He was very . . . strung out. Emotional. When we talked in the afternoon, I felt quite sorry for him. Not that I let him see.'

'Why ever not?'

'He despised any show of kindness. He just thought it meant you were weak.'

'He sounds a bit sad.'

'Don't waste your finer feelings,' said Suhami. 'That's when he took the knife don't forget. Oh – put the bloody things back. No – wait. . . .' She picked up the watch and with one quick movement thrust it towards him. 'Here – have it.'

'What?'

'Take it.' He stared, incredulous. 'Go on.'

Christopher swallowed. His eyes turned slowly to the watch as if pulled by a silken thread. 'You can't mean it.'

'Why not?'

'I don't know. It's so incredibly . . . so. . . .' He knew the longing was vivid on his face but couldn't help himself. 'Who does it belong to?'

'Me. He always said he'd leave me everything.'

'But you can't just. . . .' The same thread now lifted his arm, uncurled his fingers, stretched out his hand.

'Of course I can.' She made a sort of dart towards him, dropped the watch in his palm and withdrew.

'Are you sure?'

'Quite sure.' She had already moved quite away. 'Sell it if you like. Buy yourself what the agents call a nice des res. But please don't wear it if you're anywhere near me.'

Christopher slipped the watch into his pocket. It weighed nothing. He was excited by the magnitude of the gift but also faintly aggravated by the casual manner in which it had been offered. Almost dangled under his nose. He then got the notion that the whole business was some sort of test which, by accepting the watch, he had failed. He was certainly aware of a tension emanating from her that he didn't understand. Then it struck him that it might be some sort of consolation prize and that she had already decided to go her own way without him. This perception made him angry and not only because of the humiliating 'pay off' connotations. He would rather have Suhami than any timepiece, no matter how magnificent.

It was gone three by the time Barnaby and Troy drove up to the Manor House and May greeted them. She was looking wondrously flamboyant in a multicoloured striped djellaba with a beaten copper belt.

'Ah – there you are.' As if they had been personally summoned. 'I'm so glad. I've something to tell you.'

219

'Oh yes, Miss Cuttle?' Barnaby followed her into the hall. The house seemed still and quiet but for the faint clatter of crockery. He noted and commented on the marvellous spillage of painterly light from the lantern.

'We bathe in it, Chief Inspector. We saturate our psyches. At least once a day. Never underestimate the healing power of colour. Perhaps you would care . . . ?'

'Another time, perhaps. What did you wish—?'

'Not here.' She walked speedily off, beckoning as she went. This was accomplished by holding her arm straight up above her head and swivelling her hand back and forth. Barnaby was reminded of a submarine's conning tower.

Her hair was piled on top of her head today. A shapely coronet of loops, waves, sausage-like curls and a frilly fringe which, on a women less formidably Rubenesque, might have been described as saucy. They followed her without difficulty. Indeed such was the magnetic pull of her flowing draperies that it seemed impossible to do otherwise. She ushered them into a room, glanced intently up and down the corridor, then closed the door.

After these urgent preliminaries, Barnaby expected an immediate flood of informative speech, but she waited – wrinkling her splendid Romanish nose and delicate nostrils. Eventually she said, 'There are some extremely negative, not to say thorny vibrations here.' Her gaze swivelled sternly between the two men. 'I rather think it's you.' Troy raised his eyebrows, Joe Cool. 'I must ask for a few moments' grace to re-establish positive ions and restore my vitality index.'

She sat down at a small round table covered by an orange bobble-fringed chenille cloth, rested her elbows against the edge and closed her eyes. A minute ambled slowly by, followed, as is the way of things, by several more.

Is there anybody there? wondered Troy. He hoped it wasn't his Aunty Doris. He'd owed her fifty quid when she'd got knocked down by a Ford Sierra and she'd an edge to her tongue like a buzz saw.

'Oh! Buoyant rays!
Float in me restoring quantum peace
Effloresce and harmonise in Vesta's all-seeing eye
Ida and Pingala – cross my nodes.'

At the first declarative boom, Troy nearly jumped from his skin. Barnaby studied his shoes, refusing to catch his sergeant's eye. He noticed another larger table in the far corner holding many bottles of bright liquid. Nostra for the credulous no doubt. May inhaled and exhaled deeply a few more times, looked around and gave a calm and welcoming smile.

'There. Isn't that better? Are you quite comfortable?' Barnaby nodded. Troy continued to stare thornily out of the window.

'I did not sleep last night as I'm sure you can appreciate but, resting briefly before luncheon, I fell into a slight doze during which I was visited by the green Master Rakowkzy. He gives advice on legal matters, as I expect you know, and he said I ought to talk to you.'

'I see,' lied the chief inspector, rather stymied by this 'hey presto!' introduction.

'It isn't anything to do with the Master's elevation but another matter entirely. I'd been worried for some time and had just decided to talk to Christopher about it when the meteor fell and that put it right out of my head. We didn't realise at the time it was a portent.' Mistaking the controlled blankness of Barnaby's expression for incomprehension, she added kindly, 'That means omen, you know.'

'Yes,' said the chief inspector.

May glanced over to the window where Troy was pressing his head hard against the pane. 'I say – is your sergeant all right?'

'He's fine.'

'I'm afraid,' said May, 'I can no longer play the dromedary with my head in the sand. There is definitely something going on.'

Dear God, thought Barnaby, up to our oxters in murder and there's something going on.

'It all started after Jim Carter left us.'

'I don't recall the name, Miss Cuttle.'

'No. He died before you met him.'

Barnaby didn't even try on that one. 'And who was he?'

'Oh, a dear person. One of our longest-serving members. He had an accident – a fatal fall. I'm surprised you don't know about it.'

'Not our pigeon – accidental death.'

'There was an inquest.' May regarded Barnaby in a rather judgemental manner as if he'd been caught smoking in the bike shed. 'It was a day or two after his death when I was on my way to the laundry that I overheard the argument. Or a bit of it. The door was ajar in the Master's sanctum. Someone said: "What have you done? If they decide on a post mor—" Then they were shushed and the door was closed.'

'Did you see who it was?'

'There was a screen in the way.'

'Was it Mr Craigie speaking, do you think?' Barnaby leaned forwards as he spoke. Troy stopped massaging the window and turned into the room, his eyes wide and sharp. The air tightened.

'I don't know. The voice was so knotted up. But when the inquest came and there was a proper coroner's report and everything seemed to be all right, I thought I was probably reading too much into it. Then, a couple of weeks later, I was woken by a noise in the middle of the night. Soft bumps as if furniture was being carefully moved about and slidy sounds like the opening and closing of drawers.'

'Where was this?' asked Troy.

'Next door – Jim's room. It was never locked so why do all this creeping about? Why not just go openly in the daytime?'

'Perhaps a break-in,' suggested Barnaby.

'Not at all,' said May and explained about the person running down the side of the house.

'Didn't you think of contacting the police?'

'Well, you know, we don't do that sort of thing here.' May gave Troy a smile with a consoling pat in it. 'I'm sure you're very good but it might have caused real psychological damage.'

'Do you think he – or she – when running away could have heard your window open? I assume they would know your room was adjacent.'

'I suppose that's possible.' She glanced up at him with clear bright eyes. 'Is it important?'

Troy took in the question with a mixture of awe and disbelief. Here was a woman who drove a car, handled the company finance, dealt with banking matters and looked after sometimes quite large numbers of visitors. All these accomplishments existing alongside a shining belief in archangels, extra-terrestrial domestic and legal help, plus an astrally spot-on blade artist who'd despatched the head gaffer, no messing. He watched her giving the chief, who was looking excessively pained, a gentle touch on the arm.

'Are you feeling quite well, Inspector Barnaby?'

Barnaby cleared his throat, a dryish scrape. May appeared concerned. 'A tense larynx can conceal grave kidney problems.' This formidable diagnosis having being received calmly, she added: 'I can get my passionflower inhaler in a twinkling.' Barnaby went into a constrained but unequivocal retreat.

Doesn't want that at his time of life, observed Troy. Randy old devil. Should be slowing down.

Barnaby sensed that May was disappointed. She shook her head a little sorrowfully but her opulent assurance remained undimmed. It was plain she was one of those people who must always be helping others. He had no doubt that she was genuinely kind, but suspected that the kindness would manifest itself in a rather narrow application of her own principles to the problem in hand, rather than a real attempt to seek out the supplicant's needs.

'Perhaps we could have a look at Mr Carter's room?'

'There's nothing there. All his things have gone.'

'Even so. . . .'

'A tip, Inspector,' she set off still talking, 'which you should find very useful. Pull up an amaranth by the root – Friday of the full moon otherwise it doesn't work – fold in a clean white cloth, which must be linen, and wear next to the skin. This will make you bullet-proof.'

'The police supply garments for that purpose, Miss Cuttle.'

'I say – turn left – do they really?' She became intensely interested. 'Are you wearing one now? Could I have a look?'

May's eyes shone and her amber globe earrings shone too. She found herself thinking that being involved in an investigation was proving to be quite exciting. And wondered perhaps if the Windhorse, in refusing to give houseroom to a radio or television set or printed matter of a non-spiritual nature, was not only blotting out all negative vibrations but also a certain amount of lively colour. I should get out more, she thought, and felt immediately shamed by such disloyalty.

'Would you say I was "helping with your inquiries", Inspector?' she stopped outside the room next to her own. 'I've often wondered exactly what that phrase meant.'

But she had hardly formed the words when the door had been opened, herself courteously thanked, and the door closed again.

Barnaby and Troy looked about them. The place was as neat as a sailor's. A minimum of furniture. Two pale oak chairs with high slatted backs which a smart dealer might have sold as Shaker, a single bed, a card table, a wardrobe containing an empty shoebox, the label showing smart Italian loafers, and a chest of drawers. There were three hooks screwed into a plain piece of wood on the far wall. The coverlet on the bed was white roughish cotton, the sort found on iron bedsteads in men's lodging houses. It was hospital-cornered, stretched with tight rigidity over the thin mattress. This straining air of self-effacement sat well with the rest of the room. It had such a feeling of puritanical restraint that any loose fold or wrinkle would have appeared pushily voluptuous. There was a text on the otherwise bare walls: God Is A Circle Whose Centre Is Everywhere And Circumference Nowhere.

Troy checked the chest of drawers. Empty. Barnaby stared around, wondering at this apparent confirmation of the necessary link between physical discomfort and spiritual attainment. He thought of mendicants in hair-shirts, self-flagellation, yogis sitting in caves for years – matty-haired, ash daubed and smelly; of martyrs rushing into flames or the jaws of great tawny cats. The chief inspector could see neither rhyme nor reason to it. He loved his comforts. A well-used armchair at the end of the day. Or a hammock on a summer evening, glass of wine to hand, music pouring through open French windows. He loved – how he still loved – going to bed with Joyce. Or sitting by a warm fire, sketching the still unblurred lines of her profile.

The chief inspector was not given to dwelling at length on philosophical matters, not only because he didn't have the time but also because the pursuit seemed to him ultimately arid. He tried to live decently. Cared for his wife and daughter, did a worthwhile job as well as he was able and supported half a dozen charities when subscriptions were due. He had few friends, having been content to spend the little spare time that was his lot with his family, but the friends he did have had good cause to be grateful for his attention and concern if they were troubled. Overall he reckoned he hadn't done too badly. Well enough, perhaps, to tip the scales positively should there prove to be such a metaphysically mischievous joke as Judgement Day.

'Not much to show for a life, is it sir?' Troy had wandered over to the book shelves. Three wooden planks separated by neat stacks of amethyst-coloured bricks. He crouched, pulling out a volume from the bottom layer. 'There's a book here on wolf messing.' He passed it over. 'My autobiography by R. R. Hood.' And chortled.

Barnaby could never decide whether his sergeant's happy appreciation of his own wit was truly ingenuous. It seemed unkind to think so. He looked at the spine. The tome was by Wolf Messing, described on the jacket as 'Russia's greatest psychic healer'. Barnaby pulled a book of his own out. *Deathing: An Intelligent Alternative for the Final Moments of Life* by Anya Foos-Graber. Much cheered by the news that there was going to be a choice, the chief inspector was only sorry that poor old Jim had failed to grasp the principles. Either that or he'd been given no time to bring his intelligence into play.

'Better check them all – you never know.'

The two men pulled out each volume, shaking them, leafing through. Barnaby, expecting to find evidence only of cultural vassalage to the East, was pleasantly surprised. Sufism, Buddhism, Druidic Lore, Myths and Legends, Runecraft, the Rosicrucian, a Jung primer. There was also the *I Ching*, books on UFOs, *The Tao of Physics*, and the *Arkana Dictionary of New Perspectives*. They were mostly paperbacks and all second-hand. Top whack three pounds seventy-five, the cheapest twenty-five pence.

'He must have had some personal stuff, Chief?' Troy riffled through the last volume and put it back carefully. 'Most people have got at least a birth certificate, a few photographs. You can't exist with just the clothes on your back and a few books.'

'Monks do.'

'Oh well . . . monks.' Troy's tone was so deeply uncomprehending he might have been referring to men from Mars. Barnaby picked up *The Meaning of Happiness*. What man would not?

'One here by a yogi, sir. Yogi Bear actually. Ten exciting ways with porridge.'

'If all you can find to do is make daft jokes you can clear off and interview Mrs Gamelin.'

'Right. Any idea where she is?'

'You've got a tongue in your head. Ask. You know what we want.'

I know what I want. A nice long tasty puff. Troy opened the door and nearly fell over May who immediately offered to take him to Felicity. On the way she gave him many an encouraging glance, stopping at one point to suggest that he should refrain from cutting his hair so short as it served as an antenna for cosmic forces.

'The Temple of Victory on Venus is open to our consciousness on the seventeenth of this month. Would you care to join us for a little healing ceremony?' Troy looked exceedingly nonplussed. 'You do need healing, you know. Very, very badly.' Thinking his silence meant indecision, she continued, 'And we treat the whole person here. You see when you're ill outside you just get some drug on prescription. Or if you're hospitalised surgeons pay attention to the organ in question and not the person behind it at all.'

Troy who had spent his entire adult life searching for a female with just such a talent for disinterested application, checked a hankering sigh. 'Yeh . . . well . . . bit busy at the moment. New baby and that. . . .'

Leaving Troy on the landing, May entered Felicity's room then re-emerged saying, 'She's awake but her force-field is still very low so would you—'

'We'll be fine, Miss Cuttle.'

Troy hardly recognised Felicity. She was sitting in bed propped up by pillows, straight hair tied back with some sort of plaited stuff, wearing a blue silk robe. The nicest thing about the following interrogation, to the sergeant's mind, was that he smoked all the way through without asking her permission. This minuscule bit of point scoring (sans-culotte 5, aristo nil) was rather undermined by the fact that she hardly seemed to notice, let alone be at all put out.

In fact she didn't seem much more *compos mentis* than yesterday. And hardly remembered where she was sitting on the dais or who was next to her. Troy wondered if she'd just blotted the murder out. Let's face it, being in the same room while one was being committed was enough to unbalance anybody, and if you were ten pence short of a quid to start with. . . .

Questioned on her feelings regarding the McFadden Fund and its disposal, she became quite agitated and said she'd known nothing about it. On being told her husband certainly had, she added, 'Trust him.' Then, 'He'd fight it with everything he'd got.'

'It's the girl's inheritance, Mrs Gamelin. Up to her surely?'

'Whose money it was would make no difference.' She became

extremely distressed and started tossing her head about. Troy
decided to open the door. Before he had reached it she launched
upon a startling breakdown of her husband's physical and mental
distinguishing features. Troy, full of admiration at this talent for
picturesque abuse (the mildest phrase being 'frog-faced illegiti-
mate avaricious prick'), quite missed the fact that it was couched
in the imperfect present. When Felicity, panting, rested once
more upon the pillows he said primly, 'I don't think that's
very nice, Mrs Gamelin. He has just passed away after all.'

At this Felicity gave a loud cry and fell out of bed, hanging
upside down in a sort of swoon. May came running in.

'You stupid bugger, Gavin,' said Barnaby on their return to the
station.

'Well, how was I to know? She was lying there looking like
death warmed up. I assumed someone must have told her the
good news by then. Sir Sinjhan Farty was round there at ten
this morning.' He glared sullenly at the floor. 'I get blamed for
everything round here.

Whipping boy I am. Should have been a plumber. Or a lines-
man like my dad. But even as these grumbling alternatives
formed, Troy recognised they were dishonest. He had always
wanted to be a policeman, loved being a policeman, would never
wish to be anything else. But there were times when the carping,
the paper work, the brown nosing and double-declutch hand-
shakes, the soft attitudes of outsiders who never had to scrape
up the mess, the political in-fighting, the need to button your lip
if you wanted to get on and a thousand other day to day irritations
all coalesced and threatened to overwhelm him.

Noting the tightened mouth and strawberry patches on Troy's
cheekbones, Barnaby recognised that he had been unfair. The
assumption that Felicity had been told of her husband's death
was not an unreasonable one, although no doubt his sergeant
had handled matters unskilfully. Troy's modest level of academic
achievement was a very sore spot and calling him stupid was
striking where it hurt. Normally the chief inspector would have

thought 'tough' and let him get on with it. Today he was feeling benevolent.

'Mistake anyone could have made, Sergeant.'

'Sir.'

That was all it took. Troy's ego was back from the mender's in no time. Already he was wondering if this new indulgence was encouragement enough to broach the subject of Talisa Leanne tactfully. He murmured a few words. Just an oblique reference, nothing specific. Receiving an absent-minded nod, he immediately leapt into hyperbolic speech delineating the baby's charm, beauty, growth rate (height, teeth, hair, nails), speech development, teddy bear (handling and interrogation of), musical accomplishments (creative timpani-playing with saucepan lid) and artistic creativity. The latest drawing, Blu-tacked to the fridge, was the dead spit of her nanna's poodle.

Barnaby easily tuned out. He was back in the bare-boned room thinking about Jim Carter. A man serious in his devotions and friendly in his ways. And about the fragment of overheard conversation.

'What have you done? If they do a post mor—'

A post mortem? What else, two days after an unexplained death. So Craigie (perhaps) and at least one other had been afraid of such a procedure. And now Craigie was also dead. Were the two linked?

Speculation was fruitless at this stage. A waste of energy and a great spoiler of concentration. And God knows, thought Barnaby, I've enough on my plate to be going on with. The new information would have to go on the back burner and bide its time.

It did not have to bide long, for the very next day some information became available which threw a new and deeply disturbing light upon Jim Carter's death.

Chapter 11

Breakfast chez Barnaby. Cully and Joyce were sharing the *Independent*. Tom was sawing at something very soft, very pink, wet, white and streaky.

'I wish you'd cook bacon properly. Why can't we have it crisp?'

'Last time I did it crisp you said it was burnt.'

'It was burnt.'

'Talking of food,' Cully folded the paper and rested it on her knees, reached for another brioche, 'how's the chef-ing coming on, Dad?'

'I shall have to miss this week.'

'I mean for tomorrow night, silly.' She slathered on nearly white butter followed by lashings of black cherry jam and, without waiting for a reply, started reading again.

'I've done the first course but it might be wise to get something from Sainsbury's to follow up.'

'*Sainsbury's.*'

Joyce said, 'Don't talk with your mouth full.'

'This is my engagement dinner we're discussing. Plus my birthday.'

'I'll take us all out when the case is finished. Somewhere really nice.'

'Not the same.'

'I see that awful tycoon's made the front page.' Joyce opened up her section. 'With, I assume, an obit inside. I wonder what it says.'

'Did not suffer human beings gladly,' replied her husband.

'Bad as that?'

'I suppose it'd be a bit pushy to ask for a piece?' Barnaby stretched out his hand to no avail. 'Why do I never get what I want in this house?'

'We all love you, Dad.'

'I'd rather you let me have a look at the paper.' Barnaby wondered how long it would take before the press discovered that the newly deceased millionaire had been present only hours before when a murder was committed. No time at all was his conclusion and he hoped the Golden Windhorse was prepared.

Cully was chuckling again and the paper, held by slender fingers tipped with hot pink nails like glossy almonds, trembled. She was wearing a man's silk foulard dressing-gown, her long dark hair piled up and loosely pinned on top of her beautifully shaped head. A curl fell forward and she pushed it back with unmannered grace. Or was it mannered grace? It was never easy to tell where the daughter left off and the actress began. Barnaby had to remind himself – observing the sweet curve of her cheek, the soft unblemished apricot skin and baby fine golden down on her forearm – that this was a girl who'd been around. On the pill at sixteen, she'd also taken soft drugs during a punk-rock phase. Something she only told him about when it was over and done with. And now here she was, five years and God alone knew how many lovers later, looking as exquisite and untouched as a newly opened rose. Ah youth . . . youth. . . .

'What on earth's the matter Tom?'

'Mm?'

'Have you got indigestion?'

'No thanks to that bacon if I haven't. Well, if I can't share the paper,' he scowled at his daughter, 'perhaps I can share the joke?'

'A man who thought he'd been unfairly sentenced broke into the judge's chambers during recess and boiled his wig in an electric kettle.'

'I don't believe that. I do not believe that.'

'It's true.'

'Show me.' It almost worked. The paper was nearly passed across. Then at the last minute snatched back.

Joyce laughed, started to read out bits from her section; the weather, a recipe, a detailed account of someone squatting up a tree to save the whales.

'Won't find many whales up there,' said Barnaby.

'There was another car bomb at the weekend,' rustle, rustle. 'The victim was someone in the UDR. It says he's emigrating to Canada.'

'Quite a blast then.' Cully grinned at her father.

'That's not very funny, darling.'

'Is this murder at Compton Dando' – Joyce peered over the edge – 'the one you're working on?'

'Yes.'

'Why didn't you say so?'

'I did.'

'You just said "out Iver way".'

'What does it—'

'That's absolutely typical.' Joyce folded her paper and slapped it on the table, upsetting a salt cellar. Barnaby's hand crept out.

'Don't you dare!' snapped his wife.

'Do you know what's got into your mother this morning?'

Cully gazed out of the window at the flowering jasmine – refusing, as she always did, to collude or take sides.

'Don't discuss me as if I'm invisible, Tom. It's infuriating.'

'All right. So what's supposed to be typical of me this time?'

'You don't talk to me.'

'My God, Joycey – I've been talking to you about my job for twenty years. I'd've thought you'd be glad of a break.'

'And – what is worse – you don't listen.' Barnaby sighed. 'I bet you don't remember Ann Cousins.'

'Who?'

'I thought so. My friend at Compton Dando.'

'Ah.'

'Last year after Alan died this Manor House lot did a workshop called New Horizons, which she thought might help. A great

233

disappointment as it turned out. All style and no content. We both went.'

'What? Why didn't you tell me?'

'I *did* tell you.' Joyce smiled with a certain grim satisfaction. 'In great detail. Even when your body's at home your mind's at work. You have no interest in anything I do.'

'That's grossly unfair. I'm always down at the theatre painting scenery. I never miss one of your shows—'

'You missed the last one.'

'Two children had been abducted. Or perhaps *you* don't remember—'

'Poppy Levine's getting married.'

Cully's voice, loud and clear, sliced through the deepening acrimony. Her parents, choosing to believe their daughter was becoming upset, immediately ceased hostilities.

Cully, merely bored, continued: 'In a skirt up to her cleavage and sequinned leggings.'

'I'm late.' Barnaby got up. 'We'll talk about this visit of yours when I get home.'

'Suddenly I'm interesting,' said Joyce sourly. She got up, too, and moved behind Cully's chair where she lowered her greying curly head and scowled at the wedding picture. 'Six husbands and she looks about twenty-one. How does she do it?'

'Rumour is she sold her epidermis to the devil. Look at that.' Cully flicked the paper hard with her nail. 'It really gets me the way they always print how old a woman is. Poppy Levine, thirty-nine, marries cameraman Christopher Wainwright. No mention of his age – Dad!' The *Indy* was snatched away. 'Don't be so bloody rude!'

Barnaby scanned, shook out the relevant page, folded it.

'There's an interview with Nick Hytner on the back of that . . . *Dad*. . . .'

'What is it?' said Joyce. 'Something to do with the case?'

'Sorry.' Barnaby shrugged on his jacket. 'Take too long to explain.'

'There you go again. That's exactly what I mean.' The door

slammed. Joyce turned to Cully and repeated herself. 'That's *exactly* what I mean.'

Troy sped along the A40. Fast, easy, relaxed, enjoying his superior position as the one who knows. His passenger did little drum rolls on his blue-denimed knees. Before that he had played with a packet of Polos in the glove compartment, then fiddled with his seat belt until Troy had sharply instructed him to desist.

'But what does he want to see me for?'

'I couldn't rightly say, sir.'

'I'm sure you could rightly say if it suited you.'

Troy was not to be provoked. Nor was he unwise enough to show his pleasure at having a member of the great British public sweating away, supplicant and vulnerable, at his side. He was especially pleased that it was Wainwright whom he'd had down as a swaggering bastard – although in the sergeant's book this meant no more than a simple refusal to be struck all of a heap at the sight of a CID warrant card.

'I expect it's about the murder?'

'Probably, Mr Wainwright.' Troy tightened his lips to check a smile. He'd really enjoyed saying 'Mr Wainwright'. Playing the bloke along. He enjoyed it so much that, swinging into Uxbridge turn off, he said it again.

'Won't be long now, Mr Wainwright. Five minutes at the most.'

Barnaby was at his desk re-reading statements when a blue Orion zoomed past his window and redirected into a sensational curve before braking savagely a hairline from the station wall.

The chief inspector buzzed for three coffees and they arrived stimultaneously with Sergeant Troy and his companion, who sat down, looking even paler than usual, convinced he had just narrowly escaped multiple windscreen lacerations at the very least.

'What do you want to see me about?' Christopher accepted the coffee, drank it very quickly then said: 'Mind if I have a cigarette? They're rather frowned on at the Windhorse.'

To Troy's chagrin (the No Smoking sign was plain enough), Barnaby told Wainwright to go ahead. Catch me going ahead, thought the sergeant. I'd be hearing about it to the end of time, plus replays. Christopher shook out a pack of Gitanes and offered them round. Both men declined, Troy with a marked slaver. The cigarette was lit, vigorously inhaled and the first question repeated.

'I take it you haven't seen today's paper?'

'Not allowed. Too much external stimuli impedes one's journey to a higher plane.'

Barnaby was sure he deduced a whisper of sarcasm. 'Poppy Levine was married yesterday.'

'Again?' said Christopher. 'Well, it's kind of you to let me know, but surely a simple phone call would have sufficed.'

'Rather a coincidence really.' Barnaby folded the *Independent* to a quarter square. 'The groom was a television cameraman.' He passed the paper over.

'Why not? We're hardly an endangered species.' He glanced down. 'What a ghastly – ' A catch of the breath. Barnaby grabbed the paper just before it knocked over a coffee cup. There was a lengthy pause then Christopher said, 'Sod it.'

'Quite.' Barnaby began to read. 'The groom, who was at Stowe with the bride's brother, has recently returned from shooting a film in Afghanistan. After a whirlwind romance and a wedding at Chelsea Town Hall, the happy couple returned to the bride's house in Onslow Gardens. Next month they take a delayed honeymoon in Santa Cruz. So . . .' he dropped the paper into his wastebasket, 'that tells us all about Christopher Wainwright. What we'd like to know now of course is – who the hell are you?'

The man facing Barnaby screwed the stub of his cigarette out in his saucer, fished in the pocket of his cotton Madras jacket and shook out another. 'Do you think I could have some more coffee?'

Delaying tactics. Won't get him anywhere. Troy stepped into the outer office to find Audrey on the telephone and the only other policewoman present comforting a scrubber who was faking tears that wouldn't have deceived a baby. Reluctantly he got the coffee himself, managing even during this brief and extremely simple procedure to project an air of put-upon truculence wildly disproportionate to the task in hand. When he returned, the interviewee was still staring over Barnaby's head and punishing his cigarette. The chief had a notebook in front of him and a Biro in his hand. Wainwright accepted the coffee, sipped a bit, stirred a bit. Barnaby waited until the cup was empty then said, 'Answer the question, please.'

'That's rotten luck.' He nodded at the *Independent*. 'He'd only just met her when we had lunch. Bowled over though, went on and on.'

'This lunch, I presume was before you moved to the Manor House?'

'Directly before. I ran into Chris in Jermyn Street. He'd been buying shirts at Herbie Frogg's. I was going to the cheese shop for some sausages, which should give you some idea of the delicate gap between our respective incomes. It's quite true that he was at school with Levine minor and so was I. A spiteful little prig he was too. Wriggling in and out of people's conversations and assignations, and beds.'

'Stick to the point.' Barnaby could easily sound more angry than he was. A useful accomplishment. The false Christopher Wainwright hurried on.

'We went for a drink in the Cavendish then he suggested lunch at Simpson's over which he told me in interminable detail about his glorious rise in the BBC and this trip to what he kept calling "the roof of the world", although I'd always thought myself that was Tibet. Then he started on Poppy. I couldn't get a word in so I just switched off and concentrated on the glorious protein. We had some trifle and when the bill came he picked up his jacket – we were sitting on one of the banquettes by the wall – and couldn't find his wallet. Said he must have left it at the shirt-makers. I got lumbered with the bill for forty-eight quid. I was furious, being nearly broke at the time. Specially as I was sure

237

he hadn't lost it. He was always tight as a tick at school. Locked everything up – even his face flannel.'

Barnaby was hunched forward, elbows on desk and hardly aware of the increased fumage. He made a forceful beckoning gesture of encouragement with his left hand and 'Christopher' began to speak again.

'I needed to visit the Golden Windhorse. To look around the house, get to know the people. Search their rooms and belongings if necessary. I couldn't do any of those things under my own name.'

'Which is?'

'Andrew Carter.'

Troy looked quickly across the room and watched his chief absorb the name and settle back, easing off the pressure. As if a point of no return had now been reached and the unravelling could safely be left to continue on its own.

'Jim Carter was my uncle. I don't know if the name means anything to you?'

'I'm familiar with it, yes.'

'I believe he was murdered. That's why I'm at the Windhorse. To find out why. And by who.'

Barnaby said: 'Wild words.'

'Not when you hear my reasons.' He pulled out an envelope and produced a photograph. 'My bona fides by the way. Such as they are.'

He passed the picture over. It showed a laughing fair-haired boy of perhaps ten or eleven years old, on a donkey. A man in early middle age, also blond, held the reins. The boy looked straight ahead but the man, so alert as to appear anxious, was studying the child's face as if to reassure himself as to his safety and enjoyment.

'There's certainly a likeness.' Barnaby did not return the picture. 'But very slight.'

'That why you dyed your hair, sir?' Troy was now behind the desk picking up the snap.

'Hell – is it so obvious?' Nervously he smoothed the dark cap.

'Yes. I thought it might lessen any resemblance. He brought me up – my uncle – after my parents were killed. He was tremendously kind. He couldn't afford to keep me on at Stowe but apart from that I wanted for nothing. I didn't notice of course how much he went without himself. Children never do.' He held out his hand for the photograph. 'I was very fond of him.'

'I'd like to make a copy of this, Mr Carter.'

Andrew hesitated. 'It's the only one I have.'

'It'll be returned before you leave.' Barnaby passed the picture to Troy who took himself off with it. 'When did you last see him?'

'Some time ago. Our relationship was close but we didn't meet all that often after I left home. I was eighteen. We had a row. I got involved with someone who was married and a lot older. It was the only time there was any real conflict between us. He said it was morally wrong. He was old-fashioned like that. He got really angry. His disappointment made me feel guilty and I stormed off. The rift didn't last five minutes nor, oddly enough, did the affair, but I never lived permanently at home again.

'I was a bit of a drifter I'm afraid. I liked being on the move and picked up work wherever I happened to be, sometimes abroad. I did grape-picking in France and Italy, moved on to a ski lodge in the Alps. Worked in a circus in Spain – lion tamer of all things but they were poor toothless animals. Went to the States – couldn't get a work permit. Dodged immigration for a bit then had to come back. I even did a stint on the Golden Mile at Blackpool, working the amusement arcades. All very picturesque. Or sordid, according to your age and tolerance quotient.'

'But you always kept in touch with your uncle?'

'Of course. I wrote regularly. And I always went to see him between sorties. He'd feed me up a bit. And he never lectured although he must have been sad at the way I turned out. Just accepted me for the grey sheep that I am.'

These last few words were spoken so quietly that Barnaby had to strain to understand. But there was no mistaking Carter's expression. His eyes were burning with a heated mixture of anger and despair. The muscles in his jaw strained with the effort to stop his mouth from trembling. Troy came in with the photograph and some more coffee but Barnaby signalled sharply for him to wait.

'So when did your uncle go to the Windhorse?'

Carter took a deep breath and long moments passed before he spoke again. He seemed to be bracing himself with great effort for the next step as if it would bring him to the very kernel of his unhappiness.

'He wrote to me about joining when I was in the States. I must admit I wasn't altogether surprised. He'd never married. As a child of course, I was glad. It meant I didn't have to share him. And he'd always been a bit . . . well . . . reclusive. There were periods each day when he'd ask to be left alone to just sit quietly. In meditation, I suppose I'd call it now. Nearly all his books were religious or philosophical. Bhagavad-Gita, Tagore, Pascal. I remember them all throughout my childhood. They're mostly still in his room at the Manor House. It really broke me up when I found them. . . .'

He paused again, this time pressing his knuckles against his mouth as if to dam some unseemly rush of emotion. When he removed his hand, his lips were white. Troy discreetly slid the photograph back on to the desk.

'It was eighteen months before I got back to England. I moved into a bedsit in Earl's Court, then I wrote giving my address and phone number and told him I'd come down for a long weekend as soon as I'd got a job sorted. He wrote back saying how much he was looking forward to it. He hadn't been well – some sort of stomach upset. Then a few days after the letter this arrived.' He picked up the envelope again and drew out a sheet of lined writing paper which he passed to Barnaby. It read: *Andy, Something terrible has happened. Will call you at eight p.m. tomorrow (Thursday) from village. Can't use house phone. Make sure you're there. Love, Jim.* The last sentence was heavily underlined.

'I never heard. On the Friday I hung around till lunch time, then I rang the Manor House. I simply couldn't believe it when they told me he had died. My whole family just . . . gone. I sat for hours trying to take it in. Then I went out and got good and drunk. Believe it or not it was well into the next day before the two things – the letter and his death – sort of connected up.'

'Are you suggesting he was deliberately killed to keep him quiet?'

'Of course I am.'

'Isn't that a bit melodramatic, Mr Carter? The terrible news could have been all sorts of things. Of a medical nature perhaps?'

'He was only in his late fifties. And his health, apart from this upset I just mentioned, was always good. They told me it had been an accident. "A tragic accident." ' He turned the phrase into a spit of disgust. 'I found out when the inquest was and went along, sitting upstairs in the gallery. And that's when I discovered for certain I was right.'

Barnaby's coffee was by now stone-cold and even Troy had forgotten the half cup of scummy liquid hanging at a dangerous tilt from his finger and thumb.

'Up until then although I was deeply worried and suspicious I had nothing definite to focus on. But when I heard the medical evidence *I knew*.' He leaned forward gripping the edge of Barnaby's desk. 'The doctor said Jim had been drinking. That he smelled of whisky and some was spilt on his lapel. That was absolute nonsense. In his first letter he told me the doctor had given him some tablets for this intestinal infection and had warned him most specifically not to drink, as alcohol would have a very unpleasant perhaps even dangerous effect. An unnecessary warning as my uncle never drank anyway.'

Barnaby gave it a moment then said: 'Is it your belief, then, that someone who knew this forced him to drink and it killed him?'

'That would be a bit uncertain. I think it much more likely that they killed him then poured the stuff down his throat to make it look as if he'd had a drunken fall.'

'Easier said than done, Mr Carter. Deglution – like most other bodily functions – ceases upon death. A corpse – forgive me for being blunt – cannot be made to swallow.'

'It should have been brought out at the inquest, nevertheless. I was banking on that.' Carter became angry, raising his voice. 'I thought that's what post mortems were for.'

'Pathologists are busy men. He may have had other jobs waiting. A pm starts at the head . . .' Barnaby suddenly had a spectacularly vivid picture of just what this involved and felt momentarily queasy, 'he got to the neck, saw that it was broken and stopped there.'

'But . . . don't you analyse stomach contents? All that sort of thing?'

'Only if there are suspicious circumstances. This obviously appeared to be straightforward. It's a pity,' he folded up the letter and placed it under a paperweight, 'that you didn't pass all these doubts on to the police straight away.'

'What could I prove? The cremation had taken place before the inquest – they made sure of that. All the evidence literally gone up in smoke. Also, I thought that if you did take me seriously and started questioning people they'd be on their guard, clam right up and I'd get nowhere.'

'Have you had any luck?'

'No.' His expression became dark and sombre. 'Not a bloody whisper. I was very careful. I'd been there a month before I asked anyone anything. And then I was casual about it. Mentioned him only in passing. I thought this would be acceptable – even half expected. You know how curious people are after an unnatural death. I hoped it would be assumed my questions fell into that category. All I discovered was what he was like as a person, which I knew already.'

'Did you find anyone reluctant to speak. Feel they were hiding something?'

'No, damn it. I did wonder at one point if they were in it together.' He caught the quizzical look of a rough grey brow. 'It has been known.'

'I'm aware of that.' Barnaby, who had long since rested his pen, now put it and the pad aside. 'Surely it's a bit unlikely no one at the Manor House knew of your uncle's medication and the possible side effects.'

'I doubt it. The problem of alcohol wouldn't come up. The place is dry, you see.'

'*Dry?*' The word, coloured red for horror, flew from the sergeant's lips. Troy looked sternly round as if a fourth party were present, concealed perhaps in the filing cabinet, infelicitously interrupting.

'You didn't search his room by any chance?'

'How did you know that?' He looked briefly impressed.

'You were heard.'

'Oh dear. That's bad.'

'Were you looking for anything specific?'

Andrew flushed. He looked awkward and for the first time since the beginning of the interview, insincere. He blustered for a moment then shrugged, turning his hands palms-upward in a gesture of exculpation. 'This is going to sound awfully mercenary so soon after he died but yes, I was looking for a Will. He'd sold his house when he moved to the Windhorse. Nothing grand. A three-bedroom terraced in what years ago was the non-posh bit of Islington. Now of course there's no such thing. He got a hundred and eighty for it.' Troy gave a low whistle. 'I went to Barclays where he always banked, but they weren't holding a Will and they'd tell me nothing about his affairs.'

'Perhaps he put it into the commune?' suggested Troy.

'That's not how it works. You don't have to buy in. People just pay their way. And in any case it's not something he would have done. He didn't have to take me in and bring me up, but once he did our attachment to one another was total. I was his next of kin and I know he would have left the proceeds from the sale of the house to me. Certainly in preference to a bunch of strangers.' His voice rose again on the final words then he paused. Breathing slowly in an obvious attempt to calm down, he reached for a third cigarette.

'Perhaps you'd let me have your address at Earl's Court, Mr Carter?'

Barnaby picked up his pen once more.

'Twenty-eight Barkworth Gardens. Easy to remember because it's my age.'

'You say the morning of your uncle's death you hung around waiting for a call till noon. Were you alone?'

'Part of the time. Around half ten Noeleen – an Australian girl next door – asked if I'd like some coffee. We had it in her flat. The phone's on the landing and she left the door open. Why do you ask?'

Barnaby capped this question by another. 'What are you going to do now your cover's blown?'

'No reason why it should be.' He fielded two disbelieving looks. 'There's no newspapers, radio or telly at the house you see.'

'It's all over the tabloids, Mr Carter,' said Troy. 'Maybe display boards, too. You don't have to buy a paper. Just be in the blasting area.'

'I don't know about that. I was in the village this morning and I didn't notice anything. Anyway – it'll be a one-day splash won't it? All over by tomorrow. I think I'll keep my mouth shut and my fingers crossed.'

'You're going to have the fourth estate crawling out of your Tudor woodwork any minute now,' said Barnaby, 'what with the murder and Gamelin's death. No point in telling them your name's Christopher Wainwright.'

'Hell. I suppose not. Then of course Trixie might have seen it. If she comes back – '

'Comes back? What do you mean?'

'She's run off.'

'What!'

'We discovered it just before lunch.'

'Why on earth didn't you notify us?'

'Oh there's nothing sinister. She went of her own free will. Taken all her things.'

244

'It's not for you to decide what's sinister and what isn't!' shouted Barnaby. 'You were all instructed not to go anywhere without informing the police.'

'It's not as if she's involved – '

'She's a witness in a murder inquiry, Mr Carter. And a possible suspect.'

'*A suspect* . . . but isn't . . . I thought. . . .'

'The case is still open.' He watched that sink in. Saw the implications take root and his visitor's subsequent alarm.

'I must get Suze away. I'll tell her the truth. She'll understand. Why I had to pretend, to lie. Won't she?' He sounded uncertain. 'I'm not bothered what the others think.'

'That's a foolish and careless attitude, Mr Carter,' said the chief inspector. 'If your suspicions regarding the death of your uncle are correct – and I tell you frankly that I would not be at all surprised if they were – then someone at the Manor House has already killed two people. And they'll not hang about, I assure you, if they feel a need to make it three.'

'But why should anyone want to kill me? I haven't discovered anything.'

'Then it might be sensible to publicise the fact. And also,' concluded Barnaby, 'to watch your back.'

In the kitchen the Beavers were clearing up after lunch, Heather washing and wiping, Ken (hop, rest, 'aah!' hop) attempting to stack.

'When I think of all that sprout timbale.' She sounded quite peevish.

'You haven't thrown it away?' Ken was naturally aghast. Throwing away was the irredeemable sin. Everything, even the contents of the vacuum bag, went on the compost heap – which at the Windhorse obtained to an almost iconic status. It was lovingly tended, dampened, activated by Garotta, forked sides to middle, gee'd up with a little lime and gently compressed by Arno's wellies. Worms were thought specially beneficial and many was the *lumbricus* going modestly about its day-to-day affairs that would suddenly find itself tenderly whisked from terra firma and sent flying through the air to land, like as not, on a heap of rotting egg shells.

'Don't be silly,' Heather now replied. 'We can heat it up for supper.' She tipped the Ecosudz down the sink. This, too, was not wasted. All water, (bar that from the loo), was diverted via an elaborate ganglia of tubes and hoses to the herb garden which remained ungratefully sodden-rooted and spotty-leaved. 'Oh – do be careful. Here – let me. . . .'

Ken, balancing as best he could to put a stack of plates away, had almost toppled over. 'Sorry . . . a myriad thanks. A bit difficult getting earth-centred today.'

Pouring out the hyssop tea, Heather reintroduced a topic which had kept them awake and chatting the previous night well past sleepy-bye time. 'Have you thought any more,' she said, 'about what we're going to do if. . . .'

Ken shook his head. He drank a little tea, lifting and stretching his top lip in a rabbity fashion to keep his moustache dry. 'Something might turn up today.'

There was no need to elaborate. They both knew that 'something' meant a Will.

When the matter was being discussed earlier, Ken and Heather had looked very higher-planeish and disapproving, being drawn in, they made clear, quite against their own selfless and delicate inclinations. But later, *à deux*, they had to admit that facts were facts no matter how the nut roast crumbled. And that uncertainty had entered their lives in a big way.

They were very contented at the Windhorse and had become deeply attached to the idea of sleeping beneath a solid roof, washing in hot water and staying fairly warm. Neither wished to rejoin the hipoisie of which their memories were keen. Both recalled sharply lurching about the country in leaky caravans and filthy buses. Hounded and moved on none too gently by the police, or hard-faced, granite-hearted landowners for whom the words 'care and share' might never had been invented. Wearily shifting from one smoke-filled bivouac to the next, crouching round a listless fire surrounded by snapping ribby dogs and whining children. Breaking ice on cattle troughs to make tea, shoplifting – Ken had especially hated shop-lifting – and outbreaks of violence at dead of night if the local barbarians sussed their arrival. Heather had been woken once by the roar of motor cycles to find fiery rags burning on her pillow.

Neither of them had any idea of course, in those far-off Gandalfian days, that they harboured such a multiplicity of psychic gifts. Yet, now, here was Ken chosen to be a channel for one of the greatest minds the world has ever known, and Heather visiting Venus and being sent back with outstanding powers of healing.

It was mainly because of their work that they were anxious to retain the Windhorse base. They saw it as a haven where the ailing and spiritually bereft could come and be succoured. Should the house prove to have been deeded to some unsympathetic stranger or, worse, be enclosed by Government fisc, where would these poor souls go? Where, come to think of it, would Ken and Heather go? Property was theft, of course, but even if that were not the case they had no savings with which to buy. And no children to qualify for council housing – Ken, (on top of the leg), having a quite minuscule sperm count.

Even ordinary day-to-day expenses might prove to be a problem. The DSS, when first approached for Income Support a year ago, had been especially unimaginative. In vain had Heather explained the importance of their work: the ripple effect (a loving smile in Uxbridge warms a heart in Katmandu) and the thousands of pounds her ministrations saved the NHS. The department had been equally short-sighted over Ken's claims for a disability allowance, rapping boringly on about the need for a conventional examination plus X-rays.

'That'll be the day,' Ken had retorted defiantly, 'when I trust my body to some chemical-dispensing allopath and his cancer-forming rays.'

Heather had proved loyal in support, crying, 'Why not just send him to Chernobyl and be done with it?'

Good old Heth. Ken watched her now, languidly taking the mugs to the sink, rinsing them out. She was wearing a cheap white cotton boiler-suit through which the outline of her homely black-knickered bottom clearly showed. Having removed the crystal, her forehead rose naked, high and bumpy – giving a quite erroneous impression of towering intellect.

'Far be it from me,' said Ken, lowering his voice, 'as you know. But I couldn't help wondering if Suhami will still want to give her money to The Lodge now the Master's gone.'

'Oh, I do hope so!' cried Heather. 'Even if one manages to remain personally non-corrupt, unearned wealth is still the most enormous barrier when mutating to harmonal soul-rule.'

'Right.' Ken reached for the bread bin. 'Is there any jam left?'

'I've just put it away.' She crossed to the cupboard. 'And you sat there and let me.'

'Sorry. Do you want a slice?'

'I shouldn't.' Ken sawed off one more. 'Funny, Trixie running away like that, don't you think? After Guy Gamelin died. I wondered if . . . well . . . if they might have been in it together.'

'They didn't even know each other.'

'She said that afterwards but May saw them driving off together the afternoon he arrived. Before he'd supposedly met any of us.'

'Probably after a bit of rumpy-pumpy.'

'Ken, honestly!' Heather applied a slab of pear and rhubarb stick to her bread. 'For a highly graded planetary light-worker you can sometimes be awfully coarse.'

'Human nature, Heth. Who are we to judge?'

The telephone rang. There were three: one in the office, one in the kitchen and one on the hall table. Heather let it go saying: 'It'll be business of some sort. May's in the office.'

But if May was, she did not respond and eventually Heather, sighing, 'As if I didn't have enough to do,' picked it up.

Ken watched and listened, becoming more and more intrigued by his wife's disjointed and seemingly harassed response.

'. . . but she's not here . . . not at the moment . . . I really couldn't say. . . . Oh I wouldn't have thought so. . . . No, no –

it's not at all that sort of place. We. . . . Well, I was present myself as a matter of fact . . . Heather Beavers. Writer, Healer and Priestess . . . priestess. MPFS . . . I'm not trying to spell it – those are my qualifications. . . . Gosh I'm not sure about that. We live communally here you see. Talk everything over together. . . . Really? That's not long . . . will you? I could ask – hullo? Hullo?'

She rattled the receiver before hanging up and turning to Ken, her face stretched taut by the muscular effort needed to conceal the intensity of her reaction.

'That was the *Daily Pitch*.'

'Earth-bound profaners,' said Ken automatically.

'Oh yes – of course. They wanted to talk to Miss Gamelin – Suhami. I said she wasn't here.'

'Quite right too. Thank God someone caring took the call.'

'We must protect her, Ken. That's vital.'

'Evoke the crystalline hordes.'

'Trouble is . . . après moi le déluge, ducky.'

'Ay?'

'That's what this woman said. This reporter. We're going to be absolutely besieged.'

'Tory lackeys.'

'Absolutely.' Heather looked around the empty kitchen and spoke more quietly. 'They're so slick. After she'd kind of trapped me into admitting that I was there when the murder took place she began talking about an exclusive. Start counting your noughts my love – all that sort of thing.'

'Christ.' His voice had gone quite pale.

'I know.' Heather locked her fingers in a vain attempt to control a shudder.

'What a load of shites. You'd never feel clean again. . . . Would you?'

'I should say not,' agreed Heather, painedly studying the interlacing digits. 'On the other hand . . . I got to thinking, Ken. Like – you know – what are we about here?' She waved at the honest home-made loaf and sturdy jam. 'What are we into?' Her husband screwed up his eyes sternly and frowned. 'Cooling the ego – right? Thinking of others, putting them first. Now here's an opportunity to protect a bereaved sister – we could speak to them and draw the flak from her on to ourselves who are better able to bear it.'

'Ohhh . . .' Ken groaned, mangling his crust in self-abnegation. 'Sorry sorry sorry. . . . Of course you're right. Poor Suze. Once again Heth you show the way.'

'And it would mean more merits for our karma.'

Her husband laughed and shook his head. 'Seems it's impossible to get away from the ego entirely. Look – how would it be, just to reassure both of us, if I checked it out with Hilarion?'

'She'll be ringing back in a minute.'

'A minute is all it takes.' And Ken straightened his spine, crossed his eyes, concentrated on the tip of his nose and tuned in to the Intergalactic World Brain.

May had not answered the telephone because she was upstairs starting on what she had already recognised would be a lengthy and most formidable task. Nothing less than the reclamation of the soul of Felicity Gamelin. May had started simply at the most basic level, for physical strength must first be restored.

Now, stroking Felicity's thin hand and holding her in the light, May poured all her energy, (hardly at its peak after the last two days), into the pale motionless figure. She was working quite alone for Felicity seemed to have no will at all. She simply lay, dull eyes staring at the ceiling, looking as if she were about to shrivel up and die.

May's gentle consoling voice had been rippling on for half an hour when Felicity suddenly turned and looked at her. May saw cold, hard stones resting in ivory sockets.

'I hated him.'

'Ssshh.'

'I hated him. So why aren't I glad?'

'Because it is not in your true nature.'

May had seen that straight away. The aura, though tattered,

was surprisingly well balanced. Quite a lot of pink and green, even a little blue. Not at all like that young policeman with red flickers everywhere. What a way he had to go, poor boy. May laid her hand on Felicity's brow, picturing divine love flowing down her arm, through her fingers, and entering Felicity's body to heal and comfort.

'Danton called him my mid-life Croesus.'

'Is Danton a friend?' asked May.

'No.' A ghostly thread of sound. 'Not at all a friend. Just someone I used to know.'

These few words seemed to exhaust her but she murmured something else before rolling her head away again. It sounded like 'chaos'.

'Our Master used to say that there is an order within apparent disorder, and I'm sure that is true. Just be still my dear and quiet, and all the mud – all the unhappiness – will settle and things will become clear and bright. You have lost your way Felicity, but together we will find it again.'

Felicity lay back on the pillow, her hand resting in May's. Gradually she felt stealing over her a most delicious lethargy. Her limbs felt so heavy they might have been melting through the mattress. May's voice came and went: deep, rhythmical and soothing like the ocean's tide. Felicity slept.

Arno was pulling radishes for a side salad, stopping sometimes to wave encouragingly to Christopher who was tying up runner beans at the far end of the garden. The radishes were poor forked things quite unlike the glowing crimson globes promised by the seed packet. One of them was covered in little scales and plainly destined for the bonfire. He tried to arrange the rest on a wooden plate brought out expressly for the purpose, but no matter how he turned them they always finished whiskery-side upmost and looking faintly rude.

He had been attempting, as a way of keeping his mind off sorrowful things, to compose another haiku but it was not to his satisfaction. Aware that nothing would ever be good enough this last one, ('Tumultuous heart, *requiescat in pace*, on the breast of your slave') seemed especially inept. It even omitted his adored one's name.

He had hardly seen her today. He understood. Felicity's need was great. Anyone could see that she had been very ill. But Arno's heart was heavy, too. He had said his prayers before going to sleep and on rising, but not with any hope of comfort and certainly with no sense of homage. More out of habit really, because once he had promised his mother he always would. Never forget, she used to tell him, that Jesus loves you. Personally he'd never felt this and, even if it had been true, would have gained little consolation – for who wanted to be loved by someone who loved everybody? And then only because it was their job.

This attention-drift brought him back to the Master's death from which his thoughts had briefly strayed. How utterly dreadful it had been. And how changed they now were. No one put this into words. No one looked squarely into another's face and said: 'You are quite changed'. But it was true. Arno could not describe precisely how. But people seemed somehow . . . smaller. Their humanness a shade diffused, their benevolence slippier, their vitality diminished. Perhaps this was what that poem meant. 'Any man's death. . . .'

Arno pinched himself. His Zen awareness seemed to have quite vanished over the last forty-eight hours. He was living not in the moment but in the near and dreadful past, the image of his dying teacher frozen on the retina. The constant comings and goings of the police distracted and alarmed him. Yesterday they'd searched the house. Today they'd been again, taking away all sorts of tea towels. Arno was especially concerned on Tim's behalf. When frightened, who knew what the boy would say? That chief inspector, surprisingly brief and restrained though the manner of his questioning had been, looked like the sort to try again.

Heather caught Arno's eye, not for the first time. Over the last hour she had ballooned up and down the drive at least three times. Arno thought at first this was part of her daily work-out until he noticed that she stepped outside on to the pavement, scanning the High Street between each run. Perhaps something had happened since he left the house. A development in the case. If so, it was his duty to hurry back. How reluctant he was to do this. Somehow, out in the sunshine, things looked fractionally less appalling. Reasoning that he'd soon be called if needed, Arno turned back to his vegetables and so missed the cream car swinging through the Manor House gates.

Ken and Heather had got ready at some length for the *Daily Pitch*, aware that there might be photographers and that it was their duty as representatives of the Golden Windhorse to look their very best.

Thankfully Hilarion had given a positively radiated blessing on the project. Indeed the great chohan had been not only unequivocal in his support but also generous with his explanations. Zedekial must know that, on the other side, the word 'money' was solidly anchored in the pink, atomic cellular light of manifest neutrality. Put simply, the stuff could be used for good or ill. Naturally as Pan-earthed cosmics, he and Tethys could be entrusted to fulfil the latter part creatively.

Once this detail had been tidied away, the Beavers had discussed the situation at great length, mainly from the possible viewpoint of the other residents. Eventually, regretfully, they had come to the conclusion that their willingness to touch pitch, even on behalf of another, was fraught with the possibility of being misunderstood. This perception grasped, the next brief step (from virtue to pragmatism) was quickly taken. They decided that their sacrifice on behalf of Suhami should remain a secret. After all wasn't it in the Bible – the left hand not knowing what the right hand was doing? The upshot of all this prosing was that Ken and Heather decided it would be wiser to take their long spoons and sup with the devil elsewhere.

Which is how Heather came to be resting against the old rose brick of the crinkle-crankle wall now gilded by the afternoon sun

to deep umber. She was frowning and peering right – the direction from which a London-leaving car might reasonably be
expected to arrive. But the Citroën CV, PRESS disc on its windscreen, approached from the left and was through the open gates
and half way up the drive before she noticed.

Semaphoring wildly, Heather started to run. Fast and graceless, flip-flops alternately slapping against the soles of her feet
and the gravel, she cursed her misdirected attention.

The car was already parked and two people had got out. *If
they rang the bell*. . . . One of them was standing in the porch,
the other, fingers steepled against the light, was peering through
a closed window. Calling on Artemis the swift-footed for assistance, Heather panted and lumbered on.

The female half of the duo watched this approach, lips compressed for it was an amusing sight. Mistakenly encouraged into
lime green (Ken said it matched her eyes), Heather had piled up
her hair to emphasise her neck, and she'd gilded her eyelids and
brows to emphasise the hierophantic nature of her calling. She
wore a nuclear receptor and the pyramid bounced on her vast
bosom as she ran.

'Terry . . . hey. . . .' The girl was wearing a mini-skirted
denim suit, cream tights and spiky high-heeled shoes. She carried
a black patent-leather bag almost as big as a brief case. 'Get a
load of this.'

'Blimey,' said Terry. (Short-sleeved check shirt, jeans and
trainers.) 'Weight-watchers' disaster of the year.' The Pentax
flew into his hands and clicked as Heather crossed her hands
back and forth over her head. They stood together, waiting.

'Hi. You, Mrs Beavers?' She stepped out, tipping forwards
slightly on the towering heels. 'Heather?'

Heather nodded, leaning on the porch frame, cheeks like
sweating beetroots, hair collapsing. Terry took a couple more
pictures. One of these, very cruelly angled indeed, made her
look like a washed-up dugong.

He said, 'Lovely bash, darlin. Yours is it?' and went off without
waiting for a reply, walking backwards, click clicking all the time.

'I'm Ave Rokeby.'

She had a really nice voice, decided Heather. Soft and kind and interested. A little humorous. Not at all like that common aggressive photographer. She was holding out her hand. That wasn't so nice. Long bony fingers with crimson nails like birds' claws. Quite witchy in fact. About to shake it, Heather realised she was clutching a Walkers 'Salt and Vinegar' bag picked up from the pavement. They laughed as she transferred it to the other hand.

'Bit of a problem . . .' said Heather getting her breath back, 'vandalism.'

(Vandalism? A crisp packet?)

'Compton Dando's rather a spiritual desert. No one's really soul-aware.'

(So what's new?)

'We link up with extra-terrestrials of course for inter-planetary cleansing. . . .'

(You do what?)

'But Hilarion says till our akashic records are given egoic clearance, earth will remain locked into the same lethal agenda.'

'Hilarion? Your husband?'

'Oh . . . oh.' Heather chuckled, slopping in all directions. 'Hilarion's been dead for hundreds of years.'

(Je*sus*.)

'But you still talk to him?'

'Ken does. He's clair audient. A channel for the great ones to come through. He wrote all Shakespeare's plays you know.'

(Did I leave a number at the office?)

Ave sat down in the porch and produced a tape recorder from her bag and a mike like a bulbous grey sponge. 'I just want a bit of background. If you could tell me briefly how many people live here, what your general beliefs are. If you're into UFOs – that kind of thing.'

But Heather had hardly drawn attention to the multi-stellar glories of the soon-to-be-expected Venusian reconnaissance before Ave was asking how Guy Gamelin came on the scene and what could Heather tell the *Pitch*'s readers about the habits of the murdered man.

'Are there a lot of young girls here for instance?' Heather looked bewildered. 'Boys then?' Even more so. The mike went back in the bag. 'OK, I'll fill in the details later.' Ave rose and lifted the wooden latch on the front door. 'This is the country all right. Leave your place unlocked for two minutes in London, somebody does you over. Terry. . . .' Her voice raucoused up a notch. 'We're going in.'

'Right.'

'Could you please keep . . . if you wouldn't mind . . . not shouting. . . .'

Heather's heart, only just settling down after her tempestuous marathon, was once more beating fast. She wondered where Ken had got to and looked round anxiously. A vague belief in the law of averages left her certain that if a house held eight people, the time must surely be close when one of them should appear, or at least glance out of the window.

'Ave . . .' she plucked at the denim arm. 'Miss Rokeby. . . .'

'Ave's fine.'

Terry pushed past Heather and a moment later all three were in the hall. Ave said, 'God – this smells like my old convent,' and started to wander round, the metal tips on her heels savagely scoring the venerable boards.

''Ullo, 'ullo.' Terry was standing by the round table which held the pamphlets and wooden bowls. Ignoring the 'Guilty' card, he picked up the one marked 'Love Offering'. 'This where you put your names when you want a bit is it?' He sniggered and turned his attention to the reading matter. *Hugs and Laughter Workshop. How to Nurture Your Spiritual Tool.*

'Who turns out this stuff?' He waved Ken's *Romance of the Enema*.

'Different people.' Heather went over, saying pridefully, 'We're all writers here. My husband's responsible for that one. It's done terribly well. The Health Shop in Causton sold out the first week.'

'No shit?' said Terry, throwing the leaflet down.

'Could I ask you,' Heather restacked neatly, 'please to. . . .' But he was off again, shooting the staircase and gallery.

'Ave?'

'Uh-huh?' She was opening the elder of the chests, dragging out some curtains.

'The thing is we decided . . . Ken and myself . . . that we'd rather talk to you outside. In the village perhaps. There's a nice little pub—'

'Forget it.'

'I'm sorry?' Away from the sunlight, Heather could see how sallow the other woman's skin was, how dry her hair. Despite the mini skirt she wasn't really young at all.

'We talk here because this is where it happened, OK? And Terry'll want some piccies of the actual room.'

'You can't do that!' Horrified, Heather looked round and round again as if the very suggestion might materialise wrathful inmates. 'The Solar is a holy place kept strictly for prayer and meditation.'

'You could have fooled me,' said Ave, and she and Terry guffawed.

'Human interest, darlin',' said Terry. 'A quick flash won't do it any harm.' He danced about as he spoke. On the move all the while, the camera nosing everywhere. Reversing images, pinning them down. Wheeze, click. Wheeze, click. Hammer beams, stone Buddha, the glorious lantern. Heather stared, both fascinated and repelled by the impersonality of the thing. It was horrible – like something in a science-fiction film. A black and silver one-eyed metal brain between two hairy paws, swinging, staring, recording. Threatening. A movement in the corridor made her jump.

But it was only Ken. He approached limping, left arm folded diagonally across his breast – the hand, open-palmed, resting against his shoulder. The right hand held a flower. He was draped in a mass of dingy cheesecloth with a green sash and he wore his

257

headband with the blue tiger's eye crystal. His moustache was newly trimmed.

Murmuring, 'Blimey – a master of the universe,' Terry clicked again.

'Where have you *been*?' Heather ran to her husband. 'Leaving me on my own!' Then, noting his look of displeasure, 'it's not my fault. They just pushed in.'

'Not to worry.' Ken put her calmly aside. 'I'll handle everything now.' He approached Ave and bowed, the crystal swinging out and clunking back again. 'We will only discuss matters relevant to the current issue off the premises. So . . . if you please. . . .' He walked to the door opened it and waited.

Ave returned to the chest and discovered some old copies of the *Middle Way* and a broken lamp shade. Terry knelt in front of the Buddha, screwing himself right round in an attempt to get a wide-nostrilled distortion of its calm and placid countenance. This action had hiked up his jeans, and nylon socks became clearly visible. They seemed to express his essential philosophy. One was covered with the word 'get' in many languages, its fellow said 'stuffed'.

Ken cleared his throat and said, 'Excuse me –'

'I've tried all that,' cried Heather. 'Why don't you *listen*?'

Tension combined with all the running had started a pain in her chest. Control of the situation had quite slipped away, if indeed it had ever been within her grasp. She sensed an unpleasant tightening in the atmosphere. A determined energy running back and forth between the two visitors. They hardly conferred, yet seemed to know each other's ways like a crack team of whippers in.

'Where's this solar, then?' When there was no reply, Terry said: 'Come on, come on.' A hard Cockney barrow-boy whine. Cam orn . . . cam orn. . . . He bounced on the balls of his feet, perky and aggressive, a boxer looking for an opening. 'Did you ask us down or didn't you?'

'*Ask you down*?'

The words boomed out above their heads and, briefly, Terry

and Ave were disoriented. Then they saw at the top of the grand staircase a female figure magnificently clad in a flowing multicoloured robe, the bodice of which was adorned by a glittering crescent moon. A lofty mass of auburn hair added to this creature's already splendid height.

Terry muttered, 'Funky bisons,' and took aim. Dimly in the light from all this reflected radiance, he perceived another person. A slender girl in a green and gold sari positioned, like a handmaid, one step behind. As the flash went off, she turned quickly away, covering her face with a fold of silk.

Now why do that, Ave thought?

'Explain yourself.' A further rich vibration. It was like listening to the opening chords of some grand oratorio.

'It's our glorious free press.' Suhami spoke quietly into May's ear. 'Exercising their divine right to muckrake.'

'This is private property.' May began to descend, billowing in plenipotentiary splendour. Her feet, encased in damson velvet slippers thickly studded with brilliants, appeared and disappeared beneath the hem of her gown like gorgeous little boats. 'Who are you?'

'Who are *you*?' replied Ave, like someone out of *Alice*. Raptorial fingers hovered near the starter button of her machine.

'That's of no importance.' Clickety click, wheeze click. 'Stop doing that!'

Briefly Terry held his fire. He was staring hard at the less exotic of the two women, and coming to the conclusion that she was no more a Chatterjee than he was despite the vermilion caste-mark. The brown skin was simply tanned white skin, plus the face was really familiar. Where had he seen her before? He closed, raising the Pentax. She took up a pewter plate from the second of the wooden chests and threw it, striking him sharply on the side of the head.

'Do you frigging mind, lady?' he shouted. 'I'm trying to take some pictures here.'

'Dear child. . . .' May turned, showing a shocked and distressed countenance. 'That is not the way. Not the way at all.

What would He have said?' Suhami burst into a storm of weeping.

'Now look,' said Ave, putting down her bag and microphone but in a manner that made it clear this was temporary. 'I hate to pour cold water on all this virtuous indignation but we were invited here – right, Terry? So let's stop carrying on as if it's a break-in to rape and pillage the ancestral marbles.'

'You must be mistaken,' said May firmly.

'Ask Mrs Beavers,' replied Ave.

All heads turned to where Ken and Heather stood looking greatly discomposed. Apprehension, embarrassment and exasperation vied for supremacy on their features. They kept screwing up their eyes and exchanging 'you say – no you' grimaces. Eventually Heather spoke.

'There's been a misunderstanding. This person rang up and I completely got the wrong end of the stick. She gave me the impression that some sort of interview was already fixed and all she needed was directions on how to find the place.'

'You're wasted here, kiddo,' said Ave. 'You should be in Westminster.'

'Heather's right,' chimed in Ken. 'I was standing by the phone at the time.'

'I put the idea of an exclusive to them.' Ave spoke directly to May. 'They asked me to ring back in five minutes. When I did they said fine – come on down. Apparently they'd talked to some astral wanker called Hilarion and he'd okay'd the whole shoot.'

'Is this true, Heather?'

There was a long pause then Ave said, 'If things are going to start getting tacky, I think I should say that all my incoming calls are taped.'

'Of course it's true!' burst out Suhami, staring at the Beavers with contemptuous disgust. 'They've sold us. You've only got to look at them.'

'Don't talk to me like that!' cried Heather. 'It's all very well for you. Rolling in money all your life. Maybe if I'd got half a million to chuck about—'

She broke off, clapping her hand across her mouth, horrified at such impious backsliding. Ken, looking sheepish and responsible, as though his wife was some large ill-tempered pet that he had failed to keep under control, started to pat her in a clumsy manner.

Terry, who had been listening with lip-curling relish to this tirade, now realised why the girl looked so familiar. He stepped back a little then sideways, trying to frame her head and shoulders while she was still distracted. What he really needed was a bit of elevation. Stairs no good – he'd just get the back view. He looked around, saw the perfect spot and climbed. Ave too had twigged the girl's identity. She picked up the microphone.

'What was your father doing down here, Sylvia? D'you think he was involved in the murder? Were you having an affair with the victim?'

'Aahh. . . .' Pain flared in the girl's voice. 'You're vile. . . . Isn't it enough to lose him? The dearest man. . . .'

'He *was* your lover then?'

'*Go away* . . . for God's sake go away!'

'If I do, you'll only have the others on your back. You won't be able to step outside without being blinded by cameras and deafened by questions a whole lot nastier than the ones I've just put. But give the *Pitch* an exclusive and they'll leave you alone.'

Terry, climbing on to the Buddha's plinth, waited for this untruthful suggestion to work. It frequently did. Even intelligent people fell for it. Desperation mainly. Better the devil you've just been introduced to. Pity saris were so high-necked. She'd got lovely tits.

May was making a great effort to re-draw her karmic blueprint. Sensing that the visitors were in some way demonic, she had conjured her guardian angel and saw him now, beating his great wings, directly beneath the lantern. She pictured her bones and tissues being flooded by the pulse-beat of his celestial light. She would need all his support. How quickly and easily these people had appeared, no doubt through the great tear in the house's protective shell made by the Master's death. The woman was speaking again.

'I said – if you give us an exclusive you'll be left in peace.'

'Such a collusion would be against all our principles.'

'We'll pay. Lots.'

'That is precisely what I mean.'

'The community uses money, surely, like everyone else?'

'The community!' Ken stared, stunned. 'But I thought – ' Heather gave him such a violent nudge in the ribs he almost fell over.

'We'll make the cheque out to the Golden Windhorse then you can fight it out amongst yourselves.'

'We are not like that.' May spoke with simple dignity.

'Everyone's like that if there's enough swag on the table.'

At this point Terry, having rammed an air-pumped Reebok into the discreet drapery of the statue's crotch, was poised for a tasty full-length frame of the Gamelin profile. As he took it, she emitted a shriek of fury.

'Look where he's standing! That's a rupa. . . .' Terry winked and clicked, again getting an immaculate shot of her beautiful, frenzied face. 'A sacred thing. Get off . . . *get off*!'

An anguished and muddled hesitancy momentarily seized the group. The outrageous violation shocked them into immobility. Suhami stared around, silently imploring, her eyes glazed with misery.

The pause was brief. Suddenly an urgent stream of flying cheesecloth passed them by. Ken, having sussed an opportunity to make perhaps some tiny measure of amends, hurled himself with great force at the Buddha's plinth – knocking over the floral tribute and getting cold water and lupins in his face. Gasping for breath, he scrabbled at the slippy stone, heaving and straining upwards, crumbs of grit beneath his suffering nails. Reaching Terry's foot, he gripped the Reebok's laces and tugged.

Locking both arms around the statue's neck, thus turning away from Ken, Terry started to kick backwards savagely with his free foot. Ken received a couple of painful blows in the shoulder. There was no problem at this distance in reading Terry's socks although their directive seemed, given the behaviour of the feet, to add an unnecessary gloss. At the third blow, Ken released the laces and went for Terry's ankles.

Briefly, almost gracefully, he was swung out on the end of an even more violent kick only to go crashing face-first back into the plinth. Grappling more and more fiercely, he tugged at the denim calves, thighs and cheeks in a grotesquely literal representation of male bonding. The end came when he reached, and seized, Terry's groin.

With a yelp the photographer wrenched his head and shoulders round and started spewing obscenities into Ken's upturned face. This sudden violent movement shifted the statue. It made a slow grating sound like a large stone being dragged from a wall.

There was a concerted intake of breath as, open-mouthed and breathless, people watched the fixedly smiling figure shiver. Then it tilted forwards, but slowly, the main mass of it still balanced safely on its axis. Still able to rock safely back into position if only its dangling necklace of human flesh were removed.

Ave uttered a piercing cry. 'Terry – let go!'

Terry was panting, face made grimly triumphant by the fact that he was still hanging on in there. Then he made the mistake of turning outwards to see how all this derring-do was being received. This unwise redistribution of body weight caused the statue to tip still further, this time past the point of no return.

It fell to the floor with a deafening crash. Terry, twisting in mid-descent, landed inches from its powerful skull. Ken was not so lucky.

THROUGH THE
MAGIC LANTERN

Chapter 12

Troy came in bright-eyed, crisp as a nut, the baby having slept right through. He smelled of Players High Tar and Brusque, the plebeian's two fingers at *Chanel Pour l'Homme*. He hung up his jacket, stared at Barnaby who was gazing out of the window and said: 'What are you doing?'

'I'm studying for the priesthood, Sergeant. What does it look as if I'm doing?'

Oh dear. A sarky day. A sarky day spent looking at a face like a slapped arse. Not the day to bring out the new pictures of Talisa Leanne standing up all by herself apart from hanging onto the back of Maureen's chair. To be fair to the chief, he was not looking at all smart.

'You OK, sir?'

'So so. I didn't sleep too well.'

'That a fact?' Newly refreshed, Troy was not really sympathetic. He was one of those people who, offspring permitting, could sleep hanging by a toenail from a clothes-line. He went over to look, for the umpteenth time, at the blow-up and said, 'I've been thinking.'

This was a process Troy used sparingly. Too much thinking, it seemed to him, just got you overheated. He observed, he listened, he made neat notes. He was scrupulously accurate and sometimes intuitive. What he did not go in for were long periods of rigorous introspection plus a precisely argued follow-through.

Barnaby said, 'Uh huh,' and waited.

'This Tim, look where he's sitting.' The chief inspector had no

267

need to look. He knew the positions by heart. 'Actually kneeling at Craigie's feet.'

'So?'

'Now see where the Gamelin girl is, on Craigie's left. The three of them in fact make an upended triangle. All Tim has to do is jump up and turn and he'd be facing them both – right?' Barnaby agreed. 'I think that might be what he did. And in the semi-darkness, plus all the confusion with the old dingbat going it on the quilt, he stabbed the wrong person.'

'You mean he was trying to kill Sylvia Gamelin? But why?'

'By all accounts he worshipped old Obi. This man was his sun, moon, stars and the last bus home. But what has the lad got to offer in return? Total devotion, that's it. Well, you can get that from a dog can't you? Now here comes this girl, young, beautiful, all her marbles, plus she's about to offer the community a whacking great hand-out. Might Riley not see this as a moment of threat? Believe she's trying to buy her way into the Master's affections and push him out?'

Barnaby frowned. Troy continued, 'Probably seem an overreaction to you and me, but don't forget he's mental. He won't reason logically.'

'It's slight but just about feasible. In a state of extreme jealousy he might panic and react in the manner you describe.'

Troy flushed and tugged at his shirt cuffs: a habit when he was pleased or embarrassed. 'That might explain his wild reaction to the death, Chief. And why he said it was an accident.'

'Mm. The whole matter of emotional relationships is one we haven't even started to go into. These enclosed communities can be like pressure cookers, especially the spiritually orientated places where showing antagonism is frowned on.' If Barnaby sounded irked it was because he resented people who purported to have annexed goodness to themselves. 'And it's not unusual for a leader with exceptional charismatic gifts to be adored in a physical as well as an emotional way.'

'You mean he was knocking somebody off?'

Barnaby winced. 'Not necessarily. I suppose what I'm trying

to get at is that because we never met him when he was alive we can't appreciate – no matter what his followers say – quite how dynamic his personality really was. Or how strong his influence might have been.'

'True. Didn't look much lying on his back with his toes turned up. I still don't see though. . . .' Troy abandoned the diagram and sat down facing the desk. 'D'you mean he might have been influencing someone in the wrong way?'

'Perhaps.' The truth was that Barnaby did not know what he meant. He was simply cogitating aloud. Positing ideas, throwing them away, playing with others. Guessing at unseen connections, maybe guessing wrong. When he was younger this had been the stage in a murder inquiry that had alarmed him most. The dreadful malleability of the whole thing. Grasping at a conversation here, a suspected motive there, a physical clue (that could surely be proven and pinned down), only to find them all evaporating under closer scrutiny.

Each setback would further knot him into apprehension. He sensed, not always in his imagination, disappointment in his performance and increasing pressure to get his finger out, from his immediate superiors. He never forgot the first case that he brought to a successful conclusion. His feelings of exhilaration qualified immediately by a disturbing sense that there had been no 'spare' to fall back on. That he had made it mainly through luck and by the skin of his teeth. And that the success might never be repeated.

Now he was somewhat more at ease with ambiguity and had enough confidence not to panic, believing that sooner or later deliverance, in the shape of a newly discovered fact or freshly made connection or slip of a suspect tongue, was at hand. Occasionally they were not and failure was the result. Not the end of the world as he had once thought, but meaning simply that he was no different from other men.

At the present moment the case was barely two days old and he was waiting on many things. Firstly for the PM report and information from the lab on the fibres of a coarse apron and several towels removed from the Windhorse yesterday. He was niggled about this thread. Not knowing its origins or how it came to be there meant not knowing its importance. It might be of no moment; it might be crucial.

Then someone was trying to chase up the real Christopher Wainwright and George Bullard should be ringing back on the subject of Jim Carter's medication. There were a couple more Arthur Craigie soundalikes on the way although Barnaby had little faith in this conviction of Troy's, springing as it did merely from Gamelin's hardly unbiased description and a false hairpiece. Attempts were being made to check on Andrew Carter's story but so picaresque were his meanderings (if truthfully described), that it was going to be far from easy. Barnaby had also obtained a copy of the coroner's report and inquest on the boy's uncle and could see that re-opening the investigation might prove problematical. All members of the community were provably elsewhere at the time of Carter's death but the letter and scrap of conversation could not be ignored. Trixie Channing was not on the computer so she had not, as Barnaby had previously suspected, skipped bail. This meant a composite had to be built up and circulated, all of which took time. Barnaby was by no means as convinced as Andrew Carter that 'nothing sinister' had occurred just because all the girl's gear had disappeared when she did. Trixie had been scared of something at the time of her interview and Barnaby now regretted he had not pushed harder to find out what it was.

'You still set against Gamelin, Chief?'

'I suppose I am.' In fact Barnaby was no longer even tempted. Quite why he could not say. Partly irritation at being so forcefully presented with a scapegoat. Partly Gamelin's genuine rage that he should have been so used. Then there was the motive. Seemingly so straightforward, on closer examination it proved to be much less so. Barnaby believed, when it came to the push, Guy's daughter would come before her ducats. He appeared consumed by a fierce despairing need to regain her affection. She had made her feelings about her teacher plain, so her father must have known that harming Craigie would scupper his chances of a reconciliation for good and all. Neither was the man's removal any sort of guarantee that Sylvie would not hand the money over. It may well have made her even more determined. Finally, and to Barnaby's mind most telling, there was the nature of the beast. Gamelin struck him as a perfect example of the take-what-you-want-and-pay-for-it-type. Certainly the chief inspector could see Guy committing murder but felt it would most likely be on a blood-boiling impulse rather than as the end result of skilful plotting. Then he'd have stood up and shouted – maybe even boasted – about the deed before throwing as much money as it took at the best defence lawyers in the business. No – Barnaby was sure it wasn't Gamelin. What he didn't understand, yet, was why the dead man had pointed him out.

Audrey Brierley brought in more information on the dead man's possible alter egos. Troy grabbed the sheets and perused. Freddie Cranmer? Not only too young but also known to be covered in exotic (i.e. obscene) tattoos. The next one, though, seemed possible. Albert Cranleigh. Fifty-seven. Early form, mainly petty swindles and flogging stolen goods. More elaborate cons. Phoney mail-order ads. Insurance and mortgage rip-offs. Then he pulled a really big time share scam. Made a packet that was never found. Got picked up in Malta. Did four out of seven. Released 1989. Exemplary prisoner, but then fraudsters usually were.

'This fits, sir.'

Barnaby listened as Troy read aloud. All the while the sergeant was nodding with enthusiasm, his vivid brush cut dipping and rising like the crest of some perky marsh bird.

'All that fits,' said the chief inspector at the conclusion, 'is that they're within a few years of each other's age. Apart from Gamelin's accusation, quite understandable under the circumstances, we've no reason whatsoever to regard Craigie as a con man.'

He watched the outline of Troy's jaw tighten. Troy with an idea was like a cat at a mousehole. It was his strength and also his weakness, for he never knew when to give up and go home.

'If you remember,' said Barnaby, who only remembered himself because he had gone over the statements the previous evening, 'Arno Gibbs mentioned the community's bursary help and donations to charity – Christian Aid and suchlike. That hardly tallies with your theory.'

'But they all did that, Chief – the big villains. Look at the Krays. Hand-outs, boys' clubs, boxing trophies. They were always spreading it.'

'Grass-roots support. The publicity encourages recruits. What we've got at the Windhorse is not tsarism but a pantisocracy.'

'Oh yeah?' Troy winked and clicked his tongue against his teeth.

'An organisation where all members are equal.' Barnaby read his subordinate's mind. 'Not one run by women.'

'Fair enough.' An understandable mistake, mused Troy, being as how most of them had minds like bags of frilly knickers. 'I still think I might get some mug-shots.' He looked mutinous.

'Leave it. They've enough on their plates out there already.' The buzzer went. It was Winterton, the communications relations officer for what was already and inevitably being called the Gamelin case. He had the press permanently on the end of his line and did Barnaby have any new morsels to throw at them.

'Reword what you threw them yesterday.'

'Thanks Tom. You're a great help.'

'Any time.' Barnaby replaced the receiver. When he looked up the room was empty.

Arno was walking in the orchard. It was quite early. Still a few tendrils of blue mist about and, surprisingly, a glitter of frost on the apples. Over his head shone the bright dagger of the Morning Star. Through the night he'd hardly closed his eyes, but was not at all tired.

He was carrying a pottle lined with strawberry leaves and making his way to where 'Stella', their self-fertile cherry, was fruiting. The tree was awkwardly draped with an arrangement of

272

net curtains garnered from various jumble sales and loosely sewn together. They were far from bird proof and several starlings flew out screeching derisively as Arno approached. He picked what cherries were left, balanced his basket on the flat of the cucumber frame, then neatly, with his pocket knife, cut away any nibbled or waspy bits. He piled the rest carefully into a little pyramid, the un-maltreated sides facing outwards. But the result was far from satisfactory and a long way from the plump black glossiness to be found in supermarkets.

Normally Arno accepted the unsprayed imperfection of his produce with resignation, but he wanted to tempt May. She had hardly eaten a thing at dinner the previous evening and no wonder, given the disastrous earlier imbroglio. Arno had fretted ever since, fearing (for truly love is blind) there'd be nothing of her soon.

Holding the basket upright very carefully, he recrossed the lawn and noticed now that the sun was up, that the grass had lost its earlier crunchiness and felt soft and dewy. As he neared the house and came to within sight of the main gates, he hesitated – walking till the last minute in the shadow of the yew hedge then peeping out to get the lie of the land.

Ave and Terry had not been wrong about the deluge. Arno had found an old lock and length of rusting chain and secured the main gates just in time. By early evening there was an unpleasantly noisy crowd out there. It was a bit like a scene from some old silent movie where revolting peasants storm the Bastille. Photographers had been standing on the crinkle-crankle wall and the ambulance had had quite a job getting through.

But at the moment things were quiet. The early birds were up and about but not, so far, the worms. However, Arno was not the only early riser. He was turning the corner of the house when a ground-floor window was flung open. It was May's room. A moment later a sublime chord floated out into the pure air. Arno's heart stopped briefly then, exhilarated, thundered on.

He stepped back in the shelter of the ivy and stood quite still, lifting and swivelling his head round, yearning towards the open casement as a flower to the sun. The golden sound flowed out into the fresh morning brightness, supremely melodious, twining round Arno's heart strings, binding him ever tighter to her, the dearest of musicians. He leaned back and closed his eyes, dust falling unnoticed from the ivy into hair and beard. The world reduced to the flashing movement of a cellist's bow.

She was playing an old Catalan folk song. An exile's lament full of majestic melancholy. It always made Arno sad, yet so harmonious was the structure of the piece and so tender the rendering that when, in a final parabola of exultation, it finally came to an end, he experienced not sorrow but a sensation of pure gladness.

He looked down at his offering. The pyramid of cherries had collapsed and they were rolling about any old how. Even the strawberry leaves no longer looked pristine. The disparity of his gift, compared to the one which had just been so gracefully and splendidly offered, struck Arno with an humiliating sharpness. He tipped the cherries into the flower border and set off to return the basket to the potting shed.

The cellist laid down her bow and moved to the open window to perform her salute to the sun. She would need all the energy she could muster, especially today. Her healing gift – for that was how May hyperbolised a naturally kind heart – would be needed as never before. She raised her arms and watery-green silk fell away, revealing their glorious dimpled strength. Crying out, 'The divine in me greets the divine in you,' she bowed low seven times, knowing that each genuflection drove into the heart chakra love and a strength both cosmic and divine. After this she had a long soak in the bath, wrapped about with milky essence of the common fumitory, did a few Yoga stretches and some alternate nostril breathing and, feeling much more able to face the day, went down to start the breakfasts.

But May must have been longer about her ablutions than she realised for when she entered the kitchen it was already full of people. Only Tim and Felicity were absent.

Heather was at the sink doing the dyna/solar water. This

274

involved wrapping sheets of variously coloured litmus-paper around filled plastic bottles, then securing the paper with string. They were then placed outside in the full sun whereupon the energy from its rays gave the water a powerful electromagnetic charge.

Heather was keeping a low Martha'ish profile, humbly going about tasks to which, a mere twenty-four hours ago, she had given not the slightest heed. She had plaited her hair, winding it severely around her head, and was wearing what could only be described as a thing of self-effacing grey. Aiming for the appearance of a diligent and compliant *Hausfrau*, she looked more like a wardress in a spectacularly punitive prison camp.

Ken sat silently by the range. He had accepted what had so far come his way (a glass of mate and some muesli) with many florid expressions of gratitude, but without any attempt to develop these thanks into a more personal exchange. He projected the air of a man knowing his place (a niche in the chimney corner), and glad of it. Indeed, even had he wished to move, Ken could not have done so for his right leg, broken in three places, was completely encased in plaster.

Ken was deliberately not playing on this. Heather had agreed, whilst trying to settle him half way comfortably in a small bedroom on the ground floor, that they could only hope the community would, unnudged, come to recognise the measure and quality of his sacrifice and set it with a sensitive and generous weighting allowance against the measure and quality of his betrayal.

Pulled from beneath the Buddha in agonising pain, Ken – as much to his own surprise as anyone else's – had behaved with calmness and bravery. Struggling not to cry out, he had taken May's rescue remedy and, when the pain then got worse rather than better, gritted his teeth and held back the tears. Loaded on to the stretcher, a faint smile upon his wax-like countenance, he even managed a small wave and an injunction that no one was to worry. Truly, nothing became Ken's sojourn at the Windhorse like the manner of his leaving it.

Arno got up as May came in, asking if she would like something to eat and a cup of freshly made Luaka tea. May smiled and shook her head. 'You're in the middle of breakfast, my dear. I'll get it.' Arno's cheeks bloomed at the endearment. She plugged in their long, rackety toaster. This was very old but most efficient, hurling zebra-striped squares of bread into the air the moment they were crisp. When the machine was full a dozen would fly up together, somersaulting gracefully in the air.

May thought how quiet it was. Usually during the meal times there was a steady run of chatter and laughter. Now hardly anyone spoke. Janet sat uncomfortably, her chair tilted on to its back legs, picking at the knees of her corduroy trousers. Christopher and Suhami, drinking real coffee, sat together yet not together. He looked at her frequently, once bringing his face round until it lay sideways just in front of her own, humorously trying to evoke a response. She shook her head and turned away. Even the sound of cutlery seemed muted thought May, watching Arno replace a knife by laying it with excessive caution on a side plate. She noticed his rather high colour and hoped he wasn't sickening for something. Three people incapacitated was more than enough.

Heather, having finished insulating her bottles, whispered at the air, 'I'll just take these outside,' and tiptoed from the room.

May's toast sprang up and, simultaneously, the telephone rang. Picking up the receiver with one hand and catching her slice with the other, May exclaimed, 'By Jupiter! That's hot.' Much to the caller's consternation.

The rest of the room, disunited in their anxiety, listened intently. Was it news of Trixie? Of the Master's murder? Was it a bank or solicitor with information about a Will? Attempts were made to flesh out the gaps between May's disjointed speech.

'. . . tombs? Certainly not. We're making our own arrangements. And I must say I think it very crass – oh, your name is Tombs? Why didn't you say so? . . . ah – I see. Yes, that's certainly a problem. . . . We shall indeed, let me think a moment. . . . No, I'm sure none of us would wish to do that.

They're not at all pleasant. Look – tell you what – in the wall of our vegetable garden there's a wooden door. Earth well-trodden underneath so there's a bit of a gap. . . . Oh, could that be done? How extremely kind. A quarter of an hour then? Many thanks.'

'What was all that about?'

'Miss Tombs, Christopher. From the village post office. The man can't deliver, our gates being locked. She said did anyone want to go down—'

'*No!*' cried Suhami.

'Quite. You heard what I suggested. She's going to put the letters in a plastic carrier bag for us.'

'I'd quite forgotten about the post,' said Arno. 'We will have to sift it carefully. People may wish to come here now for all the wrong reasons.'

'I'll go for the letters.' Chris drained his cup. 'Come with me, Suze?'

'I don't want to.'

'We'll go via the terrace. No one can see us from there. I've got something to tell you.' When she still didn't move, he added, 'If you hide in here you're letting them win.'

Suhami got up and followed him, not because of the goad in his final words but because it was easier than arguing. Her limbs felt heavy, her head stuffed with sorrow and guilt.

They walked through the herb garden towards the lawn, the gravel soft and warm beneath their feet. Weeds grew there and wallflowers: the tiny dark gold semi-wild variety that smelled of vanilla and pineapple. The path was edged with cockleshells bleached bone-pale by the sun and wind.

He took her arm and it lay, heavy and indifferent, against his own. Chris experienced a sudden uprush of alarm lest what she felt was not a temporary freezing of emotion due to the shock of the murder and yesterday's intrusion, but a permanent change of heart towards himself. At the thought that he might lose her his throat tightened in panic. He should have explained the true situation much earlier. The longer he concealed it, the worse it would look. He had courted her under false pretences for reasons

277

that seemed to him not only excusable but also essential. But would she see it like that? He recalled the bitter plaint that people always ended up lying to her.

He half stopped, irresolute, wondering how to frame the truth to underline the necessity for untruth. In the end he did nothing but walk on.

Just before lunch the PM report arrived. Barnaby had the sheets out of the folder before Audrey had left the room. He scanned them quickly. Troy said, 'Any surprises?' and received a glance that seemed to him slightly sympathetic.

'Craigie didn't smoke although he used to. Didn't drink. Last ate about nine hours before he died. Cause of death a non-angled knife-thrust puncturing the right ventricle which does away with the idea of Gamelin striking from behind.'

Barnaby waited and Troy made shift to conceal his irritation. The old man was inclined to indulge in the theatrical pause whenever an especially meaty revelation was in the offing. It ran in the family. You had to make allowances. What bugged Troy was that when *he* tried to do it, he was told to get a bloody move on. Dutifully he produced the feed-line.

'That it then, sir?'

'Not quite.' Barnaby laid down the report. 'He was also suffering from bone cancer.'

'*Cancer*!' Whatever Troy had expected it was not this. Barnaby could not have wished for a more satisfactory response. Troy sat down in the visitor's chair. 'What – bad?'

'Bad as it gets. They say he had a few months at the most. That explains the wig of course.'

'Sorry?'

'If he was having chemotherapy he'd probably lost his hair.'

'But would he go in for that sort of thing? You know what they're like up there. Wouldn't he be exposing himself to some wonky universal ray or stuffing herbs up his nose?'

'If you remember, he was at the Hillingdon on the day Riley was found. Gibbs said Craigie was a regular hospital visitor. It's my guess that all of them were told this to account for his frequent attendance.'

'You mean he didn't want to upset them till he had to.'

'Precisely.'

'Saint Arthur after all then.' Troy's mouth turned down clownishly in disappointment. Even his bright quills of hair drooped.

'We'll check with the hospital of course, but I think it'd be wise to abandon your idea of the wig as part of an actor's performance.'

Troy put on his shrewd look. He shrugged, pursed his mouth, nodded. Judicious, not convinced. 'How do you see this affecting the murder, Chief?'

'Don't know. If Craigie really succeeded in concealing it, probably not at all.'

'The murderer couldn't have known. Who's going to risk years in the slammer if all you've got to do to see your victim off is hang about for a few weeks.'

'If time wasn't a problem, no one.'

'Right. On the other hand . . . wo hay . . . what about this? Knowing his days are numbered, wishing to spare all and sundry unnecessary aggro, our hero tops himself.'

'Psychologically, I'd say that's quite sound. But he would never have done it like this, causing the maximum pain and confusion. I see him as the sort to put his affairs in order and take an overdose, leaving a note on his bedroom door. You know the sort of thing – don't come in. Call an ambulance.'

'OK. Say . . . um . . . someone knows, yes? He's had to tell them to get the future straightened out and he – or she – can't hack it. Can't bear the thought of poor old Obi's increasing deterioration, so they do a spot of mercy killing. A quick thrust and it's one halo less down here, one more on the pearly hatstand.'

'Same argument. They wouldn't choose that way.' Barnaby tapped the report. 'Unnecessarily dangerous and messy. They'd slip something into his muesli.'

'Spose so.' Blocked at every turn, Troy gazed rather shirtily at the VDU. It would serve some people right if they were stuck with a teak head who got one idea a year, and that out of a cracker at the Christmas thrash.

'Sorry, Gavin.'

'What?' Troy feigned bewilderment. 'Oh – that's OK. Just thinking aloud, you know – like you do. Right,' he got up, 'I think I'll grab an early lunch. Usually fish, end of the week. I'd better try some. Supposed to be good for the brains.'

'The ancient Chinese had got it taped. They gave their suspect a mouthful of rice. If he spat it out it meant his salivary glands hadn't dried up. Ergo – he was telling the truth.'

'What if he just didn't like rice?'

'Half an hour, maximum. And bring me back some sandwiches.'

When Chris and Suhami returned to the kitchen, they brought a fairly well-filled bright green bag and tipped the post on to the kitchen table. Two small parcels and around a dozen letters.

Janet's quick eager fingers picked them over. There was nothing for her. Flinching from a glimmer of pitying concern in Heather's eyes she got up and started to clear away the coffee cups.

'Heavens,' said Arno, tearing open an envelope, 'there's a booking here already for our hydro/massage weekend.'

Shake Hands With Aphrodite had been well publicised in Causton and Uxbridge and discreetly small-aded in one or two magazines. Several bubble-effect motors had been purchased to gussy up the community's staid, claw-footed baths. Alternatively, if dry, the workshop would take place in the lake.

'Here's one for you,' said Chris. 'And May.' He held out a long narrow envelope of heavy cream parchment, immaculately inscribed in heavy type and franked.

'For both of us?' Arno took the letter, pleased but puzzled. May, as bursar, got a great deal of mail but himself hardly any.

He could not imagine, he said, why someone should be writing to them jointly.

'Can't you?' said Chris, looking excited and exasperated at the same time. 'It's from a solicitor.'

'Do you think so?'

'Of course. They always look like that.'

'I think Chris may be right,' murmured Heather timidly.

'We must find May at once.'

'Open it,' said Suhami. 'It's addressed to you as well.'

'Nevertheless I prefer to wait till she is present.'

'May was with Mrs Gamelin earlier,' said Heather. 'Shall I fetch her?'

'I'll go,' said Suhami.

Felicity was lying back on her pillow, eyes closed, a little fringe of milk on her top lip. May was seated by the bed. Suhami came in quietly and closed the door.

She crossed to the bed and stood looking down. She had not seen her mother for years without what Felicity called her 'war paint' and realised that had they passed in the street, she wouldn't have recognised her.

Felicity's hair was tied smoothly back and she was lying on the pony tail, so there was nothing to soften the fastidious sharp lines of jaw and cheek. Even in deep repose she looked desperately unhappy. All of the Gamelins, thought Suhami. All of us. . . . With an unexpected movement of the heart, she noticed that her mother's unpainted brows were flecked with grey.

'Is she going to be all right, May?'

'That rather depends on whether she wants to be. At the moment all we can offer is quiet and rest. I suspect that her mind and body have been greatly abused.'

'Yes.' Suhami turned away. After all there was nothing she could do. Too much time had passed. There was not even the memory of affection. 'There's a letter for you.' She moved off, not looking back. 'The general opinion seems to be that it's from a solicitor.'

Having decamped to the office, Arno was now sitting behind

the old Gestetner and, with Chris's help, was sorting things into piles. As he had anticipated, most were inquiring about future events. One or two were bills, some sought healing appointments. He rose as May entered, holding out the parchment envelope. She tore it open at once.

'It's from a Mr Pousty of Pousty and Dingle. They want to see us.'

'What about?' asked Arno.

'Doesn't say.' May crossed to the open window and held the letter out, facing the sun. After a few moments her arm began to tremble. She brought the paper back in and laid it against her cheek, breathing deeply. 'Well, the news is certainly good. I should ring up, Arno, and make an appointment.'

Arno was not able to speak with Mr Pousty who was now on holiday in the Cairngorms, but was told that Hugo Clinch would be delighted to see them at two-thirty p.m. that very afternoon.

A man in his mid-thirties, Mr Clinch wore a beautifully cut electric-blue suit, a lighter blue silk tie and a dove-grey waistcoat. His shirt was pale canary yellow as were the crimped and crinkled high waves of his hair. He had an awful lot of large, very clean teeth.

The office was light and airy with a reproduction of Annigoni's 'Queen' on one wall and long narrow photographs of various cricket elevens on the other three. There was a bag of golf clubs resting against the filing cabinet and a silver-framed photograph on the desk, showing Mr Clinch with a fencing guard under his arm and a rapier in his hand.

Arno, who would have felt happier with a few old-fashioned proficiency certificates, saw May settled then sat down himself. No sooner had he done so than the door opened and a lady wearing a hat like a varnished mushroom and looking old enough to be Mr Clinch's grandma, staggered in with a tray of tea things. Arno sprang up and assisted her. She croaked gratefully at him and tottered off, leaving a niff of lavender in the air.

After refreshments had been dispensed – Lapsang Souchong

and Lincoln biscuits – Mr Clinch commiserated with his visitors on the unfortunate occasion of their friend's demise. This brief legal obsequy accomplished, he drew towards him a grey metal box with 'Craigie' stencilled in white letters on the side and smiled. All the teeth sprang to their stations. Arno marvelled at the pushy thrust of sparkling white enamel and wondered how on earth he ever managed to close his lips.

The Will was brief and simple. It concisely described the property known as the Manor House, Compton Dando, Buckinghamshire, then stated that this property was left jointly to Miss May Lavinia Cuttle and Mr Arno Roderick Gibbs. The solicitor waited a discreet moment, eyes tactfully on his green tooled blotter, then looked up expecting to see joyful rapacity wrestling with a more seemly expression of respectable mourning as was usual under such circumstances.

He saw Mr Gibbs pale as death, gripping the wooden arms of his chair obviously within the grip of some devastating emotion. In sharp contrast, Miss Cuttle's countenance, already vivaciously embellished, blushed deeper by the minute. She cried out, and began to weep copiously.

Mr Clinch, momentarily shocked into a natural human response, fumbled in his desk cupboard and brought out a box of tissues. Eventually, when his wastebasket was half full of brilliantly coloured wet paper and a rose or two had returned to Arno's cheeks, the solicitor offered some more tea. When this was refused, he passed an envelope over to Arno whom he regarded as being slightly less distraught than his companion. It was inscribed to them both in the Master's writing. Arno rose saying, 'Do we have to read it now?'

'Of course not. Although there may be matters arising you might wish to discuss. It would possibly save making another appointment.'

'Even so, I think we need time to absorb all this. Certainly Miss Cuttle. . . .' He looked anxiously across at May who still appeared rather swimmy. Even the green cockade on her little red tricorne hat looked limp.

'No Arno,' she said. 'Mr Clinch is right. More sensible to read it now.'

'Then perhaps – if you wouldn't mind?' Arno passed the letter back, not trusting his voice to repeat the dead man's words. The solicitor drew out a single sheet of paper and began.

'My dear May and Arno, You will know by now the contents of my Will and the burden I have placed upon you. My greatest wish is that the work of the community, the healing, the offering of refuge and the sending out of the light continues and I believe that I can safely leave this matter in your hands. I regret I am unable to bequeath any monies to assist you in this enterprise. Should the difficulties of running and maintaining such a large and elderly property become insurmountable, then I would suggest that it is sold and a smaller one purchased. You might then consider investing the difference, thus assuring some sort of future income. I commend to you, also with feelings of complete confidence, the safety and welfare of Tim Riley. My love to you both. God bless you. We shall meet again. And it is signed,' concluded Mr Clinch, 'Arthur Craigie.'

There was a long silence. Both legatees knew the absolute impossibility of finding an adequate response. Mr Clinch, forewarned, whipped out a fresh box of Kleenex. He then stared tactfully out of the window as the silence continued and was miles away when Miss Cuttle sprang to her feet. A dramatic gesture of affirmation brought her cape into vigorous play. Blinded by whirling arcs of pleated amber silk, Mr Clinch grabbed at his inkstand and the framed picture of himself *en garde*.

'We will keep the truth alight. Won't we, Arno?' she demanded, turning damp and shining eyes on her companion.

'. . . oh . . .' Arno could hardly speak. At this linking . . . this official linking from beyond of his name with May's, he felt quite incoherent. Then, in case she doubted even for a moment his full and loving support, he managed to choke out, 'Yes, yes.'

Mr Clinch promised the deeds of the house in due course, saw them through the outer office where the lady in the mushroom hat was feeding some goldfish and, with a final dazzling smile, waved goodbye.

Driving down Causton High Street, May said, 'Do you think we should drop into the police station?'

'Hum?' Arno was still not really back to earth.

'They said to let them know if there were any developments. I suppose finding the Will could be said to come under that heading.'

'Well. . . .' The truth was Arno wished to keep May to himself for as long as possible. Just the two of them snugly enclosed in her noisy little Beetle. May, declaiming behind the wheel, himself absorbing all like a happy sponge.

'Next on the left, isn't it?'

'I'm not sure.'

It was. May parked neatly in a place marked 'visitors only' and climbed out. Arno said, 'Will you leave your bag?'

'Good heavens, no. We're always being warned about that.' May removed her embroidered hold-all and locked the door. 'Some policeman is bound to see it and then I'd get ticked off.'

'Perhaps he won't be here – Barnaby,' said Arno as they pushed the big glass door marked 'Reception'. 'He might be out on a case.'

'Then we'll leave a message,' said May. There was a white button next to a card saying *Please Buzz for Attention*. May buzzed loudly and at length. 'One thing I'm not up to is talking to that youth with the frazzled aura. One gets pulled down by people like that for days.'

A constable strode up, glaring crossly at May's gloved digit. She released the button, stated their errand and they were taken over to the CID block and shown into Barnaby's office. Troy, Arno was pleased to note, was absent. Declining any sort of refreshment, May told him their news. The chief inspector, once he had recovered from the shock of being faced with a walking traffic light, asked if either of them had anticipated such a bequest.

'Indeed not.' May appeared shocked, almost offended.

Arno said, 'Such a thought never crossed our minds.'

Barnaby thought that was probably true. They really seemed the most artless pair. Quite without the usual insincere smiles and false declarations of concern wherewith the human race is wont to oil the wheels of daily commerce. May produced the letter and sat watching as he read it. When he had finished, Barnaby thanked her, noted the telephone number and handed it back. They waited on his comments. May, ingenuous and calm, her face momentarily smoothed of emotion. Arno, proud but slightly awkward beneath his unsought mantle of authority.

'Do you think anyone else knew of Mr Craigie's plans?'

'I'm sure not,' said May. 'If he didn't tell us and, after all, we are the recipients – who would he tell?'

'A splendid windfall, then,' Barnaby smiled.

'It is,' said May sternly, 'a great responsibility.'

'We do not see it as a personal gift,' added Arno. 'But more as something left in trust.'

Barnaby frowned. The sentence struck a chord of memory. Reverberated. What was it? He fretted for a moment then let it go. He got the impression that Arno wished to say something else and gave him an encouraging raise of the eyebrows.

Arno correctly interpreted the signal but remained silent. The fact was he would have liked to ask about progress in the case. If the police were any nearer to finding the murderer. But, remembering May's conviction that their dear Master had been removed by supernatural means, he kept silent.

Barnaby cleared his throat and they looked at him expectantly. 'I have some news for you. Something that showed up on the PM report.' He explained the nature and advanced condition of the dead man's terminal illness, feeling the news should be of comfort. If anything could blunt the dreadful savage edge of murder it must be the discovery that one short, brutal act had saved the victim from a much more painful fate.

Eventually May, her hand to her forehead, said, 'How typical of him not to have told us. How very brave.'

'Yes.' Arno nodded. He then made the same connection Barnaby had. 'That must be why he visited the hospital so often. And why he was tired when he came home.'

'You do understand now, Inspector,' said May, 'how right I was. This explains it all.'

'Right in what respect, Miss Cuttle?'

'Why that he was magnetically transported. Divine intervention, you see. His reward for a just and loving life. The shining ones wished to protect him from further suffering.'

There seemed little more to be said. Barnaby thanked them for coming and came round from behind his desk to show them out. Miss Cuttle bent and picked up her bag. Barnaby, holding the door handle, stared. May faltered, then stopped.

'What on earth is it, Inspector?'

Barnaby said, 'Could I have a look at that, please?' and held out his hand. He felt instinctively, even before she passed the bag across, that this was it. Returning to his desk, he laid it down, aware as he did so that his fingers trembled slightly. The bag was thickly embroidered: roses, lilies, smaller blue flowers all entwined with looping stems of emerald green. The background was filled in by ferns. It was gathered loosely into long handles of light polished wood. Barnaby was familiar with the shape. Joyce had a similar one in which she kept her knitting. 'Would you mind if . . . ?'

He parted the handles and May, looking rather bewildered, said, 'By all means.'

Outside, every square inch of the bag was covered. It was the interior he needed to see. It was beautifully neat, all ends of the vividly coloured wools darned in and clipped off. The seam had been trimmed quite close but enough fabric was left for him to be sure he recognised the thread. Receiving May's even more bewildered permission, he snipped a bit off and returned the bag. By this time she and Arno were reseated.

'On the evening of Mr Craigie's death,' asked the chief inspector, 'do you remember the whereabouts of this bag?'

'I had it with me.'

Barnaby's stomach went down with a disbelieving thud. 'All the while?'

'Certainly from the time I began my regression. Let me explain – when I entered the Solar after having done my preliminary cleansing I placed my bag by the door then took my usual position. I'd just settled when I became aware of a slight shiver. Now, during regression one sinks very quickly to what we call alpha level. The temperature drops, the skin cools so if you're cold to start with it can become quite uncomfortable. So I asked for my cape and Christopher went and got my bag.'

'And brought it straight to you?'

'Yes. He pulled the cape out and handed me the bag. I put it down on the floor, sort of by my side, tied on the cape and we were "in business" as they say.'

'Didn't anyone else handle the bag?'

'No.'

'They must have.' Barnaby spoke half to himself.

'I can assure you they did not.'

'What about when you left it by the door?'

'I was the last person to enter the room. No one went near it.'

'Did you have it with you all day?'

'Well . . . on and off you know. As one does. Part of the morning it was in my room.'

In any case that was not the problem. The knife could have been put in at any time, although common sense surely dictated that such a move be made as near to the last minute as possible to avoid discovery. Anyone could have opened May's bag. In fact someone did. *Andrew Carter.* Could it really be the case that in the dim light he had not sussed the contents?

'Do you remember what else was in your bag, Miss Cuttle? Apart from the cape?'

'My rescue remedy of course. One never travels without that. Crystals – some green aventurine, a little pyrite and snowflake obsidian. Zodiac calendar, ash twig for divining, pendulum – the usual stuff. All jumbled up a bit at the moment I'm afraid. I had to hit a reporter with it to get out of the gates.'

Barnaby's elation was fading fast. He would send the snipping to the lab, and he was still sure that it would match the thread caught up on the knife hilt, but the discovery now seemed to obfuscate rather than clarify. He pictured the concerted rush down to the figure apparently *in extremis* on the quilt. The murderer seizing the bag, scrabbling round for the knife, running back to the dais, stabbing Craigie, rejoining the throng. The whole process could hardly be more ludicrous. He became aware that Arno was speaking.

'I'm sorry Mr Gibbs?'

'I said, there was another bag.'

'*Another bag*?'

'Of course,' exclaimed May. 'I'd quite forgotten. I made one for Suhami's birthday. She so liked mine.'

'Using the same sort of canvas?'

'Not just the same sort. From the same piece. I had some left over you see.'

'I don't suppose,' Barnaby paced his voice with some effort, 'either of you noticed whether she brought it into the Solar with her?'

'Indeed she did,' said Arno. 'Put it down by her feet.'

'On the dais?'

'Yes.'

'Aaahhh.'

'She wouldn't be parted from it,' said May. 'Liked it so much. Is all this of any help, Inspector?' Barnaby said he certainly thought it was. 'You've got a frog in your throat,' May observed kindly. The polished handles of the bag yawned. 'May I suggest a piece of alehoof cough candy?'

It was four p.m. and Barnaby was waiting for Troy to return from the Manor House where he was interviewing Sylvia Gamelin. The inspector lingered in front of his blow-up, picturing her standing on the right of Craigie's chair, bag by her feet, knife in her bag.

Did she know it was there or didn't she? May had said Suhami wouldn't be parted from her present but that sort of sweeping exaggerated speech was common enough. Phrases like 'If I eat another mouthful I'll explode' or 'We think the world of you' were not meant to be taken literally. Suhami certainly had put her bag down or at least taken her eyes off it at one point during the day, if not several.

On the other hand if she did know it was there. . . . The girl was perfectly placed to deal the blow. A single step forward, turn and she'd be face to face with the victim. And if everyone else had fled leaving a single frail old man and a strong young woman? But what earthly motive would she have?

Barnaby wandered back to his desk, riffled through the papers and photographs and picked up her statement. He knew it almost by heart as he did most of the others. He remembered her anguished crying and her enraged accusations against her father. Barnaby was not a man to be easily taken in, and certainly not by tears, but he had believed the emotion to be genuine.

He read on. Like everyone else she had been quick to mention that Gamelin had been indicated by the dying man. She had also been quick to describe that her father had the perfect opportunity to take the knife and glove. But who had left him alone in the kitchen? And if he had taken the knife then and concealed it successfully about his person, why risk transferring it to her bag at a later time? He could not even have been sure that she would take it into the regression.

And if they were running two murders here – which he thought more than likely – what was the connection between the death of Craigie and that of Jim Carter? Suhami had certainly been there long enough to be involved in the earlier death and was physically quite capable of pushing someone downstairs but, even if she hadn't got a cast-iron alibi, there was again no apparent motive.

Troy entered, full of conversation. 'Got the clippings from her bag, Chief. Dropped them off at the lab. I said dead urgent. They said tomorrow morning.'

'I've heard that before.'

Troy unbuttoned his jacket, put it carefully on a hanger and produced his notebook and a copy of Suhami's earlier statement. Then he sat down, hitching up his immaculately creased trousers.

'Confirms everything the other two said. Got the bag for her birthday. Certainly kept it with her to the extent that she didn't take it upstairs to her room but it was in the kitchen for some of the day, in the dining room and one time she left it on the hall table.'

'Did you ask if she put anything in it?'

'Yes. She did. Wanted to feel . . .' Troy checked his notes, 'she was using it straight away. Some make-up, a brush, packet of tissues, some combs for her hair. Thus helping out the murderer, because he'd hardly put the knife into an empty bag. Next time she picked it up she'd just open it to see what was inside.'

'Unless they were in cahoots.'

'Yeh. There's that.'

'Does she remember when she last checked it?'

Troy looked down again at his tightly written pages. 'Didn't open it after she put the stuff in at all. In the Solar, put it down at her feet. Didn't see anyone touch it. The rest is a mystery. Would you think that narrows it down, Chief? I mean to the four who were closest to her?'

'Tempting to think so. But the rest are no more than a sneeze away. I don't think we can count any of them out at this stage.'

'Not even poor old Felicity Smackhead?'

'Not even her. Did you tell the Gamelin girl why you were asking about the bag?'

'Didn't have to. She's sharp even if she is all tricked out like a Tandoori chicken.'

'How did she take the idea?'

'Dead upset. "That I should unwittingly supply the means . . ." blah blah blah. . . .' Troy raised his hands into the air, squawking in a shrill falsetto.

It was so bad Barnaby laughed. Troy, who thought his chief had laughed because it was so good, tugged at his shirt cuffs.

Then Policewoman Brierley appeared holding some gritty-looking black and white prints.

'Your shots, sir.'

'What shots?'

'You put a request in.'

Barnaby stared at his sergeant. 'Sorry, Chief.'

'What did I tell you?'

'They're the last ones.' Troy took the photographs and asked what the chances were of rustling up some coffee.

'I'm busy.'

'Make that two would you, Audrey?'

'Right away, sir.'

Right away, sir, muttered Troy inside his head. You wait till I'm a DCI. I'll make you jump! I'll make you all bloody jump. He glanced down at the pictures. Glanced down and was held.

Barnaby was reading over his sergeant's notes when he sensed Troy approach and stand in front of him. After a moment, irritated by all this silent looming, he looked up. Troy, pale with triumph, laid the shots on the desk then slowly straightened up. The movement reminded Barnaby of a successful athlete bending to receive his medal. Barnaby didn't look at the pictures. He didn't have to. Troy's face said it all.

'You were right, then?'

That would be his lot Troy knew, but it was enough. Balm to the soul. And no one could take it from him. He had had a hunch, cold water had been thrown on it, he had persisted. And it had paid off. Who said nice guys finished last?

Barnaby finally took in the mug-shots of Albert Cranleigh. Prison-cropped hair, stubbled chin, lips pressed defiantly together. Eyes hardened into dark pebbles from the flash or perhaps by years of chicanery. A very long way from the pious smile and silvery flowing locks of the sage of the Golden Windhorse. Yet the two men were undoubtedly one and the same.

Janet had slept in Trixie's room last night. Burrowing down in Trixie's bed, inhaling traces of unsubtle perfume. Deceiving herself that an imprecise hollow in the pillow and creased outline on the bottom sheet were shadowy imprints of her departed favourite: her *mignonne*.

She woke into a cloud of unfocused dread. She had been walking along a narrow country lane when she came across an old churchyard. Drawn in, much against her will, she stumbled over a tiny mottled gravestone embedded in the grass. Bending down, she saw engraved the date of her birth and beneath this a second date partially obscured by moss. She started to scratch at the velvety green stuff when the stone changed its shape and texture, becoming red and slippy and rather soft. It started to move beneath her fingers, pulsing gently, and she backed away in horror.

Now, climbing stiffly out of bed and into the clothes she had thrown over the green flock velvet armchair the night before, Janet strove to shake off this grisly fantasy. Drawing on navy, strap-footed trousers, she caught sight of her lardy thighs dimpled with cellulite beneath seersuckered skin. Cover up quickly. Pulling the zip she remembered how Trixie had teased her about the trousers. Saying they were all the latest rage and poor old Janet was in fashion at last.

She buckled on a strap of watered silk threaded through a wafer-thin watch that had belonged to her great aunt. Then she went back to her own room, splashed her face with cold water and punished it dry with a huckaback towel. She dragged a brush through her tangled hair without looking again into the glass. She could not think of food (she had hardly eaten since Trixie disappeared), but her mouth was unpleasantly dry and she craved a cup of tea.

There was a smell of burnt toast in the kitchen. Heather sat at the table eating muesli, engrossed in *The Secret Commonwealth of Elves, Fauns and Fairies*. She closed the book when company arrived and got up, an intensity of sympathetic understanding flaking her features.

'Aloha Jan – go in peace.'

'I've only just got here.'

'Let me get you some tea.'

She spoke in what Janet always thought of as her 'Little Sisters of the Syrup Pudding' voice. The way people did when filling the God-slot on Radio Four.

'I'm perfectly capable of getting my own tea.'

'Of course.' Unoffended, Heather backed away, showing her lack of umbrage by a loving smile. 'Some toast perhaps?'

'No thanks.' The very notion filled Janet's mouth with bile. She thought she might be sick.

'You could have some butter – as a special treat.'

'*No thanks, Heather.*'

'Right.' But Heather's finely tuned antennae had picked up a shiver of despair. She rubbed the palms of her hands together, conjuring all her therapeutic powers, then drew them slowly apart, knowing that a powerful current of restorative energy now sprang between the two. She crept up behind Janet and started moving her hands about just above the other woman's shoulders. Janet leapt round, cup in one hand, tea bag in the other, and shouted, 'Don't *do* that!'

Heather stepped back. 'I was only trying to help.'

'Help what for heaven's sake?'

'. . . well. . . .'

'You don't know do you?' A dignified and compassionate silence. 'Has it never occurred to you Heather that you have absolutely no diagnostic gifts whatsoever?'

Heather, red-faced, mumbled, 'I can see that you're unhappy.'

'So I'm unhappy. Why shouldn't I be? Or you – or anyone else come to that. It's a condition of life. What makes you think it can be instantly erased? Or that we'd be any better for it if it were.'

'That's ridiculous. No one develops a radiant holistic soul by being miserable.'

'How on earth would you know? You've got about as much chance of developing a radiant holistic soul as I have of becoming Miss World.'

'I'm really glad you shared that with me.'

'God—' Janet flung the tea bag back into the box. 'Talking to you is like wrestling with a vat of marshmallow.'

'I can see you're pretty stressed out right now, Jan.'

'Shall I tell you what really stresses me out, Heather? Almost more than anything else in this depressing, loveless mouldy old universe. This vale of tears. Shall I share it with you?'

'I wish you would dear.' Heather's face was cheesily transformed by pleasure.

'It's being called bloody *Jan*.'

'Right. Fine. Now we have a scenario to talk through. Just remember, whatever comes out, that at the psychic edge I'm OK and you're OK.'

'Well actually, Heather, you have always struck me as being very much not OK. In fact I'd go as far as to describe you as fat for your age and a pain in the bottom.'

'You're missing Trixie—'

'Oh shut up. *Shut up!*'

Janet ran away. Through the side door, across the smashed flagstone, down the terrace steps and across the lawn. She didn't stop running till she reached the orchard where, amidst a drift of ox-eye daisies, she flung herself down. Early little green and red striped windfalls bumped under her back. The spirit of the place, the warm air, mocked her misery. The very words 'love, light and peace' were like stabbing swords.

She thought, I can't stay here. I must move on. Not to another community, I'm obviously no good at living en masse. She had tried it many times (sometimes her life seemed nothing more than one long vagrancy), and it had never worked. Some places had been better than others. All, like the Windhorse, offered 'love' – demanding in return merely a posture of credulous submissiveness. Mostly they seemed to see the spiritual life as just constantly pretending to be nicer than you actually are. Janet felt there must be more to it than that.

She had exposed herself to all the orthodox religions in turn, hoping to catch faith rather as one caught a tropical disease, but had proved to be immune. Occasionally though, deeply moved by a poem or some music, or when meeting someone who seemed to have got it shiningly right, everything that she had read and thought or otherwise absorbed seemed to click into an immensely satisfactory whole. Briefly, the mysterious arid muddle in her head would be resolved, taking on a brilliantly clear and finished shape. But it didn't last. By nightfall, like Penelope with her shroud, Janet had undone her certainties of the day and gone to rest as confused and lonely as before.

She had been made aware that such vacillation was far from healthy (Heather said negativity made warts on the mind), but did not really see what she could do about it. Whoever called religion the science of anxiety had known his stuff. It was apparently impossible to negotiate with God – whoever he, she, it or that was.

She was unhappily rambling thus when she noticed the carrier. Fawn and orange today, pushed under the little wooden door. The post! Janet scrambled to her feet and hurried to pick it up.

The bag was quite full. She tipped the letters out and straightaway saw the long blue envelope. She knew, even before turning it over, that it would be addressed to Trixie. Checking the rest – nothing for her – Janet bundled the letters away and hurried back to the house. She dumped the carrier on the hall table and ran up to her room.

In the kitchen Heather, having tilted Ken's leg up on to the unlit range so that the blood could flow, was pouring tea all round. The company had stopped gathering in the dining room, even for dinner, once the formal highlight of the day.

The Windhorse routine, which used to be of such worshipful importance, seemed to have quite disintegrated. Members got up (or didn't) when they liked and snacked on the hoof. The news letter hadn't been sent out, neither was the roster of tasks attended to with anything like the usual diligence. It was either glanced at and forgotten, or ignored altogether. The laundry room was full of washing that awaited pegging out, and the frequent sad tonk of Calypso's bell indicated that even the goat was at the end of her tether. The centre had not held and there was no doubt that things were rapidly falling apart.

Heather passed round the giant jar of honey from more than one country and continued her report of Janet's unkindness, being careful to avoid the slightest hint of criticism.

'I could see she was upset and all I did was try to trace the cause-initiating agent – you know? So I could offer a positive seed-thought. And she just turned on me.' Heather's gooseberry eyes moistened as she dissolved Ken's honey and took the mug over. Ken nodded his thanks and gave his wife's hand a comforting squeeze. This morning his nose, though still smashy, had lost its angry, blood-engorged appearance and was now a brownish yellow. The little cuts in the skin were healing up quite nicely.

'I expect,' May said, 'she's worried about Trixie.'

'Of course,' said Heather. 'I do understand that. At least I try to. Trouble is I've always been so boringly normal.' She sighed as at some capricious miscarriage of genetic justice. She and Ken exchanged normal and excessively boring smiles. 'But when she said I wasn't a healer—'

'*Not a healer*?' The leg nearly slipped from its iron support.

'I know.' Heather managed a light laugh. 'I nearly threw that withered ovary from Putney in her face.'

'I'm sure Janet didn't mean to be unkind,' said Arno. 'We're all under a great deal of strain at the moment. I personally am extremely worried about Tim.'

A terrible change had come over the boy. Only Arno was permitted in his room, the door was locked against all others. Tim refused to have the curtains opened but enough daylight filtered through for Arno to discern, and be dreadfully shocked by, his rapid deterioration. Sleep and weeping had puffed out his normally taut, unblemished skin. His cheeks, hummocks of scarlet flesh, were criss-crossed with tear tracks and enseamed where he had pressed his face in the mattress. Crusts of yellow glued up his eyelids.

When Arno had tried to change the pillowcase, which was stiff with sweat, he had to ease Tim's fingers from the edge one at a

time, gently coaxing the fabric free. Then the fingers, so bony
and strong, had gripped his arm in terror. Arno had sat patiently,
speaking words of consolation and reassurance.

'It's all right . . . you'll be all right. You're safe, Tim. Do you
understand me?' He paused and Tim's eyes rolled wildly as if
searching every shadowy, reeking corner of the room. 'There's
no one here. No one will hurt you. Can't you tell me what you're
frightened of?' This time he paused for much longer, stroking
Tim's burning forehead with his free hand. 'He wouldn't like to
see you like this.'

At these words, gently spoken though they were, Tim gave
forth a series of desolate strangled hiccups. Arno, full of concern
for the boy and paralysed at his own inability to comfort,
despaired. 'You're not worried about the future, are you? I tried
to explain yesterday that May and I have the house now. We'll
always look after you. The Master left you in our care. *He loved
you Tim. . . .*'

'Do you not think, Arno,' May's voice recalled him to the
present, 'that we should perhaps talk to someone at the hospital?'

Ken and Heather looked at each other in open-mouthed consternation. Never did they expect to hear such a renegade phrase
beneath the Windhorse roof. Every allopathic remedy from the
mildest analgesic to major life-sustaining surgery was regarded
with equal and grave suspicion. They had both been devastated
yesterday when news of the Master's terminal illness and the
treatment he had been receiving was revealed. Even now they
could hardly believe that he had deliberately turned his back on
the embarrassment of restoratives available in his own home.

'I feel if we do that, May,' replied Arno, pained that for the
first time ever he was about to disagree with his heart's delight,
'he will feel betrayed. And might never trust us again.'

'I understand,' said May. 'And I hate to ask for professional
help. But we can't just leave him up there. Oh – if only the
Master were here.'

'He will earth again, May,' called Ken from his home on the
range.

But the words seemed to shrivel on the air and offer no comfort.

Meanwhile, directly above their heads, Janet was curled up on the padded window-seat. She had withdrawn the blue envelope from her pocket and turned it face upwards with trembling fingers. A second-class stamp. A Slough postmark. Masculine writing (of course it would be), yet not an especially strong hand. Why, then, was she so sure? Was she simply projecting her own jealousy and resentment?

Maybe she was wrong. Perhaps the letter (perhaps all the letters) came from Trixie's mother or sister. Or a girlfriend. But whoever it was must be quite close otherwise why write so frequently? And given this closeness, there was surely a pretty good chance that they knew where she had gone. Janet began to pick at the flap then stopped.

What if – being such a regular correspondent – no need had been felt to include an address. In that case she would have violated Trixie's privacy for nothing. Because of course that could be the only legitimate reason for opening the envelope. To contact Trixie and persuade her to return. She must know that, as witness to a murder, she'd be in trouble running away. For all Janet knew, the police had already sent out a description. Surely it was her duty as a friend to find Trixie and persuade her to return? Naturally she would not *read* the letter. She tore at the flap and pulled out a single sheet of paper.

Dearest Trix, You won't believe this – I can hardly believe it myself – but Hedda's gone. It's true. Ring or just come. Love oh! love V.

Janet slammed the sheet of paper writing-side down upon her knee. She felt cold with shock. And a terrible concentrated desolation.

So that's why Trixie had run away. To be with this man – this V – who had ill-treated her before and was no doubt at this very moment doing so again. Janet had read about women who kept returning to husbands who knocked them about. Such behaviour had always seemed to her totally incomprehensible. No one had ever hit Janet and she was sure if they did she would walk right away and never look back.

She recalled the day Trixie arrived. She'd had terrible bruises on the side of her jaw and, on her neck, fierce red nail-marks. Thinking of it, Janet gave a shudder, a single involuntary jerking of trunk and limbs, after which she sat quietly for a long time.

But eventually, with great reluctance, as if forcing her gaze upon some unpleasant scene of despoilment, she looked again at the sheet of paper. There was a brief address. *Seventeen Waterhouse*. Presumably in Slough to match the postmark. If it isn't, thought Janet, I'm lost. And even if it is there's not a lot to go on. No street, road, drive or crescent. No villa, avenue or close. The post office might be able to help.

Janet made herself read the note over and over again, working on the principle that any word or series of words if studied, or spoken aloud for long enough, loses all meaning. And thus the power to wound. She couldn't honestly say this was entirely the case here. Sharp pinpoints of distress still penetrated and a single thrill of jealousy but, eventually, although her hand had not quite stopped quivering, she began to feel a little calmer. And, with the slow curling away of that first swamping pain, rationality returned.

For instance – why should she take it for granted that 'V' was male? True, Trixie (or, more vulgarly, Trix) was the writer's 'dearest' but what did that signify? Strong affection was all. No reason to assume a romantic interest. Same with the concluding form. Who didn't sign their letters 'love' these days. Even to mere acquaintances. Of course there was that rather fervid repetition, but that could simply mean the writer had an enthusiastic nature.

The more Janet thought about this, the more likely it seemed. As for the obviously foreign Hedda, she was probably an au pair living in the house – with whom Trixie had not got on. Now she had left, it was OK to go home.

It was not until that moment, after all her angst-ridden reasoning, that Janet saw how stupid she was being. For of course Trixie had gone before the letter arrived. The two things could not possibly be connected.

About to scrunch up the paper, she checked herself. Nothing had changed in one important respect. V, even if not actually sheltering Trixie, would probably know where she might be found. So the next step must be to ring Slough Post Office and seek out a more detailed address.

Janet got up. Doing something, she immediately felt better. To her surprise she also felt hungry. She took an orange from her fruit bowl and set out to find an unattended phone.

'Where's the *Indy*?'

'I'm sitting on it.'

'God, you're mean!'

'That's right.'

In the corner of the Barnabys' kitchen the washing machine clicked and swooshed and swirled. When Cully was home it was on, and usually full, every day. A smell of frying bacon and coffee mingled with the scent of summer jasmine, a great swag of which hung over the open window. It had been a close night and the air was oppressive and still.

'It's not as if you're going to read it. You're just thinking about the case. Isn't he, Ma?'

'Yes.' Joyce turned the bacon with a fish slice.

'So who is it?'

'Who's what?'

'The man in the black hat.'

'Don't know.'

'Pooh. Three whole days and don't know.'

'Watch it,' said her mother. 'He's big but he's fast.'

'It sounds really weird, this Windhorse. Do they dance starkers under the moon? I bet they're all having it off. They do in covens.'

'It's a commune not a coven.'

'Same difference. What do they wear? Wampum beads and ethnickers?'

'More or less.'

'Don't see how you can wear less,' said Joyce.

The toaster popped and Cully got up, gathering the soft folds of her dressing gown (pale-grey marbled silk this morning). The robe was far too long but she had found it in a period second-hand clothes shop in Windsor and fallen in love, saying it made her feel like Anna Karenina. Joyce said she'd end up tripping over it and doing herself an injury. Cully jacked up the toast and glanced down at the frying pan.

'Turn it off! Turn it off!' She grabbed the fish slice, removed the bacon and reached for a plate.

'I'm making it crisp.'

'It's already crisp.' She tore two sheets from a paper towel roll and started to pat the rashers. 'Any crisper and it'll self-combust.'

'Now what are you doing?'

'Saving him from a heart attack.' Cully put the plate and some fresh toast in front of Barnaby. The bacon was perfect. Then she went back to her seat and said, 'Tell me some more about your suspects?'

'What on earth for?'

'Because I might have to play a hempen homespun one day.'

'Ah.' Of course, acting. Everything came back to that. 'Well, there's someone who channels spirits and whose wife visits Venus when she's not organising fairies to help with the washing up—'

'I wish she'd send some round here,' said Joyce.

'And a woman who reads auras – very worried about mine by the way, even if no one here is. Says I should harmonise my spleen.'

'How can people believe such pottiness?'

'Tunnel vision,' said Cully. 'Isn't that right?'

'It's a mystery to me,' said Barnaby who saw no rhyme or reason in regarding the world as other than it was, and could not have done his job if he had.

'All cults are the same. You just have to blot out everyone

and everything that doesn't agree with your beliefs. As long as you can do this you're OK. Bet they don't have a radio or telly.' Barnaby admitted that this was indeed a fact. 'Dangerous though, being isolated. Once the real world breaks in you're finished. *Pace* our late dominatrix.'

'Oh, do stop showing off,' said Joyce, still cross about the bacon. . . . She brought her coffee over to the table and sat down. 'So one of those spiritual souls has committed a murder?'

'Perhaps two.'

'Oh?' She put in too much sugar then didn't stir. 'You're not talking about that man who fell downstairs?'

Barnaby stopped eating. 'What do you know about it?'

'Ann told me. We met for coffee just after it happened. The village was in a high old state. Everyone convinced he'd been vilely done to death. They were terribly disappointed with the verdict.'

'Why on earth didn't—'

'And I told you that very same evening.'

'I don't recall—'

'I always tell you about my day. You simply never listen.'

There was a far from pleasant silence. Then Cully grinned at her father and spoke. 'This big white chief – the one who got spiked? Was he one of your charismatics?'

'Oh, definitely.' Barnaby took a deep breath and prepared to put his irritation aside. 'Silver-haired and silver-tongued. Seems to have held everyone spell-bound.'

'The Romans thought a good rhetorician must, in the nature of things, be a good man.'

'Hah.' He spluttered and put down his tea. 'They'd have got it wrong with Craigie. He's a con from way back.' Briefly the Chief Inspector wondered, when the past of their beloved guru was laid bare, how his communicants would take it. Some no doubt, already blind with faith, would continue blind even in the face of irrefutable evidence. God knew there were enough historical precedents.

'Got to go. I'm picking Gavin up. Maureen's taking the baby

to the clinic so she's using the car. No doubt I shall hear every boring detail of Talisa Leanne's progress before the day's out.'

'*Talisa Leanne.*' Cully snorted.

'You were just the same,' Joyce smiled at her husband.

'Me?'

'Used to carry snapshots of Cully and press them on total strangers.'

'Rubbish.' He looked across at his daughter and winked. Cully immediately slipped into a parody of film-starish camera-hungry glamour. Lips parted, eyelashes batting madly, chin resting on the heel of one hand.

'Tubby little thing she was.' He moved towards the door. A piece of toast flew past his shoulder, striking the woodwork.

When in the hall putting on his jacket, she called, 'Don't forget tonight, Dad.'

Barnaby sensed behind the words a tugging need that had been absent from their exchanges for a very long time. It made him uneasy. They both knew the score. Over the years Cully had gradually, painfully come to accept that whereas the dads of her friends were invariably present at birthdays and school plays, sports days and holidays, her own quite frequently was not. Her tears, his guilt at the sight of them, then anger at being made to feel guilty, all left Joyce in the unenviable position of family buffer. This wore her out, leading to extremely voluble outbursts of resentment. (All the Barnabys would have won prizes for self-expression.) They loved each other but it had not been easy.

Now, as he groped for his car keys and called 'Bye' over his shoulder, Barnaby seemed to hear an echo of a hundred sorrowful childish wails: 'But you *promised*. . . .'

'What on earth's got into you?' Joyce sat down, facing her only child who had already disappeared behind the *Independent*. 'Don't read when I'm talking, Cully. . . .' She reached out and pulled down the newspaper.

'Do you mind?' Cully shook the pages smooth again.

'When has he ever promised?' Joyce paused. 'Come on.' Cully stuck out her heavenly bottom lip and sulked. 'Never, that's when. "I'll be there if I possibly can" is as near as he would ever come.'

The repetition of that long-time fail-safe rubric evoked a vivid rush of muddled recall which coalesced into one especially unhappy episode, Cully's fourth birthday.

Seven little chums, Noah's Ark cake with chocolate marzipan animals, lots of games, lovely presents and all the while the child's face turning, turning to the door. Waiting. Missing her own party by a mile. Eventually, when the guests, balloons bobbing, were waving and calling goodbye from the windows of their parents' disappearing cars, Tom arrived. But by then she was inconsolable. He was home for her fifth party and her sixth but, as is the way of children, it was the fourth that she remembered.

'Don't try and back him into a corner, love. He'll feel badly enough if he can't be here, without you throwing a moody.'

'Not half as bad as I'll feel.'

'Oh be fair.' Joyce felt anger rising and tried to calm herself. They'd the rest of the day to get through. 'For the past three birthdays you haven't been near us. Last year we tried to ring and you'd gone to Morocco.'

'This is different I'd have thought. It's my engagement as well.' She dropped the paper on the floor. 'You always stick up for him.'

'Of course I do. No I don't. Pick that up.' Cully reached out for an apple and a paring knife. 'Cully . . . it's difficult this case. I don't think it's going well. Don't give him a hard time.'

Cully looked across at her mother then, with one of the mercurial swings of mood which so enchanted her admirers and drove others mad with irritation, gave a warm and brilliant smile.

'I'm sorry . . . sorry. . . .' She leaned across and kissed her mother's cheek, slipping an arm around her neck. Joyce tried to kiss her daughter in return but Cully, already free, was getting up.

'Poor Ma.' She shook her head in what looked to Joyce very much like mock sympathy. 'Pig in the middle. Again.' And turned away. 'I'm going to have a bath.'

'What are you doing this morning?' Joyce, trying to prolong the moment of closeness, knowing it had already gone for good.

'Going to see Deirdre's baby.' The slender brown pink-toenailed feet tripped upstairs. 'Then I'm meeting Nico at Uxbridge tube. We'll be back by four to give you a hand.'

Joyce imagined the hand. She shouted over the sound of running water: 'You'd better bring some stuff from Sainsbury's. All we've got so far is eight tarragon eggs and a few ground-up cardamom seeds.'

'Kay.'

Wisps of carnation-scented steam floated down as Cully shook some Floris Malmaison into the water. Joyce picked up the newspaper and started to clear the table. As she broke up left-over toast for the birds, she played back Cully's graceful flight across the tiled floor. Recalled the skilful gathering of the heavy robe, the sinuously twining arms around her neck, the elegant half-turn of the head, the melting affectionate kiss and smooth backward dance of her retreat. From start to finish it seemed to Joyce there had been no more than one single continuous flowing movement. She and Tom had gradually and painfully realised that they were never sure when their daughter was acting and when she just was. It could be very disconcerting. Joyce felt briefly sorry for Nicholas until she remembered that he was even worse.

Mid morning. Barnaby sat hunched over his desk, a large fan cooling one side of his face, the other trickling with sweat. The dailies were scattered all over, weighted down against the artificial breeze. Only the tabloids still featured the story on their front pages and only the *Daily Pitch* made it their main headline. DID YOGI'S KILLER COME FROM VENUS? Heather, memorably unkempt, had made the front page.

Barnaby's door was wide open and showed a scene of orderly activity. Forms and more forms, photographs and reports. And dazzling green-lettered screens with yet more information. Plus of course the phones, which never seemed to stop.

Many callers offered 'vital information' about, or even solu-
tions to, the crime at the Golden Windhorse. It took more than
the fact that a murder was domestic and had taken place in a
tightly enclosed environment to stop the great British public
sticking its oar in. One anonymous caller had got through at five
a.m. to describe a vision wherein the ghost of Arthur Craigie
had appeared before him in chains, declaring that his spirit would
never be at rest until all the coloureds in his beloved homeland
had been returned to their natural habitat. The man had added,
'That's tropical climes to you and me, John,' before hanging up.

But much of the information was official and a great clearer
of the air: George Bullard rang to say that Jim Carter was
probably prescribed Metranidozole and would indeed have been
very unwise to imbibe alcohol whilst taking it; following permission from Arno Gibbs, Mr Clinch had agreed to reveal the
contents of Arthur Craigie's Will; the real Christopher Wainwright had been raised at White City Television Centre and had
verified Andrew Carter's description of their schooldays at
Stowe, meeting for drinks in Jermyn Street and subsequent lunch
at Simpson's. The only point at which their stories diverged was
that Wainwright seemed genuinely to have lost his wallet. He
had said, 'Andy paid for lunch,' sounding quite chuffed.

Noleen, Andrew Carter's bedsitting neighbour at Earl's Court,
had also confirmed that they were having breakfast for a good
half of the morning on which his uncle died. Barnaby had not
seriously thought the boy was involved, but it was not entirely
unknown for a guilty person to put up an elaborate smokescreen
of pretend-investigation to cover their tracks. Barnaby had been
less successful so far concerning Andrew's activities on Blackpool's Golden Mile, but out there in the hive someone would be
working on it.

Whether there was a link between the two cases was, at the
moment, quite unclear although it was temptingly easy to start
guessing. Sticking to facts, however, the only certainties were
that Carter had made a discovery ('*Andy – something terrible has
happened. . . .*') and had shortly afterwards fallen or been

pushed down the stairs. And that two months later Craigie had been murdered. The Master may or may not have been involved in the first death – Miss Cuttle had been unsure to whom the emotion-choked voice fearing a post mortem belonged. Assuming it was not Craigie's had he, in his turn, discovered the something terrible and likewise been despatched?

If so, that let out the Gamelin bequest, for Sylvie had told the chief inspector at her interview that she had not suggested it to the Master until the week before her birthday. And that neither of them had mentioned it to anyone else. Until Guy, of course, and that on the evening of the murder. Barnaby looked down at his pad. He often doodled as he thought, plants usually. Ferns, flowers, delicately detailed leaves. He had drawn the sharp spears and the curled-back veiny petals of the *iris sibirica*: the poor man's orchid.

'Trust' was written several times in the margin. The word had been floating repeatedly to the surface of his mind as if asking to be paid attention to. It was a constant irritation, for Barnaby presumed he knew all there was to know about Sylvia's trust fund. How much it was, her determination to offload it, her father's determination that she should not, Craigie's feigned (according to Gamelin) refusal to accept. The chief inspector drew a thick, cross line down the margin, tore off the sheet and threw it in the bin. The word floated up again. So. . . .

What about alternative meanings? Trust as in be certain of, or have faith or belief in. Trust as in lack of, falsely placed or betrayed. Certainly the last was the very essence of a con man's art. Barnaby ferreted away at this notion. Had Craigie been murdered by an acolyte who had discovered his true nature and felt betrayed? Or by some enraged victim of a previously successful scam? One of the time share losers, perhaps waiting patiently till his predator should be released. Most of them could doubtless be traced. But surely Craigie would know whoever it was, and be on his guard?

Troy came in with the lab report. He was wearing his usual tight trousers, a beautifully ironed, crisp white shirt buttoned right up, despite the heat of the day, and a narrow discreetly patterned tie. Barnaby rarely met his sergeant off duty so had no idea how formal the rest of his wardrobe might be, but at the station he never rolled his sleeves up or wore a casual shirt. Audrey had been heard to say this was because he had no hair on his chest.

Barnaby thought the reason for this sartorial swaddling was rather more complex. It was all of a piece with the sergeant's meticulous reports and scrupulously tidy working area. The second thing Troy would do when entering the office, after putting his jacket on a hanger and before calling for coffee, was to align the wire-meshed trays on his desk with the edge and twitch any disorderly bits of paper into a neat stack. Sometimes he would rub at a barely visible stain with his handkerchief.

It hardly needed a professional analyst to deduce that this was all about control. About the constant vigilance needed to keep disorder at bay. A bit glib, perhaps, to assume this behaviour to be the outward manifestation of a million inward seething resentments. A touch of the Windhorse pop psychology there. Heavens, thought Barnaby, I'll be counselling him next. He held out his hand for the expected confirmation that the shreds of canvas from Suhami's bag were identical to the filament caught up on the murder weapon.

Troy handed over the envelope and switched on the portable television to catch the eleven o'clock news. There was an interview with Miss Myrtle Tombs, village postmistress at Compton Dando, who had been so cunningly placed before an excellent still of the Manor House that she appeared to be actually standing in the drive. She had nothing to say about the Gamelin case or the house's inhabitants and was saying it with great conviction and at great length. Troy switched off just in time to hear a lengthy hiss of indrawn breath from the far side of the office.

Barnaby was staring at the paper in front of him, his mouth slightly open, his eyes disbelievingly blank. Troy crossed over, slid the report from his chief's slackened grasp, sat down and read it.

'This can't be right.' He shook his head. 'They've cocked it up.'

'The appliance of science. Highly unlikely.'

'You'll check back though?'

'Oh yes.'

Where does this leave us if they've got it right?'

'Up the bloody creek.' Barnaby began savagely punching at the buttons as if in retaliation for some mortal insult. 'Without a bloody paddle.'

Felicity was up and dressed and sitting by the open window of her room. She was wearing the contents of the pigskin case: a Caroline Charles cream silk two-piece splashed all over with poppies and wild flowers. There were some companion shoes, bright grass-green suede by Manolo Blahnik. Peep-toes and heels like oil derricks. May put these firmly away in a drawer and offered a pair of comfortable slippers instead. Before putting them on, she had massaged Felicity's feet with a little scented oil. The orangey-copper skin was like fine wrinkled paper; her ankles the size of May's wrists.

'We must feed you up,' May had said, smiling. 'Lots of fresh vegetables and home-made bread.'

'Oh I can't eat bread.' Felicity immediately added an apology. 'You're very kind but I have to stay size ten.'

'What on earth for?'

'. . . well. . . .' The fact was that all of Felicity's acquaintances were size ten and the minute they weren't they rushed off to a Health Hydro until they were again. Faced with twelve stones of blooming benevolent amplitude, this explanation seemed both feeble and insulting. 'I don't know.'

'You have a very long journey, Felicity. You will need all the help we can give you but you must also help yourself. Now, at the moment you are very weak and can only do a little, but that little must be done. It is your contribution, do you see?'

'Yes, May.' Felicity was disturbed at the notion of a contribution – feeling that her spirit, brittle as ice, might well crack beneath the strain. At the clinic, where she had lived in a cosseted dream, her contribution had been purely financial. Perhaps that was what May meant. A nervous question revealed this not to be the case. Felicity gathered up the lees of a waifish courage and asked what she would have to do.

'For now, just eat a little and rest. Then as you get stronger we shall see.'

Felicity stretched out her hand. As she did so her mind kicked up a vivid memory. Arriving home from her first drying-out, she had turned to Guy reaching out, precisely so. He had called her an emotional vampire and turned his back. But May took Felicity's hand between her own still faintly scented palms, kissed it and laid it against her cheek. Felicity felt her veins unfreeze.

'You haven't any more of that dreadful stuff that goes up your nose?'

'No, May.'

'That's right. The body is the temple that houses your immortal soul. Never forget that. And never abuse it. Now,' she gently removed her hand, 'I must go and help Janet with the lunch. There'll be some nice soup and you must try and drink a little.'

In spite of having promised at breakfast to do the main course once more, there was no sign of Janet in the kitchen. May started on the soup, chopping up Jerusalem artichokes and leeks and sweating them in a little Nutter. She had a look on the seasoning shelf, wondering what flavour might best tempt Felicity's appetite. The soup looked rather pale. May dwelt on the possibility of adding a pinch of saffron. Brother Athelstan's Herbal assured her that it 'makyth a man merry' but added a cautionary postscript telling of the Norwegian mystic Nils Skatredt who, after a heavy night on the pistils in 1462, OD'd on the stuff and died laughing. May replaced the tiny box and took down a jar of bay leaves.

Once the soup was nicely bubbling she went in search of Janet, first going up to her room. Janet wasn't there but a letter was, propped up against a copy of Pascal's *Pensées*. May opened it then took herself off to the nearest telephone determined, after their telling off over Trixie's departure, to get it right this time.

'What she says, Chief Inspector, is that she's a pretty good idea where Trixie is and if she isn't back this evening – Janet I mean – she'll ring and let us know what's happening. . . . Not at all. It's a pleasure. How are you? And that poor boy with—'

But her contact had hung up so May went to seek out the others and put them in the picture.

Janet sat uncomfortably jammed up against the burning window of a double-decker by a stout woman with two bursting shopping bags. One of them was half lying across Janet's knees but the woman made no attempt to rearrange it or apologise. When Janet got off, she saw that some squashed tomatoes had left juice and pips on her skirt.

She had changed the stretch trousers for a summer dress at the last minute. Overlong and full-skirted, patterned with harsh electric blue and tan splodges, it had a scooped neckline. This exposed the rather scrawny hollow at the base of her throat, so Janet had put on a loosely strung necklace of large transparent beads resembling old-fashioned cough lozenges. The dress had an outside pocket to which her fingers constantly and nervously strayed. Tucked in there were instructions on how to find *Seventeen Waterhouse*. (That really had been the complete address. A block of flats the post office said). There was also a bumpy home-made bag of lavender which Heather had thrust into her hand as she was coming downstairs, saying, 'It's only a teeny tiny, Jan, but it comes with all my love.'

At the terminus Janet dismounted, leaving the bus station, turning right as per her instructions, then right again. She had reached the traffic lights when her eye was caught by an exquisite little Georgian bay window – a jewel in its own right – fronting a jewellery boutique. She crossed over for a closer look.

The window was nearly empty, as is the way when the price is immaterial. Just a fold or two of ivory velour, some stunning earrings in thinly beaten bronze and a scarf. This lay as if casually abandoned, a glowing pool of lustrous, irridescent green and shining turquoise. There was a white ticket turned blank side up. Hardly aware that she was doing so, Janet went inside for a closer look.

The scarf was a thirty-six inch square of pure silk, marvellously fine and slippy. The sort of stuff people used to say could be drawn through a wedding ring. Janet imagined it thrown over Trixie's fair curls, casting a verdant shadow on her creamy complexion. It cost a hundred and twenty pounds.

Janet bought it, trying to recall the final figure of her most recent bank statement whilst writing out the cheque. They wrapped it beautifully in a flat black-and-white striped box lined with scarlet tissue and tied with scarlet silk ribbon. The shop's name, XERXES, was stamped across the top in gold.

Walking away, thrilled by her purchase, imagining Trixie's face as she excitedly removed the ribbon . . . the lid . . . the tissue and, finally, the lovely scarf, Janet felt briefly, uncomplicatedly happy. Then doubts started to rise.

When had she ever seen Trixie wear such colours? Trixie liked pastels: cream, rose, pale blue. Come to think of it, thought Janet, when have I ever seen her in a scarf? She had some, crammed into her underwear drawer, but hardly ever brought out and worn. Oh – Janet stopped dead on the pavement, causing a man to bump into her and curse. How foolish a thing to do. Stupid, wasteful. Idiotic.

What Trixie would need, what she always needed, was money. There was never a time when she wasn't short. She would look at the ravishing useless present and think: God – what I could have done with all that cash. For she would know the cost to within five pounds. Somehow she always did.

Janet stood hesitating as people surged about her and car horns blared and her lungs choked on exhaust fumes. Should she take the scarf back? Would the shop accept it? But that meant she'd turn up at Seventeen Waterhouse empty-handed and she did so want to take a present. What I should have done, Janet reflected with tardy sadness, is buy something that would be of real use. Some food. Or something to drink.

On the other side of the road there was a Marks and Spencer. With the same unheeding impetuosity with which she had entered Xerxes, Janet now dived after a group of pedestrians crossing and, a moment later, found herself in the food department.

It was a long time since she had shopped at Marks and Sparks and the shelves were a revelation. She bent over the freezer cabinet, loving the blast of cold air on her burning cheeks and picked up a box glittering with icy crystals: American Fudge Pie. She added a tub of Lemon Ice Cream. Then she turned to the made-up dishes, selecting crispy Peking Duck, Prawns Won Ton, Fillet Steak with Green Peppercorns and Salmon in pastry parcels. Into the trolley went real coffee, some double cream, a herby round cheese wrapped in vine leaves and wild strawberry conserve. A big box of Belgian chocolates. Bread of course (plaited Italian ciabatta), unsalted butter, asparagus. On the fruit counter she found two mangoes, a wonderfully scented Ogen melon and some Muscat grapes. Then she saw a cauliflower: snow-white curds tightly packed, leaves immaculately fresh. Recalling Arno's poor weevily offerings, she simply had to have it. Just as she had to have the champagne.

It was while piling these things on to the rolling check-out belt that Janet realised it might have been wiser to use a basket. There seemed to be an awful lot of stuff, some of it rather heavy. It was possible to buy carriers larger and tougher than those freely offered so she picked up a couple, adding them to her bill (fifty-four pounds and seventeen pence.)

Stepping out of the air-conditioned store was a shock. Janet stood on the baking pavement and put her bags down, trying to ignore the honking traffic. She studied her map to regain her bearings then stopped a woman with a pushchair and showed her the address.

'Straight down and turn at Caley Street.' She eyed Janet's shopping. 'It's quite a walk.'

'Oh – is it?'

'A good twenty minutes. I should get on a bus.' She nodded at a longish queue nearby. 'Fifty-seven.'

Janet had to stand on the fifty-seven but was able to put her shopping in the space behind the platform. She kept the black and white box, gripping it with one hand, hanging on to the rail above her head with the other. At the fourth stop, the bus half emptied and the conductor called, 'Here you go,' dragging her bags out.

Janet climbed down and stared around her in some bewilderment. She turned and called, 'Are you sure this is right?' but the bus was already moving off.

She was facing a large patch of scrubby ground littered with rubbish, around which reared six great cinder-coloured tower blocks. A boy clattered by on a skateboard and she caught his arm saying, 'Waterhouse?'

He shouted 'Carncha read?' and jerked a thumb over his shoulder.

A wooden board with orange and white lettering, much of it peeling off, and dotted lines to indicate covered walkways, gave the layout of the estate. Waterhouse seemed to be the furthest block away. She picked up her bags and trudged off.

Within a couple of minutes the busy sounds of the street were muted and she became aware of a quite different atmosphere. Oppressive, enclosed and curiously empty: curious because she must be surrounded by hundreds of people – a few feet away on the ground or stacked high into the clouds. Janet tipped back her head and craned her eyes upwards. No sign of human life. In spite of the glorious weather, not a soul sat out on their balcony, perhaps because there was no room amongst all the washing. No one looked down from a window either. Janet recalled how quickly the other passengers had melted away. It was really quite uncanny.

She passed two metal bins, taller than she was, smelling most unpleasant and humming with flies, and entered a walkway. She moved along quietly, anxious not to attract attention. The enclosure was covered with spray-on graffiti. It was all pretty uninventive, confining itself mainly to indicating where the observer should next go and what he should do when he got there. Janet, sweaty and nervous, was glad when she came to the other end.

But then, stepping into the open once again, she got a shock. Facing her was a group of youths straddling motor cycles. The nearest machine, powerful shiny black with a towering wind-shield, was so huge and threatening that it looked more like a weapon of war than a means of transport. All the bikes had tall masts on the back with pennants attached.

Janet stopped dead and her heart leapt. The boys stared, hard-eyed. Then one of them gave a wolf whistle and the others gave raucous shouts of encouragement. Janet thought of asking where Waterhouse was out of sheer cravenness but then decided simply to walk on. It wasn't as if they were blocking her way. She had only gone a few steps when a tremendous revving roar of sound ripped the air. Janet nearly jumped out of her skin, dropping the black and white box. The lads nearly fell off their saddles laughing.

Finally reaching her objective, she stepped beneath the con-crete overhang and put down her bags. Around her were several shabby doors numbered one to four. So if there were four flats on each level, V's would be on the fifth. Janet pressed the button marked FT and waited. She pressed it several more times and was starting to get impatient when there was a bumping and thumping to her right. A young girl appeared wearing skin-tight jeans and white winkle-pickers, dragging a baby in a pushchair down a flight of steps. A toddler followed scrambling backwards, tearful at the prospect of being left behind. The girl spoke to Janet.

'You'll stand there till Christmas.'

'I'm sorry?'

'Not working is it?' She dragged at the little boy, wrenching his arm, hoisting him down the final two steps. 'Come on. . . .' She sounded as irritated as if they had just come back from a morning's shopping instead of just starting out. 'Shift yourself for Christ's sake. . . .'

She was walking away. Janet called: 'Do you know if the

people in Seventeen are in?' The little boy started crying in earnest. The girl did not reply.

Janet walked to the base of the steps and looked up. There were eight, then a square to turn, then eight doubling back. It shouldn't be too difficult. Not as if she were in a hurry. Thank heavens she hadn't walked here from the town. As it was she felt reasonably fresh. Janet started to climb.

At the first 'platform', she had to stop to rearrange her shopping. The champagne bottle kept cracking against the side of her knee. She turned the bag round, took several deep breaths and fought her way up another two flights. Half way the sole of her open sandal caught just under the edge of the step and she nearly fell. She was careful after that, lifting her feet higher than was strictly necessary, putting extra strain on the muscles of her calves.

Resting for the second time, panting, aware of a hard, gathered pain between her shoulder blades, Janet noticed a damp stain was spreading over the black-and-white gift-wrapping on her beautiful box. She snatched it out of the carrier bag where it had been lying on top of the ice cream. Unable to face rearranging the shopping yet again, Janet wedged the box under her arm before striving and struggling on.

Next time she stopped she had a pain in her side which was more than a match for the one in her back. Her shoulders were rigid and achingly tender, as if newly beaten and the backs of her legs trembled. Her upper arm throbbed with the effort of gripping the box close to her side, and sweat ran into her eyes.

She was about to rest her bags when she noticed a foul mess by her feet. Squashed chips, greasy paper, a chicken rib-cage crawling with flies, a pile of excrement. Somehow she dragged herself up eight more steps, sitting down on the final one, resting her aching head on her knees, struggling not to cry.

She sat there for a long time knowing that she could climb no further, at least if accompanied by the bags. Perhaps she could stash them in a corner somewhere and carry on alone. Then, after greeting each other, Janet would tell Trixie all about the delicious things she had brought and they would come down together and collect them. This idea led Janet to recognise how the certainty that Trixie would be present at Number Seventeen – with or without the mysterious 'V' – had been growing in her mind. Now she saw all three of them laughing and eating Prawns Won Ton, champagne foaming down the side of slender glasses. She looked around for a hiding place.

The front doors of the four flats to her left opened on to a single narrow frontage which some three-foot-high brickwork transformed into a balcony. Janet took the bags to the far end, putting her other parcel on the wall whilst she stowed them away in the corner. Suddenly, at the window only inches away, a German Shepherd dog appeared snarling and snapping furiously. Alarmed, Janet jumped sideways and knocked the box off the edge.

Crying out, grabbing at space, her fingers brushed the ribbon then the box was gone. It fell slowly and lightly, turning over in the air. Alerted by her exclamation, the boys she'd encountered earlier looked up. She watched them move, walking towards where the object might land. Foreshortened beneath their brightly coloured caps, squat bodies and spindly legs sidling across the ground, they resembled a swarm of preying insects.

Janet turned away and began once more to ascend, grateful that at last she was able to make use of the handrail. Before she reached level four all her carrier bags had vanished. By level five the boys had kick-started their machines and were zooming between the bollards, churning up the pathetic barren earth. Tied to their aerials, along with the mock-fur tails and pennants threatening mega-death and destruction, were fluttering strips of blue-green silk.

Trixie snuggled down into the narrow bed, pressing herself against the thin knobbly ridge of her sweetheart's backbone. They had made love and slept, made love and slept. She exhilarated with pleasure, he thankful, happy but still nervous in case it was all a dream. In case his wife returned.

She had caught them once before six months ago. Had locked Victor in the bathroom and worked Trixie over. Then, after pushing her, bruised and bleeding, out of the front door, she'd retrieved Victor and made mincemeat out of him. She was a big girl was Hedda.

Trixie had fled overnight to her sister in Hornchurch then, seeing a poster in a book shop, to the Golden Windhorse. Her job in a separates boutique had been no great loss but Victor was something else. Ringing frequently, hanging up if Hedda answered, she eventually found him alone. She had told him her location and he had rented an accommodation address. They exchanged letters and sometimes anguished telephone calls. She never reproached him for lack of courage, recognising the same omission in her own character.

She kissed him now on his small neat ears and saw his irresolute mouth curve into a smile, as if remembering her presence in his sleep. The atmosphere in the room was stale and spicy. Several foil dishes from the Mumtaz Takeway were on the table and some empty Ruddles Bitter cans. Last night they had celebrated Hedda's departure. She had gone to live with a professional wrestler at Stamford Hill. All her things had disappeared so it must be true. But V was still nervous.

Trixie was not. She had swaggered happily into the flat, kissing her lover, laughing in a new and quite boastful way. On her third beer she had said, 'What would you think if I told you I'd killed someone?' Victor had laughed, 'You, pretty kitten?' and taken her on his knee. Trixie let him tease her, thinking it's a fact though and if Hedda comes back I shall tell her, and she'll see by my face it's true and leave us alone.

At the sound of footsteps along the balcony, Victor's eyes opened, becoming quickly alarmed. Trixie – although her heart beat a little faster – said, 'It's all right . . . keep quiet. . . .'

She put her arms around him and they lay huddled together beneath the duvet, absolutely still. It was not Hedda, the lightness of the step told them that. Perhaps it was someone from the council. A snooper trying to make trouble.

The letter box rattled. Trixie smothered a laugh, covering her mouth with the corner of the sheet. Victor whispered, 'Sshh. . . .' They rested motionless, hardly breathing. Victor whispered again. 'What are we going to do?'

'Nothing. Don't worry. They'll go away.'

And, after a long while and a lot more rapping, they did.

Chapter 13

The evening group-meditation on the terrace was a failure. Everyone sat on seats of thyme-fringed paving slabs, separately locked into fretful inner disturbances. When it was over there was a sad bit of discussion about the Master's funeral. They all seemed to think the sooner it was over the better. Suhami said she couldn't bear the thought of his physical shell lying in a metal drawer in the dark. He should be resting on a high catafalque she believed, on the seashore perhaps, under a benign sun. Everyone had voted for a cremation rather than a burial.

'That would be his own wish,' said May. 'Spirit of air and light that he was. Blowing in the wind.'

Ken said, 'That was a lovely album.'

He and Heather glanced with shy unease at the heirs regnant. Yesterday they had expressed their surprise and pleasure roundly, like everyone else, when May and Arno had told their exciting news – but the couple were still not sure if they would ever be well thought of or trusted again. Their smile now was the smile of people in tight shoes. From inside the house, the telephone rang and Heather cried, 'I'll go, I'll go!'

The meeting broke up. May disappeared to prepare a herbal sleeping draught for Felicity. Suhami left to milk Calypso. Chris tried to follow, was gently rebuffed, tried again and finally went into the house – his face dark with anger and distress. Heather returned, explaining that the call had been a wrong number and asked if Arno could help her get Ken to his feet ready for his walk. Ken had been told that it was important to exercise his uninjured leg and every couple of hours would have a discreet little hobble about. Now Heather suggested that, as the main gates were now news-hound free, they might take a turn around the village.

Arno watched them go, Ken complaining loudly that it was much too far, then he set off for the kitchen to wash up the supper things. He knew he should be feeling indignant about how the Beavers had behaved but the fact was that he found himself in such an extraordinary state of mind that other people's presence, let alone their transgressions, hardly registered.

It had all started yesterday. Shortly after the remarkable disquisition of the Master's Will, Arno had felt stirring within his for-so-long-timorous breast a bracing current of embryonic confidence. He was chosen! Obviously not for any outstanding qualities of spiritual leadership (Arno had never been one for self-deception), nevertheless he had been thought capable. That night before climbing into bed to fall instantly into a calm and happy sleep, he'd extended his prayers to include a request for strength to shoulder courageously his new responsibilities.

He awoke equally calm and happy, only to be gripped at once by a new and terrible idea that frightened him half to death. He leapt out of bed as if speed of movement might trick the notion into staying behind to be smothered in the pillows, flung on some clothes and rushed about his business. Throughout the day he completed not only his own tasks, but also half the others on the list.

But physical activity, he found, was no answer. However busy his body, his mind remained like a pot on the boil – throwing again and again to the surface this single and deeply disquieting suggestion. The truth of the matter was that his passionate love for May had finally got the better of him and, by linking the two of them more or less officially together, the Master's bequest had nudged Arno into such a state that he was on the point of declaring himself.

There had been many opportunities during the day but he thought none of them propitious. At one point, recalling May's veneration of all things indigo, he went into the garden and picked every deep blue flower he could find. He returned with a huge armful of lupins, delphiniums, larkspur and Canterbury bells, only to find himself rigid with fear at the thought of even presenting them, let alone stumbling into amorous speech. They were now in a bucket under the sink.

One of the problems – well, the main problem actually – was that Arno was no longer able to deceive himself as to the pure, ennobling and spiritual nature of his affection. He now knew it would no longer be enough to share with her, in happy platonic servitude, the sweet prosaic things of everyday life. To venerate her from a respectful distance. He wanted more.

'Oh,' cried Arno aloud in the empty kitchen. 'I am no higher than a beast.'

He had fought this onrush of licentiousness. His baths had got cooler, his flesh pink from loofah persecution. He had applied himself to the section in Father Athelstan's Herbal that dealt with Discharge of Troublous Humours and been instructed to gather some hyssop flowers, bake them to drive off the moisture, mix the remaining purple crumbs with some almond oil, spread the resultant paste across his tummy and lie down for half an hour with his feet up on a hassock – all of which he duly did. He felt better for the rest but his skin went blue.

He had tried to reason with himself, which had proved difficult, and to think uplifting thoughts which had proved very easy. Attempting to approach what the Master had called his innate fountain of wisdom, he was always beaten to it by Priapus, muddying up the water. So, finally, Arno had been compelled to accept this irresistible summons of the blood, comforted only by the knowledge that at least he would do the decent thing and keep these feelings to himself. And so he had. Until today.

Today it had been borne upon him that until he spoke he would have no peace. Also that, if he failed, she would be lost to him for ever. For, in spite of the Master's injunction, Arno felt he could not then further embarrass May by his continual presence. All day, like an anxious foot soldier before a fateful battle, he had been on the look out for favourable signs. After lunch one had been vouchsafed. Draining his mug of Acorna, the remaining sludge had formed itself into the shape of a perfect heart. This had cheered Arno considerably. The time it seemed was right. He only had to do it once and, after all, how long did it take to say three little words? No time. Of course there would have to be a few endearments.

At the thought of the endearments Arno's skin crawled with apprehension. Perhaps he could just place his last and final haiku in amongst the flowers. He produced it from his pocket.

> May, goddess, heart's queen
> Bitter the path without you
> Joined be. With me.

He was cheating rather on the last line, which was a syllable short unless you said 'joinèd' like Shakespeare, but it had pith and moment. No doubt about that.

Washing and drying all this time, Arno now began to put the glasses back and that was when he came across the brandy. Tucked away, in a purely medicinal manner, on the back of the oats and beans and barley shelf. With nothing really definite in mind, Arno took it down. It was a pretty large bottle and it was pretty full. He poured out a small glass and drank it.

It burned his throat and made him cough but there was no doubt, once the discomfort had worn off, that he felt better. In fact he felt so much better he decided to have another. This went down much more smoothly, engendering nothing more disturbing than a nice warm glow across the chest. Arno could feel it doing what he had always understood strong drink was supposed to do. Loosening inhibitions, magicking up the assurance he needed to accomplish his brave, foolhardy sortie. He decided to have a third, then sat down in a single swoopy motion – feeling rather blobby in the head.

For no reason a memory arrived. Some indeterminate time ago he had seen a play at an amateur theatre. Set in Russia, the bit Arno remembered had two people who were thought by all the other characters to be in love. She was packing to go away, he was standing by the door. She thought he was going to propose and he thought he was going to propose, but he never did and she went off to be some sort of governess. Arno had been very moved by the waste and pathos of the situation. He saw this recollection now as both warning and encouragement.

Lest sorrow should unman him, he had another small glass and with some difficulty made his way towards the window. He opened it and the balmy air lay warm against his face. It was pleasant but he felt he could have done with something a bit more bracing. And then he heard the cello.

She was playing the chakras which, she had explained to him once, corresponded to the seven-note musical scale. How he knew she was not simply playing the scale, Arno could not have said. A special richness in the timbre perhaps; a deeper resonance in the pause. Could one in any case *hear* colours? He stood, supporting himself by gripping the edge of the sink, straining not to miss a single thread of the glorious sound.

He felt intoxicated with joy and immensely confident. As if all the strength he would need to sustain and support them, both now and in the years to come, had been given all at once in a lump. And far from weighing him down, he soared with it. He flew. He was suddenly totally convinced she would be his – he knew it! All the exuberant unfathomable extravagance of her. As the dulcified notes flowed, Arno – in a frenzy of nympholepsy, – recreated the beloved musician and saw her not seated in an English country house, but magnificently astride a gold-rimmed cloud and surging across the heavens in a shining helmet, with bright curved shining horns. This was it! His instant of momentous opportunity. His *kairos*.

Buoyed up by all this riotous bodily excess, Arno started to tug the flowers out of the bucket. He looked round for something to tie them up with. Nothing of the right length, width or texture presented itself, so he made do with a tea towel. The strategy was to offer them, rhapsodise a while on the beauty of her soul, the sweets of her conversation and her astounding physical loveliness, bow low in a proper boon-craving manner, then withdraw. Shouldn't be too difficult. Anyone could pitch a little woo. He slipped the poem between the larkspur and the delphs and was just tottering towards the door when the music stopped in mid-scale (somewhere between the heart and the solar plexus).

Arno stood very still, all his attention straining into the silence – which continued. What could be the matter? Was she ill? He felt a shiver of fear until reason asserted itself. May was never ill. Those Rubenesque limbs, glowing eyes and that unquenchable bosom were surely not only healthy but also indestructible.

Perhaps she had simply taken a break to tighten a string. Or rest that strong right arm. But half way up the scale? As he hovered, disconcerted, clutching his bouquet, another much stranger sound came to Arno's ears. A bitter-sweet and pure sound interspersed with brief moany gurgles. He thought at first that she was singing. Certainly the manner of delivery was strangely musical. Its clear plangent quality reminded him of medieval, high-French ballads often sung to a lute. But then a sudden extra-mournful cadence brought home the appalling truth. She was not singing, but *crying*.

Unhelmed by pity and terror, Arno flew along the corridor. May was sitting in the nursing chair, bending over her instrument, bow poised as if to play again. Her cheeks were wet and her profile stamped with sorrow. Arno halted at the threshold, heart breaking at the sight. He could not speak. Could not choke out a single comforting phrase, let alone deliver his chivalric eulogy.

At first, wrapt in unhappiness, she did not notice him. Then, still clutching his unbound bouquet, Arno hesitantly stepped forwards. She turned and said simply, 'Oh Arno – I do miss him so.'

It was enough. Released, emboldened, Arno approached. Crying, 'Dearest May,' he embraced her and launched into a flood of adoring speech.

Then things got a little complicated. May rose to her feet, her expression one of confusion rather than alarm or dismay. Arno, clinging to voluptuous silk-clad shoulders, slid off. There was a brief tumultuous scrimmage, involving folds of slithery fabric, stout little legs, spires of deep blue flowers and gleaming rose-wood, followed by a howl of elemental magnitude, though whether provoked by joy or anguish it was impossible to tell.

It was nearly seven. Barnaby sat, head in hands, brain stuffed to bursting with a kaleidoscope of detail, his thoughts over-heated and stale. A labyrinth of faces, voices, diagrams, pictures. But which thread would lead him to the clear light of day? Perhaps that thread had not yet been discovered. If it was, he wondered how the hell he would find room for it.

That there was plenty of material that could be jettisoned he had no doubt, but at the moment he dared throw nothing away. His shoulders were stiff and he hunched them up and down then pressed them back to loosen up a bit. Troy was looking at his watch.

'I expect they're doing evening-chanting up at the Windhorse,' he said 'Dancing round. Or whatever daft rubbish it is they do.'

'Don't be like that, Troy. You might get born again yourself one day.'

'Strikes me most of the people who are born again should never have been born in the first place.'

Barnaby laughed and Troy looked disconcerted. The chief would do that sometimes. Sit straight-faced through any amount of little witticisms then fall about when you were being serious. 'It's getting on, sir.'

'Something might still come in.'

'Thought you said it was Cully's birthday.' Barnaby disliked the naked lechery in his sergeant's voice whenever Cully's name came up. 'Isn't there going to be a party?'

'A small one. She got engaged as well.'

'Oh yeh? What's he do?'

'An actor.'

'He'll be on telly, then,' said Troy with simple confidence.

Barnaby did not reply. He was staring down at the pile of

statements. Gamelin's was on top. Was there, buried in that printed page or on any of the others, a line of speech that could be reinterpreted? A fact looked at in a different light.

Troy observed his chief sympathetically. 'My money's on that Master Rakowkzy. Anybody gives free legal advice must be up to no good. Most solicitors charge fifty quid just to fart in your pocket.' He chortled. 'And talking of solicitors – you thought any more about Gibbs and May Cuttle? I mean – we've got a real motive there. Elizabethan manor house, acres of ground, not to mention that goat. I know they come over as innocent idealists—'

'Idealists are never innocent.' Barnaby did not look up. 'They cause half the trouble that's going. Check this.' Troy took Guy Gamelin's statement, read it through and looked blank. 'It tells us something about the murder scene that none of the others do.'

Troy frowned. 'No it doesn't.'

'Yes it does. Read it again.'

Troy read it again and then once more. 'Ohhh. . . .' He shrugged. 'What difference does that make?'

'Perhaps,' Barnaby took the statement back, 'it indicates another way of looking at things. Never a bad idea, especially if you're stuck.'

'Right.' Troy moved fast to nip any lecture on the open mind in the bud. 'Don't you want to get off now?'

'Hmn.' Barnaby half rose, still looking at the bit of paper. 'I think we'll have another talk with that mad boy tomorrow. Try and find out why he's so convinced Craigie's death was an accident. And why he's so frightened. Gibbs was definitely trying to put us off seeing him. We'll get someone else to sit in next time. Might have a bit more luck.'

'What time's it starting – the sworry?'

'Half seven.'

'Just do it nice then.'

Barnaby said 'Hmn' again, drummed his fingers on the desk, switched on his monitor. Troy couldn't understand it. Catch him hanging round the office on his daughter's twenty-first!

'I'll stay.' A quick look of surprise. 'I've missed the baby's bath and bedtime so there's no rush.'

'That's good of you, Gavin,' said Barnaby, thinking poor old Maureen. 'We've probably got all we're getting for tonight. And, of course, they can always reach me at home. Still – I appreciate it.'

'Till about nine say?'

'Fine. I can probably be back by then.'

'Course you can, Chief,' said Troy, thinking poor old Cully.

When Barnaby had gone, he hung around obediently for half an hour, drifting in and out of the main office, talking to the duty staff, taking a few calls of no special interest. Then, bored, decided to get a bite of supper in the canteen. Leaving instructions that if his wife rang, he was out and if anything at all relating to the Windhorse case came in, it was to be put straight on his desk, he went off.

It wasn't just that he was hungry. There was a new assistant on late shift. Nicely married and, by all the locker-room accounts, not entirely averse to putting it about a bit. Loading his tray with spaghetti and chips, and a mug of bright rust-coloured tea, Troy arrived at the till. He noted with pleasure the long false eyelashes, straining overall and hot pink lips. They were shiny, too, as if she licked them a lot. Perhaps in anticipation? His change came to fifty pence. Holding the coin out, the lashes did a bit of cheek-sweeping. She said, 'You ought to give that to the blind dogs.'

'Blind dogs?' Troy saw the tin and dropped the coin in, regarding it as an investment. 'Poor devils. It's not as if you can explain it to them, is it?' She looked blank. Ah well. He wasn't after her sense of humour.

Later she came round to clear. Troy patted the space next to him and when she sat down, said he wouldn't half like to be the leather on that chair. There was a fair bit more of this and a lot of sexy giggling. It was all very pleasant not to say promising, and Troy was quite sorry when a shout from the kitchen moved

Caroline Graham

her on. He ordered a double mince-slice and custard and, when he'd finished that, another cup of tea – dallying both times at the till. Then he had a ciggie, spinning it out, watching the smoke curl away. All a bit time-consuming and of course he was very sorry afterwards. But how was he to know that it would cost a human life?

Barnaby arrived home on the stroke of half seven to find the double celebration had now become a triple – for Nicholas, in his final year at the Central School of Speech and Drama, had won the coveted Gielgud medal.

He had played Oedipus, stalking the stage righteous and white clad hunting out diseased corruption and then, marled in red, finding it within himself. It had been a performance of outstanding showiness. So stylised and flamboyant in its agony as to dangerously approach parody but it had remained truthful at the heart and he had (just) pulled it off. Now, wondrously delighted by his aquisition of an agent and the certainty of the essential, life-preserving Equity Card, plus an entrancing fiancée, Nicholas was understandably on top of the world.

He and Cully were capping each other's remarks, laughing at everything and nothing. Every now and then, Cully would throw back her cloud of dark hair which was strewn with flowers. She was wearing a long scarlet cotton skirt banded with multicoloured ribbon and a white frilled Mexican blouse with sleeves so wide that several other blouses could have sprung fully formed from each one.

'I can't tell you,' Nicholas was telling everyone, as the eggs tarragon were being relished, 'how utterly appalling it was working with Phoebe Catchpole.'

'She wasn't too bad,' said Cully graciously.

'Actually,' said Joyce, 'I thought she was quite good.'

'But the size of her, darling,' continued Nicholas. 'It was like squaring up to a rhino. On "Oh – lost and damned" – you know, her final exit – she leaned on me. I thought I was going straight through the boards. The only mature student in my year and

330

they give her Jocasta. She was old enough to be my mother.'

Everyone cracked up and this time Nicholas tossed back his hair, which was long and chestnut gold. They fizzed and bloomed and radiated at each other across the table. All youth, beauty and mettlesome talent. No doubt seeing themselves, Joyce reflected tartly, as the Viv and Larry *de nos jours*. Ah well – life would soon knock the edges off. Life, the theatre, other people. Joyce felt sad, irritated and envious all at the same time. She started to collect the plates, saying, 'I can never understand why psychiatrists call lusting after your mother an Oedipus complex. Surely the whole point of the play is that he didn't know she was his mother.'

'Didn't you think Tiresias was moving?' Cully scraped up a last morsel of jelly. 'Specially in that last speech.'

'Oh come *on*,' returned Nicholas quickly. 'He's got a voice like a corncrake.'

But the greatest of these is charity. Joyce bore the dishes away thinking Nicholas was going to have to guard his tongue if he wanted to get on. She could still hear them in the kitchen, projecting like mad.

'It's great there was a female messenger,' Cully was saying. 'They're always terrific parts what with all the gory stuff happening off stage.'

'If they brought bad news,' called out Joyce, 'they were taken out and executed.'

'Blimey,' said Nicholas. 'How d'you get stuck with a job like that?'

'The usual way,' said Cully. 'Hanging round Groucho's.'

More laughter: Cully's artfully shaped, pure and poised perfectly in the throat. A chime of silver bells. Nicholas', warm, brown, shaving ad., masculine.

Joyce dished up Sainsbury's enchiladas and Basmati rice and tossed a large salad of escarole. There were two bottles already opened of some chewy Portuguese red. And Chocolate Butter Pecan ice cream to follow. She shouted, 'I could do with a hand.'

'I'm still not sure what option to take up,' said Nicholas,

harking back to his future. He had been offered play as cast at Stratford or parts at the Octogon. 'I suppose parts is the best bet.'

'Of course it is.' Cully was incredulous. 'What do you want to be? An actor – or some buskined groupie goggling at Ian McKellan's tights.'

'I thought he was at the National?'

'And you might be in a production that doesn't transfer.'

Nicholas was horrified. 'Don't they all transfer?'

Putting plates of steaming food on a tray, Joyce found Tom at her side and handed it over. 'Do try and contribute, darling.'

'What?'

'Say something.'

'I'm listening.'

'No you're not.'

'They wouldn't notice if we stayed in here and ate.'

'Don't tempt me,' said Joyce, knowing he was mistaken. Actors always notice when an audience disappears. She took in the wine and Cully poured it out, telling Nicholas the while how lucky Bolton was to have him. Nicholas said, 'Please, no idolatry.'

'Right, you two.' Barnaby's voice was loud and firm. The rebuke went unnoticed by Nicholas. Cully pulled a penitent face and smiled. Glasses were raised. 'To your future success. On and off the boards. Be happy, darling.'

They all drank. Then Cully came around the table, kissed the top of her mother's head, her father's cheek. Briefly the curtain of fragrant hair blotted out his view and he felt the loss of her, to which he had been long resigned, brutally raw and sweet.

'Thanks, Dad. Ma.' She was already back in her place.

Nicholas took her hand, curling the slender fingers within his own, raising it to his lips and saying, 'I don't want to be out of London too long.'

'For heaven's sake, Nicholas,' Joyce sounded really irritated. 'You've only left drama school five minutes. You need some experience.'

'What I'd really like,' said Nicholas, 'what would really stretch me I think is to get right away from verbal theatre altogether for a bit. Get some experience in mime. Maybe in a circus. That'd be fantastic.'

'You need to go to Spain for mime,' said Cully. 'Or France.'

'One of my current suspects worked in a Spanish circus,' said Barnaby. 'As a lion tamer.'

'Was he a roaring success?' asked Nicholas.

'We went to see a mime the night we got engaged,' said Joyce. 'Do you remember, Tom? At the Saville?'

'Course I do.' He welcomed the vivid recollection which banished all thought of work, if only for a moment. 'Had dinner first at Mon Plaisir.'

'Were they any good?' asked Nicholas. 'The company.'

'It was just one man. Marcel Marceau.'

'He's supposed to be brilliant,' said Cully.

'He was,' said Barnaby. 'Filled the stage with people. Talking to them, dancing with them. You'd swear they were actually present. There was one bit when he walked against the wind and you could see it practically knocking him over.'

'Coo,' said Cully. She and Nicholas had stopped eating.

'The best of all I thought,' said Joyce, 'was the one he finished with. The mask-maker. He had this pile of masks – imaginary of course – and he tried them on one at a time. His own face is very handsome and amazingly flexible, like rubber. All the masks were different. He held them up quickly and each time his expression was totally transformed. The last had a terrible tragic expression. And he couldn't get it off. He tugged and pulled and finally tore at the edges, getting more and more frantic. It simply wouldn't budge. But – and this is what was so incredible – although the mask didn't move you could still see what lay behind it. See his terror when he realised he was going to look like that for the rest of his life.'

Absolute silence followed this dramatic narration. Cully and Nicholas sat entranced. Barnaby drew lines on the tablecloth with his fork. Finally Nicholas spoke. 'God – I wish I'd seen that.'

'He comes back here every so often. We talk about going again but never get round to it. Isn't that right, Tom?'

There was a lengthy silence. Cully made several elegant eloquent passes before her father's eyes. Nicholas giggled and she said, 'Don't do that. It's a capital offence in this house, laughing at the police.'

'Seriously, Tom,' said Joyce, 'are you OK?' He looked so pale, so tightly folded in on himself, staring as if not knowing who she was. All three of them began to feel genuinely alarmed.

'Yes.' He took them in at last, noting their concern. 'I'm . . . sorry. Sorry. All right. Of course. Yes. I'm all right.' He smiled at them all. 'Sorry. I'm fine. Yes.'

'You're not fine,' said Joyce. 'You're burbling.'

'We should go back to Mon Plaisir, darling. For our silver wedding. Let's all go.'

'I'll get the ice cream.' Joyce disappeared to the kitchen, calling over her shoulder, 'It'll calm you down.'

She was looking through the hatch when the phone went. One harsh vibration and his chair was empty.

As the car sped through the thick night, the two men talked, getting it straight. Getting it right. Barnaby had immediately seen the truth of the matter when Troy rang his home with the new item of information. The insight that had come upon the chief inspector at the dinner table merely served to reinforce his theory.

Now, Troy said, 'Peculiar.' He signalled and slowed down, or at least accelerated less fiercely.

The Manor gates stood wide open and, apart from a single light on the ground floor, the place was dark. The Morris van was missing. As the police car entered the drive, the halogen warning lamp transformed the house into a moonlit dark-socketed shell.

They got out of the car and Barnaby knocked loudly at the

front door, also ringing the bell. Receiving no reply to either summons, he tried the knob and went inside. Troy, raising an eyebrow at this casual reworking of the police rule book, was close behind.

Barnaby called, 'Hullo?' and the word was swallowed up in the silence. The house appeared quite empty.

'I don't like this.' He moved to the bottom of the staircase and called again. 'There are eight people living here so where the hell are they?'

'It's like that ship, Chief. Found floating.'

'They couldn't have all got into the van. And the VW's still here.'

'Listen!' Troy threw his head back, staring up into the lantern. Barnaby joined him.

'What? I can't hear anything.'

'A sort of . . . scuffling. . . .'

Yes, he could hear it now. Directly overhead. As if something heavy was being dragged along. Then there was a bump and a loud cry.

'On the roof!' Troy ran out, Barnaby following more slowly. The two men retreated until they could get a good view of the top of the house. It seemed empty.

'He must be on the other side. Behind the chimneys. I'll get round—'

'No – wait.' Barnaby seized the sergeant's arm. 'Look – there . . . in the shadows.'

A pair of dark forms locked together, wrestling, struggling, dangerously near the edge. One broke away and scrambled up a nearby sloping section, the other pursued. Barnaby saw an elongated gleam of reflected light.

'Christ – he's got a bloody iron bar—'

'How do we get up?'

'There's a skylight so probably steps. You try the gallery. I'll take downstairs.'

'What about a ladder?' Both men were running now.

'Take too long. . . . (Pant, pant.) Don't even know . . . where to look. . . .' Barnaby hung on to the porch. 'You . . . go on. . . .'

'Right.'

Troy was half way across the hall when there was a strange sound above him. A gritty crackling and cracking as if a huge ball of cellophane was being violently scrunched. He glanced up and Barnaby saw his face change. Pinch into a concentration of shock and disbelief.

The sergeant jumped back just in time. A cloud of opalescent dust and fragments of brilliant glass tumbled down and, in the heart of this glittering stream, twisting and turning and crying out, the slender golden-haired figure of a man.

Everyone was in the kitchen. Heather had made some powerful tea in the twenty-cup brown enamel pot. Not all were drinking. Troy, leaning back against the draining board, shook his head as did the chief inspector. May, too, refused. Having bathed Andrew's face, both her hands were now occupied in smearing comfrey ointment on his grazed cheekbones and bleeding lips. He was sipping tea and, between winces, gazing hard at Suhami as if willing her to show some concern for his condition.

May, Suhami and Arno had arrived back within seconds of Tim's fall. Seeing the Orion, Suhami had parked practically in the porch and hurried into the house.

'Tim. . . .' She had cried out, flying across the hall, kneeling by his side, hands to her face in horror.

'There's nothing you can do, Miss.' Troy had tried to raise her up. 'The chief inspector's ringing for an ambulance. Don't touch that,' he added sharply, as she reached out to the crowbar.

'But – how did it happen?' She looked at the gaping hole in the lantern. 'Did he fall? What was he doing up there?'

That was when Andrew appeared, dragging himself along by the gallery rail. He was bleeding and his shirt and jeans were torn. The rasp of his breath, expelled forcefully in the form of shudders, seemed to fill the hall. He was mumbling something, the words becoming clearer as he approached.

'Kill me . . . tried to kill me. . . .'

Half an hour later Barnaby was repeating the phrase in the form of a question. He asked three times before getting any response.

'Why? Because he'd discovered who I really was.' The words, issuing through swollen lips, were not quite clear. There was a murmur of puzzled curiosity.

May, wiping her hands on a muslin cloth, said, 'What do you mean, Christopher?'

'My name isn't Christopher. It's Andrew Carter. Jim Carter was my uncle.' The curiosity became consternation. The others followed Barnaby's example and started to ask questions, and it took a good few minutes to quieten them down. Ken was the last to hush after asking what the point was in pretending to be somebody else.

Andrew explained about the letter, his uncle's tablets, his own presence at the inquest, the whole thing. 'I knew someone was on to me,' he concluded, speaking to Barnaby. 'I just didn't know who it was. The photograph – the one I showed you – was hidden under some shirts. I found it had been moved. Shortly after this I was attacked. A lump of iron was pushed off the roof as I was leaving the house. I lied to the others about where the stone fell. It was not on the slab where May was standing at all, but the one behind.'

'You said nothing of this to me.'

'But I did, Chief Inspector!' cried May. 'I told you when I was first interviewed.'

'I don't think—'

'I remember it distinctly. My accident? When the meteor fell?'

'Ahhh. Yes.'

'You told me to stick to the matter in hand. I didn't like to persist. Thought there might be some sort of etiquette in these matters. You brushed me aside in your office as well.'

There's no answer to that is there, my old darling? Troy took secret pleasure in his chief's discomposure, whilst glossing over

337

the fact that he would have done just the same himself.

'So why did you keep quiet?' The chief inspector emphasised the 'you' as he turned once more to Andrew.

'I felt that if I appeared ignorant of the real reason for the attack, they'd think I wasn't on to them and my position would be safer.'

'Sounds like dangerously muddled thinking to me. And that needn't have stopped you telling us.'

'You'd have come round asking questions and given it all away.'

'What evidence do you have that the whole thing wasn't an accident?'

'I went up on the roof directly afterwards. There was no way the metal chunk could have rolled off. It was a couple of feet from the edge. Also, wedged in between the chimneys, I found a crowbar.'

'The one that was used tonight?'

Andrew nodded. He looked weary, finished. 'I took it away and hid it in Calypso's stall. Yesterday it was still there. When I checked tonight it was gone. I realised that whoever took it was the one who attacked me. It turned out to be Tim.'

The others exchanged looks of deep distress. May said, 'You should never have attempted to conceal this, Christopher. It was very wrong.'

'We'll have to remember now to call him "Andrew",' said Heather.

And Ken added, 'Tomorrow I shall channel him a star name.'

'It wasn't even as if I was much of a threat. I'd been looking round, asking questions, checking Jim's room for weeks and found nothing.'

'Was that you then – in the middle of the night?'

'Yes. I'm sorry if I alarmed you, May. I heard your window open as I was running off.'

'I'm glad to have the mystery explained. And my other mystery, Chief Inspector . . . the snatch of conversation I overheard – surely Andrew's suspicion of his uncle's death renders that even more significant?'

'What conversation's this?' Andrew's tiredness seemed to fall away. 'Who was it? What did they say?'

'Who it was remains unclear, Mr Carter,' said Barnaby. 'But they seemed concerned about a possible post mortem.'

'I knew it —'

'I can't imagine why anyone would wish to hurt Jim,' said Suhami. 'He was so harmless.'

'I told you,' said Andrew. 'He discovered whatever was going on here.'

'Nothing's going on,' said Ken, 'but love, light and peace.'

'And healing,' added Heather.

'Rather than go in for vague speculation at this stage,' said Barnaby, 'I'd like to try and get straight what happened tonight. How did the fight start? What were you doing on the roof?'

'I was in my room. Ken and Heather had gone into the village —'

'Just briefly,' Heather broke in defensively, 'to exercise his leg.'

'And Suze had driven May and Arno to the hospital. He'd had an accident.'

Good God, thought Troy. If this lot ever had a day without an accident, they'd think the world was coming to an end.

'I'd taken a drink up and was reading on my bed. I hadn't seen Tim. None of us had, except Arno. I'd been reading for half an hour, I suppose, and I heard someone cry out my name —'

'Which name?' asked the chief inspector.

'My real name, *Andrew*. That's what was so odd. Then I heard his door open and I went out on to the landing. It seems pretty stupid now but I wasn't suspicious at all. It was just poor old Tim – you know? And he was coming towards me – his hair all tangled and his eyes staring – with this bar. He was . . . wielding it. Whirling it round his head. It was bloody terrifying. I backed away – my room's at the very end of the gallery and I found myself up against the door that led to the roof. So it was either up there or over the gallery rail. . . .' Suhami gave a jerky little cry of fright.

'Of course on the roof I was equally trapped. There's no way down. I dodged about at first between the chimney stacks – he kept flailing away – great chunks of brick flying around when he hit something. And then I thought if only I could get rid of it, we'd at least be more equally matched. When the halogen lamp came on it distracted him and I had a try. Made a grab at the bar and hung on. He wouldn't let go. Then he started kicking. He was quite a bit taller than me . . . long legs . . . it was very painful. So I went back to dodging about. I was crouching behind the chimney stack next to the lantern when he came by. He stood inches away, staring round, trying to suss me. I reached out and grabbed his ankles. I thought if I could bring him down. . . . But he fell backwards away from me . . . and through the glass. . . .'

The last words were barely audible. His narrow handsome face had become pale with remembered fear and clouded with misery. Andrew turned his back on them all as if the confession had marked and isolated him. There was a long heavy silence which even Ken and Heather seemed hesitant to rupture. Finally Barnaby spoke.

'So you're convinced that Riley was the person who found the photograph and attacked you on Thursday?' Andrew lowered his head. 'And was responsible for your uncle's death?'

'I believe he had something to do with it, yes. Although I'd have thought the whisky business a bit beyond him.'

'I can't believe any of this,' said May. 'It's just too terrible.'

The Beavers nodded in agreement and their eyes shone.

Barnaby turned his attention to Arno who so far had not spoken. He sat by the empty range, his left foot, encased in a snowball of white bandage, resting on a metal bridge to raise it from the ground. His body, still awash with the residue of alcohol, was also shot full of pain-killers and anti-tetanus vaccine. His mind, tortured by a certain ambiguity in May's receipt of his advances, felt full of cotton wool. He was almost sure he had not actually been repulsed or rejected, although in all the kerfuffle it was hard to be certain.

Now he became aware of a certain pressure on his bubble of drugs and dreams and struggled to pay attention. The chief inspector was staring at him in what struck Arno as a grave and accusatory manner. He felt suddenly sick. It had come, then, as he had always known it would.

'I'm sorry. . . .' They were all looking at him like that now, even May. Oh God – even May. 'I'm afraid I didn't hear.'

Barnaby repeated himself. 'Isn't it time you told the truth, Mr Gibbs?'

'Why do you say that to me?' Arno's face was the colour of his bandages.

'I think you know the answer.' Barnaby waited, then, when the other man still did not speak, continued, 'I ask because of your obvious concern for the boy. Your attempts to stop me speaking to him and, when I did, your interruptions lest he give himself away.' When the silence continued, he added, 'Come along, Mr Gibbs. Nothing can hurt him now.'

'No.' Arno looked up sadly, 'That's true.' He explained it all, then, addressing Andrew, as was only right.

'Your uncle's death I would have said was an accident, although I fear a court of law might disagree. On the day it happened the three of us were going into town, just as I described at the inquest. Tim and I were putting some fresh flowers in the Solar while we waited for the Master who had gone to collect Tim's outdoor coat. Suddenly we heard loud voices. I ran out to see what the matter was. The Master was coming out of Tim's room, followed by Jim. They were arguing. I was astonished. I'd never heard Jim even raise his voice before. At the head of the stairs they stopped – Jim blocking the Master's way and shouting, "I shan't let you do it. I'll tell everyone what I know – everyone."

'Then he sort of grabbed at the Master's shoulders as if he was going to shake him. Next – and it all happened so quickly there was nothing I could do – I heard a sort of . . . well . . . *roar* is the nearest I can get to it, and Tim raced along the gallery, seized

Jim and pushed him away. He went hurtling backwards down the stairs and broke his neck.' Gradually, during this speech, Arno's gaze had dropped towards the floor. Now he forced himself to look once more at Andrew Carter. 'He couldn't have suffered. I know that's small consolation.'

'You're right. It is.'

'Once it was plain there was nothing we could do – and if there had been *I swear* it would have been done – both of us thought only of protecting Tim. We knew that the police would have to take some sort of action even though there had been no intention to cause serious harm. The Master thought Tim might be charged with manslaughter and found . . . "unfit to plead" is it? In any case he might have gone to prison – shut in a cell perhaps with dreadful people, like the ones who hurt him before. Or be put away in an institution. Drugged to keep him quiet . . . sitting around for months or years surrounded by mad people. He was only twenty-three!' cried Arno passionately, 'and he was so happy here. We thought if we were vigilant and watched him carefully, nothing like that would ever happen again. I realise now,' he turned to Barnaby, 'especially after tonight, that I did wrong.'

'Very wrong, Mr Gibbs.' Barnaby strove to keep his voice even. He was angry with Gibbs but even angrier with himself. Interviewing Tim, wishing to cause as little distress as possible, he had deliberately not introduced the Master's name. Now, too late, it was plain that the accident the petrified boy had referred to was not Craigie's murder but the earlier death. 'You understand that perjury is a criminal offence.'

'. . . Yes . . .' whispered Arno. He seemed on the verge of tears. His trembling fingers searched for a handkerchief.

Barnaby eyed the wretched figure coldly. Knowing even then that he would not prosecute, he saw no harm in letting Gibbs sweat it out for a day or two. Or even a week or two.

'Go on. What happened next?'

'We took Tim into the garden – he was terrified, crying – and tried to work out what to do. We decided the least complicated plan, and the most sensible, would be to just carry on into Causton and do our shopping as we planned, then come home and pretend to discover the body. The fact that May – Miss Cuttle – returned first is a matter that caused us both great distress.

'The Master took Tim to the van and I was about to follow when I started to get terribly cold feet. And an overwhelming conviction that we wouldn't be believed. It just seemed so unlikely that anyone would fall down a flight of stairs they'd used hundreds of times, for no reason. So then I thought – what if he'd been drinking? There was a miniature of whisky in our medicine box. I got it out and tried to pour some into his mouth – I had to close his lips and massage his throat to try and get it down.' Arno shuddered. 'It was horrible. Then I rucked up the runner on the landing to make it look as if he'd caught his foot in it.'

'I told the Master when we were driving back. He got terribly upset. Kept saying I shouldn't have done that. Then a couple of days later, seeing how unhappy I was, he explained why. Told me that the stuff Jim was taking for his infection meant he couldn't take even the smallest drop of alcohol. He said if they did a post mortem—'

Here May gave a little cry of recognition and looked affirmingly across at Barnaby, who signalled her to be quiet.

'—and it was discovered, they'd know something was wrong. When they did, and it wasn't, I was so relieved. I took it as a sort of sign that perhaps I hadn't done anything so terrible after all.'

'Surely, Inspector,' said May, 'you can see that Arno's motives were quite selfless. He did the wrong thing, yes, but for the rightest and purest of reasons. For the love of a fellow human being.'

This unexpected, generous and completely undeserved sponsorship affected Arno deeply. Such a tumultuous wave of gratitude broke about his heart that he felt almost unable to breathe.

Sensing a natural break, Heather made a move to refresh the

giant pot whilst Ken readjusted his plaster cast on the wheelback chair to a more easeful and prominent position. He had come to regard Arno's snowball as some sort of featherweight contender in the wounded-hero stakes and had no intention of giving any ground.

May put the ointment away and wondered about going to check on Felicity. The sleeping draught had been a mild one and she might well have been awakened and alarmed by the disturbance. Suhami collected the cups of those who wanted seconds. She touched Andrew gently on the shoulder and smiled when she brought his, but could not be coaxed into remaining by his side. He had hoped his appearance might so distress her that affection would be rekindled. That terrible business on the roof, the whole bloody mess in fact would be worth it if that happened.

This time round Troy accepted a drink but Barnaby still refused.

'Jim's death may have been unintentional,' said Heather when everyone had been served, 'but the attack on Chris – sorry *Andrew*, certainly wasn't. I suppose Tim got a sort of taste for it. People are supposed to, aren't they?'

'What a spiteful thing to say!' retorted Suhami angrily. 'He's just died for heaven's sake. The least we can do is speak kindly of him.'

Heather flushed at this slur on her reputation as a non-stop fountain of compassionate concern. 'I don't think you're in any position to attack me, Suhami. After all, if it weren't for you the Master would be alive today.'

Suhami gasped and went pale. Andrew spoke up sharply. 'She was against her father's visit from the start. It was the Master who insisted.'

'I think you know,' said Barnaby, 'that as far as the Craigie murder is concerned, Mr Gamelin's visit was neither here nor there.'

Six faces stared at him, five with varying degrees of amazement. Only May, assuming the police had come round at last to her celestial way of thinking, nodded serenely. Suhami sat forward awkwardly, thin fingers locked together.

'Do you mean . . . do you have some idea that he might not have been responsible?'

'There's no doubt about it, Miss Gamelin. He was definitely not responsible. Just unfortunately in the wrong place at the wrong time.'

'Was that Tim as well, then?' asked Heather. 'In a sort of mad fit.'

'Quite impossible,' said Arno. 'He was utterly devoted to the Master. You saw how he grieved.'

'They can turn though, people like that,' said Ken. 'Even on those they love. Like dogs.'

'He was not a dog!' cried May.

'Perhaps it was Trixie?' said Andrew. 'Perhaps that's why she ran away?'

'What on earth motive could Trixie have?' said Ken. Then, to Barnaby, 'You should have told me you weren't satisfied Gamelin was guilty. I could have channelled Hilarion for you.'

'Are you saying, Inspector, that my trust fund might not have been the motive?'

'Or that the whole thing was an accident?'

'Oh no, Mrs Beavers – the murder of Arthur Craigie was quite deliberate, but it was also opportunistic. By that I mean prepared for up to a point and then, when things took a wrong turn, carried through in a most daring and impulsive manner.'

He got up, giving the impression without speaking that it was to stretch his legs, but really it was to pace up and down. Troy watched, not really lacking confidence but still extremely tense. It was thin ice the chief was striding out on. Suppositions, deductions, guesses, a certain amount of informational back-up, but no real proof. If the party in question brazened it out. . . .

'One of the most crucial components,' began the chief inspector, 'of any murder case – random killings apart – is the character

345

of the victim. What sort of man or woman were they? What makes them tick? The answer can only be found by asking people who knew. In this case they were pretty unanimous. Only Guy Gamelin demurred in painting a picture of an almost saintly man full of concern for his fellow humans. And even he admitted to being genuinely impressed during the course of their single conversation. In fact, not to put too fine a point on it, the Master was universally loved.

'But what was really interesting about Mr Craigie is that when I tried to look further into his background to discover more about him, I was unable to do so. As far as I could see he had sprung into being as a fully fledged seer a couple of years ago. Now that's very odd. It's not easy to remain unrecorded in these computerised times. If you've ever paid insurance or tax, owned a car, house or bank account you're down there somewhere. But not Arthur Craigie.'

'He had a bank account,' said Ken defensively. 'In Causton.'

'The Windhorse had a bank account, Mr Beavers. Not quite the same thing. To cover your tracks so efficiently,' continued Barnaby, 'involves a lot of determination plus a fair amount of rather iffy know-how.'

'I don't like the turn this conversation's taking, Chief Inspector.'

'Blackening the name of a person who can't defend himself is despicable,' said Heather and looked round in surprise when Suhami laughed.

'One of the reasons we found it so difficult to trace him was that Craigie was an alias. And the first of many, adopted when he came out of prison just over two years ago where he had served five years out of seven for fraud. In fact, Miss Gamelin, your father was not far out when he called Craigie a con man.'

'That is utter hooey!' May rose trembling, as near to rage as any there had ever seen her. Arno trembled, too, in sympathy and admiration. 'His astral body was radiant. Suffused with blue. That's something no one can fake.'

'I'm sure that's true, Inspector,' said Suhami. She also seemed

346

most moved and on the verge of tears. 'You might have checked all sorts of things but there's a mix-up somewhere. You've confused him with someone else.'

'Mind you,' said Ken, 'I suppose anyone who's going to be successful at a mucky business like fraud has to be totally convincing. The essence of the job.'

Heather nodded. Both of them seemed to have quite abandoned the ostentatious knowing of their place. Forgetting his alcohol/drug-infested bloodstream, Arno shook his head chidingly at this sign of breaking ranks then wished he hadn't. The result was so sensational he thought for a moment it had rolled off entirely.

'Do you mean that someone from his past broke in here,' asked Heather, 'and attacked him?'

'That's nonsense,' said Andrew. 'The only people in the room when he died were us.'

'Indeed,' agreed Barnaby. 'Although I think Mrs Beavers is right in a way when she suggests someone from his past was there. And certainly the manner of that past contributed to his death. However, it's my conviction that Craigie died not because he was a con man *but because he was not*.'

'I knew it!' May cried out in triumph. 'The aura never lies.'

'I don't get that,' said Andrew. 'You just told us he was.'

'Let me expand. When I discovered his background I naturally saw the acquisition of the Manor House – using I'm pretty sure money from a time share swindle – as a major ingredient in some grand scam. But, going into the affairs of the Windhorse, I found not only was everything in financially immaculate order but that quite an altruistic flavour hung over the place. Bursaries were given to the deserving and, occasionally perhaps, to the undeserving. People who came for healing or therapy were not charged a set fee but asked to pay what they felt they could afford. Every month a varying amount was sent to charity. And yet . . . something was going on. We have Jim Carter's letter to prove this. And tonight, via the evidence of Mr Gibbs, his spoken words: "I shan't let you do it. I'll tell everyone what I know."

'The letter, written so soon before Mr Carter's death, struck me as deeply worrying. Now that we're aware of how he died I feel it appears less so. The spoken threat however – and I do see it as a threat – remains. What did Jim Carter know and, equally important, what was Craigie about to do, that instigated such a violent response?

'My conclusion about the first half of that question is predictable enough. Jim Carter knew about the past. The second part isn't so easy. I thought if I could find out more about Carter this would help. My sergeant and I looked around his room and here, although his clothes and effects had been removed, I found two things that I thought were interesting.'

He paused and Troy, standing well back against the wall, barely nodded in an involuntary acknowledgement of the power of his chief's personality and narrative skill. There wasn't a movement anywhere. Not a blink. Nothing but total absorption.

'One of them was an empty shoe box which had once contained some extremely expensive Italian loafers. An unexpected choice for a man who spends all day at his devotions. A tiny anomaly but, as I say, interesting.

'And then there were the books. At first sight just the type that you'd expect. All second-hand – that's fair enough, not everyone can afford new books. But all the prices were marked in decimal coinage. Now Jim's nephew has told us that his uncle read devotional literature all his life, yet none of them could have been bought before 1971. In truth, as our department discovered, none of them was bought before 1990. They were part of a job lot from several second-hand bookshops in Slough and Uxbridge. Nearly six hundred altogether.'

'My uncle's collection was probably somewhere else,' said Andrew. 'Maybe downstairs in the library.'

'But you told us you recognised the books in his room, Mr Carter. And how much seeing them distressed you.'

'Do you mean they were bought just to create the right effect?' asked Ken.

'Precisely so,' said Barnaby who had helped dress enough sets

348

for his wife's drama group to know whereof he spoke. 'But what was so strange about these bulk buys is that they were collected, and in two cases paid for, not by Craigie but by Carter.'

'Jim?' May looked completely bewildered. 'But why on earth would he do that?'

'Perhaps his nephew can tell us?'

'No idea.' Andrew shrugged, opening his hands in helpless incomprehension. 'Unless, completely taken in, he was persuaded to make a contribution.'

'Oh, I don't think your uncle was that easy to take in. I'd say, if anything, the boot was on the other foot.'

'I don't know what you mean, Chief Inspector, but I do know I don't intend to sit here and listen to you malign him.' He climbed down from the table and was half way to the door when Barnaby spoke again.

'Why did you dye your hair, Mr Carter?'

'We went into all that when I was in your office. I didn't want anyone to connect me with my uncle.'

'But the likeness was negligible. I could hardly see it at all.'

'*I* thought it was there – all right? And decided to protect myself. Christ – I was nearly killed three days ago, I'm assaulted tonight by a madman with an iron bar. You'd think I'd get sympathy and understanding. Not a bloody third degree.'

'So fair on the photograph, wasn't it? Nearly white – very striking. Anyone who'd met you as a child say, as Craigie did, might easily have recognised you again.'

'As a . . .' Andrew stared around, inviting everyone to share his incredulity.

'How old were you? Eight, nine? When they worked together?' Now Andrew shook his head in the way people do when presented with something strictly beyond belief. 'I'd say this was the real reason you didn't want the police called in after your uncle's death. Not because people here might be put on the alert but because of what we might discover.'

'All this is absolute nonsense.'

'I believe Andrew's right,' said May. 'The first gathering I went to, Jim was on the platform and spoke of how meeting the Master changed his life. That was why I joined. I was so moved by his testimony.'

'You can see that old trick, Miss Cuttle, in any market place. A shyster selling rubbish and another in the crowd shouting as how the rubbish changed his life. Tell me – didn't you find staying at the Windhorse a touch expensive when you first arrived?'

May appeared taken aback at this sudden swerve in the conversation. 'I must admit I did. And was asked to charge rather more for my workshops than I personally would have liked. Arno . . . you came shortly after me, I don't know if you . . . ?'

'Yes. I remember seeing a notice in a travel agent's window just after I'd booked my first weekend and I could have had a week in Spain for the same money. Not that it wasn't worth every penny.' He looked sideways at May, blushed and turned in his toes – or at least the five that were still movable.

'But wasn't that just until the place got established?' asked Heather. 'Certainly when we joined a year later things were much more reasonable.'

'We couldn't have come otherwise,' explained Ken.

'I don't think it was a question of getting the place established at all, Mr Beavers. I think the original premise was to separate as many people from as much of their cash as was humanly possible.'

'So what went wrong?' said Ken, amending hastily, 'Or right, I should say.'

'My own belief – and this is not unheard of although the longer the criminal's in the game the rarer it gets – is that Craigie, perhaps because of his reading, his pretend prayers, his meditations, his constant exposure to people who were truthfully struggling to live some sort of spiritual life, underwent a genuine transformation. Not a grand Pauline conversion, something slower yet nonetheless quite genuine. In other words the mask became the man.'

'I knew it,' May spoke quietly. 'He could not have taught the way he did—'

'Or cared for us the way he did,' interrupted Suhami.

'And there's Tim,' said Arno. 'He related to people emotionally. He *understood* what they were really like. He was like a child in that respect, and they're not easily fooled.'

Barnaby let that pass. This was not the time to go into the matter of how tragically easily children can be fooled. He continued: 'But then Craigie became ill. Finally, I've no doubt, becoming aware that he would not recover. And this led to what I suspect is the "something terrible" mentioned in Carter's letter to his nephew. I've been aware of the word *trust* as a persistent irritating niggle and couldn't think why. I knew all there was to know about Miss Gamelin's inheritance and how – as I thought – it related to the case, so it didn't seem to be that. And then I recalled your first interview, Mr Gibbs, and realised that not one, but two trusts are involved here.'

'Really.' Arno frowned. 'I can't think . . . unless you mean the charity—'

'Exactly,' said the chief inspector. 'Craigie wished to deed the house and organisation in such a manner that no single individual had overall control. This enraged Carter who, I'm pretty sure, in spite of what his nephew told me to the contrary – had put money from the sale of his house into the enterprise. Nearly two hundred thousand pounds. I doubt if the altercation Mr Gibbs overheard was the first by a long chalk.'

'He didn't do it though,' said Arno. 'Take charitable status I mean.'

'There was no need,' said the chief inspector, 'after Carter's accident.'

'So it's an accident now?' Andrew had flushed dark red. 'You're as bad as those incompetents at the inquest.'

'It's not a good idea to take the law into your own hands, Mr Carter.'

'Well, it's not exactly shining in yours is it? How do you know what the argument was about? Even Arno who overheard them and lived here doesn't. And I must say the fact that Riley killed my uncle and has made two murderous attempts on me seems to have been pretty lightly touched on. You seem to have forgotten it was almost my death being investigated here tonight. And no doubt, if you hadn't turned up when you did, that would have been covered up as well.'

'That's unfair,' said May. 'Tim was only trying to prevent your uncle attacking the Master.'

'We've only Arno's word for that.'

'His word,' said May staunchly, 'is good enough for me.'

'The grey sheep. That's what you rather disarmingly called yourself in my office, Mr Carter, if I remember correctly.' An uninterested shrug. 'Your ex-Stowe chum by the way not only genuinely lost his wallet but was five thousand in the red by the time he'd notified Visa and American Express. One item being an antelope jacket.'

'Well it's not this one. I got it from Aquascutum months ago.'

'That shouldn't be difficult to prove.'

'If you've the time to waste.'

'What did you mean, Inspector?' Suhami was staring at Andrew Carter with sickened apprehension. 'About taking the law into his own hands.'

'I'm talking about murder, Miss Gamelin.' Although his stress on the word was harsh, Barnaby's glance was not without sympathy as it rested on the girl in the pale green sari.

'*Murder.*' Her face became drawn and, whispering, 'It can't be true,' she started to shake. Heather immediately bustled forward and enfolded Suhami in her giant bosoms.

'Of course it isn't true,' said Andrew scornfully. 'I didn't go near him. Just because you've given up on Gamelin you needn't think you're pinning this on me. For a start – what earthly motive would I have?'

'A mixture, the most dominant I imagine being revenge. One of the few things you told the truth about in my office was that you had a deep and lasting affection for your uncle. I've no doubt, as you told me you kept in touch, that you knew about the set-up here and that things were going wrong. What made you so sure Craigie had killed your uncle? Did you think that thieves had fallen out?'

'There were no thieves to fall out. At least as far as Jim was concerned. He told me in one of his letters that the man who was running things here had developed religious mania. Well, we all know how people like that can turn. Half the psychos going say God was telling them to get rid of prostitutes or rent boys or one-legged pensioners.' He broke off here to light a cigarette. Heather started coughing and waving at the air.

'You're right about the argument though. Jim felt the man was a poseur. It was only due to my uncle's constant efforts at persuasion that the prices started to come down.'

'You can think on your feet, son,' said Barnaby. 'I'll give you that.'

'You said the most dominant motive.' Ken was now also coughing preposterously. 'What were the others then?'

'Money – as it so often is. First in respect of the entailment of this place which I've no doubt Mr Carter, being his uncle's heir, regards as no more than his due.' He paused to encourage a response but in vain. 'And then of course the famous trust fund. Miss Gamelin was about to offload it. Carter was in a difficult position. He'd been pursuing her almost from the first moment he arrived yet there was still no definite engagement, let alone the chime of wedding bells. Perhaps under Craigie's influence she was still drawn to a more reclusive, maybe even celibate life. Another reason why his death may have forwarded your plans.'

'There weren't any "plans". I fell in love.' His angry glance swung from Barnaby to Troy and back again. 'Can't you see how you're upsetting her? Telling all these bloody lies.'

Suhami was watching Andrew as he spoke. She saw no traces of remorse. But then, if it was all bloody lies, there wouldn't be. Her own reaction to all these revelations was most curious. After the first shock of distress and disbelief she found she was experiencing nothing at all. A great yawning void seemed to have opened up around her. Whether Christopher had truly fallen in love with her seemed to be of no importance. She put a little gentle pressure on the memory of past emotions, recalled the moment in the byre when she had been so delirious with joy. The whole scene now seemed no more than faintly pleasurable. For the first time in her life things had gone wrong, more vilely and horribly than ever before, and she was not all over the floor in pieces. It was a mystery but a most consoling one.

'Forgive me for saying so, Inspector,' murmured Arno, 'but what you suggest is quite impossible. As Andrew has already explained and we can all confirm – he never went near the dais. Are you saying he had an accomplice?'

'An unwitting accomplice. Not to the act of murder, but of course he had to get the knife and the glove into the Solar. He was dressed – I'm sure deliberately to reinforce his "alibi" – in such a way as to make concealment about his person out of the question.'

'But how could anyone bring a knife in without knowing it?' said Ken.

'In a bag,' said Barnaby. 'There was a thread caught up on the handle proving this. Where were you positioned on the dais, Mr Carter?'

Andrew did not reply. Suhami said, 'He was next to me.'

'Yet after fetching Miss Cuttle's cape you did not return there?'

'May often had distressing times during her regressions. I thought it might be of help if I stayed close.'

'Ever done that before?'

'No, but I should think just the fact that I chose to do it then is enough to knock your theory on the head. If you're going to kill someone you get as close to your victim as possible, not as far away.'

'Ah, but you had no choice. Because you put the knife in the wrong bag. It was only when opening it to take out the cape that you realised your mistake.'

'In *my* bag!' May's voice surged to a peak of Bracknellian splendour.

'He thought it was Miss Gamelin's. They're very similar.'

Suhami groaned at this and Heather's bosoms leapt to their cradling once more.

'He did this at the very last minute, perhaps even taking charge to make sure she didn't open it.'

'Yes that's right,' cried Ken. 'He carried it in for her. I remember.'

'You would,' said Andrew.

'He was banking on the sort of disturbance which did in fact take place, but of course he expected to be close to Craigie at the time. As I said previously, this was a partly planned, partly impulsive crime.'

'I don't see how he could possibly have slipped a knife in at the last moment Inspector,' said Arno. 'He couldn't have been carrying it and it certainly wasn't on the table.'

'Yes, that fazed me for a bit. Then I remembered Guy Gamelin's complaint that he wasn't allowed to sit beside Sylvie because one of the community's disciplines was keeping to the same seat. I've no doubt that there was a cushion on Mr Carter's. The knife was placed beneath it earlier in the day. And the glove, too, of course.

'Stupidly choosing a left-handed one,' said Andrew scornfully, 'although I use the right.'

'Just an added pointer in the wrong direction. I think you simply turned it inside out then turned it back. You couldn't have known of course that Gamelin would be left-handed. That must have seemed a real bonus. As it happened, he tried to offload it behind the curtain and was spotted. I'm sure, if this had not been the case, you would have somehow managed to draw the matter to our attention. Perhaps via Miss Gamelin who was already completely convinced of her father's guilt.'

'Supposition – all of it. You're stuck, Inspector – you can't solve the problem so you've dreamed up this fantasy. And if you're going to say I killed him when I went to switch on the light you can think again. I didn't go near him at any time. Nor, as you've obviously forgotten, was I part of the group that Craigie pointed at before he died.'

355

'That's of no matter,' said Barnaby. 'For Arthur Craigie was not pointing at a person at all.'

'Yes he was. Gamelin. Ask anyone.'

'Certainly it must have seemed that way but going over things earlier tonight, I was struck by one very interesting difference between Guy Gamelin and the rest of the group. He was the only person who was standing up.'

'So?'

'That put him in the way.'

'In the way of what, Inspector?' asked Arno.

'I believe Craigie was indicating the direction from which the knife was thrown!'

There was a fair old hubbub at this. The word 'thrown' was repeated several times with varying degrees of incredulity. Heather left Suhami and ran excitedly back to Ken. Andrew burst out laughing.

'Oh – that's brilliant. In a dark room? Ten feet away?'

'Not dark – duskish. And he was wearing a brilliant white robe.'

'Impossible.'

'Not to someone who's thrown knives for a living.' The hubbub melted into a stunned silence. 'You didn't tell us that did you, Mr Carter?'

'There's all sorts of things I didn't tell you.'

'That's for sure,' said Troy.

'It was careless to mention your time at Blackpool, because we got in touch with your employers who revealed that, apart from your lion-taming skills for which they had little use, you also offered fire eating and a knife act.'

'Carny people'll say anything.' Barnaby was silent for quite a time. Eventually Andrew Carter spoke again.

'That's it is it? Your evidence against me? Well, all I can say is that if by some miracle this ever gets as far as a courtroom, the jury'll be falling off their bench in hysterics.'

Miracle is right, thought Troy. He had listened, engrossed, totally convinced, whilst the chief unravelled the case against

Andrew Carter but now the mesmerising tale was done what did they have? What did they actually *have*? A thread from a bag caught up on a knife. Everything else was supposition. No prints on the murder weapon. One quick daring movement with everyone looking elsewhere. All Carter had to do was stick to his bewildered denials and a good lawyer would have him out on the streets before you could say no case to answer. He knew that – the cunning bugger. Look at him shrugging, shaking his head, smiling. He wouldn't crack. Or make mistakes. Even if they managed to dig up some past form – so what? All that proved was he's not Persil clean. And character defamation could only take you so far. Troy tried to look at his chief but Barnaby, his face blank, was gazing at the stone-flagged floor. Finally he looked up and spoke.

'How did you get the boy to come out of his room?'

Stone the crows he's really getting desperate. Clocked the problems, no making the first one stick so going all out on the second which is even more of a no no. Riley'd already attacked Carter once and nearly killed him. Self-defence is a foregone conclusion. They won't even get him on manslaughter. Troy's expression revealed none of these ponderings but his heart was heavy. What was it the chief had said yesterday – up the creek without a paddle? Too bloody right! Troy felt a momentary flash of fellow feeling for Barnaby. Almost of affection. This sort of empathetic insight was so alien to his usual way of thinking that he was relieved to see it disappear as quickly and mysteriously as it had arisen.

Now the tension in the room had snapped, mainly because of Andrew's burst of apparently quite genuine laughter. May broke a long awkward silence by asking Arno how his foot was feeling. Suhami turned her back on them all. Heather collected the dirty cups and took them to the sink. Only Troy saw the door slowly open.

Barnaby repeated the question, '*How did you get the boy to come out?*'

'He imitated Arno's voice.'

357

Felicity was wearing her Caroline Charles two-piece and borrowed furry slippers. She looked very white but the words were strong and clear. The pressure in the room shot up again.

'Come and sit down, Mrs Gamelin.' Barnaby, his sluggish heart once more on the move, drew out a chair. She came further into the room, but hesitantly, looking frightened. Having set her down, Barnaby perched on the table's edge, his burly form concealing Andrew Carter.

'Tell me what happened.'

'I woke up wanting the loo. I put a robe on and I'd just started to open the door when I saw . . . him. . . .'

'Andrew Carter?'

'Christopher.'

'Whereabouts??'

'Kneeling by the keyhole of Tim's room. His lips were very close. He said, 'This is Arno. I've got your supper.' His voice was so different. It was uncanny. He didn't have a tray or anything but he had this terrible iron bar that he propped up against the wall. And when Tim opened the door, Christopher made a grab, pulled him outside and . . . and started to hit him with it. I should have gone for help . . . I know I should. But I was so *frightened*. I just went inside again. I didn't even ring the police. I'm sorry . . . so sorry. . . .'

'We were on our way in any case by then, Mrs Gamelin.'

'Oh – is that true?'

'Quite true.'

'Then I don't feel so. . . . I heard glass breaking. Is he all right? Tim?'

There was a deeply awkward pause. Heather went across to Felicity and said, 'Why don't I make you a nice cup of Acorna? With plenty of honey.'

Troy wondered if that was the boiled sludge offered to him the night of the murder. If so it was more likely to finish Felicity off than revive her. And that would never do because they'd need her for the trial. What a marvellous piece of luck! And she was telling the truth, it had shown on Carter's face though he'd been quick to collect himself. A nice little caution now, a neat arrest and they'd be home and dry. The chief had got up, was about to say something, but before he could do so May spoke up again.

'What you said earlier about the Master's death makes me wonder if I should have been more explicit at my first interview.'

'In what respect, Miss Cuttle?'

'Well of course I did see everything, you know.' The ground opened around Barnaby's feet. I am not hearing this, he observed silently, and there's an end to it.

'It's all in my statement.' The only one he had hardly bothered to go over, recalling it as a load of supernatural claptrap, signifying nothing. 'A silver dart? Flying overhead?'

Oh Jesus! Oh bloody hell. He didn't know whether to laugh or cry. Cry of course. What else? With another life gone. The chief inspector had a sudden searing sense of shame. He recalled Joyce's fierce accusation that he never listened and his own earlier attempts to stop Troy exploring the con-man theory. It seemed no one could be right but himself. Fortunately the sergeant had gone ahead anyway but if he had not. . . .

My arteries are hardening, thought Barnaby. And I don't like it. He realised May was addressing him.

'I'm afraid I felt at the time,' she said, 'that you were simply not ready for more detailed esoteric knowledge. But perhaps I was mistaken.'

Yes, perhaps you were, you dozy old bat, thought Troy, noting his chief's look of crumbling devastation. The sergeant's reaction was not entirely sympathetic. He had been on the receiving end of the instruction always to keep an open mind too often not to feel a sting of satisfaction. There was also the undeniable fact that this discovery slightly eased Troy's own guilt. His sole defence, should Barnaby notice the fifteen-minute discrepancy between the time logged for the Blackpool information and his sergeant's phone call to Arbury Crescent, would have been of the truculent 'How was I to know?' nature. Which was of course no defence at all. Now there'd been a pre-emptive strike. For if the chief had been more attentive to May Cuttle's statement not only the boy, but also a great deal of time and money would have been saved as well.

The caution was completed. Troy buttoned his jacket and moved forwards, prepared for trouble. But there was none and five minutes later all three men were in the car and on the way to the station.

Troy drove. Barnaby sat in the back, Andrew Carter sullenly at his side. He had vehemently denied Felicity's story, saying that she'd probably been hallucinating. Anyone could see she was brain-damaged by years of booze and drugs.

'We'll test the bar for prints.'

'Test away. I've already told you I made a grab at it when we were on the roof. Plus I carried it down to my room the time before.'

'If that's all you did, that's all they'll find.'

Barnaby watched Carter's face as he spoke. All he saw was a smirk of bravado. The man leaned back, crossing one leg high at right angles across the other knee. As he tugged at his sneak-ered foot the soft hide of his jacket hitched up and Barnaby saw the glowing circle of light on his wrist.

'Where d'you get that?'

'Present. My nearly-but-not-quite fiancée.'

'She's had a lucky escape.'

'Me, too. She was as neurotic as hell. Always rapping on about her inner life. Can I smoke?'

'Not at the moment. Tell me – just as a matter of interest – did you know she was living at the Windhorse before you arrived?'

Carter paused as if mulling over the possible consequences of a truthful reply, then said: 'Yes. My uncle wrote to me. He recognised her.'

'From an engraving in the Buddhist scriptures no doubt?'

'It's no crime to look out for a rich wife. If it was, half the male population would be inside tomorrow.'

'You ever been inside?'

'Of course not.'

'You said you were "working" the arcades. That's thieves' cant.'

'A slip of the tongue.'

But in the weeks leading up to the trial more and more information on both the Carters came to light. Faced with facts that made his previous protestations frankly untenable, Andrew Carter, on the hottest legal advice the sale of his watch could buy, decided to plead guilty to the murder of Andrew Craigie.

Filling in the background, he admitted that his uncle, after watching a television programme from America showing an overweight guru with a fleet of Rollers supplied by adoring underlings, had visited his old sparring partner in Albany prison and sold him the idea that they should pool resources and set up just such an establishment in this country. This they had done and much was made at the trial of the deliberate annexation of Carter's contribution after his death, leaving the accused, as lawful next of kin, virtually destitute.

Andrew Carter – thin, hollow in cheek and eye – touchingly, perjuringly, described how, on the night of the murder, he had finally been driven to reveal his true identity and begged for even a small amount of money to set against the share that was rightfully and morally his, but all to no avail. Craigie, he told the court, just laughed in his face.

Defence counsel, the brilliant Gerard Malloy-Malloy, in a dazzling closing speech, dwelt at length on the character of the deceased confidence trickster. He revealed such a string of heartless swindling farragos and deceits that the wonder in everyone's mind was not that someone had killed Craigie, but why on earth it hadn't been accomplished years ago.

Carter's plea of 'Not Guilty' to the murder of Timothy Justin Riley was upheld. Felicity's history of instability and drug-dependence, plus the fact that she had taken a sleeping draught a bare hour before supposedly seeing Carter lure Riley from his room, made her appear an unreliable witness. Counsel reduced her to tearful hesitancies in no time. All the smeary mass of prints proved was that both men had handled the bar.

Evidence was offered as to the dangerously aggressive and violent behaviour of Riley. He had caused the death of the accused's uncle and had also made an attempt on the life of the accused which was only foiled by the quickest thinking. (Here the piece of metal was produced.)

No one but Andrew Carter ever knew the real reason why Tim had to die. Troy had hit on it whilst tossing ideas about, but the supposition had been one of many not to be pursued. The fact was that, caught up unwillingly in the rush down to May, Tim had indeed been distressed at being separated from his beloved Master and was making his way back when the knife had been thrown. He had seen the action, looked back, seen the murderer. And been seen in his turn.

Carter was sentenced to eight years in prison, of which he served six and a half. Having left the residue from the sale of his watch in the hands of a shrewd investment analyst, by the time he was paroled the amount had substantially increased. A few weeks later, wearing most of it round his waist in a money-belt, he skipped the country.

He travelled around Europe for some months – living high, spending and gambling until some serious unpleasantness in Marseilles involving a marked deck in a poker game caused him to move on. He flew to America then, choosing to land at San Diego, attracted by the idea of the sunshine state. He hired a car there and drove up the coast. Unfortunately, just outside Sausalito, he was waylaid, savagely beaten and robbed of all he possessed by a couple of *mafiosi* disguised as New Age shamans.

EPILOGUE

Sylvie Gamelin left the Manor a few days after the case was solved, refusing her mother's offer of the keys to the London house and moving instead into an anonymous hotel in Victoria. Here, for over a month she stayed in her room, resting, coming out just to eat at the in-house restaurant and, once, to visit the family solicitor.

The revelations about Arthur Craigie (as she now could not help thinking of him) had shocked her deeply. Accepting that his conversion – which had taken place before they met – was genuine, Sylvie still could not regard his teachings with the uncritical admiration of former times. This seemed to double the sense of loss she felt at his death and also add confusion, so that she felt unable to grieve cleanly.

The lengthy breathing space at the hotel helped sort these feelings out and she began gradually to appreciate that the veracity of the insights received were independent of her teacher's moral character. And to know that her experiences during meditation were not a matter of self-indulgent conjuration. They were true, if mysterious, encouragements that she was right in her decision to seek a way of life that included some sort of spiritual discipline.

It was during this period that a letter, forwarded from the Windhorse, arrived from Willoughby Greatorex asking her to come and see him. She went with some reluctance, expecting a firm avuncular lecture on the future disposition of her trust fund only to find that the matter in question was the reading of her father's Will. Guy had left all of which he died possessed to his daughter. Although Sylvie always knew this to be his intention, she was still dismayed when it turned out to be so. Before she left, Sir Willoughby handed her a large manila envelope – saying that it was her father's wish that she should have it. He did not know what it contained.

Back in her room, Sylvie put the envelope at the back of her wardrobe and tried to forget about it. She did not need further reminders of her father. One of the things that occupied her most during this period of solitary introspection was the knowledge that, although innocent of the murder of which she had so vehemently accused him, Guy had died knowing that she believed in his guilt. And, whilst her feelings towards him in a general sense had not changed, she bitterly regretted this single misapprehension. Several times, sitting quietly and trying to get some sort of sense and order into her thoughts, she had tried to 'reach' him by closing her eyes and concentrating so intensely on his image that her head began to swim. All this mental activity, however, was in vain. Guy remained resolutely unreachable and so, presumably, unaware of his daughter's remorse.

Eventually she opened the envelope, tipping the contents out on to the bed. She had half expected to find share certificates or insurance policies and was nonplussed at the sheets of folded paper, photographs, ticket stubs and programmes that tumbled all over the duvet. She picked up the topmost piece of paper and smoothed it out.

It was a school report; Christmas term 1983. There were a lot more. Every one, in fact, from that year until she left. Plus paintings, maps and scientific drawings and a lace-edged collar lumpily embroidered 'S.G.' that had mysteriously vanished soon after she brought it home. There was some sheet music and one piece, 'The Robin's Return', had been vividly inscribed by felt-tipped pens. A lock of hair twisted into a rubber band. She remembered when it had been waist-length she had insisted on having it cut, simply because her father said he loved it long. She found some ticket halves attached to a postcard of a gorilla on which was written *Our Day At The Zoo*.

She sat working through the pile, not always reading, sometimes giving things scarcely a look. But gradually, and at last, she came to know the extent of his loneliness and pain. Absorbing it, she let it mingle with her own. At the very bottom of the collection was a smaller sealed envelope with her name on. It held a letter which begged her forgiveness. The writer understood that his protestations of affection were unwelcome but perhaps, now that he was no longer present in person, they could safely be accepted in the sincere and loving spirit in which they had always been offered. He wished only for her happiness. She had been the single undeserved joy in his life. He was, always, her devoted father.

Sylvie held the letter for a long time. She sat completely still until the room grew quite dark, making of her profile an inky silhouette against the sodium-orange glow from the streetlights. She felt disturbed and regretful to the point of anguish. She thought back across the years of their estrangement and, in the light of the letter and the poignant heap of mementoes, no longer saw his observance and pursuit of her as spiteful and oppressive. She remembered him hovering in the doorway opposite her apartment, trying to hide when she came out, herself screaming abuse across the street.

Now she thought, what had he done after all that was so terrible? Neglected her, as no doubt thousands of busy parents did their children and then tried to make up for it, grossly overplaying his hand as he did in every other area of his life because he couldn't help it. It seemed to Sylvie, the single piece of paper quivering in her hand, amazing that she had been able so easily and continuously to harden her heart against him.

The Master had said, 'Try to know each other in that which is eternal.' She had not tried to know her father at all, and now the letter was all she had and to lament over the omission all that she could do.

These perceptions made her so miserable that she was driven

from the hotel to walk the surrounding streets. Around and about she strode through piles of damp yellow leaves, hardly taking note of passers-by and her surroundings, briefly resting sometimes on a bench before striding on fiercely. She would walk until exhausted then return to her hotel and sleep. Once she found a public garden and whiled away a whole afternoon concealed amongst the shrubs, trying to empty her mind and attend only to her breathing as she had been taught – but with little success. Regret, that most suffocating and sterile of emotions, consumed her in a way that drained the present of light and warmth, rendering a peaceful future seemingly impossible.

She had passed 58 Eccleston Square several times before realising that it was the home of the Buddhist Society. And several more before she rang the bell and pushed open the shining black door. But after the first visit she came nearly every afternoon, usually spending her time in the library, reading a little but mainly just resting in the silence. At first she avoided looking at the carved rupa which reminded her of the grotesque fracas that had taken place at the Manor House. But, as her visits continued, and she began to feel increasingly at home if not at peace, this recollection occurred less often.

She started to attend the Saturday meditation class and joined a weekly discussion group which was addressed on one occasion by Thannisara, a Buddhist nun. Attracted by the Bhikkuni's air of collected contained attention, her grace and warm regard, plus the fact that she laughed a lot, Sylvie went to stay for a few days at Amaravati – a Buddhist monastery near Great Gaddesden to which the Venerable Sister was attached.

After several such retreats she bought a small cottage nearby and gradually, in the rôle of lay helper rather than embryonic nun, began to spend a great deal of her time at Amaravati. She worked in the kitchens or the garden and on Open Days and family retreats she especially enjoyed helping to look after the children. Gradually her inner and outer life meshed more and more closely and harmoniously with that of the community, and she was content that this should be so.

Once a week she met and talked with Sister Thannisara. During these times, as if the woman's presence gave some special dispensation, Sylvie would either stumble through pain-filled and self-accusatory recitations or lash out and blame others – anyone and everyone – for her present unhappiness. She would go over and over the same ground until gradually the words became null and void, like ashes in the mouth.

Guilt slowly seeped away and her mind, instead of feeling like a suppurating wound, each day became a little clearer, a little more purged of dead matter. She began to consider the idea of visiting her mother. But she hardly thought of Andrew Carter during this time of healing, and, by the end of the first six months, he had quite faded from her mind.

Coming to Ken and Heather, what is there to say that the reader (provided he or she owns a television set) will not already know? Perhaps only the briefest details regarding the manner of the couple's departure will suffice. This took place the morning after Tim Riley died.

The Beavers appeared – or rather presented themselves – at breakfast, standing on the satin-smooth stone floor with heads sacrificially bent, shoulders bowed, hands pressed together as if linked by invisible chains. Calais could have been engraved upon their hearts. They said they had not been able to sleep since their surrender to cupidity and so painful was their distress that they now had no alternative but to remove themselves from the Manor House for good.

The others argued back. Forgiveness was plainly on the cards, no strings attached. Ken cried, 'Oh! Coals of fire,' but still would not be moved. They packed their few belongings and within the hour were gone, walking and hobbling down the gravel drive with even Ken's plaster cast looking ashamed of itself. They did not look back.

The following weekend the *News of the World* (having rung up during the evening meditation on the terrace and doubled the whack of the *Daily Pitch*) carried part one of their exclusive story. Nothing was left out, though much was included that was fictional.

Much was made of Heather's visits to Venus. Also, of the assistance given on her daily round of common tasks by various elohim and other spritely little scarperers. All this being presented under the heading 'Elementally, My Dear Watson.' Two weeks later they were invited to appear on *Wogan* where, no doubt, the intention was to have a little gentle fun at their expense. If so, the experiment misfired for half way through the programme Ken suddenly went into a trance, channelling Hilarion and the Crystalline Hordes with such dynamic authority that the switchboards were immediately jammed by callers wanting to book appointments. And when the first message came through from the other side (it was Cosmo Lang, late Archbishop of Canterbury, wishing to apologise for his part in suppressing the Church Report On Spiritualism And Communication), the studio went wild.

After this it was just a matter of time. Within days Ken and Heather had been taken under the wing of Baz Badaistan, second only to Malcolm McLaren in the promo business. They were soon channelling to packed houses up and down the country. These sessions were always concluded by a demonstration of healing by Heather. Smiling celestially, she would place the tips of her fingers on the forehead of the supplicants who then obligingly fell back into Ken's arms. If they didn't, the pressure from Heather's fingers would increase until they did.

From the first their television audience-participation programme, *The Perfect Medium*, was a huge success. Ken and Heather, in jewelled and sequined kaftans, would laughingly try to beat each other's astral points on the Karmic Klapometer whilst simultaneously clobbering *Coronation Street* in the ratings. Heather always finished with a casual strum and a song the latest of which, 'Shake A Little Ether and Smile, Smile, Smile', quickly rose to number one in the charts.

In spite of their determination to remain unencumbered by earth-anchored cogitations and material goods, the Beavers quickly accumulated so many of the latter that they were compelled to purchase a four-bedroomed penthouse on Canary Wharf to put it all in. Here a housekeeper and secretary run their lives, for Ken and Heather are both far too tied up with cosmic decrees and divinations, with business meetings and plans for a second TV series, to concern themselves with day to day affairs. Next year – Europe and the States.

Seventy-six Beauclerc Gardens, W11, was a tall narrow four-storey building with elaborate iron balconies rather like those to be found in New Orleans. You couldn't miss it, for it was painted indigo and had a bright yellow sun smiling down from the roof.

It was owned by The Lodge of the Golden Windhorse, an organisation devoted to meditation and healing, and consequently regarded as pretty much run of the mill by the rest of Holland Park. The village of Compton Dando on the other hand, where the group had previously been sited, had murmured 'Good riddance' on the news of their departure. One or two inhabitants even going as far as to cross themselves excitedly as the removal vans went in.

The new house was divided neatly into four. Basement: two large rooms for interviewing, counselling and group workshops. Ground floor: reception, book stall and library. First floor: general treatment rooms. Top floor: private accommodation. This comprised a large and comfortable sitting room, a tiny bedroom with shower and a fitted kitchen.

Janet lived in the flat which had been specially converted and was given rent-free in exchange for twenty-five hours' administration work per week. In fact Janet did much more than this, having discovered both a talent and a liking for the job. She ran her reception office, the beautiful high-ceilinged sitting room full of flowers, with flexible precision like the captain of a ship. So far she had refused all offers to bring in paid assistance. There were three telephones and a computer on her vast leather-top desk. On the wall, posters of coming events and a large calendar studded with dressmaker's pins with coloured heads.

The thing that surprised Janet most about her new rôle was how easily she had slipped into the welcoming side of things. Meeting people, giving information, making suggestions as to various courses and methods of treatment. She was playing a part, of course. The real Janet (the old Janet) standing aside watching, often with a caustic shake of the head, would have been hopeless at it. She shook her head, too, over the silky tweed skirts and slippy, narrow jumpers and as for the haircut. . . . Felicity had brought that about, tactfully suggesting that perhaps corduroy bags and a wiry untamed mop might not be quite the thing for a receptionist.

Janet went out quite frequently now. When she had first moved to London, she had been wary of leaving the house – both fearing and longing for an encounter with Trixie. (Slough was not that far away.) When she finally did start going shopping, she 'saw' Trixie at least once on each occasion. One time she ran after a blonde girl in a knitted beret and followed her all over C & A's until the girl, who was not Trixie at all, threatened to call the manager.

But, eventually her apprehensions began to fade and if she saw someone now who even vaguely resembled her former friend she would look the other way until they had passed. Or even cross the road perhaps, to avoid a meeting. Time had put her former enthralment into a far saner perspective. She saw what a pathetic figure she must have cut and flinched at the memory. In the matter of day-to-day existence she was still not happy and still believed that such was never to be her portion. But she was not unhappy and occasionally experienced moments of content-ment.

The tentative, awkward yet persistent beginnings of a friend-ship had sprung up between herself and Felicity. They would talk occasionally, sometimes at great length, about philosophical matters which puzzled Felicity and to which Janet had no answer. In the late spring they went to the open-air theatre in the park and once Janet suggested a concert at the Festival Hall. She chose a programme much lighter than the one she would have preferred, but Felicity had no knowledge of classical music and Janet was anxious not to put her off. She was delighted when, after borrowing various tapes and compact discs, Felicity expressed a liking for Palestrina. They had had supper one evening, sitting in the gathering dusk on Janet's iron balcony, listening to the *Missa Brevis*.

Felicity's appearance was much changed. She was plumper and her hair, left to its own devices, was now the colour of pewter and wrapped in a shiny French pleat. Her inward transformation, though continual, was of a daunting, hesitant and frequently alarming nature. But May's hand was always present should Felicity stumble, which she did all the time.

They shared a house two doors away from Number 76 which had also been purchased with money from the sale of The Manor. This had raised over a million pounds, four hundred thousand of which had been safely and ethically invested, the interest being used to fund day-to-day running expenses, modest salaries, outreach projects and bursary assistance for the financially impoverished – of whom there seemed to be many. All four members of the organisation agreed that, although sending out the light was of the very essence, sometimes practical help was even more important. Very occasionally this kindness was abused but their serene and good-natured collective heart stayed steadfast through all adversities which, in any case, were minor compared to those in the recent past.

Arno had a garden flat in this second house, which was also home to an elegant tortoiseshell cat. Although a stray, it had the most exquisite manners – being both timid and refined. He named it 'Calypso Two' after the goat – now browsing, supercilious as ever, on a Welsh hillside.

Arno felt extremely blessed. In fact, as his joy increased, he sometimes felt he might burst under the strain. To his amazement and relief, his earlier florid declaration of undying love had not resulted in immediate banishment from May's sight. And when, sober and desperately contrite, he promised unconditionally to withdraw his offer and never, ever refer to the matter again, he received only a kind and gentle chiding. He thought at first she was merely being sympathetic, for he was in considerable pain from the injury caused when the spike of her beloved cello had gone through his foot. But later conversations soon revealed that her affection, too, had been quite seriously engaged for some time.

Almost a year later, and on the day our story ends, four people gathered in the vestibule of Chelsea Registry Office. Felicity in a full-length rainbow dress and Janet, clad in lilac silk and clutching a nosegay of rosebuds. Arno wore his best suit, steam-pressed to a shining gloss. The bride arrived radiant, carrying an extremely large bouquet of flowers in every conceivable shade of blue.

As the shimmering column of white satin and lace, crowned by a wreath of orange blossom and foaming clouds of veil, sailed across the carpet and came to rest by his side, Arno tilted his newly hennaed beard to its most triumphant angle ever.

Five minutes later it was all over. Everyone kissed everyone else and the groom, happy beyond his wildest exaltations, led his lawfully wedded wife out to greet the world. May Cuttle (star name 'Pacifica') had finally and for ever become May Gibbs. And Arno's Valkyrie queen.